SKY OF SEVEN COLORS

SKY
OF
SEVEN
COLORS

RACHELLE NELSON

COASTAL VILLAGES

THE
GRAY
EARTH

Where the sky of seven colors
Meets the waters of our lands
When the new one has walked on silver
Eyes of hue and golden hands

— VERSE 1127 OF THE ANTICIPATORY WRITINGS

1

On my seventeenth birthday, I hiked into a forest and disappeared. It was Andrew's idea. The forest, not the disappearance.

Pine trees flashed by my window as we drove along a dirt road. Cloud cover deepened the shade of the woods, promising a summer storm.

"Your dad's okay with us coming up here?" I sat in the middle seat of Andrew's pickup, my leg a breath from touching his.

His mouth tilted up at one side. "I always explore when I come for Christmas."

That wasn't an answer.

"By the way, you're invited this year, if you want . . ." His invitation trailed off. He glanced over at me, then back at the road. "My mom would kill to have another girl around."

Christmas with Andrew Knoll. That would be something. I watched him drive and felt myself smile.

We pulled onto a long driveway, stopping in front of a two-story house. Large window panes glistened beneath gables, reflecting the evergreen forest that surrounded us.

I eyed the structure. "You call this a cabin? I'm pretty sure it's bigger than my house."

When I had imagined the place, I always pictured logs and mud.

Andrew laughed. "It's not as great as it looks. The hot water tank goes out half the time. Besides, we're not here for the cabin. We're here for the trees."

The Knolls owned a hundred acres in the mountains above town. Private, gated property. Andrew's mom liked to say the woods were haunted. Andrew said they were beautiful. I was just glad to be outside. To be with him.

I slid out of the truck onto the pavement. The air smelled like rain and pine sap, a welcome change from the dry valley below.

"Tree therapy." Andrew closed the truck door and flashed a smile. "You ready?"

I nodded and followed him to a path on the other side of the driveway. Tree therapy was our thing, an excuse to spend time together over the summer when we weren't in school. I had learned about it in biology class, how some doctors prescribed walks in the woods to help their patients. So now, that's what we called our hikes.

But today's hike was different. Special. It was the Saturday before my seventeenth birthday, and this was our way of celebrating.

Last year, my mom had thrown a party. Balloons and cake and half the town on the guest list. That was before she got really sick. This year, Andrew claimed birthday planning dibs. As if someone was going to fight him for it. I didn't want a party. Too many questions about how I was doing. Questions I didn't know how to answer, now that she was gone.

The trees were better than anything I could have asked for.

Ferns and branches brushed our shoes with dew as we made our way along the path.

"Who built this trail?" I asked.

"My great-grandpa cleared it. For good reason." Andrew quickened his step. "You'll see soon enough."

For a while, we walked in silence. I didn't mind the quiet. Liked it, even. We always acted like tree therapy was a joke, but I actually thought there was something to it.

A breeze blew my hair over my shoulder, snagging the thin strands on a branch. I stopped, caught. Things were always getting stuck in my hair. Jacket zippers. Door handles. But I refused to cut it. It was the same long chestnut as my mom's, though hers had been thick and curly, not a curtain of limp snares.

Andrew laughed, reaching to help me detangle.

"Thanks." I lowered my hands and let him work at the snag.

This close, I could feel his warmth. I was always aware of him. Especially aware of the distance between us. My heart beat faster and heat crept up my neck. Great. A blush would make my skin even patchier than normal. I hoped he wouldn't notice.

Andrew wore a linen shirt, snug across his broad shoulders, complementing his olive skin and amber eyes. Those were the kind of eyes a girl could get lost in, if she looked too long. Which is why I never did.

At first, when we started hanging out in my freshman year, I hadn't noticed him in that way. Since then, things had changed between us. Part of it was him—he had grown into himself. Part of it was me.

Andrew was the one who sat beside me at the funeral. And after the funeral. He was there when I finally let myself cry, his hand in mine. Sometimes, I thought there was more than friendship between us. But he never said anything, so neither did I. Things were good the way they were. I didn't want to mess that up.

Except things weren't going to stay the way they were, and I knew it.

In a few weeks, I would start my senior year of high school. Andrew would go to college.

I shook my head, pulling myself free from the branch, creating space between us. I lost some hair in the process.

Andrew removed my loose strands from the pine needles, holding them out to me. "You're always leaving your mark."

I smiled. "Call me Gretel. It's my trail of breadcrumbs."

"You won't need it. We're almost there." He put a finger to his lips. "Listen."

It was barely audible. Beneath the bird calls and the forest noises, a roar droned, the sound of river rapids.

"It's just a little further." Andrew quickened his steps as he led the way.

After two more bends in the trail, we came to the top of a ridge, overlooking a ravine.

I took in a breath at the sight. Across the ravine, a waterfall poured over the edge of a high cliff, crashing into a spray of mist below us. Bright green moss grew on the rocks behind the falls. With the dark sky and the vivid color, it looked like another world.

It was beautiful. A place untouched by sadness.

To my surprise, my throat tightened with emotion. This was better than tree therapy.

"What do you think?" Andrew asked over the sound of the falls.

I swallowed back the threat of tears, another thing that made my skin pink. "It looks like it should be in a national park. How does no one know this is here?"

Andrew stepped closer to me. "Knolls know. They just don't care. My grandpa's brother fell here as a kid. It was . . . bad. He died. After that, they closed the place to the public. It was way before my dad was even born, but still no one comes out here. My parents like jigsaw puzzles and they hate getting their shoes dirty. You're the only one I've ever shown. Hopefully it's not a lame surprise."

He was watching me.

I grinned and took a deep breath, taking in the scent of green things. "It's amazing."

"It's even better up close." Andrew motioned for me to follow him further down the trail.

He was headed into the ravine. My shoulders tensed. Right now, the path was wide enough to stay away from the edge. But what if it became narrow or steep? I had never been good with heights. Even the Ferris wheel made me want to puke, and it had safety rails.

I didn't move to follow Andrew.

"Don't worry." He came back up the trail. "The path is only tricky at one spot. This is the easiest way down."

He took my hand and gave it a reassuring squeeze, then let go. I closed my empty hand, wishing he had held on longer.

"It's easy for you." I edged along the path close behind him.

"You're not scared of anything." Not heights, or people. Or real birthday parties.

"That's not true." Andrew didn't elaborate.

He was probably trying to make me feel better. My list of phobias was too long: spiders, strangers, driving. It hadn't always been that way. Last year, when everything went wrong, it was like my brain realized bad things can happen. I started worrying about the bad, focusing on it. But good could happen too. Like this hike. Like Andrew.

"Hey," I said. "Thank you for bringing me here."

"It's better with you." Andrew looked back at me. "Now, since this is technically your birthday party, I think it's time for games."

"And cake?"

"If you insist." He pulled a crumpled paper bag out of his backpack and tossed it to me.

"What's this?"

"Open it."

The bag smelled sweet. Inside were two enormous oatmeal cookies. My favorite.

"I was joking about the cake. But this is better." I took a bite of a cookie. Sugar and butter melted in my mouth.

Andrew took a cookie for himself. He packed the empty bag away. "I wasn't joking about the games. You ready for truth or dare?"

I laughed. "You sure you can handle it?"

We had played before. Last time, it ended with Andrew having to eat a concoction of ranch dressing, sandwich cookies, and pickles.

"Well," he said, "since you're the birthday girl, you get to go first."

"Fair enough."

We kept walking, pausing to climb over a log that had fallen across the trail.

"Truth," I said.

"Perfect." Andrew brushed dirt off his jeans. "Do you have any regrets?" He didn't look at me when he asked the question.

Regrets. I tried to think of an answer that wouldn't ruin the hike. There were things I wished had never happened. Cancer. Death. Things I couldn't control.

"I regret not eating both cookies," I said.

"Come on. You picked truth. You owe me a real answer."

"You're supposed to ask me something easy. Like, what's the worst birthday present you ever got."

"Your mom gave you a pair of red shoes with glitter last year," Andrew said. "You hated them. But you pretended like you didn't."

He was right.

"Okay," I said. "Real answer. When I was in fourth grade, I took this field trip to the zoo. I waited for everyone else to ride the carousel before me. I was nervous, I guess. But I wanted to ride the horse. By the time I got in line, it was time to leave. I know it's dumb . . . but it's a regret."

"Acceptable answer." Andrew guided me to the inside of the path, away from a raised tree root. His hand was warm on my back.

"I used to ride that carousel all the time when I was a kid," he said. "I'm sorry you never got to."

"You were probably first in line," I said.

"I was."

"You probably cut in line."

"I did." Andrew grinned.

That smile made something flutter inside of me. I looked down, concentrating on my steps. "Truth or dare?"

"Dare."

I rolled my eyes. Andrew always picked dare.

"Before you decide the intensity of the challenge," he said, "keep in mind that I did bring my first aid kit. So we're good to go."

I didn't have a dare for him. I wanted to keep talking. "What do you regret? I dare you to tell me the truth."

I expected Andrew to fight me on this. He liked his dares. But he was silent for a moment. He turned to me and held my gaze, his eyes serious.

"The truth." He paused. "Actually . . . I did want to talk to you about something."

I could hear in his voice that the game was over. My stomach tightened. "About what?"

He put his hands into his pockets. "Meg, I'm going to be leaving soon—"

I interrupted, panic washing over me. "But you're not leaving today."

This was the one subject I didn't want to talk about. No matter what he was about to say, he was leaving eventually, and nothing could change that. We would be apart for a whole year, except for Christmas. He would probably meet some college girl from the city with silky blond hair and a rock-climbing gym pass. Today, I would avoid heights, parties, and this conversation.

I took off down the path, past Andrew, hugging the safe side.

"Meg—" The sound of his footsteps followed behind me.

I laughed, passing it off as a chase. When I came to a patch of pinecones on the ground, I had to slow down or risk stumbling. Andrew passed me and stopped, blocking the trail. We stood facing each other.

"I need to tell you something," he said. "Will you listen for a second?"

I nodded, my smile fading. Whatever this was, he wasn't going to let it go. He took a step closer. My head tilted up to see him.

"I know I'm leaving . . ." he went on. "And I don't know where that leaves us."

Us? I tried to stop him with my eyes, to beg him not to tell me that things were going to change between us. End between us. Whatever we were.

Andrew searched my face like he was looking for something.

"What are you trying to say?" I asked.

He ran his hand through his hair, a gesture he only made when he was frustrated. I held my breath.

"What I'm trying to say is—It's just . . ." He dropped his hand to his side. "It's just that, after everything this year, I didn't want to move too fast. And then we never moved at all. And everything's been the same for years, but it's not the same for me anymore. I can't leave without saying something."

My heart leapt to my throat.

He took a deep breath and spoke in a steady voice. "I'm in love with you, Meg."

I froze, my eyes locked with his.

He kept going. "I've been trying to show you for the past year, maybe longer. I'm sorry if that's weird for you to hear, but it's true and I need to say it out loud."

My breath grew shallow. Raindrops flecked my cheeks.

Neither of us had ever said I love you—not in that way—but I had felt it a hundred times and tried to hide it. I had spent all that time keeping silent. I had trained myself to push aside my feelings. Now, I stood there, trying to wrap my brain around what he had just said.

I waited too long to reply. I felt it in the awful moment when he looked away.

Andrew scuffed a rock with the toe of his shoe, his hair curling in the rain. "So . . . I guess I wanted you to know that. If you didn't already." He turned and kept walking, deeper into the gully, speaking over his shoulder. "We're about halfway to the bottom of the falls."

In a minute, when the rush of feelings slowed, when I caught my breath, I would figure out what to say. The right way to say it. I walked behind him, chewing the inside of my lip.

Within a few paces, the ground transitioned from packed earth to slick gravel. A thin stream of water trickled under our feet. I turned up my collar, steadying myself.

Andrew tried to smooth over my silence. "Maybe you'll want to do a sketch?"

I always had my sketchbook. Leather bound and weather worn, it sat in the bottom of my backpack, which was slung over my shoulder. I made an entry in those pages on every hike we took. Andrew made a big deal out of each drawing. It was another reason I loved him, another reason to tell him so.

I opened my mouth, ready to speak, hoping that the right words would come out.

And that was when Andrew fell.

2

The rock under his feet slid down the damp edge of the ravine, taking him with it, destroying several feet of the trail. Andrew tumbled, too long, too far. His body landed against a boulder with a sickening crack and he rolled through slick underbrush.

"Andrew!" I went cold, sick from the adrenaline flooding my veins.

He didn't answer. He lay motionless, thirty feet below the path.

I didn't think about the height, or how I would climb back up, or what would happen if I fell too. My body just moved. I lowered myself onto a landslide of mud and grass. My legs shook and gravel dug into my hands as I scrambled my way to Andrew.

When I reached him, I knelt at his side, slow, afraid of what I would find. His eyes were closed. A deep gash ran along his temple, seeping blood into the dirt and rocks. To my relief, his chest rose and fell, a sure rhythm. He was breathing.

Thank God he was breathing.

"Andrew?" My voice quaked and I swallowed hard. I squeezed his hand, trying to wake him up. "Andrew?"

He didn't respond.

I knew better than to try to move him. He could have injured his spine, and there was no way I would be able to carry him back to the truck. I smoothed his damp hair out of his eyes, leaving a smudge of mud on his brow.

Tears blurred my vision as I leaned my face close to his and whispered, "Andrew, I'm sorry." I didn't know exactly what I was apologizing for, but I felt regret in every rattled bone.

Could he hear me? Blood trickled down his face.

I needed to get help. Now.

I fished Andrew's keys out of his pocket and pressed my sweatshirt against his wound, trying to stop the flow of blood. His face was already turning purple, a bruise spreading. He didn't move.

"I'm coming right back. You're going to be okay."

I dug my foot into the side of the ravine. There was nothing to hold onto but flimsy plants and loose rocks. As I climbed, my foot slid through the mud, almost back to where I started.

After minutes of desperate crawling and slipping, I had only made it partway to the path. I never liked to take my bag off on our hikes, never set my sketchbook down. What if it got dirty? It was part of me, part of us, full of too many precious memories. But it was slowing my climb. I couldn't afford to be slow. I threw my backpack into a bush and held onto its branches, trying to catch my breath and hold my position.

My chest tightened and words welled up inside of me. A prayer. Not that my prayers had ever been answered before, but I couldn't stop myself.

"I'll do anything," I said. "Just let him be okay."

A strange noise came from the trees above, like paper being torn, or a harsh whisper. The air rippled. I blinked. Pines bent beneath a gust of cold wind and damp leaves blew over the edge of the ravine. The storm was getting worse.

Whatever the noise had been, I didn't have time to think about it. I kept climbing.

By the time I made it back to the path, my arms and legs were weak. I managed to jog down the trail, but the distance back to the truck seemed twice as long as it had on the way to the waterfall.

Unlocking the truck door, I grabbed my phone off the seat. One bar of service blinked yellow on the screen. I steadied my shaking fingers and dialed the three-digit number no one ever wants to have to dial.

Three days later, Andrew wasn't okay. Not in the way I had hoped. He was in the hospital, attached to tubes and monitors, eyes still closed. The fall injured his head, not his spine.

The doctor said he suffered from severe neurologic deficits, leading to a minimally conscious state.

A coma.

The longer he took to wake up, the less likely his recovery would be. They didn't know if he would ever be okay again.

I had spent three days and nights in the plastic-coated hospital chair at the end of Andrew's bed, watching him sleep, looking for signs of awareness. It was something I knew how to do, something I had practiced in the weeks before I lost my mom. The beeping of monitors, the smell of sanitizer, the hushed jargon of the medical staff. I hated that these things were familiar, that I was learning them all over again for someone else.

I only took breaks from my chair to use the bathroom, or to buy a snack from a vending machine in the hall. Every time I left, I brought back another bag of crinkle-cut chips for Andrew. They were the only kind he liked. If he woke up, would he be hungry?

Andrew's mom stayed beside his hospital bed, her eyes fixed on something unseen. She kept my chip bags in a neat stack on the bedside table, a useless collection.

I didn't know what to say to her after the accident. If it hadn't been for me, Andrew wouldn't have been distracted when the path crumbled. He wouldn't have gone out there at all in the summer mud.

"I shouldn't have gone with him." This wasn't my first apology to Ilene. "I should have stopped him."

She gave me a gentle smile. "All those shoulds will drive you crazy, Meg. We never liked him running around in the woods, even when the ground was frozen solid. But that's Andrew. The best of him and the worst. You were there to call for help. That's what matters."

"He's always been there for me." I tried to hold back tears. Ilene didn't need to deal with someone else's feelings right now.

"That's also Andrew. His dad's not good at emotional stuff. Andrew's the opposite. He would have helped me through this, if he weren't the one . . ."

Andrew's dad, Dave, paced the halls outside the little hospital room. He frequently left to "get coffee" for Ilene.

I swallowed, wishing I could help, not knowing what to say. How could I reassure her when I didn't know what would happen? I moved from my chair and rested my hand on her shoulder.

Tears spilled down her cheek and she patted my hand. "He'd be glad you're here. You know he's already homesick and he hasn't even left for school yet. You're a big part of that."

"Then he'll have to come visit next semester."

Ilene smiled through her tears.

I hoped with everything in me that there would be a next semester.

When Ilene left the room to get lunch, I stole her chair beside the bed and slipped my hand into Andrew's. His was square, fingers calloused at the ends from playing guitar strings.

"I'm so sorry." I ran my thumb over Andrew's knuckles. His hand stayed limp in mine. "If you can hear me, things are going to be different when you wake up. Different between us."

How active was his mind? There were so many things I wanted to tell him.

"Are you dreaming in there?" I asked. "I've been having dreams. It's—"

Andrew's mom returned with a paper cup of coffee, Dave in tow. I jumped out of her chair.

"It's okay," she said. "Stay."

I did stay, late into the night. Eventually, I fell into a shallow sleep. The dream came again, the same one that came every time I had dozed off since Andrew fell. Wind whispering through the trees. A voice. What was it saying?

Ilene woke me up. The clock on the wall read 12:04 AM.

"You've been sleeping in that chair for three nights," she said. "You need to go home and get some rest."

"I can't." My voice sounded bleary. "What if—"

Ilene stopped me. "If anything changes, we'll call you." She hesitated, then met my eyes. "Dave and I need some time alone with him. Just mom and dad and son. I know you understand. We would love it if you came back tomorrow afternoon."

Of course. There would be things they needed to say to him too. Alone. I hadn't been thinking of that. My cheeks heated as I nodded and grabbed my hoodie.

Ilene settled into the chair, a fuzzy blanket over her lap. Dave took a seat in his own chair, rarely used. They didn't know it was my actual birthday. No one did.

"Call me," I said.

Ilene gave me a tight-lipped smile. "He'll be okay."

Would he?

I headed home to my uncle Peter's place, a six-block trek from the hospital. I had moved in with him after the funeral, though I wasn't convinced he had noticed. It was better than my dad's place. I didn't have to switch schools, and there was always food in the fridge. If Peter didn't notice me, at least he didn't mind me being there.

When I got back to the house, my uncle's beagle, Pete, greeted me, his tail wagging ferociously. Who names a dog after themselves? Pete's food and water bowls were empty, as usual when I wasn't around. The human Peter was probably at his girlfriend's place for the night.

"I'm sorry, buddy." I poured a bowl of kibble.

Pete scarfed it up.

In my room, I sat on my bed and stared at a note Andrew had given to me days earlier. He had folded it into a paper plane.

> Dear Meg,
>> Be ready to leave at 10 a.m.
>> Wear good shoes.
>>> Yours always,
>> The Surprise Birthday Planner

I imagined Andrew's fingers around a pen, forming letters into words. He had tried to make his messy handwriting fancy, curling the lines at the ends.

Pete laid his head on my lap with a soft whine.

"Do you know you're drooling on my jeans?" I scratched him behind his ears.

He stuck out his tongue, increasing the flow of drool into his fur. No wonder he had smelled so bad before I moved in and started giving him regular baths.

"It's a good thing you have me."

But who did I have?

For a moment, there had been a glimpse of something in my future. Andrew wasn't leaving our friendship behind when he left for college. Not after the way he had looked at me, the things he had said. What might have changed between us if I had spoken up? What would we have become if he never fell?

But he did fall.

Out of all my petty fears, loneliness was the worst, and the most real.

I settled into my bed, Pete curled up beside me. It was the middle of the night, and I was restless. But in order to dream, you have to sleep. And I wanted to dream.

The dreams in the hospital chair had given me a sick feeling, triggering memories of blood-soaked dirt. At the same time, a part of me hoped for them. I wanted to see the forest again, to go back before it all happened.

That night, as I slept beside Pete, the same dream returned.

The forest trail was muddy and mist hung in the air. A voice spoke to me in the breeze, a whisper. Was it Andrew? I left the path and walked into the trees. Would Andrew be there? His amber eyes open, a smile on his face? It was all I wanted. I trudged further into the pines, my ears straining to hear the voice.

Like always, I awoke too soon, before I could hear what the whisper was saying. Pete snored beside me. Early morning light pierced through my window.

That was when I decided to return to the forest.

It was unreasonable. Pointless. So why couldn't I shake the idea? The waterfall had been a special place to Andrew. It was where he told me he loved me. Maybe I wanted to relive that moment?

No. That wasn't a good enough reason to risk another rock slide. I needed more excuses to return.

I had forgotten my backpack and sketchbook in a bush on the side of the trail. Those pages were full of memories that only Andrew and I shared. Days spent in the trees together. If I left it there for too long, the drawings would be ruined by weather.

That excuse seemed almost good enough.

But underneath all my justification, I knew the truth. It was the dreams. It was the way they made me feel, like going back would mean something. Like it was important.

But I knew that was senseless. It wasn't important. Yet I couldn't just sit around all morning, waiting to go back to the hospital. I needed to move.

I poured Pete a generous bowl of kibble, then double-checked the stove before heading out the front door. Lately, that had been a new fear, digging at the back of my mind. What if I left the oven on and burned down the house? I hadn't even cooked anything. But what if?

The screen door swung shut behind me, the keys to my uncle's spare sedan clinking in my hand. Peter liked it better if I asked before borrowing the car, but he probably wouldn't notice I was gone. I would be back in time to go to the hospital in the afternoon.

It had been a while since I had driven. It wasn't that I couldn't. I had my license. It was just another "what if." When I turned the ignition, my heart drummed in my ears. I sat there for a moment before shifting into gear.

The drive to the Knoll cabin took an hour. An hour alone with my thoughts. At least I was out of the house.

I ignored the No Trespassing signs on the road to the property.

The cabin driveway was empty. I parked and let my legs carry me to the trail. Dew dripped off leaves and pine needles crunched beneath my boots. I ran my fingers along the trees, feeling their spiny branches. It should have been a terrible place for me, after what had happened. But there were good memories here too. I pictured Andrew again, untangling my hair, helping me over a log, the way he looked at me when he told me how he felt.

I repeated my whispered prayer.

"I'll do anything."

I had meant it. I still meant it. I would climb the ravine barefoot or drive the car off a cliff if it would help. But it wouldn't. I had tried it all when my mom was sick. Praying, begging, researching alternative cures. I was powerless.

Once I reached the gravel section of the path, I hugged the inner rim, away from the edge, more cautious than Andrew would ever be. My heart raced, warning me to turn back. I ignored it. I had come this far. Why not get my bag?

I neared the mud where the path had fallen away. Over the edge, near the top, my grimy backpack hung on the branches of a bush, where I had tossed it during my climb.

I stood there, frozen, working up the courage to near the edge. I hadn't given it a second thought last time. Now, it made me queasy. I sat in a crouch, anchoring myself against a tree root in the path. With the tips of my outstretched fingers, I reached down and fished the bag off the branches, pulling it up to safety.

Grief washed over me again, fresh, like upturned dirt. Andrew wasn't gone yet. He still had a chance. But that was what they had said about my mom. It was happening again, the same as before. Both hospital stays mingled together in my mind until I felt numb.

What if I had fallen instead? Andrew would have had his family to help him through it. I wouldn't want him to watch me bleed, like I had watched him. But his mom needed him. No one needed me.

A breeze flurried my hair, and a sound came from the trees. It was the same noise as before, when I was climbing up, like paper being torn. Like a whisper, loud enough to be heard over the falls. I took a few steps along the path, deeper into the ravine, toward the noise. Wind wasn't supposed to sound like that.

A voice spoke. This time, I could distinguish the words.

"Do you see her?"

I jumped, my eyes searching the trees. There was nothing but shadows and branches.

"Hello?" I wasn't sure where to direct my voice. "Who's there?" Another hiker, trespassing?

A second voice whispered, sharper and clearer than the first. "I do not see her. I feel her."

Ilene's old ghost stories about the Knoll property crept into my mind. I pushed them away as quick as they came. I wasn't the kind of person who believed in ghosts. Or haunted dreams. Not in real life. So why was I here?

"Are you sure it is a girl?" the whisper asked. "We need a girl."

"It is her," the second voice said. "It is time."

Time for what? Clammy sweat formed on my palms. I needed to get out of here. I turned my body, but I never took the first step.

Something like an icy finger pressed against my spine. I tried to twist my neck so I could see my attacker, but I couldn't move. I couldn't even scream. I was paralyzed.

Cold spread over me, expanding to cover my skin. The chill sank deeper and grew so cold that it burned. Pain overtook thought, and lightning flashed behind my eyes. I collapsed onto the trail. My vision went dark.

I awoke on lumpy grass and pine needles, my head throbbing. My eyes strained against hazy light that filtered through the trees. The sun was going down.

That wasn't right. It was supposed to be morning.

Memory returned. The icy attack. The voices in the wind. I went rigid and tried to sit up, but my stomach lurched. I swallowed hard against a bitter taste in my throat. With my hand, I searched the forest floor next to me. My bag had fallen off my shoulder when I passed out. I tangled my fingers in the straps and clutched it to me.

The sound of heavy footsteps approached from behind. I closed my eyes, pretending to sleep.

"Do you really think it is her?"

"Why else would she be here?"

The voices were close. Right above me.

They had a foreign accent that I couldn't place. Deep, gravel tones, like rocks grinding together. I struggled to keep my breath steady.

"But does she have color in her eyes?" asked the first voice.

"They all do. Eyes and hair. And she is old enough. He will be happy about that."

They were talking about me. My hair. My eyes. Who else could it be? We were alone in the woods. My heart leapt into my throat. What if they attacked again? I couldn't just lie there like I was asleep forever. I probably wasn't fooling them, anyway.

Who were these people? Ignoring the tug in my stomach, I rolled over and opened my eyes.

As it turned out, they weren't people at all.

Two figures towered over me. Tall wasn't the right word to describe them. They were long, much longer than a person should have been. Their slender limbs stretched too far. Enormous eyes, lined with white lashes, peered at me over high-bridged noses.

Everything about them, from their teeth and skin to their clothes and hair, ranged in shades of white and gray. Even their lips were ashen. They wore loose trousers and rough-spun sweaters that fell to their knees. Worse yet, they had no shoes. Their dirty toes curled free in the grass.

I stared at them, too afraid to look away, unsure of what I was seeing.

They stared back at me.

The smaller of the giants whispered to the larger one, "Her eyes. Perfect."

At the sound of the creature's voice, I scrambled to my feet, muddled thoughts colliding in my mind. They couldn't be human. They couldn't be real. But here they were, right in front of me. Real enough. Was I going crazy? I didn't care. I was too afraid to doubt myself.

Run. I knew I should run. Instead, words tumbled out of my mouth in a strained squeak.

"What are you?"

The taller giant bent its neck forward in an almost bow. "I am Proce, and this is my companion, Von."

The other turned to Proce. "The human did not ask for your name."

"I heard her. She asked, 'Who are you?'"

"What," Von said.

"Excuse me?" Proce raised its bushy brows.

"She asked, 'What are you?'"

"Oh."

They both looked at me again.

My head throbbed and my vision blurred. I searched the trees for a path. Which way to the car? We were in the thick of the forest, no trail in sight. The ground spun, and I lost my balance, sitting heavy on the forest floor. My bag weighed me down.

"She is not recovered yet," Von said. "She needs rest."

The big one, Proce, bent low and did the worst thing I could have imagined. It touched me, its long fingers wrapping around my middle. Then, it lifted me into its arms.

A scream tore from my throat. I kicked my legs, struggling against the giant, but it slung me over its shoulder. I tried to claw at its pale skin with my fingernails. It cradled me closer until I had no range of motion.

We were moving. It was taking me somewhere.

Von followed behind, directly in my line of sight.

"We will not harm you." The smaller giant offered a toothy smile. "Do not be afraid."

"Let me go!" I thrashed until I was out of breath. When that didn't work, I went limp in Proce's arms, trying to make myself heavy. Despite its size, the giant felt like a normal person. Solid bones and warm skin.

"Good," Proce said. "Stop fighting. You need to recover. I am sorry to have to carry you, but it really is best. Now, you asked what we are. So you have noticed that I am not a human?"

A blind person wouldn't have mistaken them for humans. Not for long. I pushed my arms against its shoulder, fighting for an inch of distance between us.

"I do not think she is ready to listen," Von said. "The journey here was hard on her. But her sickness will fade in a little while."

"We can at least explain some things," Proce argued. "We have waited such a long time."

Von's mouth went tight. "Go on, then. But not too much."

Proce did go on, presumably speaking to me. "We share the same earth with humans, but once removed. That is the best way I can say it. Normally, we would never be able to see or hear one another, but Von and I have called you to cross over. Have you heard of thin places? Groves of trees and corners of cities where the separation between one earth and another grows thin. You are in such a place now. We are between earths."

I fell against Proce again, unable to push away anymore. "Cross over?" My voice croaked. "Are you . . . you're ghosts?"

"I am not a ghost." Proce let out something like a laugh, chest rising and falling beneath me. "Though Von might be one."

"Do not tease," Von snapped, directing the next comment to me. "I am sorry. Proce can be oblivious. You have never met anyone like us. How are you supposed to know if we are or are not ghosts?"

It was difficult to focus on anything but Proce's wiry arms encasing me. I studied the trees as we passed, looking for somewhere to hide when I escaped. I wouldn't be able to outrun them, but maybe I could disappear. Maybe I could fall asleep and wake up and all of this would be over.

After a while, Proce carried me out of the trees into a narrow meadow. Across the meadow, the falls crashed into a river, surrounded by marshy streams. We were at the bottom of the ravine.

Ahead of us, a cobblestone path wound through wet grass, ending in a stone structure with a thatched roof. A thin line of smoke floated from a chimney. Flowers had been planted along the front step. The whole building was impractically tall, like the giants. Was it theirs?

I scanned the meadow. Something was wrong with this place. It was the sound. The streams splashed over rocks. The giants' feet thudded against the cobblestone. But the waterfall, which should have been deafening at this distance, was completely silent. I could see it, but I heard nothing.

Even the sky was wrong. The sun should have gone down already. I woke up in the forest at sunset. Since then, the sky hadn't darkened one shade.

What was this place? Between earths. That didn't mean anything to me.

The giants made their way to the stone house. I stiffened in Proce's arms, ready to fight before I allowed myself to be carried inside.

To my surprise, Proce set me down outside the entrance. Von was right, my headache and nausea were almost completely gone now, faded during the journey through the forest. My eyes darted toward the trees, toward my escape. It was the first time I had been able to look up since Proce carried me. I had planned to run as soon as my feet touched the ground. Instead, I stood there, disbelieving what I saw.

Beyond the tree line, where the top of the ravine should have been, there was nothing. Just trees, and then empty sky above. The rest of the forest, where we had just come from, was gone. My uncle's sedan, the Knoll cabin, the trail. They had completely disappeared.

I backed away from Proce and Von. "Where am I? Where's the cabin?"

"Do not worry about your house," Von said. "We will share ours with you. You should let us know what kinds of pillows humans like for sleeping."

"You know what I'm asking," I said. "Where did the forest go?"

"We will explain when we go inside." Proce bent toward me again, as if to pick me up.

I jumped out of reach and bolted toward the trees.

3

I didn't look back. At any moment, unnaturally long fingers might have snatched me from behind. I willed my feet to move fast, flying past the tree line, dodging branches and jumping over rocks.

When I couldn't run anymore, I slowed to a brisk walk and heaved deep breaths, looking over my shoulder. I pulled my phone out of my bag, now that I was away from the giants. No service. Two percent battery life. I was on my own. Would I be able to find my way back up the invisible hill with the invisible cabin and car? After a long incline through the woods, the trees opened up in the distance.

The road.

I hurried my steps toward the clearing, then stopped.

The open space was not the road, or the cabin driveway. Somehow, I had turned around and gone straight back to the meadow. I peered out from the shadows of the trees. The two giants stood on the cobblestone path, facing one another in conversation. Were they planning to come after me?

I backed away slowly, sinking into the shadows of the trees, hoping they hadn't seen me. When I was far enough from the clearing to feel invisible, I ran again, searching for anything familiar: a trail, a footprint, the mudslide where Andrew fell.

But there was nothing.

Only undisturbed forest. No matter which direction I went, I eventually ended up back at the same tree line, looking out across the meadow to the falls.

Proce and Von stayed in the meadow. Sometimes I found them standing outside their cottage, sometimes they rested on a boulder beside the stream. Most of the time, they watched me as I approached the clearing, as if they knew when I was coming. But they never moved to chase me.

How long before anyone would show up looking for me? Would they think to check the Knoll cabin? Probably not. There was no reason for me to come here. They would find Peter's sedan at Christmas. In six months.

The sun never moved, so I had no idea how much time passed while I wandered the forest. Hours? A day? Maybe more. I was used to walking everywhere in town, since I had become nervous behind the wheel. Peter had even sold my mom's car. This was different from a walk. It was a restless battle with underbrush and dew, a panicked trudge toward nothing.

Once, while I hid at the edge of the meadow, I watched Von go to the stream to take a drink. My legs ached and my mouth felt like cotton. I needed water.

I leaned against a tree, out of sight. My chest shook with a sob and sweat dripped from my forehead. How could I be so stupid? Andrew had almost died in these woods, and I had decided to come right back because of a dream. A feeling.

Von finished slurping water and retreated to stand beside Proce. The giant straightened its tunic and folded its arms, scanning the tree line. I ducked further into the forest, as if I could hide. They knew where I was. Where else could I go?

Reality sank in. The giants didn't chase me because I couldn't get away. Every direction pointed back to them. It was impossible, but it was happening. I had tested it dozens of times now.

Why had they brought me here? When I was a kid, my mom read stories about giants that ate the bones of humans for dinner. I shivered. This wasn't a story. It was real. Inescapably so. And I didn't want any part of it.

When Andrew fell, I had been there to call for help. Now, I would have to be my own help—to calm myself and make a plan. No one was coming to rescue me.

I took a deep breath. What next? If I was ever going to get out of the forest, I needed to survive. In order to do that, I needed water. It had been a while. Too long. I probably needed food and sleep too, but I would start with hydration.

Like a cautious rabbit, I left the tree line, my eyes fixed on Proce and Von. They watched me, but they didn't move.

I scurried to the far end of the stream. If it was safe for a giant to drink, would it be safe for a human? The water flowed transparent over multicolored pebbles.

"Drink," Von shouted from across the meadow. "You need to refresh yourself."

I flinched at the sound, ready to retreat, but the giants stayed put at a safe distance. Von's invitation made me nervous. But if the water was clean enough for a giant, it was probably okay for me to drink. And they hadn't chased me yet.

In a hurry, I cupped my hands beneath the surface of the stream and brought water to my lips. Cold liquid hit my empty stomach. I took in a quick breath and realized how hungry I was.

I had to make a choice. The meadow was a cage, an outdoor prison without walls. The giants were my jailers, but they were also my only source of information. I could wander the woods until I collapsed, or I could talk to Proce and Von.

From far away, their figures looked almost human. But they were too large to be familiar, too thin. When they moved, they possessed a slow grace I only knew from the animal kingdom, like a giraffe or an elephant. Their white hair should have made them look old, but it didn't. It made them look otherworldly.

Proce and Von. I said their names in my head again. Somehow, having names made them less terrifying. It made what I was about to do seem less crazy.

I rose to my feet and walked toward the giants, my shoulders back, my steps deliberate. I focused my gaze on the distant meadow, past their faces, so I wouldn't have to look into their huge eyes. Could they see my fear?

When I was close enough to talk without shouting, I stopped, every nerve on edge.

The giants remained motionless, unblinking.

What was I doing?

"Proce and Von." My voice shook and I cleared my throat. "Can . . . can you tell me how to get out of here?" It was direct, but it was all I could think of.

I braced myself, ready for Proce to lunge at me again. Instead, both giants sat in the grass, stretched out their legs, and leaned back, like spindly picnickers.

"It is easier to talk when we are at your height," Von said. "Now we can hear you better."

They were taller than any human, around ten feet. When they sat, their faces were close to my level. I took three steps back.

"You cannot go home," Proce said.

Of course. It couldn't be that easy.

Von gave the other giant a sharp look. "You are going to scare her even more."

Proce shrugged. "What was your plan? She is going to find out eventually."

"Yes. But we can tell her gently."

"That is fair. We will discuss it all with the human and then decide what to do."

My lip trembled. I didn't want to lose it in front of the giants, but I was hungry, and exhausted, and confused.

"You have to put me back," I said. "You said you don't want to hurt me, but you attacked me." I stopped myself from saying more. I wasn't in any position to be making accusations.

"We did not attack you," Proce said. "I carried you. For your own good. Von thinks it was not safe for you to walk after the call to cross over. She is sometimes right about these things."

She. Proce called Von she. I examined Von more closely. There was something almost delicate about her, compared to Proce. She was smaller than the other giant, though still enormous by human standards. Her brows were less wooly, and her cheeks curved, soft. Both creatures had silky white hair that trailed down their backs, but Von's was decorated with silver beads and tiny braids. Proce had wider shoulders and a sharp jaw. He was a he-giant, and Von was a she.

Von pursed her gray lips. "You ran around the forest all day and night. I am glad you have decided to be reasonable now."

A full day and night. A sun that never moved. By now, Dave and Ilene would wonder where I was. They had enough to worry about without a missing girl in the mix. Heaviness settled over me, making me want to sit. I fought it, staying as straight as I could.

"Can you tell us your name?" asked Proce.

Maybe they wanted to eat me, but why waste time with conversation if I was a meal? Not that I was going to completely rule out that theory. Either way, I needed them to keep talking. If there was a way out of this creepy forest, they knew it.

"I'm Meg."

Von tilted her head at me. "You need to eat something. We have prepared grain in the house. Will you come?"

My stomach churned with hunger. I searched Von's face. Was she a killer? There were a few soft lines around her eyes, crow's feet, but I couldn't tell her age. I couldn't tell much. Except that she wanted me to trust her, which made me trust her less.

"If I go inside your house, will I be free to leave again?"

Proce answered, "We will not keep you, though you cannot go far. We are all limited to the boundaries of this place, in between."

"Yes. I noticed."

I glanced back at the half-missing forest. More than anything, I wanted to run to the car and drive away. Driving wasn't as bad as I had made it in my mind, and it was definitely less nerve-racking than anything I had experienced in the last day and a half. I wanted to go back to the hospital, to find Andrew awake and well. But that wasn't possible right now. If it was ever going to happen, I needed to stay alive. Stay strong. I needed food.

"I'll go inside for just a minute," I said.

Von showed all of her teeth. "Good."

Both giants rose to their feet, towering over me. I backed away and stumbled on a patch of grass, my legs exhausted from running up and down the forest. They watched me as I caught myself.

"I can walk to the house by myself," I warned.

"Yes, you can." Proce gave one nod, then headed down the cobblestone toward the cottage.

At first, the giants walked faster than I could manage, their long legs swishing over the ground. When I fell behind, they noticed and slowed their pace.

"We will wait for you," Von said.

I trotted behind them, keeping distance between us.

When she reached the cabin, Von swung open the front door. A sweet smell wafted to us, like baking bread. Proce ambled inside.

Von stood clear of the entrance and motioned for me to enter. "You are welcome in our home, Meg."

I edged across the threshold, barely breathing.

The interior walls of the one-room cottage were constructed from forest materials. Crooked tree limbs and river pebbles framed smooth walls of earthen clay. A hefty fireplace stood in the corner of the room, topped by flat stones that held a kettle and a skillet. Next to the fireplace sat two absurdly tall chairs and an enormous, rough-hewn table. Knitted cushions of various sizes crowded the corners of the scrubbed wooden floor, and a glow from the fireplace added to the twilight from the window.

The room looked lived-in, almost pleasant. I took comfort in the visible lack of bones or blood stains.

Then I noticed the writing. On each wall, from corner to corner, were lines of neat script, written in black. I couldn't read the words in the twilight.

Von entered behind me and Proce closed the door. I pressed my back to the nearest wall, eyeing their movements. The door latch might be too high for me to reach if they locked it, and Von stood between me and the exit. Even if I managed to run out that door,

I would still be trapped in the forest. My situation hadn't changed. So why was my heart drumming in my chest?

"I will prepare a place for you." Von moved across the room, slow, as if I were a wild animal she had cornered. She combined together a cushion and a giant-sized stool.

"This is where you will eat." Von gave the cushion a brusque pat. "Come."

The stool would be a table for a human, the cushion a seat. From a high shelf, she took dishes of food and placed them on top of the stool.

I waited until she backed away, then eased my stiff body onto the cushion. It was almost high enough to be a chair. The stuffing was lumpy. I slid my bag off and set it on the floor. Relief eased my tense shoulders, tired from hours of walking.

Proce and Von settled into their places at the giant table.

I inspected the dishes in front of me. There was an oval bowl, filled to the brim with what looked like broth. Next to the bowl sat a cup of gray liquid and a plate, heaped with a massive portion of silvery grain. Why was it metallic? Was it safe to eat? I couldn't think of a good reason for the giants to poison me. If they wanted to hurt me, there were easier ways. At this point, I was hungry enough to try it.

I reached toward the cup, but Von stopped me.

"Not yet."

The giants closed their eyes and lifted their arms into the air, stretching out their gray fingers.

I flinched, ducking away from them. What were they doing?

Sound filled the room. A low, wordless melody, hummed from the giants. They were singing, their coarse voices mingling together. The song only lasted for a few seconds, then Proce and Von opened their eyes.

Von rested her hands on the table. "Now we eat."

"Now we eat." Proce took a long swig from a huge cup.

My human-sized dishes looked like the miniature version of the giants', carved from wood. My spoon was too long and my cup was too small, just big enough to hold a few swallows. I had never used dishes like these. Had the giants carved them, anticipating human guests?

I lifted the bowl to my lips. When I tasted the salty broth, hunger took over and I gulped it down, warming my empty stomach. Onions floated in the soup, adding a bite to its savory flavor. When the broth was gone, I tried the silver stuff, scooping it up with my awkward spoon. The grain looked like metal, but it tasted like toasted wheat.

Von watched me eat. "Did you like my soup? We used the green onions from your earth, along with our white. I hope the color is enough."

"It's great." I tried to smile.

Now that I had food and water, a part of me wanted to get as far away from the giants as possible. But I needed information, and this cottage was the only place to get it.

Proce wiped his mouth on his sleeve. "Of course, she does not understand why green onions are special. She does not know about her own color, just as fish do not know they are wet."

Von rolled her eyes. "Go on, tell her then."

I didn't care about color, or onions, or whatever they were hinting at, but I listened to every word they spoke, hoping for a clue about how to get away.

Proce straightened his shoulders. "Our earth is a pale land. You may have noticed how our skin is gray? But you are covered in color. Your earth's sky has seven shades, so vibrant you take them for granted: red, orange, yellow, green, blue, indigo, violet. As the humans call them. When Von and I first came here, we could not stop staring at the green plants and the blue water. It was all we did for days. I even forgot to eat."

"I never thought I would see a day when my brother would forget to eat."

Proce shot Von a look.

Brother and sister. They were siblings. A family of giants.

Something about that made me feel safer. Almost. I set down my spoon. My stomach was too full, uneasy after days of hunger.

"We gave you too much food?" Von asked.

There was still a mountain of grain left on my plate.

Proce eyed the food. "I could eat the rest, if you are not going to finish . . ."

Both of the giants' plates were empty. The last thing I wanted was for either of these creatures to be hungry. I picked up my leftover food and held it out to Proce. He took it and shoveled the rest of the grain into his mouth.

I shrank away from him, leaning into the cushion. My back ached and my eyes felt like sandpaper, tired from the sleepless hours in the trees. If I had been alone in the cottage, I could have fallen asleep in two seconds. With the giants beside me, I could barely blink, let alone sleep.

Von got up from her place at the table and cleared her dishes into a wooden box. After she put her plate away, she sat on the floor, far enough away to keep me from panicking. Now that she was lowered to my level, I could see her steady eyes in the firelight, orange reflected in liquid gray.

"You must have questions for us?" Von asked.

Really one basic question. How was I supposed to get back to my car? But they weren't going to answer that. I went with something else.

"Why am I here?" Suddenly I was afraid of what their answer would be.

Proce got up from his chair and settled onto the planked floor beside Von. Von took in a breath to speak, but Proce beat her to it.

"I am glad you asked. We have waited long years, hoping for one such as you. We brought you here to become the wife of our king."

What was given is taken away

Oh peace, return through the new one small

She will walk upon silver

Oh sleep, return upon her call

- VERSE 1126 OF THE ANTICIPATORY WRITINGS

4

I blinked at the giant. A wife? My breath grew shallow.

"Proce!" Von glared at him. "You are saying it wrong." She turned to me. "It is not quite like that . . . Well, I suppose it is. But we were going to ease you into the idea before it happens. If it happens . . ."

"Of course it is going to happen," Proce said. "Look at her. She is exactly the way it was written. Once he sees her, he will agree. She needs to be prepared."

"True." Von relented to Proce's reasoning.

I wanted to pretend like I hadn't heard the giants, to go on sitting in a comfortable house with a meal in my stomach. But the words sank into me and my whole body trembled. I clenched my hands together to keep them from shaking. This was dangerous. Not the kind of danger I had first imagined, but maybe worse.

"Um . . ." I bit my lower lip. "I . . . It's getting late." My cushion slid against the floor as I stood. "I need to leave."

Von frowned. "Meg, you have not slept for a whole night and a day. Feel how exhausted you are."

Then she sang, humming a melody, her deep voice surprisingly lilting.

In my mind, I wanted to get up and walk out of that house. But my body wanted to rest and listen to Von sing. Her voice washed over me, and I sank back onto the cushion.

As the song went on, I did feel exhausted, and the cushion felt luxurious. Why had I thought it was lumpy before? I lay down, nestling my head against it. Just a nap. A short sleep and then I would leave.

The song ended, but the drowsiness stayed.

"I have helped you to relax with my gift," Von said. "For your own good. It will wear off once you have slept for a time."

Her gift? I curled my legs against my body, finding the most comfortable position.

Von kept talking, her voice velvety and deep. "While you rest, Proce and I will tell you a story. This way, you will not be alarmed by anything you hear. It is a very important story, so you must listen. There are things you need to understand before you decide."

I nodded, eyes closed. My mind felt fizzy, like fresh seltzer water.

Proce spoke. "The king began his reign in the season of the grain festival. The grain in that year was—"

Von interrupted. "She does not need to hear about the crops. What does that have to do with the story?"

"I am getting to it. If I will be allowed . . ."

Von sighed.

"Now, as I was saying," Proce continued. "The grain harvest was abundant. The holds were full enough to sustain us for many seasons."

"I suppose the grain was relevant," Von relented. "More of us would have died during that cold without that harvest."

"Exactly."

"We should tell her the history of life. Otherwise, how will she know why we need her?"

"I will tell it," Proce said. "This is the history of life: In the ancient days, our people were given a burdensome choice. We could either choose new life, or long life. Humans have new life. Many new children are born to you every year, adding to the generations before them. Your numbers grow, covering the earth. In the king's library, it is written about humans—"

"Proce. Enough about humans. She knows that already."

There was a pause, with whispers I couldn't quite hear. Then Proce raised his voice.

"Von would like you to know that our people chose long life instead of new life. We live for a thousand years, sometimes longer, but our numbers do not grow. We can only, at best, bear enough children to replace the last generation. Compared to us, you are still new in years. Though you are old enough to be a bride."

I opened my eyes halfway and pushed myself away from the cushion. Who was getting married? Von hummed, and I laid my head back down.

"Good," said Von. "Now, tell her about the cold."

"Do you want to tell the story? Because we agreed I would do it."

"Then do it."

Proce cleared his throat. "I will tell you about the cold. In order to live long on the earth, some of us must have times of sleep, to restore us. We sleep every night, just as you do, but when the cold comes, we may sleep for many years. It is one of the gifts."

"There are many types of gifts," Von said. "But the King's Gift is special. It is given only to him, and it is for the benefit of us all. He must bless our sleep, or we cannot have it."

"Now for the king," Proce went on. "Early in his reign, he took a wife. Queen Elia, beautiful and cunning. We mourned for years when she died, and the king grieved deepest of all. When the cold came, he lost the strength to bless our sleep. It was the first time we stayed awake in all of history. We believe some of the King's Gift has died with the queen."

Proce took a deep breath and let it out. "Sagac, our cousin, passed before his time during that season. And we lost two of our village elders."

This part of the story awoke an odd ache inside of me. *Before his time.* Why did it hurt to hear those words?

"Without the sleep, we are not ourselves. Von can no longer heal more than one or two ailments in a day. There are few healers in our region. Others cannot use their gifts at all. We hoped the

King's Gift might recover with time. It has not. The cold is coming again." Proce's voice deepened. "I am only a Cropper, but I was given a gift for words. I studied the Writings that foretold how we might regain our sleep and avoid death. They speak of a girl with colored eyes. Only a human could fit that description. It was not by chance that Von and I found this place."

"I found it first," Von said. "And then I told you."

Proce ignored her. "There was no time to tell anyone else. We rushed to hold open the gap between earths. Thin places are a rare thing, only found once in a lifetime. They come and go at random, opening for an hour or a day. Never long. The time has been extended before, using a gift. But to hold it open for so long, we did something that has never been tried. We entered the gap, halfway into your earth. Von has more gifting than most of us. It is why I believed we would survive. Though I was not certain. We cannot go home without the thin place closing. We don't know how to enter all the way into your earth. So we have stayed here, in between."

"Even for us, plenty of years have passed since then," Von said.

"True. But we had a responsibility. We had to wait for a human. Though he is young, the king has been without a wife for longer than he should. He believes that a marriage to a human will return the fullness of his gift. The Writings do speak of these things. I agree with the king's interpretation."

At the word 'marriage', my cushion became decidedly less comfortable. I turned onto my other side and tugged at a fistful of my hair.

Von hummed and I settled.

"You must listen," Proce said. "It has been two hundred years since the last human came to our earth. That was before the queen died. Since then, we began to doubt we would ever find another human, now that we needed one. In two more years, the cold will return. We can feel the change in the air, even from here. When it comes, we can be ready. The king will be able to bless our sleep, because we found you. Soon, you must decide if you will go with us, to our earth."

My eyes fluttered and I tried to sit up.

"That is enough," Von said. "We should end the story and let her sleep."

Sleep. The word melted me into me, and I drifted into a fitful slumber.

My body rested but my mind was active, wandering through a misty dreamscape. In my dream, the forest was white, as if every leaf and twig had been covered perfectly with frost.

A silver-dappled pear hung among shimmery leaves, rustling in the wind. How strange to see a fruit tree in a pine forest. I reached up to pluck the pear from its stem, then I brought the fruit to my mouth, feeling its smooth surface against my skin.

As my lips parted to take a bite, a voice spoke.

"No," it said. "Don't."

I looked at the pear again. My skin burned where it touched me. I dropped it. Pain shot up my arms, and my hands blistered. The calluses on my palms peeled away, revealing red flesh.

Something moved behind me, but I couldn't look away from my wound. My lips burned and my throat ached. Then, a stranger's pale hand touched my palm with a gentle finger, and cool relief replaced the pain. The skin on my hands smoothed, better than it was before, and the blisters disappeared.

The tall stranger stood beside me. His sharp features had the look of a boy who had recently become a man. Maybe early twenties. Black hair framed his ashen face, skin tight and too hard, like the blood had been drained from his veins. And there was something wrong with his eyes. The irises were ice-white with dark rims.

"You're not safe," he said. "When you come to my earth, you need to find me."

5

I awoke in the dim cottage, my neck stiff from curling up on the cushion. Twilight still shone through the window. Apparently, between earths, the sun never moved. The room was empty, the giants nowhere to be seen.

Good.

With a rush of adrenaline, the previous day's events crashed to the forefront of my mind. The giants' meal, Proce's story, my forced sleep.

When would they try to call me all the way into their earth, to meet their king? I couldn't let that happen. I couldn't even contemplate the future they had planned for me. Did they think I would just go along with everything? Maybe they thought I was lucky to marry their king. I shuddered and forced my thoughts elsewhere.

Proce and Von could do things I didn't understand. When Von sang me to sleep, they called it a gift. It felt like a weapon to me. They didn't want to eat me, or to hurt me, but that didn't mean I was safe.

What about my strange dream? Had it come from the giants, or from my subconscious? Something about it felt too compelling, like the dreams that had brought me back to the forest. The white-eyed man was right about one thing. I was in danger.

I slid off the cushion and crept to the door, my nerves on end.

Where could I go? It was irrational to run away. All the forest paths led back to the meadow. But there was one direction I hadn't tried yet. The waterfall cliff. It might not take me back to my car, but maybe I could get out of the ravine. That was good enough for now.

With outstretched fingers and tippy toes, I flipped the high latch. The door cracked open, letting in twilight. No giants in sight. I stepped across the threshold.

Nothing moved. No gravel voices called to me. There was only the sound of the stream. I clenched my hands into fists and raced toward the waterfall cliff. My body still ached from my run in the woods, but my heart raced, urging me forward.

As I came closer to the falls, the ground grew marshy. Water soaked through my boots and into my socks. I picked my way over boulders and crags until I reached a sheer wall of rock, crisscrossed by the occasional ledge. Never in my life had I wanted to climb anything, let alone a cliff. But what if this was a way out?

I steadied my breath and pulled myself up, not thinking, just moving. If I let myself think, I wouldn't be able to do it. I crept higher along the ledge, toward the water. How strange that the falls could rush by without a sound. The wind whipped off of it, and I could smell the damp. But it was silent. What if the water was still in my earth, not stuck between? Maybe that was why I couldn't hear it.

I edged closer, where the ledge grew thin and wet, reaching out my hand, stretching toward the stream. A piece of rock crumbled beneath my boot, clacking on the boulders below. I clung tighter to the cliff, wind from the falls in my hair, spray soaking my jacket. The loose rock wasn't enough for me to lose my balance, just my nerve. My knees felt weak.

There was another sound from below, but I was too scared to look. It was the sound of steps. Long strides against mud.

The giants were coming.

I pivoted, searching for a higher ledge, too fast, too careless. Fear made me clumsy. My foot slid against moss. I couldn't stop it. My hands scrambled for anything to cling to, but I couldn't find a hold on the wet rock.

With my fear of heights, I had imagined this moment a thousand times. A premonition of falling through the air, unattached and out of control.

This was worse than I imagined.

I let out a scream as I tumbled from the cliff. Was this how Andrew felt when he fell? His had been a mudslide. Mine was my fault.

When I hit the ground, bone cracked against rock. I moaned and rolled onto dirt. Pain ripped through my leg as I gasped for breath, lying still. I was awake. Alive. It was my body that was hurt, not my head. Sweat and water ran into my eyes.

Proce knelt at my side.

"Don't touch me," I moaned. "Leave me alone."

"We will not leave you alone. You are hurt."

I strained my neck and dared a glance at my leg. My stomach heaved at the sight. Blood poured through ripped jeans and my shin bone protruded at a gruesome angle.

"I need an ambulance . . ."

"You need to be less stupid."

Von crouched at my other side. "It will be alright."

How could it be alright? We were miles from a hospital, trapped in some weird meadow.

She placed her large hand over my shin.

"Don't!" I tried to pull away, but movement was excruciating.

She opened her mouth and sang. Was she putting me to sleep again? That wouldn't stop the bleeding. I needed a doctor.

Her voice entered my ears and filled my mind, overwhelming the pain. It was the same feeling as before, as if something effervescent had been poured over my head. When the song faded, my leg itched.

It itched, but it didn't hurt.

How?

Von removed her hand. The jutting bone was gone, replaced by smooth skin. The only evidence of the trauma was a thin white line where my wound had been, visible through the cuts in my jeans. I bent my knee as a test, tensing for anticipated pain. None came. My leg felt better than it had before I fell, all the stiffness gone.

I looked up at Von, searching for words. She wasn't looking at me. She was still crouched, gasping for breath, like a sprinter at the end of a race.

Proce supported Von with his reedy arm. "Was it too much?" She steadied herself against him. "I am fine."

Proce's mouth went tight and he scooped me into a hold, carrying me toward the cottage. I didn't try to fight him this time. I kept my eyes on Von. After a moment, she rose to her feet and followed behind.

What had she just done for me?

We trudged through the marshy boulders. Soon, the three of us reached the house.

"You have behaved foolishly." Proce hoisted me over his shoulder as he opened the door. "Von will not be able to heal again for some time. She is exhausted. And you cannot be trusted to stay safe."

He set me on the floor, then brought a blanket to Von. She wrapped it around her shoulders and lay against a pile of cushions, her breath heavy.

I was still too shocked to be grateful for Von's gift, but in that moment, it became difficult to see her as a monster. She looked softer to me now, after her healing song, almost vulnerable.

I leaned down to inspect my leg, running my fingers over the silvery scar.

It was a miracle. Impossible. Amazing.

And that miracle changed everything for me.

If I had gone to a hospital, I would have been treated by doctors in sterile white gloves, wielding needles and plastic tubes. My recovery would have taken months. What if Von had been there when Andrew fell? What if she could be with him now?

My mom had faded slowly. She was sick for nearly two years before the end. I had felt powerless, sitting in those hospital rooms.

But Von wasn't powerless.

And her power opened up a path in front of me, a path I had never imagined could be possible.

The giants wanted something from me. All I had wanted was to go home, until now. What if I wanted something else, something only the giants could give me? What if they could undo what had happened to Andrew?

Proce walked to the door. With a dry click, he fastened a metal bolt at the top, too high for me to reach on my own. I was locked in.

"I promised you could leave our house at any time, but I did not know you would harm yourself." Proce stoked the coals in the fireplace and set the kettle on the flat stones. "Much of Von's gift is taken to hold open the thin place, ensuring we have a way home. It makes healing difficult here. You may not leave again until we are certain you can be safe. You do not know what is at stake if we lose you."

But I did know what was at stake. I remembered their awful story. They thought I was the key to their problems. I wasn't, but it didn't hurt that they believed it.

Von sat up, her voice raspy, her eyes on Proce. "What if she is not willing? What if she will not go with us?"

"We must—" Proce began.

I interrupted him. "I need your help."

Both giants looked at me. It was the first time I had spoken since the healing.

Von shook her head. "We have already told you, we cannot send you back. We can only call you deeper into our earth."

I didn't trust that she was telling the truth.

"It's something else. You believe I can help your people. They're at risk?"

"Yes," Von said. "The cold happens fast. One day, it is summer, the next, cold. We never know how long we will sleep. This time, we do not know if we will be able to sleep at all."

I looked each creature in the eye. "I also have someone who's at risk. He's injured. If you can heal him—" My voice broke. "Can you heal him?" I had no idea how to get to Andrew, but maybe they did.

"What is the human's ailment?" Proce asked.

"He slipped and fell." My throat tightened. "Like me, but he hit his head." I looked at Von. "When can you heal again?"

She sat up from her pillows. "When did this happen? Six days ago?"

"About then." It felt like a lifetime ago.

"Did it happen here, in these lands?" Von asked.

"At the top of the ravine."

The giants shared a meaningful look.

"The boy," Von said.

Proce gave her a slight nod, then turned to me. "We sensed you here with the boy, six days ago. We have waited for a girl for years, but only the boy ever came here. Sometimes, a woman would come close. But never close enough."

I thought of Andrew's mom. She said the woods were haunted. Had she heard the strange whispers? Would the giants have taken her, if she went into the ravine?

"You didn't take me the first time I came down here," I said. "You waited."

"You were at the edge of the thin place," Proce said. "Your presence was faint. You left before we could call you to cross over. Others came. Men. They left with the boy. When you returned a second time, we were better prepared. We knew where you would be."

I remembered the voice in the trees, as I climbed to get help for Andrew. "You were there when Andrew fell."

"We did not know he was hurt," Proce said. "We can only sense a mere presence across the thin place. Using our gifts, we sent a beacon with you. We gave you dreams, asking you to return. And then you did."

"The dreams . . ." I was shaken. "You tricked me."

"We did not trick you," Proce said. "We only asked. You responded."

"We have been here for sixty-two years," Von said. "Then you came."

Sixty-two years? An ominous timeline settled into place. Andrew's great-uncle had died in the ravine as a boy. The giants would have arrived around that time, when the Knolls closed off their property to hikers. Andrew was the only one who had explored the ravine since then, and I was the first girl to wander into the woods, into their trap.

"You made him fall." I backed against the wall of the cabin. They had been there when I fell too. Did they injure me just to heal me?

"We would never harm a human," Proce said. "Though I can see how you might think that. Sometimes, the truth is more simple than we like. Did you know I have also broken my arm and my foot among these trees? Though I healed long ago. This is a treacherous place, and I am not surprised your human fell. Thin places are always this way, wild and hidden. They appear in the smoke of a fire, deep in churning waters, beneath a poison tree. There are often accidents. We feared a girl would never come down here, until you arrived."

I said nothing, unsure what to believe.

Proce sighed. "You have no reason to trust us. But I can show a mark, from where I fell." He pushed up the rough fabric of his shirt sleeve, revealing a silvery scar along his elbow.

"Proce does not lie," Von said. "He is not good at it."

"That is true," Proce agreed.

Maybe he was telling the truth about everything. About being stuck in the meadow. Maybe not. Either way, Von had the power to restore Andrew's life. I had seen it. That was what I needed to focus on now.

"If you didn't hurt Andrew, prove it by healing him," I said.

"Should we see?" Proce asked Von.

"Yes."

Proce took a step toward me. "I will need to touch your arm. Do not be afraid."

He bent down and reached his fingers toward me. My stomach tightened and I pressed myself against the wall.

"Think of the boy." Proce wrapped his long fingers around my forearm. "Picture his countenance and think of his location. You should close your eyes."

I kept my eyes wide, fixed on Proce. "How is this supposed to help?"

"If you care about your human, do as I ask."

I forced my eyes closed and imagined Andrew's face. Tawny skin, amber eyes, and shaggy hair. The kind of face that made people want to know him as soon as they met him. I envisioned his hospital room, and heard the beep of the heart monitor.

Proce hummed without melody and the room seemed to shift beneath my feet.

"You are right," Proce withdrew his hand. "The human is not well. We have not the strength to heal him from here, and we cannot go to him."

I opened my eyes. I knew they wouldn't send me home. It would ruin their plans. But why not this? I needed something to bargain with. Bargaining for Andrew felt right. Like there was a purpose to all of this.

"I'll never cooperate." I said. "You can't watch me forever. I'll keep running away and falling off cliffs. But if you help me . . . it might be different."

"We cannot do it," Proce insisted. "We are not gifted enough. We never will be. But the king may be able to do it."

That would mean leaving the thin place and going to the giants' earth. That was exactly what they wanted me to do.

"How do you know you can't help?" I asked. "How did touching my arm tell you anything?"

"I could sense his presence through you," Proce said. "We are always tied to the ones we love. You are ungifted, but the bond is strong between you and the boy, so my gift was enough to assess him. He may live for many weeks. Long enough for us to reach the king. It is your best chance."

"You could be making everything up," I said.

"Yes, but I am not." Proce tilted his head to one side. "I will describe the human. He is as new as you. His skin is more golden, and he has a cut on the left side of his face. He lies in a white room, surrounded by machines."

Andrew's injury was on his left side, and he had a darker complexion than me. I doubted the giants knew what a hospital room looked like. Maybe Proce really had seen Andrew. I knew almost nothing about these gifts.

Von scooted closer to us, along the wooden floor, her eyes intent. "If we take you to the king, will you join us and cross into our earth? It has to be of your own will. Will you come?"

I held my breath and looked up at their high faces. Next to the giants, I was like a child. If I went with them, how was I ever supposed to get home again? I wasn't scared of their king, because I didn't believe their story. It was too bizarre. Too unlikely. Whoever this king wanted to marry, it wouldn't be me.

It was the crossing I feared. Moving further from my earth. But if there was a chance for Andrew, I had to take it. It should have been me that fell and hit my head, not him. Maybe this was my way of setting it right.

"If Andrew can be healed," I said, "then I'll go with you." The words constricted my throat. What had I just agreed to?

"Of your own will?" Von asked.

"Why is that so important?" They had already taken me against my will.

Von looked away. "It damaged your body when we called you in between."

"Yeah, I remember the cold," I said. "And the headache."

"The next crossing will be worse. Here, we are closer to your earth than ours. To go all the way to our earth . . . will be difficult. If you resist the call to cross over, it may kill you this time. You must commit to it fully in your mind."

"How?" I asked.

"Resolve your will," Von said. "When the call comes, do not fight it."

I shivered at her words and thought of the burning cold that had brought me to the meadow. "What if I don't go with you?" I asked.

Proce used a metal rod to stir the coals beneath the kettle. "We will stay with you. In two years, we may die. Or we may live. We do not know yet what will happen without our long sleep this time. If we die, the thin place will close, and you may die too. If we live, we will not abandon you here. We will watch over all your days. But we cannot send you back to your earth, no matter what you choose."

Staying in the meadow forever wasn't an option. Losing Andrew wasn't an option. I had said I would do anything if he would be okay. This particular anything had never crossed my mind.

"Okay. Of my own will."

Proce's eyes went to Von's. "It is written."

"It is written."

I sank to the floor and leaned against the wall, staring at nothing in particular. The giants thought I could help them. I couldn't. I was just a random girl who had wandered into their forest. But I would go with them. I would ask their king for help. Beyond that, I didn't have a plan.

Von scooted closer to me on the floor planks. "You are like us. We did not want to leave our earth. I did it for the future of those I love. Not every human has survived the crossing into our earth, but you will. Because you want it. That makes you strong."

Wanting another miracle didn't make me strong. It probably made me stupid.

"When will we go?" I asked.

"Soon." Von showed her gray teeth. "Our earth is beautiful, in its way. We are eager to return."

Had it really been sixty-two years since they left? How old were Proce and Von?

Proce poured something gray from the kettle into two large bowls and a miniature cup. He handed out the steaming drinks, then settled onto a cushion. "We will not leave too soon. First, you must be prepared."

6

After an hour or so, Von recovered from the healing. She bustled around the cottage, rinsing grain and stirring a pot of broth while Proce stretched out on the floor.

I cleared my throat. "So . . . I'm supposed to prepare for the crossing? How?"

"Von wants you to eat first." Proce kept his voice low, as if Von might not hear him. "But if you are ready now, we can begin. We must prepare your mind. Not just for the crossing, but also for what lies beyond. Do you have any questions about our earth?"

I thought for a moment. "The Writings you mentioned . . . The ones that made you come here. What do they say?" The more I knew about the giants' plans, the better.

"You can read them for yourself," Proce said. "Many find joy in it. The words are perfect and true." He waved a hand at the lines of writing, inscribed on the wall in black ink. The sentences stretched around the entire room. A whole book's worth of scribbles.

I squinted at the letters, but they were foreign. I couldn't read them. "For now, could you read the most important parts to me? Just the ones I need to know."

"I do not need to read," Proce said. "I am gifted with words. I will recite the key verses from memory."

He began to sing in soft rhythm. His voice filled the cottage.

"Where the sky of seven colors
Meets the waters of our lands
When the new one walks on silver
Eyes of hue and golden hands

What was given is taken away
Oh peace, return through the new one small
She will walk upon silver
Oh sleep, return upon her call."

When he finished his song, Proce raised his eyebrows with a knowing look. "So now you see."

"See what? How is that supposed to be about me?"

Proce's smile disappeared. "Is it not obvious? In this thin place, the waterfall is high on the horizon, as if water meets sky."

"So if I climbed up the falls I would be in your earth?"

"It does not work like that," Proce said. "The description is a metaphor for this thin place. There has never been one like it. It was foretold. The Writings speak of a new life, with colored eyes and golden skin. You are just as described, and we found you in the correct spot."

"That's not me. I don't have golden skin. I can't even get a tan."

"Every human has golden skin compared to us," Proce said. "And you are the first human girl we found."

"So I'm supposed to . . . walk on silver? And then you all will be able to hibernate or something?"

Von set a plate of grain on the stool in front of me. "It would be difficult to understand if you did not know our ways. To walk on silver is to be married. We weave shoes for the bride from silver grass. I will weave your slippers for you, Meg." She gave me an encouraging smile.

I took a bite of the nutty food. It went down easy. "I promised to go with you. I never promised to marry anyone."

Better to be clear.

Von looked away from me. "We will see."

Proce helped himself to a plate of the grain.

"Not yet," Von scolded.

Proce lifted his hands and hummed, more brief than before. I set down my spoon until they finished.

"Why do you sing?" I continued eating.

"Croppers sing for many reasons." Proce took a huge bite of onions and spoke with his mouth full. "Before a meal, we sing to honor the ones we eat with. It reminds me of the Writings. I will quote to you—"

"No more quotes," Von said. "She knows about the Writings now. She can read them for herself, since you insisted on scribbling them all over our walls. What we need to prepare her for is the Regents."

When I finished eating, Von clattered the dirty dishes into a basin and opened the cottage door. "Meg, will you walk the meadow with me? I need some time outside."

"I will walk too," said Proce.

"In that case, I need some time inside . . ."

"Never mind." Proce slumped his shoulders.

I followed Von out the door, jogging to keep up. They were letting me out now. But not out of their sight. I wouldn't run away again. There was too much at stake.

Von took a path that curved around a formation of boulders. On the other side of the boulders stood tall rows of silvery plants. They reminded me of the giant's metallic grain.

"This is where we grow our food." Von sat on a rock. "Fields are the best places for lessons. I will teach you."

I sat on an adjacent rock. "I'm listening."

"Have you wondered what our king looks like?" she asked.

"Well . . . yes." How was a giant supposed to marry a human? Even in theory, it didn't seem plausible.

"Do not worry. In our earth, we have no humans, but we do have a variety of peoples. Proce and I are Croppers. The king is a Regent. Kings always are. Regents are smaller than the Croppers.

Otherwise, he would make a terrible husband for you." Von let out
a chuckle.

"Cropper," I said. "Like crops? You're farmers."

"Yes. We used to have a different name for ourselves, in the old
language. As did the Regents. But now, we call each other what we
are. It is easier that way."

"Isn't a Regent someone who rules in place of the rightful king?"
I had learned the definition of the word at some point, probably
from a history book. Maybe from a fairy tale. Now, I was living a
fairy tale. A cautionary story about monsters in the woods.

"The Regent king is our rightful king," Von said. "Though I
don't know the exact origin of the name. Croppers have trusted
Regents to watch over us for generations."

"What are Regents like?" I was afraid to hear the answer. Would
the king be more shocking than Proce and Von?

"They are . . . particular. When you enter the King's House,
most of the Regents will be won by your color, but there are families
among our capital city who will not be pleased by you. Some hoped
the king might marry one of their daughters. Not all of the Regents
value Cropper sleep as they should. They don't need the sleep."

As far as I was concerned, any of those daughters could have
the king.

"I don't want to make enemies. I just want a healing."

"As a human, you will be under the king's protection," said Von.
"But he cannot be with you always, and the other Regents will
judge your worthiness. Kings like to keep their people happy. Your
life among them will be . . . easier if you win their affection."

"How am I supposed to do that?" I asked.

"They will expect a certain manner from you, in dress and
speech. Those kinds of things are important to Regents. I can help
you to be loved by them, but you must commit yourself to learning.
Will you do this?"

I needed their king's help. If that meant winning over these
Regents, I would try. Maybe I could convince one of them to send
me home. It sounded like they were the ones in charge.

"Okay," I said. "I can learn manners."

Over the rest of the day, I worked to remember everything Von said.

"You must always wear your hair in an upward sweeping fashion for evenings. All of the Regents do it like this."

Von piled her wispy hair on top of her head in a sloppy bun, pinning it in place with a silver comb. It was a mess of braids and beads that somehow made her look even more bizarre, revealing the tips of her pointed gray ears. With her long nose and wide-set eyes, she reminded me of a deer.

Von drilled me again and again on proper greetings.

"The ladies bow this way." Von bent forward with her palms facing outward. "The Regent males bow like this." She crossed her arms over her chest.

After the tenth time we practiced, I bowed with my arms crossed, purposefully getting it wrong.

"Like this?" I teased, lowering my voice to sound as manly as possible.

Von didn't think it was funny. "I am trying to make sure you remember."

What would Andrew have thought of me, teasing a ten-foot giant? What would he have thought of Proce and Von?

"How do Croppers bow?" I asked.

"We do not. We only follow the Regent manner when we must."

Over the next several days, the sunset twilight of the meadow never changed. There was no way to tell time, only cycles of sleeping and eating and going out for walks. The wind never blew and the crickets never chirped. I never saw a bird—not even a spider. I asked Proce about it once, but he didn't know what a spider was. I liked the sound of that.

At every breakfast, Proce used his gift to check on Andrew. He would sing a guttural tune. After a while, I became aware of a deeper sound, beneath Proce's voice. His touch carried an electric glow, an almost buzz. When I asked him about it, he said it was his gift. I would close my eyes and picture Andrew's face, then the gift would warm my skin.

"Your human is unchanged," Proce reassured me. "He still sleeps."

I believed him. I could somehow sense it too, like a rope of awareness, pulled taut. I felt Andrew's presence, dull and veiled behind sleep. He hadn't changed for the worse, but he wasn't getting better.

The giants followed me everywhere. They slept beside me. We ate together. If I went for a walk, they insisted on joining me. They only left me alone when I bathed in the hot springs. It was a thin brook that ran through the meadow, made evident by little curls of steam that rose into the air. Hot springs were common in these mountains, but most were too warm to swim in. Near the falls, the spring mixed with cold water, forming a shallow pool of warm.

The first time Von saw me washing my face in the pool, she ran to the cottage and returned with a tiny jar. "This soap is made from a plant. It is not as fine as the soap in our earth, but we made the best we could." She handed the jar to me. "We will give you privacy." Both giants retreated to the cottage and closed the shutters.

I took off my boots and my jacket, but I left my jeans and t-shirt on. They needed washing as badly as I did. It was my first bath in days. The jar was filled with a fibrous mush that lathered and left my hair with more tangles than ever. Sand and pebbles stuck to my toes, and the water smelled like sulfur. I soaked until the skin on my hands wrinkled, thankful to be alone.

When I got out, I sat in the grass, wrapped in a knitted blanket. Tears came, tears I hadn't allowed myself to shed around Proce and Von. They leaked like pressure from a valve. All of it mounted up into one: The fall, the hospital, my terrified run through the woods. By now, even my uncle would know I was missing. I tried not to imagine Dave and Ilene, worried for their son, now worried for me.

Soon, before I was ready, my solitude ended.

Von reemerged from the cottage and strode across the meadow, silver comb in hand. "I can arrange your hair . . ." She peered at my damp strands.

"Thanks, but I'm good." Would she notice my face? I always turned pink when I cried.

"I have never seen colored hair before." Von took a step closer. I inched away.

"No." My voice sounded harsher than I had intended.

Von looked at her feet. "I just thought it might be nice."

She sat in the grass, at a distance, and put her comb into her shirt pocket. Was she pouting?

Why did I feel bad? She had kidnapped me.

"Okay." I moved to sit in front of her. "But just this one time."

I threw my hair over my shoulder.

Von looked happy as she pulled the comb out. She wiggled up behind me, her torso twice the height of mine. As she worked, I didn't feel a single tug or snare. She hummed a gentle tune and twisted my hair into a smooth braid. Smoother than I could have managed. Her song didn't carry the buzz of a gift beneath it. She was singing for the sake of singing.

"There," she said. "Now you are as polished as a Regent."

From then on, she combed my hair after every bath. She stopped asking for permission, and I stopped protesting, though I still was tempted to roll my eyes every time she pulled out the comb.

Proce wasn't as helpful with my preparations to meet the Regents.

Von explained. "I am a healer, and so I have spent more time in the city than Proce, although he would like more excuses to visit the king's library. I suppose if Proce found a book about Regent customs, then he would become an expert. Otherwise, he does not care."

Proce quoted his sacred Writings to me often, and he loved to ask questions about humans. Apparently, he had read books about humans, but they didn't tell as much as he wanted to know.

"Do all foods in your earth have color?" he wondered. "Do

different colors have different flavors? And how far can you travel in a day, with such short legs?"

I did my best to answer his curiosities, but each answer led to a new question.

One evening, in the cottage, I pulled out my sketchbook. I wasn't in the mood to draw, but I wanted the comfort of home, of seeing a time when I was free.

I flipped through the pages, smiling at the earlier sketches, when my work was new. They were mostly landscapes, but a few were of Andrew. I stopped on one, hovering my finger over the charcoal lines. It was a good likeness, for my skill level. I wanted to touch the drawing, to trace the contours of his face. But I didn't want to smudge the image.

Proce leaned over my shoulder. "You are an artist."

"Not really."

"It looks like him." Proce nodded at the drawing. "Except he is much more colorful, in real life."

"I have colored ones." I flipped the page.

It opened to a more recent sketch. A drawing of the river outside town. In the sky, above the trees, I had painted a dozen hot air balloons, brightly colored with acrylic. The river was real. The balloons were from my imagination.

"Are they flying animals?" Proce asked.

"They're balloons. They trap air inside here, to make it float. People ride in the baskets." I pointed to the different parts as I explained.

"You have flown?" Proce raised a brow.

"No. I'd be too scared. I just like the idea." I liked to imagine being weightless, above everything.

Von sat beside Proce on the floor. She had been listening too. "It is a nice idea. Your art must be very popular in your city."

"Andrew's the only one I show."

"And your family?" Von asked.

I didn't know how to answer her, and I didn't want to explain about my mom, so I shook my head.

Von's face went still and she watched me for a moment. "In your earth, I think you are alone. In our earth, it will be different. You will never be alone again."

That was what I was afraid of.

On one of our evening walks, I caught Von staring at me. The giants were always staring.

"Why do you keep looking at me like that?" Did I seem as strange to them as they did to me?

Von looked away. "I always knew you would have eyes of hue. But they are not just one color. They hold a yellow ring, like your sun. It is nice to look at. I am sorry."

"You really haven't met any other humans, have you?"

"You are our first," Von said.

They were my first giants. I had probably done my fair share of staring.

"The last human who crossed over had skin as dark as your tilled earth," she said. "I wish I could have seen it. She passed soon after I was born."

"How many other humans have crossed over?" I asked.

"Only eleven, in all of our histories. And we are an ancient people."

I halted in my tracks, an idea occurring to me. "How do you know they didn't already fulfill your prophecy? Why does it have to be about me?"

"Our sleep was not under threat when they came." Von kept walking. "Now, we need you. It is time."

After we circled the meadow, I skipped rocks on the surface of the stream. Proce reclined in the grass. Von only allowed him to come on our walks when she was in a good mood, and she strictly forbade him from any long-winded stories or quotes.

Von joined me at the stream, throwing a stone. It plunked into the water without a hint of a skip.

"Mine does not bounce like yours," Von complained.

"You need to throw smaller rocks." I showed her the stone in my hand. "Flat ones, like this."

"I am throwing small ones." She picked up a rock the size of a goose egg.

Von threw the rock with a splash, and we both laughed. Von's shoulders shook with mirth, her breath low and raspy.

"I have never seen you laugh before," she said. "You will be a lovely bride for the king."

In an instant, all my laughter disappeared. I set down my skipping stone.

"I'm tired. I'm going to go lie down in the house."

I headed back to the cottage, the giants in tow. What was I doing, laughing with them? Von wanted me to like her, to be her pet. The worst part was, when I forgot myself, I did like her. Her easy smiles and gentle manner hid her true intentions. She wanted to use me. And, in turn, I would try to use their king.

The giants were beyond anything I could have made up. Ancient and child-like. Their slow, lithe steps carried them faster than I could run. Their voices thundered and purred. I only understood about half the things they talked about, and I couldn't help but be curious, ask questions.

In the cottage, Von began preparing our next meal, filling bowls with water and measuring silver grain from a cloth bag.

"How do you know if you have a gift?" I asked. "How does it work?"

She dumped a mound of onions into broth. "My first gift was healing, and it is still my strongest gift. When I was very new, I came across a besmonn with a broken wing. I knew what I must do. My gift flowed, healing the animal. The gifts do not belong to us. They are given to us to be used for a purpose. They whisper to us.

The greatest among us are not the most gifted. They are the ones who listen to their purpose, no matter how small."

I was already prepared with my next question. "How do you know how to speak English?"

How could the giants possibly learn my language without going to my earth, or being around humans?

"We do not speak the human language," Von said.

"Von does not," Proce corrected from his chair at the table. "I have studied human words in the library and I can say things in their tongue."

Proce demonstrated for us, uttering nonsense in a stilted manner. "*Flores crescunt in agris.*" He looked pleased with himself. "That is called Latin. It means 'flowers grow in fields.' There are a few phrases recorded in the old books about humans. Though not as many as I would like."

Von gave Proce a look, then turned back to me. "Meg, you do not speak your own language, either. Not anymore."

"Of course I'm speaking English."

"You are not," Proce said. "You are close enough to our earth now to experience our language gift. When you crossed over, you lost your words and found our own. It may take some time for you to comprehend the differences. You will see them, eventually. Long ago, we had many ways of speaking in our earth, as humans do. We still have books written in those languages, and most of our names come from the ancient tongues, but now we speak only one. It is a gift that unites us, and you will share in it."

He had to be wrong. I wanted to believe that Proce was speaking English, but I couldn't deny the odd shape of his mouth as he made the sounds. He spoke in straight, clipped tones. If I let my mind wander, there was something foreign about the sound that I hadn't noticed before.

I squinted at the clay wall of the cabin. It was covered in a meaningless script, neatly written in black lines. "You're lying," I told Proce. "If I'm speaking your language, then why can't I read your writing?"

"I do not know." Proce eyed the wall. "I hope you will be able to when you cross into our earth fully. It is a wonderful thing, to read the Writings."

How could I forget my own language? It couldn't be true. And, it wouldn't matter unless I went home. Before I could do that, I had a goal to accomplish.

That night, as we settled onto our cushions, Von continued her lesson about Regents. "You will attend weddings with the king someday. He comes to almost all the weddings in the cities. Regent weddings, and even Cropper weddings."

"Do Croppers ever marry Regents?" I asked.

"Of course not. A child would never be born." She yawned and stretched her arms. "We are too different."

"I know Regents are smaller," I said. "How else are you different?" Would these other creatures be terrible?

"Some consider Regent gifts to be higher than ours," Von said. "But that is not true. Their gifts are only different, not better. Croppers are close to the earth and the people. We heal and we grow. Regents guide, and they see what is to come. There are some exceptions, of course. Every once in a while, a Cropper is gifted with words, or a Regent can call down a sprinkle of rain. But overall, we need each other."

"How can the king heal Andrew, like you said, if that's a Cropper gift?"

"The king and the queen carry gifts of both Croppers and Regents. They must, in order to lead both peoples. The king is our most gifted healer."

I settled deeper into my blanket and hoped she was telling the truth. "You said that other humans have crossed over into your earth. Can you tell me about them?" I wanted to know if any of them had crossed back.

"I am sorry you will not meet them. Each of the human women died many years ago. They had long, good lives by human standards. You may meet their children, although you will not be able to detect their human ancestry. The women married Regents, and they birthed Regents. Lady Analese was our last human. She bore seven children."

"All the humans married Regents? Hasn't a human man ever crossed over?"

"Not that we have heard of. If only humans did not die so soon. It is a great tragedy."

Proce joined the conversation by singing a verse from his cushion on the other side of the cottage. His low voice, rough and thick, reverberated through the room.

> "Sun below and sun beyond.
> Our time may end, but time goes on.
> What has been will be again.
> What is now has always been."

"Was that another prophecy?" I asked.

"No." Proce stretched out beneath his blanket. "It tells of the past, not the future. There are many kinds of Writings. Croppers learn to sing some of them as children."

Von's second yawn was even wider. "Proce remembers every word he reads or hears, even without a song. It is unusual for a Cropper. Tomorrow, when we have rested, we can teach you a song."

I wasn't done asking questions. "How did the other humans get to your earth?"

"They wandered into thin places," Proce said. "Trapped in between, without their own giftings to free them. The Regents saved them by calling them through. Some say they found the thin places by chance. I do not believe in chance. Humans are a gift, and the king will be glad to have you."

"He will be a good husband," Von said.

Silence settled between us.

"Now I have a question for you." Von rolled onto her side to look at me with her large eyes. "Who is the human boy to you?"

"He's . . . my best friend. And kind of my family."

"And you hoped for a future with him?"

"Yes."

Von frowned, upset by my answer. "Your future has changed now. It is not a small thing to ask for a favor from the king. It could place you in a delicate position. Things may be rushed faster than you are ready to accept. Maybe Andrew will awaken on his own?"

She waited for a response.

"His chances aren't good. It's been too long. If he doesn't wake up, he only has a few months. Maybe weeks. I've already been here for days. I want to rush things."

"I understand. But make sure you are fighting for the boy, not for a future that cannot be."

How could I make Von understand? "Would you save your people from the cold, even if you couldn't go back to them?"

In the dark, she gave me a long look, then a deep nod.

"Then you understand," I said. "Thin places and Regents and kings . . . it's a lot to wrap my head around. So by getting Andrew healed, I'm making it count for something. All of this has to mean something."

"It means a great deal to us." Von rolled onto her back and closed her white lashes.

Soon, Proce drifted into sleep, snoring from his corner of the cottage.

I tried to picture the king, but all I could imagine was a shorter version of Proce, wiry and big-eyed, with a gaudy crown and a red robe. No, it wouldn't be red. Nothing would be.

7

That night, I dreamed again of the frosted woods with the white-eyed man. I saw him more clearly than before. Black, shining hair fell to his shoulders. Beautiful hair. He didn't speak to me. He stared, a level gaze. Something in that look made me want to run, to turn away. Before I could move, I woke up, sore as usual from sleeping on the cushion.

"You slept long," Von greeted me as I opened my eyes. "It is time for the morning meal."

How did she decide when we should eat? The sun never moved, and Proce was always hungry.

My dream stayed with me throughout the day. Why did I keep seeing the same man? I had some weird dreams before I ever came to the waterfall. The usual stuff. Going to school and realizing you're naked. My teeth falling out. But nothing so vivid. No one so real. I wished I would dream about home instead. I couldn't even escape this place in my sleep.

After breakfast, Proce found me outside the cottage. I sat on a boulder, gazing into the clear brook. A tiny, perfect leaf twirled on the surface, caught in a miniature rapid.

"How much longer until we go to your king?" I kept my eyes on the leaf. I was tired of sitting around the meadow, hearing story after story about the Regents and the Croppers. Every day that Andrew stayed in his coma, his chances of recovery lessened.

Proce cleared his throat. "The Writings have not given detailed instruction on timing. I can only trust that all will come to pass as it should today."

"What do you mean?" I looked up at Proce, my head tilted back to see his face.

"You are past the initial shock now, and you have learned much."

I stood. "Today? Are we crossing today?" My breakfast churned in my stomach.

"Yes. It will weaken you. You must heed our instructio—"

"When? Now?"

"After our next meal. The sun will be high in our earth, and it will warm us. We can do it then."

"How much longer?" I twisted my hands together, to calm my nerves. "Why does it always seem like you know what time it is?" I added.

"Croppers have senses beyond sight. We will call you, when we are ready." Proce walked back to the cottage, quicker than any human could travel.

I squinted at the twilight horizon. How many days since I had seen full daylight? I closed my eyes, imagining the warmth on my skin. What would a colorless earth be like?

Then, without warning, a familiar, icy finger pressed viciously against my spine.

It was happening.

They were calling me to their earth. But why now? Proce was supposed to come find me. The cold spread into a burn across my skin, the same as it had the first time.

Wait! I wanted to scream, but I remembered what Von had told me.

When the call comes, do not fight it

I tried to ignore the pain. I tried to resolve my will. The cold sank into me, searing every nerve. I felt myself slip away as I held onto one thought.

Anything.

I had said I would do anything.

My mind hovered on a precipice. If I didn't tread carefully, I would fall to my death. Then my vision went dark.

When I regained consciousness, light filtered through my eyelids.

The sun.

We made it. And now my head hurt worse than I could ever remember. I opened my eyes and squinted against white. Gone was the dusky meadow. Gone were the colors of my own earth. Gone was my backpack with my sketchbook. I had left it in the cottage.

Proce and Von sat cross-legged on silvery grass, peering down at me.

"You have done well," Von said.

I pushed myself up from the ground and glared at Proce, my hand pressed against my temple. "You said it would be later. I didn't have time . . ."

"I am very sorry about that. If you knew the call was coming, you might have become nervous. Often, the anticipation of pain is worse than the pain itself. We knew you wanted to cross, but we did not want you to be afraid. This crossing was much further than your first, more dangerous. If you fought it, scared, your body could have been damaged. That kind of an injury would be difficult to heal. Maybe impossible. You did well, Meg. You are whole."

"You lied to me." Why did that bother me so much? "And I left my book." It was my glimpse of home, of Andrew. I could picture exactly where it sat, beneath a cushion on the wooden floor of the giant's home.

"You always carry it." Proce sat up, urgent. "Why did you not have it with you? I didn't think—"

"Proce." Von snapped. "You didn't check?"

I said nothing.

Proce's shoulders slumped, and he shook his head.

Von leaned forward. "Oh, Meg. To lose such a thing . . ." Her eyes glistened, worried.

But I didn't want her pity. I didn't want her apology. They had tricked me and taken me. This was nothing new. I looked away.

"It had to be sudden," Von said. "We were trying to keep you safe—"

I cut her off with a fit of coughs. My throat burned and I swallowed back a wave of nausea.

Von moved closer, handing me a bowl of water. "You need to rest. The call is not easy."

The water eased my throat and I lay down.

"We will stay here for a short time until you are ready." Von leaned back on her elbows.

The day was hot enough for sweat to form on my upper lip, a relief after the cold of crossing. A white sun shone above us, lighting up the gray sky. I closed my eyes and opened them again, as if that might bring the color back. As if the problem was with my vision and not with this place. Everything looked wrong.

I sat up and plucked at the grass. Silver. Just like the Writings said. Von wanted to weave my wedding slippers from that silver. The blades released a sweet scent, sharper than the smell of grass on my earth. Like something herbal. I had thought the giants' earth would look like an old black and white photo. Vague and muted. Instead, the grass was vivid. Too shiny. Perfectly outlined. I blinked again, a momentary escape.

Von reached down and ran her fingers through the grass, breathing deep. She caught eyes with Proce. "Sixty-two years waiting, and now we are back."

How long until I would return to my home?

The giants looked different in their own earth, no longer diminished by twilight. No longer paled against the colors of my earth.

I studied them. Long, high-bridged noses. White hair, flowing loose. Muscled bodies wrapped in rough-spun cloth. Wild and earthy, they belonged here, in the noon light.

We sat in a clearing next to a river. It flowed over the edge of a dual-ridged cliff, rushing into the ravine below. The tree line of a deciduous forest stretched out behind us. The scent of musty leaves replaced the clean pine from the Knoll wood. Trees fluttered in the sunlight, casting lacy shadows onto the ground. Every plant, leaf, and blade of grass grew in shades of silvery white and metallic gray.

My eyes darted from trees to rocks to sky, as if I might find a piece of color among the glittering perfection. Despite the monochrome, the landscape was beautiful.

And it was terrible.

I didn't belong here.

Proce pointed at the river. "Those waters no longer flow into your earth. The thin place has closed. The color is gone."

After a long rest, Von took my hand. My fingers looked bright and delicate against her gray skin.

"Come. We have a long journey ahead of us."

Proce and Von took painstaking, short steps, trying to match my pace. Their movements were stiff, their long legs confined to something unnatural. That didn't last for long.

My cough shook my whole body.

"You must not walk anymore," Proce said. "You are still recovering." He swept me up into his arms and let his pace stretch free.

Under any other circumstance, I would have protested, but my legs ached and nausea weighed me down. I leaned against Proce's shoulder and tried not to cough on him. "Thank you."

A path led us through the leafy forest. The trees were old growth, tall enough to stretch high above the giants' heads. We didn't stop for meals. Von handed us clumps of toasted grain as they carried me down narrow paths and over craggy boulders. The giants walked late into the night, sometimes singing.

Proce's chest rose and fell against my ear as he took breaths.

> "Bless the new ones
> Bless the grain
> Sun be bright
> Bountiful rain
>
> Though Seven Cities

call me away
I will sing to you
on your wedding day."

"Sing with us," he said. "You must know the words by now."
He had sung it to me before, in the meadow.
"My head hurts too much." I covered my ears. "For singing . . .
or listening."
Von frowned. "I will heal you tomorrow, when my gift is
replenished."
"Von is usually a powerful healer. The crossing took more gift
than we should have used. But it was worth it."
As the night stretched on, Proce tucked me into his enormous
bag, then strapped it to his back. I barely fit. It was more restful
than walking, but you couldn't call it comfortable. I dozed lightly,
my knees scrunched into my chest. I longed to stretch out on soft
grass, or even Von's cushion.
"We are close," whispered Von
I opened my eyes and squeezed open the top of Proce's bag,
peeking out into the night. I couldn't see anything.
"How are you walking in the dark?" I asked. "You're going to
trip. Or get lost."
"It is a Cropper gift," Proce said. "We can always see the earth.
We are born this way."
Of course they could see in the dark. They were already strong
enough to carry me for miles, and they were ridiculously fast. Why
wouldn't they have night vision too? There was no hope of running
away. There never had been.
I looked over Proce's shoulder. Stars shone in the distance.
No, not stars. Lights.
They flickered close to the ground, moving like white flames.
"HOOOOOOO!" Von yelled.
I flinched, startled by the sound.
"HOOOOOOOOOOO!" Distant voices returned her call.
The lights moved toward us. Proce ran, jostling me up and

down in the bag. I fought to keep my view. Soon, the glow of white torches surrounded us, torches held by long, pale hands. Strange giants stood within my sight. I sank deeper into the bag, peeking out with just one eye.

Proce and Von laughed heartily. Booming voices joined in from every direction. They weren't laughing at a joke. It was the sound of a reunion, the kind of laughter that comes with friendship. Spontaneous. Unbidden.

A jumble of large figures gathered together, huddling in the torchlight. One by one, they rushed forward and clasped both hands together with Proce and Von, locking fingers before letting go. They patted Proce vigorously on the shoulders, shaking the bag on his back. I gripped the straps with rigid arms.

"We hoped you would return soon!" a giant exclaimed.

"Somebody, go get Urma!" a voice called.

I gaped at the giants from my hidden perch on Proce's back. Their rough skin ranged from ghostly white to dark gray. Some were even larger than Proce.

"No need to get me. I am right here." A female pushed her way to the front of the gathering.

The others quieted. She reached up and cupped Von's face with her leathery hands, then pulled both Proce and Von into an embrace, squishing Proce's bag, and me, inside of it.

"My children . . ." Tears shone in the giant's wrinkled eyes. "I have waited for this time."

Their mother. I had never imagined the giants having a mother, but everyone has a family. Why should my monsters be any different?

"Have you returned alone?" The mother furrowed her bushy brows.

Von looked to Proce, a secret smile on her lips. I ducked back in as he slid the bag from his shoulders and set me gently on the ground.

I shrank into my hiding spot, though I couldn't fully fit.

"It is time to come out." Proce pulled down the edges of the bag, exposing me to the crowd.

Silence settled over the giants.

They were a terrible gathering of creatures, gracefully tall and clad in flowing tunics. Their pale wisps of hair glowed feather-white in the flickering torches.

What a sight I must have been to them, like a wild creature, tiny and strange. My brown hair and pink cheeks, a dirt-stained jacket, and blue jeans, torn where I broke my leg. I had never felt so small in my life.

The mother took a torch and shone the light on my face. I recoiled.

"Look at me, new one." She placed a giant finger under my chin. "We need to see your eyes."

I lifted my gaze, and was blinded by the white flame of the torches.

"Eyes of hue." She spoke loud enough for the crowd to hear.

The creatures broke into raspy chatter and pressed in closer. A gray hand grabbed a strand of my hair. I jerked away and glared as hard as I could.

"Enough!" Proce boomed.

He closed the bag and hoisted it up, with me inside. My body crashed painfully against his back. Crammed into the small space, I couldn't see what was happening, which was almost worse than being exposed to the giants.

"She needs rest." Proce said over the din of voices. "We must keep her healthy."

I didn't hear a reply, but the others must have agreed. The bag swayed as Proce walked away and the clutter of voices receded.

"Let me out!" I pushed at the top of the bag.

Proce untied the straps and I poked my head out, taking deep breaths of fresh air as I bounced with his stride.

"Where are we going?"

"Home." Von grinned.

Soon, we came to a cottage. It was larger than the one from the meadow. The windows were decorated with a mosaic of silver beads, glittering in the torch light. Von led us inside and lit the hearth. The main room contained gracefully crafted chairs and tables. The polished wood and clean lines were a far cry from the rough-hewn furniture Proce and Von had used in the thin place. A soft rug cushioned the floor. Big, rectangular doors hinted at additional rooms or closets. Rows of hand-painted mugs and bowls hung on one wall.

"The night is a gift." Proce disappeared through one of the doors.

Von made a pile of blankets and cushions near the hearth. "You should sleep."

I didn't think I would be able to do much else. I took off my jacket and nestled into the blankets, shivering with a feverish chill. My cough tore at my throat. Von offered a mug of warm water and I drank it all before laying my head down.

I didn't remember falling asleep, but a while later, a noise woke me. I bolted upright. The fire had died and the cottage was dark. Near the door stood the shadowy outline of a giant, smaller than Proce or Von. Smaller than any giant I had seen, though lanky as a Cropper.

"Who are you?" My voice was hoarse.

The giant faced me for a moment, then turned and ambled out of the cottage, closing the door behind itself.

I reached for my jacket and my boots. What if I needed to run?

The boots were where I had left them. But the jacket was gone.

I removed the blankets and stumbled from my cushions. I had to find it. The jacket was a piece of my home, worn in a green pine forest. I spun around twice and groped at the floor in the dark.

"Peace, new one." Von emerged from her own pile of cushions, her outline barely visible.

"Where's my jacket?" I coughed and my chest ached.

"My mother sent a young Cropper to retrieve your yellow garment. They are sewing a gown for you now. The child is shy of strangers. I am sorry she frightened you."

I sank onto my blankets and rested my hand on the carpet where my jacket had been. They had taken everything from me. Why not this too?

"I don't need new clothes," I said. "I have human clothes."

Von left her sleeping place and came to me, tucking a blanket around my shoulders. "You need a Regent gown, if you are going to meet the king."

We slept late, long after daylight. Pale sunbeams poured through the ornate window panes. I heard Von get up. She sat at the table and sipped water from a massive bowl.

I rolled off my cushions and groaned, my head pounding. I felt like I had the flu.

"The day is a gift." Von beamed at me.

I rubbed my bleary eyes and coughed. "Doesn't feel like one."

"Oh. I only meant to use a common greeting." She thought a moment. "I guess I never said it before, when we were in between. It did not feel right . . . there."

Von brought me a cup of water and opened one of the interior doors. "There is a spout in here. You should bathe before your meal. Then, we will visit the village and see the others."

"Do we have to?" I pushed tangles behind my ears.

"They are eager to meet you. Proce and I will stay with you the whole time. The Croppers will be easier than the Regents. It is good practice."

I reminded myself that I had agreed to this. I needed these people to like me. I needed their King's Gift.

In the other room, a spout poured water into a wooden basin, large enough to swim in. I had to hoist myself over the edge and I could barely reach the tap. The water was cold, but at least the room was private and there was real soap. After the bath, my dirty jeans and shirt stuck to my wet skin. Did giants have laundromats?

"Hmmm." Von looked me up and down as I emerged from the bathing room. "At least your hair is clean. That will have to be enough for now." She worked through my tangles with her comb. "No braid today. We will let them see all your color, loose and unhindered."

Breakfast was grain and some kind of white fruit. It was sweet and buttery, and we scooped it from its shell with spoons.

Von wore a new tunic, crisp and gray. "Proce went to our mother's home this morning. We must meet him."

We walked down a cobblestone path, the blazing sun soaking into our skin.

Proce greeted us from another cottage. "The day is a gift!" He strolled beside us. "Are you stronger after sleeping?"

"I can walk by myself." Each step cost me. My lungs were congested and I fought to breathe.

A gathering of cottages sprawled along a river. Silvery fields stretched out on both sides, irrigated by shining canals. Beyond the fields, forested hills rolled into black mountains.

I stayed close to Proce and Von as we approached a broad circle of flat ground. At the center, a crowd of Croppers gathered. There must have been at least one hundred giants. They looked like a grove of aspen trees, long and white and fluttering. I hesitated, falling behind.

Von beckoned me forward. "Come, Meg. No one here will harm you."

I didn't move. The clamor of unfamiliar voices rang in my ears. Proce and Von had told me stories about Croppers and Regents, but I hadn't really comprehended their numbers. They were a community, a people group, and I was a stranger.

It was becoming too real. The gray earth. And the king.

I couldn't be the bride he was waiting for. It was too random. Too weird. But Proce and Von believed it with all their hearts. And that had begun to make me uneasy.

Von came back and took my hand. "Come on."

The voices died down. Every gray eye watched me from above.

Only days before, I had faced Proce and Von in the meadow. I had feared death then. What was I afraid of now?

Plenty.

Under normal circumstances, I didn't like crowds of humans. Not even humans I knew. This was a crowd of monsters.

But if I retreated to the cottage, I would only delay the inevitable. It would give them something more to stare at. Something to talk about, probably. Better to go willingly than to be a spectacle. I pulled my shoulders back and walked into the crowd, my chest tight.

Up close, the giants were more trousers and bodies and arms than they were faces.

"Proce!" A broad-shouldered giant emerged from the crowd. "We must meet your companion!"

The other Croppers took a seat in the grass, along the edge of the clearing, forming a half circle around us. An audience. When they sat, I could see their faces without straining my neck. They watched us, expectant.

"Meg, this is Erno." Proce spoke loud enough for all the Croppers to hear. "He is among those who watch over these fields."

Erno took a step back, so our eyes could meet. "I am skilled with water and plants. If you should ever need my help, I will share my gifts." He pointed toward the river. "I built at least half the canals you see. It is easy, if you know what you are doing. The water flows all the way from the Polaris. When you are queen—"

"Friend," Proce said. "There is plenty of time later to show her the fields. If you want to hear of our journey, you must let another Cropper speak besides yourself."

At this, the crowd erupted into laughter.

"He had to make up for you, Proce!" A weathered Cropper guffawed, his raisined face split with a smile. "With you gone, who else would speak endlessly?"

Another peal of laughter burst from the giants.

Proce chuckled. Erno did not.

A dark look passed over his face. "We thought you and Von were lost to us. The elders might have died, had you not returned when you did."

"But we did return," Proce said.

"It took you long enough. The cold is almost here."

Proce stood at his full height. "You think we do not know that? You think we did not risk our lives for this?"

"If it had been me, I would have come sooner. Everyone waited around for a human, as if the cold would not arrive."

Proce sighed. "If you sit, I will tell you the story. Then you will know what took so long. She is not going anywhere. There is no rush."

Proce patted Erno's shoulder, as if to ease the tension. Erno sat among the others, though he didn't look happy about it. Proce and Von stood facing their people. I screened myself behind their legs.

"We have hoped for this day," Proce began. "We are pleased to return to you, especially with such news." He looked down at me, then back to the Croppers. "Now, I will tell you the story of what happened. Later, we will write a song about it together."

Several Croppers gave a loud whistle.

"We will sing with you!" a voice yelled.

Proce waved a hand, waiting for them to quiet down. Then, he began his meandering story. He couldn't have hoped for a better audience. The Croppers listened to each word, sometimes stopping him to ask for more detail.

The story began with many quotes from the Writings. Then, Proce told of how he and Von had found the thin place. "We used the very last reserve of our gifts to go in between. But then, the color strengthened us again. We were blessed to have grain seeds with us. Otherwise, I fear we might have starved. The sun never moved, and the days were not warm, though they were not cold, either."

The Croppers gasped and asked a series of questions about gardening. Proce cited every difference in climate and soil, though he couldn't explain how the plants grew without the sun. "And the grass was green! Even weeds had a color."

Von spoke up. "There was beauty there. Yes. But we hoped each day that our years would not be wasted."

She described how they found me, and called me in between. "Meg did not trust us at first. Yet, after she saw our kindness, she agreed to come with us. She is a brave human, and she will help the Croppers. We have barely more than two years until the cold comes. Before then, Meg will save our sleep."

It wasn't exactly true. She was making me look good.

Von knew that I had only agreed to cross over because of the King's Gift, not because of her kindness. I had no idea how to save their sleep. I barely understood what the sleep was. In Von's story, I was a hero, and she was the herald of the good news.

Proce ended by quoting a familiar passage from the Writings. This time, he sang it in a somber tune.

> "She will walk upon silver
> Oh sleep, return upon her call"

A murmur arose from the seated giants.

"It is written." The whisper rippled through the audience.

Von stepped aside, her pale legs no longer shielding me from the gaze of the Croppers. They stared, and their silence grew, resting on me. Was I supposed to say something?

Proce's mother stood, and rescued me from the eyes. "Aggi, will you bring the gifts now?"

A Cropper stepped forward. She would have been tall for a human, but the other giants dwarfed her. Her long white hair fell in silky twists, shining with silver beads. Round eyes peeped shyly over soft cheeks. She lacked the usual lankiness of Cropper features.

She was a child, I realised. A new one. I searched all the faces in the gathering. She was the only child present in a crowd of adults.

Aggi approached us with wide eyes and a shy smile. She carried a bundle, wrapped in silver leaves.

"Here it is." She handed the bundle to Proce's mother.

The elder giant unwrapped the gift with long, crooked fingers. Then she held the contents out in front of her for the whole village to see.

They murmured their appreciation.

"I am Urma," she said to me. "Mother of Proce and Von, and most elder among the village. As a leader of these Croppers, I welcome you, Meg. We spent the whole night sewing this gown for you."

I took a step forward to see what she held. White, delicate fabric flowed from Urma's fingers. It was a small garment. A human-sized gown, stitched with iridescent thread that shone in the sun. From the shoulders hung a pearly cape, embroidered with bright yellow flowers. The color was striking against all the gray around us. Yellow, from my rain jacket, torn apart and repurposed.

The murmur of the crowd grew into yells and whistles.

Urma handed the dress to Von. "Before you go, we will fit the gown to your correct size. But first, Meg, you must sing for us!"

Sing? She couldn't be serious. The crowd shouted their enthusiasm, patting one another on the shoulders.

I put a hand over my mouth and shook my head at Von.

She bent close. "Croppers love to hear new songs. This is their chance to hear a human voice. They will not let you leave until you sing."

"I don't know any songs!" I protested.

"It does not have to be long. We have not heard any of your music before, so anything will be good."

Silence returned, demanding a performance.

I stared at my feet, highly aware of every second that passed. I coughed, trying to clear my congested lungs. Von laid a hand on my shoulder, humming her gift. My breath eased.

I always liked to sing, but only in my car, or in the shower. I had never performed a solo for a human, let alone one hundred giants.

Talking to them seemed impossible. Now I was supposed to sing? I tried to think of songs, but all the lyrics jumbled in my mind.

I remembered what Proce and Von had said about language. They thought I wouldn't speak English anymore, after the call to cross over. I hadn't believed them when they told me, but now I knew it was true.

I couldn't remember a song. Nothing from the radio. Nothing from a concert. I searched my mind. What about Christmas music? Nothing. None of the words rhymed in my head. They didn't fit with the melodies. I had a vague inkling of childhood tunes.

All the giants stared at me. I had to do something.

I opened my mouth, panicked, singing the only thing that would come out. The words formed by instinct. I barely understood them. The less I tried to understand, the easier they flowed.

> "Twinkle, twinkle, little star . . .
> How I wonder what you are . . ."

As I sang, I gained confidence. My voice rang out, a little high, but clear enough. The familiar consonants reminded me of my earth. I smelled pine and saw dusky-blue skies in my mind.

> "Up above the world so high,
> Like a diamond in the sky.
> Twinkle, twinkle, little star,
> How I wonder what you are."

The last note trilled into silence. My cheeks burned as I looked at the Cropper audience.

The giants exploded with whistles and shouts.

Von patted my shoulders, too vigorously. "You did well! It was not the skill of a Cropper, but we cannot sing so high."

Aggi smiled at me from the crowd. I smiled back and gave her a little wave. Her eyes followed my hand, but she didn't return the gesture. Did giants wave? I laughed from relief. It was over. I had sung to giants.

The laugh caught in my throat and turned into a cough. My chest filled with fluid again. In my coughing fit, the field spun. My vision blurred for a moment before clearing. I fell to one knee. The giants quieted as I wheezed.

Von grabbed my shoulder, her face tight with concern. "The call was worse than we feared. I will try to heal you again." She hummed a melody. Her touch returned a fraction of my strength, but I still couldn't breathe freely. I didn't stand up.

"She needs to rest." Proce picked me up and held me over his shoulder. "Her journey has been long."

Erno spoke. "You will probably take your time getting her to the Polaris too. I am tired of waiting. You should let another Cropper take her."

"Like you?" Proce asked. "Von and I found her. She knows us. I will not hand her over to another."

"As long as you hand her over to the king," Erno responded.

Proce didn't reply.

Urma and Von followed us back to the cottage. As we left, I saw the other Croppers turn toward one another, their voices low and their eyes narrow.

I spent the evening in my pile of blankets, sipping broth. The setting sun was a delight after so many days in twilight.

"Proce, can we check on Andrew? What if he's worse?"

He knelt beside me and touched my forearm. I closed my eyes to visualize Andrew. The familiar hum of Proce's gift warmed my skin.

This time, something was different. I saw Andrew, asleep on white sheets, a tube protruding from his nose. A shadow of scruff grew on his smooth cheeks, and a foil balloon floated next to his bed. But this wasn't a memory, or an image I conjured. I wasn't imagining it. The picture went beyond my own mind. It was real. I could feel it.

I took a breath and opened my eyes.

"I saw him. Not a memory . . . it was him. He's still . . . it's not better."

"Yes," Proce removed his hand from my arm. "I saw it too. His sleep is growing deeper, but there is strength in him yet. We have time to meet the king."

"When will we go?"

"Soon. Probably tomorrow."

"Do you think—" I started, then faltered.

"Yes?"

"Why can't Von heal my cough? Maybe some things can't be healed . . ."

"Von could heal your human, if he were here. It is only distance that stops her." He stood and began to pace. His footfalls caused the floorboards to shake.

"Then what's wrong with me?" I asked.

Proce stopped and took a long breath. "Your sickness is something we do not understand. We must ask the king. I will prepare for our travels tomorrow." Without another word, Proce left the cottage.

Von was resting in another room, drained from her many healing attempts. I blew steam from my broth and took another sip. My throat burned.

How had I ended up here, miserable on the floor of a cottage? It was because of my own decision to return to the falls. Why had I done that?

I sat upright, my stomach fluttering with panic. Wait, why had I returned? What had happened before Andrew fell?

I thought as hard as I could, but the memories wouldn't come. Everything before the meadow was fuzzy. I felt like I was trying to sing another song without knowing the lyrics.

What could I still remember?

Andrew. I remembered Andrew. But what were his parents' names? How had we met?

My mom . . . she was gone. But how long ago had I lost her? That part of my life was a blank space.

I stood, my hand pressed against my forehead.

"Von!" I shouted. "Von!"

A wooden door sprang open. In quick strides, Von crossed the cottage and knelt by my side. "What is it? Are you growing sicker?"

"Something's wrong with me. I . . . I can't remember . . . Why can't I remember?" I gave her a wide-eyed stare.

Von laid a hand on my shoulder, but I shrugged her away. "What did you do to me?"

"I wish I had done something. If it were my fault, maybe I would be able to fix it . . . We heard this might happen, but we hoped it was not true. The humans who are called to cross over . . . They sometimes forget their own earth. Some forget more than others."

I sat down hard, bruising my knees.

"I am sorry . . ." Von said.

I didn't look at her.

She picked up my empty bowl of broth. "Would you like another soup?"

I didn't answer.

My eyes glazed. I heard her footsteps and the sound of a creaking door.

I let my mind rest for two heartbeats, then I looked within, facing the blank places.

I thought of Andrew, and I remembered the night after my mother's death. We had been friends for years, but something changed that night.

"You shouldn't be here." I open the bedroom window to let Andrew through. He has climbed my uncle's arbor to see me.

"You shouldn't be alone. You don't have to talk or anything, unless you want to."

I feel numb, though my hands are shaking. "I don't think I can talk . . ."

Andrew wraps his arms around me.

I lean into him, my feet bare on my uncle's gritty floor. "Don't let go."

"I won't," he says.

And he doesn't.

As I sat in the Cropper cottage, I held tight to the memory of that hug. Andrew had stayed with me the entire night. I wouldn't forget that. Would I?

I searched my mind for more memories and I tried to picture my parents. I could see my mother's face, feel her warmth. There was still a hollow spot inside of me, a deep pain where her loss had torn me. I didn't think I would ever forget that, but I didn't remember my dad. I didn't even know his name.

I had to remember, to hold onto the memories. A part of me was slipping away—the part that made me who I was. It was happening fast. I needed to act quickly.

What was most important? Everything. I wanted to keep it all. But there was one thing, above all, that I couldn't afford to lose. My purpose—the reason I had crossed over.

I tried to think.

I stood and went to Proce's room. Rows of books and piles of paper lined the walls. I searched until I found what I was looking for in an oversized desk drawer. The huge pen was made from clear glass and filled with jet-black ink. I picked up a piece of iridescent paper. It reminded me of the stitching in Urma's dress.

A pen and paper had never struck me as miraculous until that moment. Now, they were the most valuable things imaginable. I could write words, words I wouldn't forget, words I could keep outside of my own mind. I wavered for a moment, awkward pen in hand. Then I scrawled the words I should have said before.

I love you Andrew.

I read the paper over and over. I wouldn't forget. I wouldn't lose this part of myself. The girl who loved someone.

Had I written in my own language? Or did I somehow spell out the Cropper dialect? It didn't matter. Either way, it meant something to me. I folded the paper as tightly as I could and tucked it into my pocket. Aside from the clothes I wore, it was now my only possession.

8

Later that evening, Urma returned to oversee the fitting of my new dress.

"You must remove your old clothes." She pointed up and down at my jeans and T-shirt.

"I-I'd rather keep them on." My voice rasped.

Urma gave a stern look. "I can smell you from here. Your clothes must be washed, I do not care how color-rich they are." She held out her hand, as if I would strip down right there and pass her my clothes.

If it had been Von, I would have protested, but something about Urma made me think twice before arguing.

"Alright . . ." I stood on tiptoe to open the bathroom door. "But first I need a bath."

Urma took a step to follow.

"In privacy," I added. "Then I'll bring out my clothes."

Once the door was securely shut, I undressed. The bathroom spout poured chilly water into my hands. I splashed my face and hair, then wrapped an itchy towel around myself. It covered all the way to my ankles. I cracked the door open and peeked my head into the main room.

Urma sat in the corner on a stack of cushions. "Have you had enough privacy yet?"

Clutching the towel, I handed her my stiff jeans and T-shirt. She placed the clothes into a mesh bag, holding them at a distance.

"They don't smell that bad," I grumbled.

"Stand right here." Urma took my shoulders and positioned me in the middle of the room. She unfolded the delicate white-yellow dress she had made for me and billowed it over my head.

I wiggled my arms into the sleeves.

Urma reached underneath and whisked away my towel. "No need for that."

"I can do it myself!" I rushed to pull the skirt down, and my lungs quaked with a series of coughs.

"What do you think of your gown?" Urma eyed her handiwork.

The garment rested gently against my skin, light and cool, made for the white-hot sun of the gray earth. The delicate fabric had a floral scent.

"It's nice." I ran my fingers over the gossamer stitching.

"I told Ota that she made these sleeves too long. Wait until I show her how much fabric I had to remove!" Urma pinched bits of extra cloth, snipping away the loose parts with an oversized pair of shears. She cinched the waistline, skin tight, and pinned it in place.

"That's too much!" I twisted my body and the fabric moved with me, stretching with ease. "I don't like it so close."

"Ha!" Urma secured a yellow belt around my middle, the only whole remnant from my raincoat. "You will see how Regents wear their dresses. Then, maybe you will not complain so much."

After more stitching and cutting, Urma packed away her sewing kit. "There. It is done."

She reached for the bag that held my dirty clothes.

"Wait!" My paper note to Andrew was still inside the pocket of my discarded jeans. "I need to get something out before you take them. And . . . my clothes are the only things I have left from home."

Urma looked into my eyes. "I will be careful with them. You cannot imagine what you mean to us. To every Cropper. I thank you for leaving your home. Humans must be a brave people."

"We'll see." I coughed into the crook of my arm.

"You doubt yourself?" Urma asked.

"Not exactly . . ." I doubted the prophecy.

"The writings only tell us where we are going. They do not say how we will get there. But, I promise, you will get there."

"What makes all of you so sure of the Writings?" I asked. "Who wrote them?"

"Many Regents wrote them, but the writers are not important. The words were given from the same source as the other gifts. You will learn to trust."

Trust. I now trusted Proce and Von to care for me. To comb my hair and heal my wounds and carry me in their arms. But when it came to the Writings, I didn't trust anything. The giants thought I was the solution to their troubles. They were desperate. I, of all people, knew how far desperation could drive a person. It was why I was here.

Urma handed me the mesh bag. I opened it with shaking hands and removed my note.

Urma watched me. "I will return your clothes before you leave our village."

I nodded, and gave her the bag, keeping my note in my palm.

She flashed a toothy smile that reminded me of Von. "First, you will trust me with your clothes. Then, more trust will follow. You will see."

From a closet, Urma took a large mirror. It was full-length for a giant, framed in an oval of carved wood.

"See what you think of the fitting." She leaned the mirror against the wall and pointed it toward me.

My reflection glittered back at me. I had almost forgotten how small I was. White evening light shone through an open window, illuminating iridescence in the cloth of the dress. The snug waistline highlighted my curves, and the sleeves draped in flowing layers over my freckled arms.

Next to Urma, in the huge mirror, I looked ruddy and unkempt. Black dirt still lined the rims of my fingernails. My hair was in shambles. I hadn't washed thoroughly enough in the cold water.

"I cannot heal your cough," Urma said, "but I can do this." She laid a rough fingertip against my cheek and hummed a gentle tune. "You should look your best for the Regents."

The little bumps and red patches that usually marked my face disappeared. My cheeks became as smooth as rose petals, pale and gently blushed.

What a waste.

Andrew wasn't here to see me like this. Not a single human. At one time, I would have loved to have perfect skin—to walk the halls of my school without makeup and to feel pretty. Now, it made me feel less human, like the gray earth was changing me. All these gifts couldn't come for free.

"Can you undo it? It's . . . a lot."

"To Croppers, your color is beauty enough," Urma said. "But Regents prefer perfection. This is better. Von will fix your hair later. You have helped the Croppers, and we will help you, however we can."

I hadn't helped them. I couldn't help them. "Thank you. You must have a powerful gift, to be a leader of the village."

"I have hardly any gifts, compared with my children. The gift does not make the leader. We are given what we need, to do what we must."

Movement drew my eye to the open window. A bird, as large as a pigeon, floated into the room and landed on the windowsill.

I took a step back.

Its body looked like a white hummingbird and its face curved into a graceful beak. A silver ridge crested its head and enormous butterfly wings adorned its back. Black feathers lined the edges of the wings. The centers of the wings were clear, like glass.

The bird chirped a soft trill, and I edged away from it. Urma glanced at the creature.

"What is it?" I asked.

"A field besmonn. The besmonn keepers build homes for them near the trees. The besmonns help our crops to grow, and they made the thread I used for your dress."

I examined the glistening stitches on my sleeve.

Urma lowered herself onto a cushion, coming to eye level with me. "When Proce was a child, he loved the besmonns. He used to chase them around and write funny little songs about them. I wonder if he still remembers the words?"

I couldn't imagine Proce as a kid. "Is Aggi the only child in your village now?"

"Of course. Aggi had a sister, but she was grown and moved away by the time Aggi arrived. It is the same with Proce and Von. Proce had already lived one hundred years when Von was born. Both of them are growing old now. Von must marry soon, if she wishes to bear a child. It is her deep hope."

Urma pointed at a piece of wood furniture in the corner. It was a box, lined with thin cushions, set on rocking legs. "I gave that cradle to Von, when she became old enough to marry. Someday, I hope she can use it. If she hadn't left, there might have been another child in the village for Aggi to play with. We try to time it that way for them, if we can."

What a lonely childhood, their only siblings spaced by decades. "How long does it take a Cropper to grow up?" I asked.

"Not long enough," Urma said. "And, some days, too long."

I studied the deep lines that mapped Urma's face. "How old are you?"

"Ha!" she laughed. "Too old. In our earth, we live long. But do not worry, the king is still in his youth, not a hunched elder like me. You will see, tomorrow."

Tomorrow.

I smoothed the feather-light cape that flowed from my shoulders. It was the dress I would wear when I met the king.

In one day, Andrew would be healed. I wouldn't think about the rest.

The besmonn flapped its gossamer wings and floated away, returning to the outdoors.

Urma handed me the towel I had used before. "I must take your dress to finish the seams."

"What will I wear?" I asked.

"Von has many cushions. You will not be cold."

That night, I wore only a towel beneath my blankets, my note to Andrew hidden beneath my pillow. I hardly slept. Instead, I coughed, my thoughts reeling with the day to come.

The next morning, Von gave me a tiny bar of soap. "Wash with this today. And scrub well."

The bar was perfumed, sweet and floral.

I took as long as possible in the bathroom. I wanted the quiet morning to last forever. Eventually, I had to climb out of the wooden basin, my fingers waterlogged and my skin pink from the cold water.

My sickness was getting worse. I caught myself on the edge of the basin, and stars danced in my vision as I shivered and fought for breath.

After the morning meal, Urma brought in my dress. She had reinforced the bodice to be supportive, so I didn't need to wear anything underneath. A nice touch, since my chest had always been fuller than I liked, and I was definitely curvier than any of the long, slender Cropper women. The skirt flowed perfectly to the tops of my toes, and the cape trailed behind me as I walked.

"These go with the gown." Urma sat me down and eased a pair of glossy slippers onto my feet. "They are spun from besmonn thread."

Von combed my hair into submission and braided silver beads around the crown of my head. The rest of my hair she left loose.

"Seven ornaments." She counted them out. "It is a blessed number."

"Blessed how?"

"It is the number of wholeness. Seven Regent cities. Seven

Cropper Elders. I do not know why seven. It has always been so. Some things we must accept without explanation."

Even with explanation, I found most things here hard to accept. Giants who lived for hundreds of years. Poems that made good creatures do terrible things, like kidnap me.

Next, Von opened a jar full of shimmering powder. Her finger barely fit through the top of the glass. "This comes from the besmonns too." She smoothed the powder over my eyelids, my nose, and the backs of my hands.

"You're going to make me look all shiny and sweaty," I said.

"The Regents would wear more than I have used. But we do not want to hide your golden skin. They should see your color."

Urma brought the bag with my clean clothes. "The tunic is useless." She was referring to my gray T-shirt. "But the trousers are blue. We have not seen color so rich in a long time. It is a treasure. Keep it close."

"May I pack your clothes in my satchel?" Von asked.

I nodded my consent, thankful I wouldn't have to carry anything.

"Perhaps you could offer them as a gift to the King's House?" Von closed the flap to her bag, hiding away my only possessions. "It might win some favor. But only if you wish."

Favor. I'd need that to make my request, more than I needed jeans.

"Alright. Let's give them away." The words weren't easy to get out. A warm breeze blew through my dress, as if mocking the loss of my clothes.

I took my note and tucked it into my neckline, repeating the written words in my mind.

"It is time," said Von. "We must go."

I stepped into the hot sun, leaving Von's cottage for the last time. Proce waited for us on the cobblestone path. He and Von clasped hands with Urma and with each other, forming a circle.

Urma sang a few words.

"A father's teaching,
a mother's song,
will guard your step
when the road is long."

When the song ended, Urma spoke to her children, tears in her eyes. "I had hoped we would not part so soon. But this is the way it must be, and it is good."

"It is good," Von agreed. "Thank you for your blessing."

Urma walked with us through the village. "You must carry the human," she told Proce. "We cannot let her become dusty. And do not crumple her gown."

Urma had called me *the human*. Not Meg. To all of them, I was a creature. Maybe more so than they were to me, now that I had spent time in their earth.

Proce picked me up. I let him. I wouldn't admit it, but my lungs were burning, and I didn't know how far I could walk on my own.

Every Cropper in the village came to say goodbye. They lined the road, whistling their farewells.

"Thank you for your song!" called a male giant.

Aggi held a white flower out to me, her over-large eyes intent. "Please come back again, and bring your children, so we can play."

Children? I wanted to recoil, but Aggi was just a little girl. She couldn't understand. So, I smiled at her and took the flower, despite her unsettling comment. How much of my future did these Croppers have planned? I didn't want to think past Andrew's healing.

Urma stayed with the others as we followed a smooth road through silver fields. Distant trees promised shade from the hot sun.

Proce held me carefully, taking long steps. "Our village is the closest one to the Polaris. The Polaris is the oldest, most beautiful of the Seven Cities, and it is where the king lives."

I took a deep breath, and tried not to cough on Proce. My joints ached with every bump and jostle. "How long will it take to get there?"

"Not long, on Cropper legs. We will arrive by evening. I hope you do not mind if I carry you the whole way? You walk slow."

"It's okay."

"You can rest when we get to the King's House," Von said. "And he will heal you."

Rest. That's all I wanted to do. My head was pounding. A bed sounded amazing, but I would have settled for soft grass or a hard bench. Anything but Proce's sharp collarbone, though I was glad for his strength.

"Thank you," I said. "For carrying me."

Proce didn't respond, but I looked up and saw him smile.

"You think they'll have a bunch of questions for us?" I asked. "Like when we arrived at the village?" Would they demand to see my eyes?

"The king will likely sense you are coming," Proce said. "It is one of his gifts. His house will be prepared, and your needs will be met. Would you like to hear a story about the Royal Gifts?"

"Mmmhmm." My throat was raw, and it hurt to talk.

"It is because of the Queen's Gift that the Polaris has grown so large." Proce transitioned into his teaching voice. "I will tell you a story about Queen Arielas. She reigned 5,362 years ago."

I coughed.

Proce paused.

"Keep going," I said.

"Queen Arielas loved her people deeply. Especially the Croppers. We always have a special connection to the queens. Queen Arielas wanted us to be near to her. Because of this desire, she used her gift to raise up the city. She made towers and rooms, perfectly suited for every Cropper. This exhausted her for more than three years afterward."

Proce walked a little taller, his head high, as if he were the one doing a noble deed in a story. Maybe he was.

"Before her final days, Queen Arielas blessed the villages. She made new roads that led to the Polaris. On her roads, you will still find that your legs feel longer and your way is easier. It is part of the gift. We walk on such a road now."

I looked at the smooth path beneath Proce's feet. The stone didn't have a single crack or scam, as if it had been carved from one long slab.

"Without the King's Gift, the Regent cities could not stand," he said. "They are all gift-made. Now, the king must do the work of Queen Elia too. We have never lost a young queen. Not until Elia. She was the most beautiful of all the Regents."

"Let us speak of something else," Von said.

"Yes," agreed Proce. "I will tell you about the first City Watcher. He saved Queen Luannia from a wild beast. That was before she received the Queen's Gift. She reigned 12,281 years ago."

I half listened as Proce told the story, my head rested against his shoulder. When he finished, he started another story, and then another. Not all of them were interesting. Sometimes he just recited long lists of Croppers who had served on various councils. One list spanned over twelve thousand years. He knew the birth date of each Cropper.

I closed my eyes and allowed the rumble of his voice to distract me from my aching body.

"Croppers should keep better records," Proce said. "We leave it up to the Regents, but they are not diligent with Cropper matters. Regents write poetry best. If I were a word keeper in the Polaris Library—"

"But you are not," said Von. "No Cropper ever will be."

"But I could write it all down," Proce lamented. "And there is so much to organize. In the old days, there used to be a gifted way of searching the books, but now it is all done by hand. I can reach the tallest shelves. And Croppers can be just as gifted with words, though most put it into their songs rather than books. I cannot write prophecy, but neither can most Regent word keepers in this generation. Overall, they could really use a more meticulous eye. If they would just read my application."

"Yes," Von said. "I have heard this before. You are trying to convince the wrong person."

"You may not enjoy my stories, but Meg does. Do you not, Meg?"

"Mmmm." I shivered in the warm air, my breath labored.

In. Out. Each gasp a fight.

"She is worsening." Proce laid me in the cool shade of a leafy tree. We were in a forest once more. "Von, you must try to heal her again."

Von placed her hand on my chest, above my lungs. As she hummed, my headache lessened, but my breathing did not improve. I tried to cough, but it hurt too much.

"We must hurry," Von said.

Proce lifted me and took off at a faster pace. I focused on breathing. The day faded into gray sunset. My mind was confused, starved for oxygen. Would the sun rise again? Or would it be stuck, like the in-between place?

"Look!" Von said.

The jog took us over the crest of a hill. Through a break in the trees, our road stretched into the valley, winding alongside a river, backed by dark mountains. At the end of the road stood a black city that shone like glass in the dusky light. Domes topped mirrored towers behind rows of walls. It was building upon building, delicate structures joined together to make a fortress, sprawling across planes of lush silver. How many Regents lived there? Thousands? Tens of thousands?

"The Polaris," Proce said.

I wanted to ask about the size of the city, but when I tried to speak, I choked. My coughs were strangled, my breath croaking and painful.

Von's eyes widened. "We need to run."

And they did.

9

"Slow your feet, Croppers!" Ahead of us, three figures emerged from a grove of trees. They wore black hoods.

Proce and Von slowed their canter.

"Regents," Proce whispered to me.

The men bowed one by one, crossing their arms over their collars in the style Von had taught me. Their hooded gazes rested on me, but they spoke to Proce.

"The king sent us," said one of the Regents. "We'll guide the human to him. Thank you for all you've done. We can take her from here."

I leaned in closer to Proce. Would I have to face the king without the giants beside me?

Proce's grip tightened.

"She is unwell," he said. "We must carry her."

"Then you need to cloak her," the Regent replied. "Otherwise, she'll draw a crowd, and we'll never make it through."

He held out a hooded cloak.

"The people will wonder why a Cropper's child is wearing a Watcher's shade," Von said.

"But they will not see her color," Proce said. "And they will not guess she is a human. How could they?"

He took the cloak and wrapped it around me. I slumped beneath the cover, weak from fever.

"Time is running out," Proce said. "She needs the king."

He raced down the road. I could no longer hold onto Proce. All of my weight was in his arms and he clutched me tighter.

The Regents ran after us. Soon, the city loomed near.

"Hold the gate!" a Regent cried. "For the sake of the king!"

Proce leapt over water, followed by Von. It was the river, flowing around the walls of the Polaris.

The Regents splashed through, and darted under a high gate in the wall.

"This way!" they called.

In a haze beneath my cloak, I watched the Polaris flash by. To me, the city streets consisted of blurred lights and unfamiliar voices. Proce jostled me in his arms as he sped through a crowd of people.

No. Not people. Regents.

I caught snippets of conversation. I couldn't tell women's voices from men's.

"Croppers in the city this time of year?"

"They have the best summer fruit."

"The king has—"

"—windy lately, don't you think?"

"Make room!" the Regent who led us shouted, clearing space in the street.

My breath came in painful spurts.

"We are here." Proce carried me through a door.

I squinted against artificial light.

Proce set me on my feet, but I fell to my knees, and the cloak slipped from my shoulders. Figures moved around me, out of focus, and I heard hissing whispers. I choked, tasting blood. Bright red droplets splattered across my skirt. Red against white. My blood, from my lungs.

Von's hand rested on my shoulder, too heavy to bear. She sang a healing melody, but the fire in my lungs wouldn't be cooled. It blazed.

I couldn't breathe at all. My airway closed. My life was slipping away from me. Why had I thought I could help Andrew? I couldn't help anyone. Not myself. Not Proce and Von. Was this what my mom had felt like, when she died?

I clutched at the scrap of paper in my pocket, my note to Andrew. He would never read it.

A cool hand brushed against my cheek. It wasn't Von's tender hand. It was solid, and sure.

I blinked through dark spots in my vision. A low sound hummed in my ears. Or maybe it hummed in my mind. It was like Proce's gift, but off-key. Something about it felt itchy, unsettling. It seeped into my lungs and put out the fire.

I could breathe again.

I gulped a mountain of air and steadied myself against the floor.

"Are you well?" Von asked. "Meg? Are you well?"

"She is." A man's voice replied for me.

The king's voice.

Who else could have healed me?

I opened my eyes and stood as gracefully as I could manage, smoothing my blood-stained skirt. This was not the first impression I had hoped for.

Before me stood a man, taller than a human, small beside a Cropper. He had ashen skin, smooth over high cheekbones, his face youthful, though older than mine. A black jacket fit snug on his lithe figure. His eyes met mine. Strange eyes. The irises were ice-white, rimmed with black.

He was the man from my dream.

"And you're going to remain well," he said. "Now you're with me."

Those eyes pried into mine, deeper, until I wanted to turn away. I didn't speak. I didn't know what to say. After a moment, he looked at Proce. Relief flooded me.

"You've done well," he told Proce. "Though I might have felt differently, had you arrived moments later. She would have died."

Proce bowed his head to the man. "We did not know that the call to cross over would linger with her, and we should have brought her sooner. I understand if you wish to send me away, but please let my sister remain with the human. Von has grown to care for the child."

The man reached up and clasped Proce's hands, fingers interlaced, as the Croppers had done in the village. "I'm not sending anyone away. You've done a great thing by calling her here. When time allows, I want to hear every detail of your story."

Von bowed to the man. "I tried to heal her, but I was not strong enough. Your King's Gift was our last hope."

Her words confirmed what I already knew. Here was the king of the Croppers and the Regents. I had imagined a king like Proce, long and benign, with a silver crown. The real king was as pale as a Cropper, but that was where their similarity ended. All of his angles were sharp, like a creature built for speed. He wasn't human, and he definitely wasn't handsome, but there was something about him that drew the eye. He was grand, solid, like the statue of a young man, carved from ancient stone.

And I was afraid of him.

Why? His words had been kind.

Everything was happening too fast. Moments ago, I had been dying. Now, I needed time to think. I took a step backward, my eyes searching for exits.

The room was formed of black, glossy walls and a marbled floor. Cones of light hung from the high ceiling, like glowing stalactites. For the first time, I noticed the Regents at the edges of the room, watching with silent faces.

Some of them wore black cloaks. Others dressed in shining gowns and robes. The women's hair twisted and curled into piles of braids, swept high above pale shoulders, shimmering with besmonn dust. Their lips were painted black.

Von had been right. The Regents were more human-sized than the Croppers. But something about them looked less human. Their eyes glazed unnaturally pale, their skin stretched over chiseled features, too precise to be lovely.

The king turned to face Von. "Thank you for taking care of the human. I'm afraid it wasn't the call to cross over that made her sick.

Humans weren't created for our earth. Without the King's Gift, our air would poison her. It's a little-known fact, but it's why every human has lived in the Polaris."

Von spoke to Proce, incredulous. "You never read of this? The poison?"

The king answered, "The history books of humans tend to gloss over their weaknesses. Romanticize things. Idolize them. It's more poetry and story than real history. I'm not surprised you haven't read about human sickness. My father told me about it, when I was new. In the future, we need records with real facts. Solid research."

As the king spoke, he watched me. I felt examined. And not just by him. I edged closer to Proce and Von. They were the closest thing I had to friends in that crowd of glittering, pointed eyes.

My hair was damp from sweat, and the day's grime stuck to my skin. I was the smallest creature in the room and I hadn't managed to say a single word. This wasn't the proper introduction Von had trained me for. Was now the right time to bow? Even with all my training, I knew nothing about these people.

"She'll need me to heal her daily for the rest of her life." The king smiled. "A task well worth the effort."

10

The king turned to the Regents in the room. "You've seen her, as requested. Now go tell the others. You'll have plenty of time to stare at the human later."

They would?

The men in black cloaks opened a doorway, filing out of the room. The others followed, leaving by twos and threes. They whispered into one another's ears.

Some of the cloaked Regents stayed behind.

"Please show our guests to the best Croppers' rooms," the king said to a Regent. "I'd say they've earned their rest."

The hooded man beckoned to Proce and Von.

I took a step to follow after them.

The king noticed. "The human girl will come with me."

The human girl? He talked like I wasn't in the room. He didn't even know my name. If I was going to persuade him of anything, to win his favor and use his gift, this wasn't a good start. If I went with him, I would be alone, intimidated, shaken, and dappled with my own blood. I needed rest.

"My name is Meg. Thank you for healing me. For tonight, I would prefer to go with Von." I reached to hold Von's hand, but she shook her fingers free.

"Welcome, Meg." The king emphasized my name.

Von stepped away from me. I pleaded to her with my eyes,

begging her not to go. I couldn't explain it, but something about the king made me want to run away. To hide.

"I'm sorry," the king said. "The Croppers' rooms are not suited for humans. I'll take you to your own suite."

He gestured toward a door on the other side of the room, opposite the Croppers' direction.

I didn't move.

Von knelt beside me. "It is alright. We will only be a short passage away from you. We need our rest too."

She placed her hand on my shoulder and her gift flowed into me. It didn't carry healing. It carried courage and strength.

How strange that she was sending me away now. Back in the meadow, she had worked so hard for me to come near. Since leaving my earth, I had become used to Von's company. She was always nearby.

The king spoke. "I promise you, you'll be safe as long as you're under my protection. You don't have anything to fear. Your friends can come visit you after you're settled in."

"Tonight?" I asked.

The king said nothing.

"Proce," I said. "Do you promise that I'm going to see you again tonight?"

If the giants were leaving me for good, Proce would let it slip. He had never been able to hold back secrets from me, even when it would have been convenient. Except for once, before the second crossing. Von might lie to make me less afraid. Or at least, she might avoid the truth.

"I promise," Proce said. "Upon my own fields. Now, you must go with the king."

I took a reluctant step away from Von, and she followed the cloaked Regent, disappearing with Proce through the archway.

Another cloaked Regent stayed behind, so I wasn't alone with the king.

"Follow me." The king headed toward the other door.

I trailed behind him as he led me into a hallway with more black walls. The floor matched the walls, smooth and glassy.

The king walked slowly, waiting for me to match his pace. I ambled along, purposefully falling behind, where I could see his back. Two cloaked Regents followed us at a measured distance.

I took deep breaths, marveling at the ease in my lungs. The drops of blood on my dress were the only evidence of my almost-death.

"You're welcome," the king said over his shoulder. "For healing you."

What should I say? I settled on a shy smile and a nod.

The king was responsible for my miracle. Was he also responsible for my sickness in the first place? If not for him, Proce and Von would never have taken me from my home, into their toxic earth. I didn't like the king's talk about "solid research." I wasn't a science experiment. Would the king be another captor to contend with, or a savior for Andrew? Maybe both.

My mind wandered to memories of the waterfall meadow, where I had experienced my first miracle. I already missed the green grass and the blue skies of my own earth. My eyes were color starved. All the gray and black and white blended together. I wanted to see a human face, soft and warm. The Regents were too sharp. Almost human, but distorted, which made them worse than a creature.

"We're not so bad." The king interrupted my thoughts. He turned to walk backward, so he could look at me. "You'll get used to Regents."

"I'm sorry?" I sounded as polite as I could manage.

"The minds of humans are somewhat clouded from my vision. Still, I can see vague images. You were contemplating your own earth, and you feel unsure toward my people. Something about our faces? You'll get used to us. All the humans have."

I swallowed the lump in my throat. He could see my mind, my secret thoughts. Somehow I had known it, ever since he healed me, as if a stray piece of thread had been loose in my thoughts, causing an unacknowledged itch.

This gift was too much. It went too far. How was I supposed to convince the king of anything, if I couldn't even think to myself? I had lost my whole earth, even my memories. I wouldn't lose my thoughts too.

My hands formed fists.

If the minds of humans were cloudy to the king, maybe I could burrow deeper into that cloud. I wrapped my thoughts in opaque mist, as thick as a rainstorm. I imagined a wall of rushing water between us, a thousand miles of wind pushing him away. I dug at the itching thread with my mind and picked it out.

The king stopped and gave me a curious look. "Well done. I won't read you so easily after all."

He didn't seem displeased. That was good.

I stared at the walls as I walked. Cones of light glowed in the halls, lighting our path. We passed gleaming doors and archways. The stone was seamless, as if carved from one giant rock, like the Queen's Road. Swirls of black glass decorated the doors, spun thin as webs. The ceilings were high. Too high to be supported by the delicate arches and walls. It all looked like it would break.

After a few turns, the king stopped in front of the only unremarkable door I had seen. It was small and wooden, with a tiny silver knob.

Not tiny. A human-sized knob. I hadn't seen anything like it in weeks.

The king opened his jacket and removed a key, silver like the knob. Bright red silk lined the inside of his clothes, a hidden luxury, red as blood.

"These are the human rooms of the King's House." He unlocked the door and entered, ducking by an inch so that he didn't hit his head on the frame. A Cropper would have had to hunch through.

I was supposed to follow him, but I froze. The other Regents waited at the end of the hall. If I crossed the threshold, I would be alone with the king.

Why did that unsettle me?

And why had he taken me here himself? Couldn't a servant have done it? I reminded myself that I wanted his interest. I needed his interest to make my request. I took a deep breath and forced my legs to move, entering the room.

My eyes swept every corner of the large suite. More light hung from the vaulted ceilings. Thick carpet covered the stone floors, swirling with intricate floral designs. Everything glimmered in shades of white and gray. Something like vanilla scented the air.

A mosaic decorated the wall behind a velveteen ottoman, glass arranged in a geometric pattern. The mosaic was unobtrusive, the type of art hung in waiting rooms and lobbies. It said nothing.

Arches and doorways lined the farthest walls. What could be behind those doors? More Regents? More halls? I was lost, in a strange house, in a strange earth.

"This place was made for Analese," the king said. "Our last human. She's gone now, but I knew her when I was a child. The rooms are perfectly suited to your needs."

If the king knew Analese, then he was more than two hundred years old. Older than Proce and Von. A shudder ran through me. He had no right to look so young.

"These are your rooms now. You should look around." The king pointed to the nearest archway.

A curtain of crystals, dangling on strings, masked what lay beyond.

"Go on." He waited.

I moved toward the arch and parted the curtain. Crystals tinkled together. On the other side, a flight of three steps led to another room. In the middle of the floor, resting upon a gleaming dais, was a human-sized bed.

A real bed. Croppers liked to sleep on the floor, surrounded by heaps of blankets and pillows. Beds were something that belonged in my old earth.

Another part of the room belonged in my old earth too. A thin blue curtain hung in a window behind the bed. At home, it would have been an ordinary, shabby thing. Not wide enough to be useful. Here, in this earth, the curtain was breathtaking.

A second spot of color caught my gaze. Though it was small,

it was the brightest feature in the room. On a bedside table sat a figurine made from polished bronze. The little statue formed the shape of a woman with an hourglass figure. From her eyes shone two amber gems. She was human, as out of place as I was.

I heard another tinkle of crystal. The king stood behind me and I stiffened. His presence grew in my mind, and I hid away from it.

"The sculpture was made in the image of Analese," he said. "Her husband formed it when she passed away. Its color is valuable, and it's needed elsewhere soon. But I thought it would comfort you during your first night here."

The object was the shadow of a human. A woman, gone by hundreds of years. She was a ghost. How was that supposed to bring comfort?

"The curtain . . ." I said. "The sculpture. They're from my earth." Did the king have a way to travel there?

"Yes. A few things in our earth are from your home. Some cloth was brought by humans who crossed over. We preserved the color with our gifts. Other things, stones and metal, we called from your earth. It takes an excess of power. These things are rare, valuable. But a human being here . . . Well, it's more than many hoped to see in a lifetime."

As the king spoke, the weight of his mind returned, the itch that burrowed into my thoughts. He was trying to see inside my head. I had let my walls slip. Would I have to fight for privacy every moment I was with the king?

I pinpointed the itch, like a burr lodged between my ears. I imagined a rainstorm. A flash flood, washing through my head and dislodging the king. It worked. The itch receded. I thickened my walls again, a double sentry to keep him out. I felt better than I had since coming to the gray earth, thanks to the king's healing. Still, my head hurt with the effort of guarding my thoughts.

But I was doing it. I was winning.

"When will Proce and Von come?" I asked.

"Soon. If you need anything, send word to me through one of my Watchers. They'll stay outside your door."

I only needed one thing. I didn't turn around, but I felt him step closer to me. My headache deepened, as if I had been clenching my jaw for hours.

"Or whisper my name," he said. "I may hear you with my gift. There's power in a name."

His name? Of course he had one. He couldn't just be called *the king.* If I whispered it, would he come to me and heal Andrew? What if he said no? I had to ask in the right way.

"What are you called?" I asked.

"I'm Kalmus. And I've waited a long time for you. Tomorrow, after you've rested, I want to talk with you again."

I kept my eyes on the blue curtain as he walked away. When the outer door creaked and latched, I sank into the carpet, relieved to be alone.

I don't know how long I lay there, unable or unwilling to think about anything but the softness of the carpet, and the reprieve of solitude. The mental struggle between the king and me had held a strange power, a sense of accomplishment, as I matched him moment by moment. I had almost enjoyed the feeling, despite the headache. And that made me hate it.

Could it be true? What the Croppers said he wanted from me? He was something ancient and ominous. And I was . . . me. I was playing a game and I didn't know the rules. Or maybe I had been ignoring the rules, focused only on the end.

After a while, Proce and Von came to the human rooms. I heard their voices as soon as the door swung open.

"See here. I found the right place." Proce's voice drifted in from the entrance. "Look how small this door is. How are we supposed to fit through it?"

Von let out a snort. "Perhaps if you were less thick in the middle you would be able to fit."

I smiled. There wasn't a single Cropper that I would describe as *thick*.

There was a sound of shuffling and scraping, and maybe some shoving.

Soon, Von knelt at my side. "Are you ill again?" she asked. "Should we call for the king?"

"No." I sat up. "Please don't. I feel fine." A strange shiver ran through me at the thought of facing the king again.

"Your rooms are lovely," said Von.

Proce crossed his arms. "I will not pretend these rooms are of adequate size. Meg is a human, not a field besmonn." He eyed the ceiling and hunched his shoulders.

I felt trapped too.

"Why don't you sit down." I patted the carpet.

The Croppers reclined on the floor, straightening their cramped joints. Their long limbs looked out of place against the woven designs and sleek walls. Proce and Von belonged in wooden rooms and silver fields, their hair blowing in soft breezes. What were the Cropper rooms like?

"Maybe I could stay with you tonight?" I suggested. "I can help Von make soup . . ." I hadn't eaten since the morning meal.

Proce looked at Von and she shook her head.

"Why not?" I asked.

Von spoke first. "The king would like you to rest in your own rooms. We only have a moment to see you, then you must sleep."

"Can't you at least show me where you're staying?" I asked.

"I am sorry," Von said. "The Watchers will come for us in a moment."

I didn't have much time, then.

"Proce?" I asked. "Can you help me check on Andrew?" I needed to remember why I had crossed over, why I needed to face the king.

As soon as Proce nodded, I reached to clasp his hand. At first, he tensed at my unusual initiation, then rested his fingers against my palm. My hand couldn't wrap around all of Proce's, so I held his thumb.

"I'm ready." I closed my eyes and pictured Andrew's face.

"We are further away from the human earth now," Proce said. "Memories will especially help the connection. Think of your time together, if you can."

I took a deep breath and looked into my memory, afraid I might find nothing. In shifting scenes, memory greeted me, surrendered to the hum of Proce's gift.

I glide forward on concrete, wheels attached to my shoes. Skates. They're called skates.

Andrew smiles his approval, skating faster. He's always faster. His voice teases me. "Hurry up, slow poke!"

I fall onto green grass, the color and the smell of my own earth. Andrew is at my side.

I take his offered hand, and pull him into the grass.

He lands beside me, his shoulder warm against mine.

We laugh.

Then, the scene changed. In my mind's eye, I saw Andrew in the hospital. This wasn't a memory, or a picture conjured in my mind. This was Andrew, as he was, in that moment. Dark circles shadowed his eyes and bristly stubble grew on his cheeks, where he would normally have shaved.

I looked closer. As I watched him, his eyes fluttered and a finger twitched on his left hand.

Could he sense me? Did he know I was there? I studied his thick lashes, resting on damp skin, speckled and human. The sight of him, so real and present, made me catch my breath.

His mouth didn't move. His eyes didn't open. But I heard his voice, clear and true. *Don't worry. Keep practicing, and you're gonna skate faster than me before you know it.*

I'm right here, Andrew! I tried to speak to him, but my lips didn't move.

His eyes fluttered again. *Meg? Meg . . . come back.*

I could feel him fading, something black and inky pulling him away, a deep wound in his mind. His injury wasn't healing.

The vision disappeared, and I was back on the king's carpet with the giants. I closed my eyes, blinking back tears. If I kept them closed, would I see Andrew again?

We sat in silence for a long moment before I opened my eyes again.

"He spoke to me." I let go of Proce's thumb.

He pulled his hand away. "I heard it too. That was . . . unusual. Your color burns brighter in our earth. It has enhanced my gift."

"It was really Andrew?" I asked. "It felt like him."

"It was him," Proce said.

Not long ago, I had thought I would never hear Andrew speak again. But, with Proce's gift, Andrew had spoken to me from within his coma, across earths. I savored the memory of his voice in my mind.

Meg . . . come back.

He knew I was gone. Or, at least, he knew I wasn't with him anymore, at the hospital. How could I explain where I went? I barely understood it myself. He had talked about skating. He knew what I was remembering, despite the darkness in his mind. Was there a way to send him a message?

"Proce." I reached for his hand. "I need to see him again."

Proce shook his head and withdrew from my touch. "I cannot. Your vision drew me in until I almost lost myself. You have exhausted me for today."

With a low groan, he leaned back onto the carpet, as if he had just walked for miles. Von placed a hand on his arm, singing her healing. Proce had always been so strong. It wasn't a good feeling, to see him weakened.

"Proce," I said. "Thank you for today. I wouldn't have made it without you. Both of you."

Von frowned at me. She looked exhausted. "The sooner your human is healed, the better. This is not easy for Proce."

She was right. I needed to convince the king to heal Andrew soon. His injury was getting worse, like the doctors said it might.

"I'll talk to the king," I said. "Don't worry."

Von's expression softened. "When all is settled, you will be able to move on. The king is your future. That is what is best for you."

Her words stung me. I couldn't help it.

"The future's unpredictable," I said.

"The king cannot send you home," Proce said. "And he will not. You are to be his wife."

"What if you're wrong?" I asked. "Has the king actually told you his plan? Or are you just going off your poem?"

"It is written—" Proce began in his usual tone.

"I don't care what's written."

"The Writings always come to pass. Always. They told us of the longest cold season, and of our battle with the mountain beasts. Those events have already happened. And now, they told us of your arrival."

Von sat beside me, clasping her hands together. "If we could heal Andrew, we would. Can you not see we are similar? We both desire healing for our people."

Tears spilled. "We're not the same. I never stole anyone."

I wished I hadn't said that. Why was I accusing them, my only friends in the King's House? They had saved my life.

"We never considered . . ." Von began. "We always assumed . . ." She didn't finish.

Proce spoke for her. "We assumed you would want to marry the king, before we called you in between. Why would the Writings lead us to an unwilling bride?"

"This was always meant to be your future," Von said.

They would never understand. Too much was at stake for them. Maybe arranged marriages were normal for giants. Who wouldn't want to marry a king? But I had lost my past already. I wouldn't give up my future so easily.

I got up from the carpet and climbed into the human bed, pulling the covers over my face.

"Meg . . ." Von came to me.

I twisted my body away from her, pulling the covers up higher. "I need to be alone."

"If that is what you wish." Von stayed beside the bed. "But please listen first. Tomorrow, you need to lie to the king, if you can manage it. He will search your mind. Our king can be . . . proud. You must tell him that Andrew is your brother. It will go better for you if he is not jealous. Do you hear me?"

I didn't answer.

"I wish you well, Meg."

I didn't like the warning in Von's voice, but it didn't matter what they thought. It was the king I had to convince.

The Croppers left the suite, crawling through the door more stealthily than they had entered. I turned over on the bed. In the morning, I would do what I had come here to do. I would get my miracle.

After some time, the cones of light dimmed, easing the room into darkness. I took the paper note from my dress and smoothed it out onto the bedsheets. After reading it several times, I stowed it beneath my pillow. Despite the luxury of a real bed, I couldn't find a comfortable position.

Good.

I didn't want to be comfortable in the gray earth.

11

Morning sun shone through the bedroom windows, the changing light still a relief after my time spent in twilight. With all the crystal and cut glass, I would have expected a rainbow to reflect on the wall. Not here, in this earth.

All was silent in the King's House, but I was ready to start the day. Soon, I would speak with the king. Before that, I needed a bathroom, and probably a change of clothes. My stomach was hollow, ready for a meal. But my lungs were free. The king's healing was still with me.

I slipped out of the bed and went to investigate the human rooms. Aside from the three-step entrance, the only other escape from the bedroom was a narrow archway, tiled in pearly hexagons.

The arch led to a cone-lit room, larger than I had expected. A bathroom. There were more sinks, basins, and faucets than anyone would know what to do with. A glass tub was the crowning jewel, placed in the middle of the room, gilded with silver flowers. Clear bottles of various sizes sat at every basin, filled with glossy liquid.

I relieved myself in what I hoped was a toilet, and I scrubbed my hands in perfumed soap. Then, a noise came from outside the bedroom. I buttoned my dress, and rushed to the entry area.

The entrance door to the human rooms swung open, and a team of chattering Regent women flooded in.

An elegant lady directed the others, her voice shrill. "Set the tools over there—no, over there. Who brought the thread and needles?"

Glittering ladies bustled around the lobby, arranging various objects on low tables. I backed against a wall, out of the way. Despite their larger-than-human size, the Regents breezed around one another, as if they had rehearsed a dance. It wasn't graceful. It was precise.

They didn't seem to notice me. My mouth opened to speak, but the lady with the harsh voice beat me to it.

"We're here to prepare you for the king." She handed me a chalice of steaming liquid.

I took it from her and almost yelped. It was piping hot, except for the tips of the handles, which I held with careful fingers. The Regent had wrapped her marble hands around the entire cup with ease.

"Thank you." I blew on the surface of the chalice, spilling a few drops on the carpet.

The lady circled back and took the drink away from me again, setting it on a nightstand. "Can't have you making a mess of yourself." She had glossy black curls, perfectly arranged above her shoulders, and she was taller than the others.

"The king wants to see me now?" My heart fluttered in my chest.

"Not looking like that, I guarantee you."

Before I knew it, she had pulled a sharp comb from a pouch and begun raking it through my hair. I ducked away from her, but the lady brought me back with pinching fingers. I stayed, trying to maintain as much dignity as possible. If this was what I needed to endure in order to speak with the king, I would have to bear it.

"Stop moving." She pulled out the beads that Von had woven into my tangles, then threw them on the floor.

A stout Regent commented. "Croppers' trinkets. As far as I'm concerned, the cold can't come soon enough. Have you seen how many Croppers are in the city right now?"

The lady in charge let out a strained laugh. "Do you mean to ask if I've smelled them? Because I have . . ."

The others joined in a rally of metallic laughter.

My stomach tightened. Proce and Von had always spoken of the Regents with respect, even if they acknowledged their differences. I didn't like this attitude from the Regents. If anything, they were the ones who smelled. Everything here was over-perfumed.

I tried to stand still as the lady twisted my hair against my scalp. I couldn't see her work, but I snuck my fingers up once to feel a crown of braids. She flicked my hand away.

More Regent hands pressed at me with gossamer jars, painting my skin with besmonn dust. They coated my hands, my throat, and the nape of my neck. Someone laid a gown across the bed. The heavy skirt glimmered the color of iron, and blue flowers were sewn down the front. Denim blue. Von must have given my jeans to the Regents.

The tall lady followed my line of sight. "You like the blossoms? The king ordered it. Not that you need more color." She looked me up and down, adjusting an almost-pink ribbon that wound through her own curls. The ribbon was probably the scrap of some long-dead human's clothes.

"The flowers are made from my pants," I said.

"Garlian sewed them." The lady dug a final pin into my hair and stepped back. "The elder can't see a thing, but her fingers still know what they're doing."

"Hey!" snapped the stout Regent, rotund, and shorter than most. "I may be blind, but I can still hear. And I'm not that much older than you, Larlia."

I changed into the heavy gown behind a white curtain, but I needed the Regents' help to fasten the stiff bodice around my waist. They pulled the laces tight enough that touching my toes would be out of the question. Urma had warned me about this. I wished the Cropper could be the one preparing me for the day, rather than these Regents. Von's mother had been firm in her dealings. These ladies were like rocks.

The dress revealed more of my dusted skin than I would have liked. My shoulders were bare, and the back dipped low. It was a stitchless garment, flowing over my hips as if had been woven specifically for me. The Cropper dress was more comfortable, but less fitted. This gown was made with scientific skill.

"Well." Larlia took a look at me. "We did our best."

Were these the people Von wanted me to win over?

I bowed to them, palms out, as I had learned. "Thank you for your help."

They laughed again, in their rusty tones.

"She thinks she's a Regent." Larlia came close, as if adjusting one of my braids. She lowered her voice. "But you're not, are you? You're a human." She tugged a blue flower away from my gown, and let the sewn petals fall apart.

I understood her meaning. I was a blossom. A thing that would fade in a season.

I masked a pleasant expression onto my face, refusing to react. Von was wrong about the Regents. I would never win these people over.

I didn't want to.

"Well, I think she's lovely," said a young Regent with a white braid that trailed down her back. "Can't you sense her color? It's making my gift stronger. Watch this." The girl waved her hand over a ball of white thread. It disappeared, and a perfect row of white lace appeared along the neckline of her gown. "That would normally take me forever!"

"Yes," Larlia said. "I suppose it would take *you* forever." She gathered her combs and pins back into her pouch and sauntered away.

The ladies followed, scooping up their bottles and needles and bolts of colorless ribbons.

"The Watchers are at the door for you." Garlian lingered behind the others. "Best not to keep them waiting."

She crumpled my Cropper dress into a wrinkled bundle and darted through the crystal curtain.

"Wait," I said. "What will you do with my dress?"

"Don't worry. You won't have to wear Cropper rags anymore, though I'll salvage the color. Even a blind woman can sense it."

"What's wrong with looking like a Cropper?"

Garlian sighed. "Just because we need them doesn't mean we have to live like them. Clumsy. Dirty. Loud . . ." She continued her list of Cropper faults as she left the room, as if to herself. "Too big, they eat too much . . ."

I waited until I could no longer hear the women's voices, then I took my note from its hiding place under the pillow. My new dress didn't have pockets, so I tucked the note deep into the plunging neckline.

Four Regent men in black hoods greeted me when I opened the outer door. Watchers.

"We'll take you to the king's auditorium," said one of the cloaked figures.

I bowed again. "Thank you."

Their faces stern, they turned to lead the way. They didn't bow back, but least they hadn't laughed at me.

I followed the Watchers through the halls, though I didn't recognize the way from the night before. Had it really only been one night since I almost died? We stopped in front of high arches, the entrance to the room where the king had healed me.

"Go on," the Watcher said. "He's waiting."

I straightened my back and took a deep breath, reminding myself of my purpose. I would convince the king. It didn't matter what happened after that.

The Watchers followed me through the arch.

The king stood from his seat as I approached, his eyes on my dress. I stopped a few feet away, keeping distance between us. I created mental distance also. The battle of our minds began, and my heartbeat leapt to my throat. I could feel his mind, looming and present.

It was like hanging on the edge of a cliff, testing my own strength. If I held on, my thoughts would remain my own. If I fell,

I would dive into a deep pool of something unknown. A small part of me wanted to get it over with, to fall and find out what would happen. But I needed to hang on. I needed to ask for my miracle on my own terms, my reasons private.

The king addressed the Watchers. "Thank you for bringing her. You may go now."

They exited through the arch, leaving us alone.

The king had been sitting at a desk. It was made of stone, carved with detailed drawings of Regents and Croppers. The figures danced in coupled pairs and carried baskets through fields of tall grass. Shimmering glass filled the carvings, like water poured into a trench, and the whole surface had been polished to a sheen. Loose papers and books were strewn across the desk top.

The king took a step forward. I held my ground, and the wall in my mind.

He stopped in front of me and relaxed his stance. "I spend the mornings writing letters to my cities." He waved a hand toward the desk. "But I'm glad for a break."

I bowed. "Thank you for seeing me. Today, and last night." In my mind, I would fight him. The stakes were too high. Outwardly, I would be as polite as humanly possible.

"I saw you long before last night." His mouth curved into a smile, softening the angles of his face. "Don't you remember me from your dream?"

"I . . . I didn't know it was real." I had hoped the dream was my imagination, or some kind of premonition. The less the king was in my head, the better.

"I told you to find me," he said. "I knew you'd be in danger, when you crossed over. What took you so long? We almost lost you."

"I came as fast as the Croppers could take me." I met his gaze.

"In the future, you'll listen to me. Not the Croppers."

"Proce and Von did their best." I didn't want to listen to the king or the Croppers. I wanted him to heal Andrew, and then I wanted to leave.

"You're attached to your giant friends." The king's mind pressed into mine.

I strengthened my shield and stood taller, emboldened by my ability to resist. "They're the ones who brought me here. They're all I know."

"What have they told you about our lands?" he asked.

"They told me stories about Croppers and Regents . . . and about their king."

"The one called Proce is fond of stories. What kinds of things do the Croppers say about me?" This time, he didn't try to see what was in my mind, as if he wanted to hear the words I would choose. He was testing me.

"They said you have a powerful gift." That was the only story I was interested in. "And they implied that you're not as ugly as a Cropper."

"Do you think they told the truth?" The smile returned to his lips.

All of the Regents were ugly, in their way. Their perfect edges were too harsh to be beautiful. The king was less adorned and less inhuman than some Regents, and there was something about him that went beyond appearance, as if I saw his mind before I saw his face. He didn't look like the broken man from the Croppers' story, wasting away from the loss of his wife.

"Proce never lies. But I think you might be more powerful than they said."

His smile disappeared. "Tell me, do you like your rooms? Is there anything I can do to make you more comfortable here?"

Anything? This was my chance. My stomach fluttered. I had imagined this moment a hundred times during my days in between earths. I had pictured a giant king with a crown and a robe, humming a healing song for Andrew.

Now that I stood before the real king, my imagined scenario fell flat. Why would he use his gift to help some other human from my earth? What could I say?

"There's one thing you can do for me." My voice was shakier than I would have liked. "One thing I've wanted to ask you . . ."

"Good," he said. "I want you to ask me lots of questions."

He did?

"It's important. It's why I came here."

"You crossed between because my Croppers brought you. Then, they say you crossed again of your own will, just for them. Are you so altruistic?"

I took a breath. "I need to ask for your help."

"I see. Ask."

The words tumbled out. "There's a human in my earth . . . he's sick. Von couldn't heal him, but . . ." My throat tightened. "But she said you might be able to do it?"

The king studied my face and I looked at the floor. I wished my speech had been more compelling. I wished I hadn't been afraid. Most of all, I wished for the king to say yes.

"This human . . . he must be important to you?"

"He is." I didn't elaborate.

"I know the Croppers shared a certain part of the Writings with you. They hold tightly to those words."

Why was he talking about the Writings? Why didn't he answer me?

"The verses are beautiful," I said.

"In their own way," he agreed. "I look at the Writings as useful. My people believed in prophecy, so they were watchful for a way to call a human. Someone would have found a way, eventually. An opportunity. I'm just surprised it was a Cropper. Most Croppers don't even read. They prefer to sing."

"I don't have a lot of faith in prophecies," I said.

Thankfully, it didn't sound like he did, either.

"I have faith in my people. And it worked. You're here. It took a whole civilization to bring you. The truth is, I've always hoped for a human wife."

Wife.

I took a step back, my hands twisted together. This wasn't how it was supposed to go.

The king continued. "Many humans would have died upon arrival to our earth. Most have. You're ungifted, but you're strong. Even the way you guard your thoughts from me. I couldn't have asked for better."

I took another step back, my mind racing. I should have known. Proce and Von had told me from the beginning, but I hadn't allowed myself to believe them.

"I came here for your help," I said. "Not for a husband."

"I understand, but I won't miss this opportunity."

He hadn't answered me yet. Could he heal Andrew? Getting my miracle was never going to be easy. It was a desperate scramble, a foolish attempt to turn my disappearance into something good, to take back a scrap of power in my out-of-control life.

I had bargained with Proce and Von. Maybe, if I walked a thin line, I could make a bargain with their king.

"And what if I don't want to marry you?" I asked.

"You would have a terribly short life here, without a gifted husband to heal you."

It was a threat.

"This hasn't been much of a marriage proposal." I tried to sound lighthearted. The bargain wasn't going well. "Usually there's some feeling involved."

The king laughed. "I suppose it's not much of a proposal. I could have made it sweeter. Maybe I'll try again, later on, when you're used to the idea."

I forced myself to stay focused on my goal. If I allowed myself to contemplate what he was suggesting, I wouldn't be able to manage the bargain. "If you're going to demand so much from me, the least you can do is heal the human."

"You have a good point," he said. "But I can't heal him until after we marry."

"You'll have a more willing bride if you heal him first." I hated the sound of my own voice, but I would say what it took. Everything had led up to this. I had no intention of marrying the king, but he didn't need to know that. I wouldn't make any promises. Just hints.

"You should sit. We have a lot to discuss." The king pointed to a black sofa near his desk.

I went to the sofa and lowered onto the edge, my eyes fixed on the king. He sat beside me, and I fought the urge to lean away.

"I didn't mean I won't heal your human ever," he said. "I meant that I can't heal him until after our wedding. I'm not able."

"I don't understand."

"How could you?" The king relaxed into the black velvet. "I've studied humans my whole life, but you know almost nothing about Regents. It's hard to explain. First, you need to understand the colors of your earth. I want to try something with my gift to help you see."

He reached toward my hand and I flinched.

"Meg," he chided. "I would never hurt you. I have to touch you to use my gift."

Why did it feel so much easier when Proce did it? Kalmus held my hand, while I kept my fingers stiff and straight in his. His skin was too smooth, too solid against mine. Like stone.

A familiar hum filled my ears, like Proce's gift, but deeper. It didn't come from the king's voice. It came from the air, from the floor, from the walls. It reverberated inside my mind. My vision went dark, though I was still awake. I blinked furiously.

"Why can't I see?" I tried to pull away, but the king held my hand too tight.

You're seeing through my eyes. The king's voice spoke in my mind, not in my ears.

When my vision returned, everything looked wrong. I was seeing what the king saw, from his angle on the sofa.

I would have thought that a creature in a gray earth might be color blind. It was the opposite. The king's eyes were trained to see every shade around him. The room, which had once looked black and white to me, had pale green speckles running through the marbled floors. When he turned his eyes to a window, I spotted a hint of something like yellow in the sky outside. A sickly haze. The colors were sparse. Barely there, like the imitation of color.

Then, he focused his gaze on me. A shiver ran through me as I saw myself from outside my own body, alight with color. Real color. I barely recognized my small frame, vibrant against the black sofa. To him, I burned, blinding and incandescent. My hair shone like copper threads, more auburn and ember than the chestnut I always saw in the mirror. My freckled skin glowed gold. My eyes were open, staring and blank, filled with shining rings of yellow and bronze. I didn't look human. I was something else. A fairy. An angel. Or worse.

The king's vision turned inward. He was sharing his internal world with me. I sensed his gift, filling his body with white light. It pulsed with every beat of his heart, a glow of sparks too bright to look at.

My russet hair and brown eyes were no longer visible, but I felt them in the room. To the king, color was a physical experience, like heat. His gift called to the color, drawing it near. The two came together, forming something more than either could be on their own. All of this was happening without my knowledge. I only saw it because the king let me.

His gift was larger than him. It could have filled the whole earth, yet somehow, it was contained inside his body. It sensed everything around us. A Watcher stood outside the door. He was injured, a broken finger, and the King's Gift pulsed with the Regent's pain. We could feel the injury, like an empty slot waiting to be filled. The King's Gift wanted to heal, but the king held it back.

He started to let go of my hand, but I was fascinated by his gift. I held on tight, and peered closer. I could feel the whole city in his gift, and cities beyond that, and the Croppers in their fields. The light wanted to flow toward them, but something stopped it. There was a cage in the king's mind.

"Enough." His voice broke my concentration.

My vision faded back into my own eyes, and I blinked at the colorless room.

"You saw deeper than I expected." The king blinked also, as if clearing his own vision. "I still have more to learn about humans. Especially this human."

"I saw your gift. It was . . . bright. Couldn't you heal the other human now? In my earth?" I was unashamedly pleading, my miracle within reach.

"My gift is powerful," said the king. "And so is your color. But they're not strong enough to heal someone in your earth. Not yet." His tone grew sober. "We'll have to work together for that to happen."

"How?" I asked. "What could I possibly do to help?"

"When a king gets married, his wife is given a Queen's Gift. It's part of the ceremony. I've been studying the mystery, reading all the histories, even experimenting on my own. If I marry a human, I believe you won't be able to carry the Queen's Gift, though it will be fortified by your color." He gave me a steady look. "I would hold the gift in your place. With two gifts, I could reach to your earth. I could heal your human."

"You would be able to bless the Croppers' sleep?" I asked. "Your gift would be repaired?" I didn't want to mention what had broken his gift. His wife's death. It was why Proce and Von had brought me. Though they didn't seem to know about the two gifts. To them, the king needed healing.

He gave a soft smile. "Our ceremony would produce more than enough gifting to bless the Croppers. Everything is possible, now that you're here."

A ceremony. Not necessarily a marriage. Just one ceremony, and then Andrew would be healed, and the king would have two gifts. No wonder he wanted a human wife.

"Would I have to promise my love to you?" I asked. "I can't do that. And after . . . would I have to be your wife?"

The king looked into my eyes. "You don't have to promise anything. And after . . . we would have years to figure that part out."

"Has it been done before?" I asked.

"I've seen it with lesser gifts," the king said. "Analese's Regent husband was more powerful than usual. I believe it was her color, and he may have carried her portion of their marriage gift. All Regents get a gift when they marry. None nearly as powerful as a king or a queen. With two royal gifts combined into one, and the color of a human, I'd bless my people beyond any other king."

He would bless Proce and Von and their village. Urma would live through the sleep. Andrew would be healed beyond what any doctor could do. No brain damage. No recovery. He would be himself right away. Most importantly, he would be alive.

"When can we have the ceremony?" I asked.

"I would like to wait at least a year for a proper celebration," the king said. "Are you really so eager to get married?"

"He doesn't have that much time . . ." My voice was thick. "The other human."

The king studied me. "Who is he?"

"My brother." My eyes focused on my lap, and I guarded my thoughts as tightly as I could.

"You're lying," the king said. "I don't need to see your thoughts to know that. You're going to forget him, you realize? Humans always forget their own earth."

"I won't."

"You will. I think it's best if we delay the ceremony. It will give you time to adjust to my earth."

"Even if I do forget my past," I said. "I'll always remember this conversation. I'll remember that I forgot, and I'll remember what was lost." My bargaining power was growing thin.

The king's face hardened. "You're young, even for a human. There's a lot of life ahead of you. Better to let go of him."

"If you don't heal him, then I can't let go." I had no intention of letting go.

To my surprise, the king smiled. "You're trying to persuade me, but there's truth in it. The sooner we put this human behind us, the better. Will healing him do that?"

"Yes. When can we have the ceremony?" I asked again.

"You're moving fast. Don't you want to know anything about your intended husband?"

I already knew that he was powerful, and hungry for more power. That was why he wanted me. What else could I ask him? Something to flatter him. Everyone likes to talk about themselves.

"How did you become the king?" I asked.

He looked pleased. "My mother was the queen, and my father was the king. That's often how it starts, but not always. The gift chooses who it will, regardless of heritage. It chose me."

"Do you have brothers?" I asked. "Tell me about your family." Maybe someone else had enough royal gifting to heal Andrew.

"No brothers or sisters. It's difficult for a Regent queen to give birth. It weakens her. I received the King's Gift when my father died. My mother died shortly after. I was still young when I began my reign, new to life. I learned to be a king on my own."

"I'm sorry." I knew what that was like, to be alone too soon. It was one of the things I would never forget about my life.

"It's going to be different for the next king. Humans are different. You'll bear Regent sons, long before the end of my life. You're healthy enough. I sensed it when I healed you. One of my sons will likely be given the King's Gift. It doesn't always work that way, but chances are higher if we have more than one. The next king will know his father, and he'll be better for it."

My stomach curled into knots. Was he really talking to me about children? Our children?

"Something else you should know about me," he said. "I prefer my name. Please call me Kalmus."

"How soon can we have the ceremony?" I repeated my question for the third time.

He corrected me. "How soon can we have the ceremony, Kalmus."

I took a breath and forced myself to repeat his words. "How soon, Kalmus?"

When his name crossed my lips, my guard fell. I couldn't stop it. His mind rushed to search mine, but I pulled my walls back into place at the last second. It required an almost unbearable effort.

I remembered his words from the night before.

Whisper my name, and I may hear you with my gift. There's power in a name.

I wouldn't make the mistake of saying it ever again.

The king answered my question. "We can have the ceremony in two hundred days. The Croppers say the cold won't come for at least two more years. That will give us time to tour the Seven Cities—"

I interrupted. "You don't understand. Andrew's dying."

I had never said those words out loud. The truth of it crashed over me, threatening to wash away my composure.

"So his name is And-rew?" The name was clumsy on his tongue. "Andrew, the boy you won't forget."

"The ceremony has to be sooner." I held my hand against the bodice of my dress, feeling the paper note that was tucked there.

"There will be preparations leading up to the ceremony. We can bypass the tour of the cities, but the people need to accept you as my wife. There are traditions. Both the Regents and the Croppers will travel here to give you gifts, and to bless you. We'll need to visit the besmonn keep together. That's important. And, there's always an evening of dancing." He gave me a crooked smile. "It'll be an interesting night, if the others are even half as colorstruck by you as I am."

"When?" It was all I wanted to know, the only thing I could let my numb mind care about.

"Four days." The king promised. "If you insist, in four days, we will have our marriage ceremony."

I sent my thoughts to Andrew, an earth away, though I knew he couldn't hear me without the help of a gift. It didn't matter if he heard my words. I needed them as much as he did.

You have to hold on for four more days.

12

The rest of the day passed slowly. Every second ticked by in conscious time. I left the king's auditorium as soon as he would allow, accompanied by Watchers. Later, Garlian brought food to my room.

"Do you know Proce and Von?" I asked through a mouth full of bread, happy to have food for the first time that day. "My Cropper friends? Can you tell me where they are?"

"You should stay in bed and get some rest today. It's a long day tomorrow." Garlian left without another word.

I considered searching the house for my giants. Would the Watchers outside my door try to stop me from leaving? I didn't want to risk angering the king. Not until Andrew was healed. Proce and Von would check on me. I knew they would.

I waited until long after the sun went down. They never came. I had told them I wanted to be alone. But not forever. I hadn't meant it.

The night was long.

In my dreams, I wore a veil and a pair of silver shoes. Then I would wake, alone in the dark. I thought of marriage and what it would mean. I could play a bride and walk down an aisle. Would the king expect more than that? He said I wouldn't have to promise my love, and we would have years to figure out our relationship.

But he would want children. He had implied as much. And that was a thought I couldn't fathom. Not even my body would be my own.

But none of that mattered, for now. The truth was, I needed the king to keep me alive. Without his gift, I couldn't breathe. Without his gift, Andrew wouldn't live.

The next day began in an eerily similar way to the last. A flock of Regent women arrived, unannounced, though there seemed to be fewer of them. This time, no one offered me a warm drink. I didn't mind. My nervous stomach probably wouldn't have been able to handle it.

The bustling Regents selected yet another gown for me to wear. This time, charcoal gray. Its translucent sleeves hung loose, leaving my shoulders bare. Tiny crystals encrusted the waistline. Larlia painted my skin, then she piled my hair onto my head, twisting it with a blue ribbon. The other ladies complimented her work.

"Have you ever seen anyone so lovely?" said the Regent with the long braid.

Larlia shot her a poisonous look.

"What's your name?" I asked the kind Regent.

Her face lit up. "Kahlea."

Larlia scowled. "There's work for you in the linens hall, Kahlea. We're done here."

The Watchers came for me. I followed them to the king's auditorium, though I still didn't recognize any of the corridors. Had we taken a different path each time?

Soon, the countdown would begin.

Four days.

Today, day one, I would be introduced to the people in the Polaris. Whatever that might entail, I was ready to play my part.

Tomorrow, we would go to the besmonn keep. The next day, there would be dancing, and the day after that, the ceremony.

I didn't hesitate this time before entering through the archway to see the king. His stark eyes traced my bare shoulders as I approached him. His mind tried to trace my thoughts, but he couldn't break through. I felt it.

Tiny blue buttons ran up the front of his jacket. I tried to imagine how brilliant those buttons must have looked through his color-sensitive eyes.

The king smiled. I bowed.

"Meg." He used my name. "How have you been?"

"Anxious," I answered honestly. "When will we begin?"

"Sooner than I would have liked. But that's what you wanted. We'll leave through this door in a moment, accompanied by my full guard of Watchers."

We both faced the archway, and the king moved closer to me, until our arms were touching. I tensed, and stepped away.

"I know you don't trust me," he said. "I hope that will change with time. But, for today, while people are watching, we need to be close. You'll receive more kindness in the city, and in my house, if you appear to be . . . grateful . . . for our marriage"

Von had warned me. There were Regents in the Polaris who envied my position. I already knew there were Regents who disliked me.

I doubled the walls around my mind, then offered my hand to the king.

He took it with a smile and spun me around in an almost-dance. "The city has never seen anything like you. Today could be fun, if you let it."

"I'm doing it so we can get to the ceremony." I was reminding both of us.

"You do realize we'll be technically married after the ceremony?" The king's mouth turned up at one corner.

My hand went stiff in his, my stomach tight. "Only technically."

The king looked thoughtful. "Every year, Regents hold a foot race at the base of the mountain."

"Interesting." It really wasn't. All I could think about was the task ahead. The role I had to play.

The king went on. "There are checkpoints on a map where the racers have to light a fire. If they accidentally miss a checkpoint, it doesn't matter if they're the fastest. The next racer technically wins."

"Why are you telling me this?"

"We will be technically married," he said. "You can win on a technicality."

And you could lose on a technicality. But I didn't say that aloud.

A terrible thought occurred to me. "Will I have to make vows? You said I wouldn't have to promise my love . . ."

"Your only job will be to beckon the Queen's Gift."

"Good." I didn't want to lie, especially not in a ceremony.

Ignoring the king's hand in mine, I felt for my note to Andrew, tucked into my waistband. Had I promised my love to him? Had I said the words to Andrew?

A sick feeling washed over me. I couldn't remember.

I searched my mind, and my head throbbed. Worse than the looming marriage was the blank space in my memory. Every moment of my past lost was a piece of myself, gone forever.

I couldn't think of the past right now. I had a task ahead of me. After that, my future was blank, like my past, falling away like water over a cliff.

"Is there anything else I need to do today?" I asked the king.

"It would probably help if you smiled at the people. Most of them are excited to see a human. You'll be everyone's new favorite in the city."

If they were anything like Larlia, he was fooling himself. The king wanted me as his wife, but I knew I would never be the queen of these people. They were nearly immortal. To them, I was a pretty diversion, at best. A useful device. But I needed the king on my side, so I smiled up at him, practicing for the task ahead.

"On second thought, be careful with that smile," the king said. "Every Regent man in the city will fall in love and be jealous of me."

I laughed at the idea. "I'm sure I look as weird to them as they do to me."

The king gave me a lingering glance. "You're right. Humans have an odd kind of beauty. Delicate. But it's still beauty, and we're not blind to it. It's more than just color."

I felt heat rise to my cheeks. If humans could have children with

Regents, then I had to admit we weren't completely different. But the thought made me more than uncomfortable. I turned my head away and sank into silence.

Hand in hand, we exited the halls of the King's House. I suspected he walked slower than his natural gait, to accommodate my height. We stepped through a set of high glass doors, into the open city.

The air smelled like summer rain. Humid. Warm. It made me think of blue skies and green grass. Neither would be found in the Polaris. The city looked like an extension of the King's House, just as beautiful, as if made by the same builders. I hadn't expected that. Shouldn't a palace be more extravagant than the rest of the city?

Black houses lined the streets, made of the usual polished stone, like opaque glass. Their roofs were domed or coned, and their doors were arched. Again, I was struck by the delicate look of the material. So high and curved and thin. How did it hold its own weight?

The street soon became a footbridge. We crossed over a clear stream. It must have flowed in from the river at the gate. The one Proce had carried me over when I arrived.

Trees grew alongside the street. Leafy vines made their way up the fronts of houses, and over archways and windows. All the plants were silver. Hardly varying in shades of gray. Though some sparkled in the sunlight.

Unlike the king's halls, the streets were not empty. Seven Watchers led the way ahead of us. Behind trailed rows of Regents, dressed in finery. They must have waited for our arrival from the King's House. Waited to take their place in line. Larlia was in their midst.

I craned my neck from left to right, looking behind, ahead, up. Taking it all in. Regents stood on the balconies of the city, watching from above. Low voices rumbled everywhere.

At the back of the procession, far behind, Proce and Von towered over the others. At the sight of them, something in me eased. They were here. The only Croppers in line. I tried to catch their eyes, but they were busy talking to the Regents beside them.

My heavy skirt bunched between my feet and I stumbled. The king caught me. I didn't fall, but we stopped. And the whole procession stopped. Dozens of creatures were moving at the king's pace. My pace.

"Are you well?" the king asked.

"There's a lot to look at." I lifted my skirt off the ground by an inch, trying to move faster. "Sorry."

"I'm showing you off to my people," he said. "But I'm also showing them to you. Look all you want."

Elder ladies joined us, trays of pastries balanced against their hips. They passed out the treats to the Regents in the city as we walked by. Crowds formed, narrowing the street.

I was on parade.

"Word has already spread to all Seven Cities," said a Regent woman who walked behind us. "Look! Even the Croppers are here, in the city. Of course, this means the most to them."

Soon, I did start to see Croppers. White hair tangled with silver beads. They stood at the backs of the crowds, looking over the Regents' heads. It was practical. They were bigger. But some sang as we passed. I wished they would come closer, so I could hear better.

At the front of the crowds, two Regent children pressed forward to get their share of the pastries. Everyone parted for them, and they were given a double portion.

A young Cropper darted into the street ahead of us and dropped flower petals in our path. She wasn't a child, but she was barely grown, from what I could tell. Her movements were soft like a deer, her hair silky. I watched her, thinking of Aggi. She stared back at me, her eyes round with white lashes. Before we reached her, she returned to the crowd.

Regents bowed as we passed them. The king acknowledged their presence with a tilt of his head.

"Smile, Meg," he whispered to me.

I forced the edges of my mouth to turn upward. "You're smiling enough for both of us."

"Today isn't about me." He laced his fingers into mine and raised my hand into the air.

Shouts of approval came from the street.

Young Regent men, clad in an array of fitted trousers and satin jackets, came forward at intervals to offer small gifts.

The first time it happened, the king held out my hand and a man put a crystal ring on my finger.

"Thank you." I let my hand fall to my side, trying not to ball it into a fist. Everyone here touched me without permission.

The king brought his face close to mine. "Don't speak. You should bow to them, but not low. Only bend your neck." I felt his breath against my ear.

The king thanked each Regent for me. I gave them a small bow, palms forward. They brought long necklaces and silver bracelets. One gave me a black feather. At first, I thought it came from a besmonn. When I held it in my hand, it was sharp, like a glossy arrowhead carved from obsidian.

Eventually, they layered so many necklaces over my head, my neck began to ache from the weight, and I had to slow my pace.

"Let me lighten things up for you." The king paused to remove some of my jewelry, and place it on his own body.

I forced a smile for each Regent and Cropper, ignoring their bizarre appearances. Some Regents had menacing, heavyset brows. Others had eyes so pale, I was sure they couldn't see at all. There were Croppers even taller than Proce, and toothier than Von.

We walked for what seemed like hours, never running out of new faces to greet, or new streets to explore. Between houses, lawns of silver grass sprawled. In some places, there were fountains with bubbling sprays of water. Through an archway, I saw a courtyard with a tree at the center. Its branches reached higher than the three-story houses it grew between.

The king never let go of my hand.

There was a short reprieve, when no one approached us for a moment.

"How many Regents live in the Polaris?" I asked.

"102,452 at the moment," the king said. "But a child is expected by tomorrow. So then it will be 102,453. If no one dies before then. We have our elderly, too."

"How could you know the exact number? You keep track of every birth and every death?"

"My gift does."

What would it be like to be alerted whenever someone died? The king's face was impassible as we walked. The pleasant mask he had maintained for the entire parade.

"What does everyone here do?"

"Do?" The king looked down at me.

"For work. And money."

Understanding registered in his eyes. "Ah. Money. We tried that a long time ago. Generations back, when Regents first settled here. But it made us greedy. Regents focused their energy on jobs they were less suited for, in order to save wealth. Mostly producing goods. The libraries were neglected. And the prophetic gifts. So we stopped that."

"How does it work now?" I looked around at the lush gardens and baskets of bread. The luxurious houses and fine clothes. No poverty in sight.

"Croppers get whatever they want. Stones. Paper. Water pipes. Regent things. Croppers grow more than enough food. Each Regent gets what they need, and they do the work they are best gifted for. We all do what we love."

So the Croppers provided food for everyone. They did seem to love their fields. But they didn't get whatever they wanted. Not their sleep. They wanted to not die.

At the thought of food, my stomach growled. It was past midday, and I hadn't eaten.

"You're hungry," the king said.

It wasn't a question. I hadn't been guarding my thoughts. The walls went back into place.

At the king's request, a Regent gave us sweet bread and a drink to share. The king took sips from the chalice while I ate. When I finished my bread, he gave me the drink, more than half left. It was dark and spiced, like the bread in liquid form. I would rather have had cold water, but the drink was surprisingly refreshing.

Later in the afternoon, my head began to ache, and a familiar sickness burned my lungs. As soon as I coughed, the king gripped my hand tighter. His gift flowed gently up my fingers, healing me until I could breathe freely again.

I had almost forgotten the gray earth was poison to me. How long would I be able to go without the king's healing before I would die? The sickness tied me to him, an invisible tether.

By the time we made it back to the King's House, the sun had disappeared behind the spires of the city, leaving behind a heathered sky. My stomach was hollow and my feet sore from a full day of walking on unforgiving stone.

The Regents in our procession followed us through the glass doors of the King's House. Once the doors closed, a rush of preparations began in the cramped hall.

"I need to change my shoes," a Regent lady complained, stomping toward a staircase.

A Regent man scurried through the crowd, holding a long piece of paper and a glass pen. "Will your sister join us for the meal?" he shouted to a lady. "I need a count."

She answered him, and he scribbled down a note.

The king pulled me aside into an empty corridor, and Watchers formed a wall in front of us, facing away. They ushered the other Regents past us.

"You did well today," the king said to me. "I know this isn't easy for you."

None of the smiles had been for him. They had been for what he could do. Did he see that?

"Thank you," I said. "Your gift helped me get through it."

"My gift will always be here for you. Now, go with the Watchers. Ready yourself for the banquet as quick as you can, and return to the auditorium. Our night is just beginning." The king nodded at a Watcher, then he slipped away through a sliding door.

Larlia met me in my rooms. She was alone this time.

"Hello," I said. "I'm supposed to get ready for dinner . . . I'm guessing you know what that means?"

"Sit," she said.

I lowered onto the ottoman, and Larlia re-pinned my hair, digging viciously into my scalp. I tried not to flinch.

"Do you know why I'm assigned to help you?" she asked.

"You don't have to, if you don't want to," I told her. "I can dress myself, if you show me which gown to wear."

"I do have to," she said. "The king assigned me. My grandfather sat on the highest council, and that still counts for something. If the king had assigned anyone of lower status, the cities would have protested. Besides, I'm the best at what I do. The Polaris will talk about these events for years to come. They'll remember what you wore, and who dressed you. Pity I'm not doing it for a real queen."

"Pity."

I wished she was doing this for someone else too. What if a Regent queen could have helped the king to heal Andrew? Or to bless the Croppers' sleep? But the king didn't want a Regent wife. He wanted me. Two gifts in one. I should have been thankful. That was my only bargaining chip, and I needed to play the game. Larlia was helping me to do that.

When she was done with my hair and my paint, Larlia laid out fresh slippers and a new gown for me. The new dress didn't have any sleeves, and the silken fabric hugged tight to my hips, my waist, my chest. Glittering swirls covered the skirt.

After I changed, I followed the king's order and hurried back to the auditorium. Long tables filled the room, seated with Regents in high-backed chairs. They talked among themselves, low voices rumbling.

The king greeted me at the entrance. Pale eyes watched us.

There was a long table, higher than the others. The Regents seated there wore the showiest clothes. Blazers with the highest collars and dresses with the most crystals. Larlia took a seat at the end. She was the only one who wasn't looking at me.

I offered the king my hand, my mouth frozen into a smile.

"Humans can't see it," he said. "But the fabric of your dress is a pale version of what you call yellow. An almost color. Not the real thing. It looks well with your eyes."

"Larlia knows what she's doing." I tried to deflect the attention elsewhere.

"I chose the dress." The thread of the king's mind pressed into mine.

Even though I was healed and well, I still found myself tired under the weight of guarding my thoughts.

"What color are your eyes?" I showed polite interest.

"Regents have no color," he said. "Not even a hint of it. Like most things in our earth. Some Croppers are almost pink, but it's not enough to strengthen their gifts. For that, we rely on other sources. I can tell you more about it later. Right now, we should eat. You must be hungry."

"As hungry as a Cropper."

The king laughed. "I once saw a Cropper child eat twelve bowls of grain."

I scanned the tables, searching for Proce and Von. "Is that why you only invited Regents tonight?"

"No," the king said. "You're looking for your friends? I honored them among the Regents during our march today, but now they're with the others. They want to celebrate with their own kind tonight. Our engagement holds special meaning for them."

I imagined the scene. All the Croppers around a white fire, congratulating Proce and Von, patting them on their shoulders. Would they sing about it? Verses and choruses, celebrating how I was captured and taken away from everything I loved.

"When will I see them again?"

"Soon." The king squeezed my hand and led me toward a table set for two at the far edge of the room.

This time, I was glad to be alone with him. I didn't think I could manage polite conversation with other Regents. My face was already stiff from the long day of smiles and nods.

He pulled out a chair for me and we took our places. Little white flames floated above the wooden table, burning without a candle or a wick. The light reflected off metallic dishes, laden with monochromatic food. There were tureens of white sauce and plates of gray leaves, like sickly lettuce. Silvery fruits had been cut and arranged on a plate to look like besmonn wings. A tray of bread, crusted with seeds, sat in the center. Some dishes were filled with unrecognizable foods.

"You should eat," the king said.

I decided to play it safe and stick with bread. As with the Croppers, the table was set with spoons and plates and bowls. Not a fork or a knife in sight.

The king ladled something lumpy and creamy onto my plate. "Try this. It's good with bread."

"I'm guessing that's not chicken?" What kinds of animals might Regents eat? The only one I had seen in the gray earth was a besmonn.

"What is chicken?" the king asked.

"It's a bird. An animal, like a besmonn." What other kinds of creatures did they have in this earth?

The king's eyes widened and he placed the ladle back in the dish. "In my cities, we don't eat animals. We don't even speak of it. I heard humans crossed that line, but I thought it wasn't true, a story told for shock."

"I'm sorry if I offended you. I didn't realize . . ."

The king's face softened. "It makes sense, in an earth where animals die young. I can understand. My people, though, won't have as broad of a view. Please don't mention it again."

"I won't."

He edged his seat nearer to mine, his voice hushed. "I need to let you know something, so you won't look surprised. I'm about to officially introduce you as my intended wife. I'm not going to use your true name. I'll give you a new one."

"Why?"

"Meg sounds like a Cropper name. You're a member of my House now. Your name needs to show it."

I made my face as blank as I could. I wouldn't show my discomfort, but I wouldn't fake approval. What was wrong with sounding like a Cropper? What was wrong with sounding like a human?

And now I was losing my name too.

Had the king been right, when he said there was power in a name? Identity. Belonging.

The king stood and the room fell silent, all eyes on him.

"You already know what I'm about to tell you, but there's still joy in the telling." His voice carried well, steady and deep. He flashed a hint of a smile at the crowd of Regents. "You have celebrated well today, and for that I'm thankful."

He took my hand and guided me to my feet, holding out his other arm with a flourish, as if helping me to stand was a grand gesture.

Regents bowed their heads in acknowledgement.

The king continued his speech. "The woman who stands beside me is not one of our kind, but she is our future. Regents have always welcomed other peoples among us. It is especially easy to welcome one so lovely."

Some members of the crowd murmured their agreement. A lady Regent dabbed at her eyes with a cloth. Was she happy for the Croppers, or grieving her own chance to be queen? They would all outlive me. But no one wants to be passed up, overlooked. The lady's dinner companion crossed his arms and leaned back in his chair.

"Her years are few, but I've come to know her, and I can see her wisdom. She has grown to love our earth and our people already. Her color will bless our gifts, and she will bear our future king. For that, we can't help but love her in return. I would like to introduce my intended wife, Alora Lucent of the King's House."

At the sound of my invented name, every Regent rose to their feet and bowed. Then, they let out a roar of sound, their voices rising in pitch. What were they saying?

"Alora!" they shouted. "Alora!"

I hated the name. The king had told them who I was, and how I felt, and what I would do. None of it was true. I wasn't wise and I hadn't grown to love the Regents. I definitely was not ready to have a child.

But no one was going to ask me what I wanted. It only mattered what their king said.

He gave me a look, and I knew it was time for me to play my part. I forced a brilliant smile, bowing my head to the Regents. With the king's hand in mine, I stood alone in a sea of dazzling gray, wishing with all my heart for a human face, or even a Cropper. Something plain and imperfectly perfect.

13

The dinner stretched on, into the night. The Regents drank chalices of black liquid, growing louder and less reserved with each round. I drank only water. One by one, pairs of Regents visited us at our table.

"I heard the good news about you two," the king said to a Regent couple as they approached. "I look forward to meeting the child you carry."

The lady beamed.

"We owe you thanks," said the bald Regent man. "Two children in only one hundred years." He looked at me. "Don't let your intended husband be too humble about all those gemstones. No other king has been able to call so much color into our earth. The birth rates are up because of it. We might end this generation with more Regents than the last. Just imagine it."

"I'm as thankful for color as the rest of you," the king said. "As you can see." He put an arm around my shoulder, and the Regents chuckled.

When the couple took their seats again, I turned to the king. "Why gemstones?"

"Their color doesn't fade with time. They're useful for strengthening our gifts, though they're difficult to call from your earth."

"Have you ever sent anything the other way? To my earth?"

"Why would I want to?" He raised one eyebrow.

Eventually, all the Regents filed out of the room, leaving me alone with the king. The auditorium was empty, used plates and bowls strewn across tables, the only evidence of the party.

The king stood and offered to help me to my feet.

I stood on my own.

"Meg." He used my real name. "I want to try something before we end the night. Something just between us, and I need your help."

"What is it?"

"I want to know what your color can do." From his pocket, the king removed a clear crystal, glinting with cut edges.

"I'm going to call a distant relative of this stone to cross over from your earth. I want to include your color in the call, to see if it goes faster. All you need to do is remain still. Don't interrupt."

"I thought it was impossible to call anything between earths, without a thin place."

"Many things are possible, with the King's Gift." He gripped my hand in his.

The room buzzed with gifted energy, and the air shimmered. The king furrowed his brow in concentration, his eyes closed. We stood like that for a long time, unmoving. After a while, my wrist grew tender where he gripped it, and my eyelids felt heavy. How late was it?

When the king gasped for air, I jumped, but I didn't make a sound. He squeezed my fingers painfully tight, then his eyes opened.

"We did it," he said.

"Did what?"

He opened his other hand, palm up. Beside the original crystal sat a new gemstone, as blue as a human sky.

"Without you, that would have taken weeks. It might have been impossible. Some stones are beyond my reach." The king closed his hand over the gems again. "It's a colorful one, almost as bright as you."

"Except my color will fade," I reminded him. "That sapphire will outlive me."

So would the king. By centuries, maybe.

He released his grip on my hand, brushing his fingers lightly over mine. "There is a kind of intensity in human life, like a flame that burns too fast. I won't take our time together for granted."

I stretched my bruised fingers and hid my hands behind my back.

"Let's get you back to your rooms," the king said. "It's well past time for sleep."

The hall lights glowed dim as we traveled the passages to the human rooms. Was it the middle of the night? Or almost morning? I hadn't seen a clock since leaving my earth.

"Was your evening tolerable?" the king asked.

"Yes. Thank you," I lied.

Nothing about this place was tolerable. I was trapped.

"Your thoughts slip out when you're tired," the king said. "I can sense some of them. You aren't happy here now. But I think you could be someday. If you let yourself."

I snapped my guard back into place without a word.

"You're not a prisoner," he said. "You're a member of the King's House. It's your house too. There are gardens, and a library. Anytime you want, I can show you around. All you have to do is say my name and I'll come to you."

Not long ago, he had threatened to stop healing me if I didn't marry him. To let me die. No matter what he said, I was a prisoner. I chose this. I even chose to rush the ceremony. But it was my only move in a game where he held all the cards.

We arrived at the door to my rooms.

"For now," I said, "I think I need to sleep."

The king bowed to me, lower than anyone had yet. "Sleep well."

He straightened to his full height and lingered, eyes on mine, as if he wanted to say more.

"Yes?" I asked.

"Someday, maybe the smiles will be real."

Then, he left.

Once inside my rooms, I heard his steps retreat down the hall. His mind receded from mine.

I didn't sleep well. I didn't want to sleep at all. Where were Proce and Von? I had seen them in the procession, but the last time we had spoken was that first night in these rooms, when I had told them to go away. I had been angry, confused. But now, I found myself missing them, longing for something familiar in this place.

I was also anxious to check on Andrew. The king could probably use his gift to help me look at him, but I wasn't going to ask. Not until it was time for the healing. He didn't need to see Andrew. My human, as the king had called him.

It wasn't like Von to stay away, even if I wanted her to. Wouldn't she be pleased about my bargain? And what would Proce think about the king's dismissal of the Writings? About the ceremony gift? I refused to believe the giants were absent by choice. The king had separated us from the very beginning. Maybe if they couldn't come to me, I could find them. I was a member of the King's House now. If it was my home too, then I should be free to explore.

I bounced off the edge of my bed and went to the door at the front of the human rooms. The door handle wouldn't turn. I twisted the knob as hard as I could, rattled it back and forth, but it didn't budge. I was locked in.

The air in the entrance room felt suddenly warm in my lungs, the walls too close. I needed to get outside. There had to be another exit.

I ran to the windows behind the bed. They weren't designed to open.

Next, I double-checked the bathroom. The mosaic walls contained an excess of basins and spouts, but there were no windows or doors.

One other archway stood in the entrance room. I had assumed was a closet.

The Regent ladies usually darted through its door several times during their visits, returning with underskirts and extra hair pins.

With no better ideas to try, I went to the arch and pushed the sliding door. It was made of smooth black glass, and my fingers left smudge marks on the cool surface.

At first, the room beyond was dark. As I entered, dim cones glowed.

My guess had been right. It was a closet. A massive closet, even bigger than the bedroom. Shelves and aisles overflowed with shimmering cloth. Plumed dresses and lace robes hung from metal hooks, and the walls were made of mirrors.

My eyes scanned the glittering display, searching for a window or a door. I caught a glimpse of my reflection. The girl in the mirror was a streak of color: ruddy brown draped over shades of peach. I was human, warm and strange to my own eyes, which had grown accustomed to the gray.

The closet was a dead end, and I had nowhere left to search for an exit. At least it was somewhere new. I closed the door, shutting myself in with the clothes.

A stone bench sat against one wall, between shelves of boots and slippers. Decorative images of Croppers and trees had been carved along the front of the stone.

The carvings were rough-hewn, the stone raw. It was unlike anything in the King's House. Regents would have polished the surface to a shine. This bench was Cropper-made. I sat and ran my fingertips along the uneven grooves.

If I had been Analese, I would have wanted Cropper things in my rooms too. A Regent bed, but Cropper art. The giants' carvings were simple. Made by large hands. The King's House must have been made by a gift. That was the only explanation for the unnatural perfection. Cropper things I could understand. They were almost familiar. Had Analese felt the same?

As I sat, my bare feet poked out from beneath my skirt. My toes were dirty and pink from the day's walk in a pair of satin slippers. Did Regent feet ever get dirty? Probably not.

I liked the dirt. From within my prison, it was my only connection to the outdoors. Dirt belonged with trees and sunshine. Where I belonged.

A faint light shone from the hollow space beneath the bench, accentuating the dust on my toes. I bent forward. Who puts a light under a bench?

I crouched on all fours and peered beneath, but I couldn't see the source of the light. It was too far underneath. I poked my head deeper into the space and kept going, crawling now.

It was a tunnel.

Even a Regent would have struggled to fit, but I made it through easily. After a short time, I emerged into a large room, filled with bright light. I stood and straightened my dress, blinking as my eyes adjusted.

The room was six-sided. A table and chair sat in the middle, and a dusty, familiar scent hung in the air.

Books.

Shelves of books covered every wall. There were rows of leathery-black tomes, stacks of gilded leaflets, and graying piles of unbound paper. Footstools edged the shelves, so that even a short human would be able to reach the highest books.

Lady Analese had lived here before me. This must have been her library. Was Analese her real name, or had she been given a new one too? Something about it sounded Regent. She might have been a Kathryn or a Rose when she arrived to the gray earth. Was she a prisoner too, or was she happy to marry a Regent man? Maybe she didn't remember her old life at all.

A large book lay open on the table. I sat and examined the dusty pages. The book was turned open to an illustration of a leafy tree, drawn in metallic ink, framed by an ornate design. The tree's roots were painted black.

To the left of the drawing were inscribed lines of beautiful calligraphy. Would I be able to read the words in my new language? At first, the letters had a strange arc to them, but after studying them for a moment, my mind organized the handwriting into coherent sentences. I could read it, though my comprehension lagged, and it made my head hurt.

I broke the silence in the room and read the passage aloud, slow, staggering, surprised to find that I had heard parts of it before.

"Where the sky of seven colors
Meets the waters of our lands
When the new one walks on silver
Eyes of hue and golden hands

Oh peace, thou hath gone until she is here
Oh gift, thou art wielded as a sword
The tree hath rot beneath the silver
Oh, new one, thou loved by our lords

What was given is taken away
Oh peace, return through the new one small
She will walk upon silver
Oh sleep, return upon her call

Where the sky of seven colors
Meets the waters of our lands
When the new one has walked on silver
Eyes of hue and golden hands"

I read the words again. And then again. They were the words
that had inspired Proce and Von to steal me from my earth.
   Their stupid poem.
   It wasn't even good poetry. The rhymes were forced and the
metaphors felt random. Maybe the flow had been lost in translation,
ruined by the gift of language that helped me understand words in
the gray earth. Not that I really understood the poem. It sounded
like nonsense. I tried to read it for a fourth time and my eyes stuck
on one line.

   What was given is taken away.

The Croppers had lost their sleep, and maybe their lives. Could I really change that by marrying the king? Just a ceremony, and everything would be fixed.

I flipped through the pages, though I didn't know what I was looking for. I found a grayscale painting of rolling hills, captioned with dense rows of text. I read a stanza.

Wisdom buries seed in a field.
The wise live long upon its yield.
Evil deeds grow tainted crops.
The wicked reap from their own plot.

It sounded like a Cropper song, written into a Regent book. I suspected it was a compilation, made by someone who belonged to neither race. A human. Analese.

A gap at the back of the book caught my eye. The pages were separated, as if a pen had been tucked between them. I slid my hand through the paper and pulled out a thin object.

The bookmark was made of shimmering glass, shaped like a tiny sword with a miniature hilt. Though the edges were dull, the tip came to a needle-fine point. As I ran my finger along the edge, the glass vibrated with a ringing noise, like a crystal goblet rim against a damp fingertip.

It was the closest thing to a weapon I had seen in the gray earth. Regents and Croppers didn't even eat with forks and knives. They only used spoons.

I tucked the little sword into my waistband, snug beside my note to Andrew. I was the smallest person in the whole city, probably in the whole earth. I didn't want to fight anyone. Still, I felt safer with a knife. I would carry it with me, a small secret. Analese wouldn't mind.

I looked around the library, appreciating the wealth of books.

Between two shelves, at the back of the room, hung a velvet piece of cloth. Gray. Like everything else. But it wasn't a tapestry. It wasn't particularly decorative at all. Why had space been made for it? What if it was a curtain, covering something? Like a window that could be opened.

I left the book for later, and pulled the cloth aside. Instead of a window, there was a wooden door with a silver handle. Even better.

The knob twisted in my hand without resistance. The door clicked open. A delicious breeze blew across my bare shoulders as I stepped through the door, into moonlight.

I had found my exit.

Silver grass shone under the night sky, lined with neat rows of white blossoms, planted in earthen flower beds. It was a garden, encased by high walls of black stone. At the center of the lawn, a fountain bubbled, water falling into a stone basin.

Now that I was free, I needed to find the Cropper rooms. I had no idea where to go. But my giants were somewhere in this house. The cool grass prickled my feet as I searched around the corner for another door. I found nothing but more unscalable walls. The garden was completely enclosed, except for the library door. A courtyard.

I was still trapped, in an expanded cell.

With nothing else to do, I sat on the rim of the fountain and let the night air steal my warmth. At least I was outside. Nothing stood between me and the sky.

Stars speckled the darkness. At night, the sky looked the same as my own earth. It didn't need to be blue to be familiar.

And that familiarity sparked a memory. I hadn't known the memory was still in my mind. I might not have found it if I looked for it. But it was there, and it came to me now.

Andrew sits beside me on grass. I can't see the color of the lawn in the dark, but it smells green. The air is cold. True cold. The sky is black, the stars sharp. Andrew's face is visible in moonlight.

We share a blueberry muffin. Blueberries. A food described by its color. Andrew tears off bits of soft pastry, sugar sticking to his lower lip.

"You don't have to show me," I say. "If you don't want to."

"You're not getting out of it." He grins. *"And I expect honest feedback."*

Andrew picks up his guitar and plays, his fingers moving with graceful precision. The music sinks into me. It's happy, with a touch of longing. It makes me miss something. I want to cry but I don't.

The song ends.

"Are you kidding me?" I give Andrew's shoulder a shove. "You had me thinking it was going to be awful. And that wasn't awful." I catch eyes with him. "It was amazing."

Andrew looks back at me. Too long. I'm scared of what he might see. Scared of how I feel. So I look away.

"My instructor thinks it will be good enough for admissions," Andrew says. "But nothing is for sure."

"If that school doesn't accept you, they're dumb." I'm not flattering Andrew. His compositions are good. It's going to be his ticket out of Twin Cliffs. And I'm going to be left behind. "Don't forget about me when you're famous."

"Meg," Andrew says, "I could never forget you."

What happened next that night? I couldn't remember. But I knew Andrew was supposed to go to school in the fall. So he must have been accepted.

The memory was simple. Sweet. So different from my life in the King's House. I played it over in my mind again and again. It was a different world, where young people dreamed of the future. Here, the future was complicated. But Andrew deserved to make music. To share his music.

I looked up at the stars. What were the lyrics to my human song?

"Twinkle, twinkle, little star . . ." My voice was thin and small in the night breeze.

Above the garden wall, a light flickered on in a tower. I stopped singing and jumped up from the fountain rim. Had someone heard me? Who would be awake so late?

I didn't sense the king's presence in my mind. I couldn't see anything through the window besides white light.

But I heard something.

It was music, drifting from the tower window, into the garden. A woman's voice sang, low and wordless.

Her voice was deep, though she lacked the rumble of a Cropper tone. The melody lilted, haunting and beautiful. It called to me in a way that made me wary. I had felt the pull of a gift before, in my dreams about the thin place.

But this felt different from the giants' call. Those dreams had been unsettling, a spectral invitation. Something about this voice soothed me. It didn't ask for anything. Instead, it extended itself to me. The tune made me nostalgic for something I couldn't remember.

Whose voice was it? Regents didn't sing, and it wasn't a Cropper. I strained my ears toward the melody, lost myself in its swells and pauses. Every time I thought the song might end, it soared again, never resolving.

I stood like that, listening, until the black sky faded to gray. The moon was gone, the white sun rising. My legs tingled, half-numb from standing through the night.

"I need to go," I whispered. I didn't know if I was speaking to myself, or someone else.

The voice stopped singing.

Had she heard me?

"Hello?" I whispered again.

I waited in the silence until the sky brightened to its full gray. No answer came.

"I'll come back," I promised, then trotted to the garden door.

Soon, I was supposed to accompany the king to the besmonn keep, one more step toward the ceremony.

I ran through the library and crawled back through the tunnel. Would Larlia already be waiting for me, ready to braid my hair? I peeked through the closet door. All was silent, the cones of light still dimmed for sleep.

As soon as I slipped under the covers of the bed, the door to my rooms clicked open and Larlia's voice came from the entrance room.

"Somebody wake her up."

Garlian pulled the sheets off of me without saying a word. I rolled out of bed. Kahlea wasn't among the ladies.

All morning, the song lingered in my mind. I wanted to meet the singer. I knew it was gifted music, but I couldn't help myself. Her voice had been friendly, and I needed more friends in the King's House. As long as it didn't distract me from Andrew's healing, I intended to find her.

14

"The Polaris besmonns are kept outside the city walls," Larlia said. "You'll have to walk there on your short legs."

She braided my hair at the nape of my neck and selected a simple, white dress for me to wear on the journey. Loose sleeves covered my arms, and the skirt ended above my ankles.

When no one was looking, I buried my note and my sword deep in a button-topped pocket. If only every Regent dress could have pockets.

The king greeted me in the hall with a long look. "You're hiding your color under your clothes."

I stopped a few feet away from him. "I like this dress."

"Don't misunderstand me." He took my hand. "You're still lovely. But why hide a flame under a bowl?"

I hoped I wasn't blushing. The compliment made me more uneasy than pleased, but still heat came to my cheeks.

We walked through an arch, into the city. The king's shoes were sturdier than usual, as were mine.

"We're leaving the Polaris?" I asked.

The king only replied with a smile and a raise of his brow.

"If we leave the shade of the buildings, I'll need my sleeves. Some humans burn in the sun."

"Some Regents, also," the king said. "The pale ones."

"I bet they don't turn pink."

He stopped and looked at me for a moment, as if I might be lying. "Because your blood is red?"

"I guess." A shudder ran through me.

"I'd like to see red blood." The king kept walking.

"What?" It was my turn to pause, nausea coming in waves. Color was a treasure to Regents. Would they cut me open to see more?

"Only in theory." The king's eyes went wide. He didn't need to read my mind to know what I had thought. "I don't want you to get hurt. I would never—"

"It's fine."

We walked in silence for a while, though the king's mind tried to search mine. I kept him at bay. There was no parade today, but some Regents and Croppers trailed behind us at various intervals, curious to see the king's human bride. Some shouted greetings as we passed. I didn't recognize any faces.

The king was dressed in a simpler fashion today. Instead of his black blazer, he wore a loose, heathered shirt. His mind pressed down on mine, always searching. I pressed back, already tired from the effort. Sweat dampened my face as we walked beneath a canopy of white sky.

"Who are the Regents who live in your house?" I asked. "The ones who were there my first night? Some of them walked with us yesterday. Are they royalty?"

I was trying to distract the king. His mind was always less heavy during conversation.

"Some are Watchers," he said. "They serve the king. And they share what they see with the people. Others are daughters and sons of distant cities, sent here to learn. And there are those who work in the King's House. Library keepers, advisors, assistants. None are royalty. Only I have that title."

It worked. While the king spoke, our mental struggle stopped.

We passed through the front gate of the city, a polished stone passage, glinting in sunshine.

For a people who weren't at war, the Regents had a lot of walls and protections.

At the sandy bank of the river, the king paused. "We'll wait here for a minute."

I didn't ask why. It didn't matter to me where we went. I watched the river flow over black rocks, the song from the tower playing in my mind, each bend in the notes fresh in my memory. If only I could hear it again.

The king joined the Watchers, speaking to them in hushed tones. I tried to eavesdrop, but they were too quiet.

"The day is a gift!" A gravel voice spoke behind me.

Von's voice.

I spun to see the Croppers approach. They took long, graceful strides. I smiled a real smile. I couldn't help it. Despite all they had done to me, all they had planned for me, it was good to see my giants again.

The king didn't acknowledge them. He was still involved in his whispered conversation.

I ran to the Croppers and reached up to clasp Von's hands. "The day is a gift."

Then I turned to Proce. The moment my hands touched his, something strange happened. My eyes fell shut. Without warning, Proce's gift responded to me, pouring out stronger than it ever had before.

I wanted to see Andrew, but I hadn't asked. It was too soon. Somehow, Proce's gift knew what was in my mind.

A vision came of Andrew, lying in a hospital bed, a world away.

Meg? Andrew's mind spoke to me, muffled beneath a blanket of pain. He knew I was there, despite his injury.

Proce ripped his hand away, and the vision disappeared.

The giant sank to his knees, close to me. He lowered his voice. "How did you do that?"

"Do what?" I asked. "I don't know . . ."

"You called my gift away, against my will." Proce cradled his thumb where I had touched him. "It hurt my hand. In a way, it hurt all of me."

"Are you sure?" Von kneeled at our level. "Do not make quick accusations."

We were interrupted by the king, who had finished his conversation with the Watchers. The giants kept their eyes on me as he joined us.

"Welcome, Croppers," the king said.

Neither Proce nor Von responded right away. After a tense silence, Von bowed her head.

"Is everything alright?" The king's eyes flicked to Proce's cradled hand. "You're in pain. Why?"

"It is fine now." Proce released his thumb. "Just a clumsy mistake."

I hoped it really was fine.

Von showed her teeth. "Thank you for inviting us here today."

Had I really stolen Proce's gift? Would he tell the king? I clouded my mind in deep shadow, so my thoughts were private. If I had taken Proce's gift, could I somehow use that ability to heal Andrew? But the king wasn't powerful enough yet. He needed the Queen's Gift to heal across earths, which would require our marriage. So stealing wouldn't save me from anything. Better not to make an enemy, especially of the one person who could keep me alive in this earth. The king would keep his promise.

Proce tightened his jaw.

"We'd better start walking," the king said.

"Yes," Proce said, too eagerly. "Let us walk."

The king took my hand and we made our way along the river. Proce and Von walked behind us at a respectful distance, followed by a few of the always-present Watchers. I wished I could walk with the giants.

"I thought you'd like your friends to accompany us today," the king said.

"Thank you. I haven't seen them in a while." I didn't ask if the king was keeping them away, but I wondered.

"I don't blame you for loving the Croppers," he said. "All of our humans have had a special fondness for their music. Regents can't sing, but humans can. I hope to hear you sing someday."

"Anyone can sing." I hoped to avoid a future performance. "It's just like talking, but with longer syllables."

"If I tried to sing, you'd cover your ears and run away forever." The king smiled. "And then who would heal you?"

I forced a smile.

As we walked, the sun grew hotter. The king hadn't healed me yet, and a now familiar malaise settled in my chest. Worst of all, with every step, I carried the weight of guarding my mind from the king. I counted my steps, letting each number add to my mental shield. One . . . Two . . . Three . . . When I reached step forty-four, my foot caught on a loose stone in the path.

I tripped, and landed on my hands and knees.

"Are you alright?" The king stooped to offer me his hand.

I stood, brushing dust from my dress. It wouldn't stay white for long. "I'm sorry."

Had the Watchers seen? Of course they had. That's what they did. They watched.

"I should be sorry," the king said. "I haven't healed you yet. Are you breathing well?"

"Well enough."

"You're obviously weakened . . ." The king searched my mind with more fervor.

I held my ground and felt a surge of my own power. He couldn't win.

"I'm not weak enough for you to pry into my thoughts." I wanted him to give up. "No matter how hard you try."

The weight of the king's mind lifted. I maintained my walls, but they were easier now.

"I didn't know you could feel it."

I tightened my lips. "I can."

"I'm used to using my gift freely. I forget that it affects you differently." He laid his hand onto my forearm. "Let me heal you."

His gift flowed, and the pain in my chest disappeared, along with the bruise on my toe where it had caught on the path. The gifted hum filled me up and made me feel more awake than I should have been after a sleepless night.

"You haven't been taking care of yourself." The king's hum stopped. "My gift tells me, but anyone can see it. You look like you stayed up the whole night. Doing what?"

"I was worried about Proce and Von. I wanted to see them. I still do." I glanced over my shoulder at the giants.

They had stopped their progress, maintaining their place in the line.

"Come walk with us!" I called.

They eyed the king.

"The king always walks alone," he said.

"You're not alone today," I responded.

After a weighted silence, the king beckoned Proce and Von forward. "Croppers. Your friend misses you."

Von grinned, and the giants caught up to us in ten long steps.

"We are honored to be with you." Proce gave a small bow.

"Yes." The king looked back at the Watchers, as if wondering who might see him alongside a Cropper.

His tone made me defensive of Proce. "Anyone should be honored to walk with a Cropper. Without Croppers, who would grow all the food?"

The king laughed. "That is fair enough. Croppers are best suited for field work. It's why they chose Regents to rule over them."

I looked at Proce. Could that be true? The Croppers chose their servitude?

"Proce has been teaching me about your earth," I said. "Maybe he can tell the story of how Regents became kings?"

"Gladly!" Proce took short steps to stay beside me. He dove into the story without permission. "Croppers lived in these lands first, before the Regents came, in the ancient times. The Regents arrived as refugees, though our history is unclear where they came from. The Croppers welcomed them and gave them grain. As you have seen, we are very good workers, and they had plenty to spare."

"You would still have grain to spare," Von said. "If you read less and worked more."

Proce looked unhappy, but he didn't retaliate in front of the king. "The Regents settled among us. They built their own cities and roads. They shared their gifts freely, prospering in every way, except for one: the Regents were forced to rely on the Croppers to grow their food. The land trusts the Croppers. It responds to our gifts. It would not open up to the Regents."

"You mean they can't farm?" I asked.

"Exactly," Proce said. "Our Cropper elders loved the Regents, and feared for their dependency. You see, they knew future Croppers could one day oppress the Regents who had once been their guests. The Regents needed something of greater value, to balance the alliance. We gave them a sacred gift. The Cropper elders gave the responsibility of blessing our sleep to a Regent. He became the first king, with the first King's Gift. The gift chooses the king now. It is a profound mystery. But both Regent and Cropper must depend on one another."

"Is that why the king has Cropper gifts and Regent gifts?" I asked.

"I wouldn't say it that way." The king's hand stiffened in mine. "I have the King's Gift."

Proce bowed his head and fell a step behind, showing deference.

"The alliance defines both groups," I said. "It's literally in your names. Croppers and Regents. You call yourself by your differences."

"I suppose," Proce said. "We are different but equal."

"If you're equal, then why are Croppers doing the hard work?" Why were Proce and Von forced to always walk behind, to bow and to placate?

"Do not despise hard work," Proce warned. "There are many Regents who wish they could do what we can. There have been those who would take it from us, but could not. And Regents work hard, in their own way. They carry their own weights."

For a moment, the king's mind tried to invade mine, a tidal wave of pressure against my walls. Then, he gave up. Or remembered his promise to lighten up on the mind reading. What was he thinking of this conversation? And why did he care so much what I thought of it?

"We're almost there," he said. "Do you see that grove of trees, where the river bends? That's where the Polaris besmonn keep is."

Before long, we entered the grove. To me, it was large enough to be called a wood, too broad to see to the other side. Leafy branches formed a canopy, offering shade. The grass grew a darker silver beneath the trees, unbleached by the sun. Among the leaves, large white flowers blossomed.

It took a moment for my eyes to find the besmonn keep, despite its size. Everything here was gray, so the metal structure blended in. It must have been built long ago, for the woods to have grown so tight around it. Branches laced with the curling bars of the keep. It was a cage. A domed structure, as tall as the highest trees.

The bars were more widely spaced than I would have expected. How would they keep the besmonns inside?

Before I could ask, we were approached by three unfamiliar Croppers. A male, a female, and a child. A family.

Proce and Von rushed ahead to clasp hands with the strangers.

"Hoooo!" Proce boomed at full volume, ruffling the hair of the young boy. "Gifted morning."

The Croppers exchanged greetings, each patting the shoulders of the others. When they finished, the family crouched low, bowing their heads to the king, and to me.

"It's good to see you." The king smiled at the family. "This is the lady Alora. I'm glad for her to meet you."

"Gifted morning," said the woman Cropper. "I am Dorl, and this is my husband, Surm. We are pleased that the king brought you with him today!"

I bowed my head to Dorl, as she had done to me. "It's good to meet you."

"Dorl and Surm are the best besmonn keepers in the Seven Cities," the king said.

Surm looked pleased. "We are inspired. The king is the best rider in the Seven Cities."

"Rider?" I asked.

Before anyone could answer, the child ran forward, stopping one pace away from me, his narrow face no higher than mine. His eyes had gray speckles in them, and his white hair was straight as straw.

"If I touch her, will she burn me?" he asked. "She is too bright."

"Cham!" His mother pulled him back several paces. "Be respectful."

I laughed. On any earth, a child was a child. I couldn't blame this one for being curious. And it was nice not to be the smallest, for once.

"It's okay," I said. "I don't mind questions. And I won't burn you."

Cham looked up at his parents. "Truly?" His eyes darted back to me.

Proce crouched down to Cham's level. "Only days ago, I carried her all the way from my village. She did not leave a burn on me." He held out his hands as evidence.

I held my hand out too, inviting Cham forward. "You can try it for yourself, if you want."

Cautiously, with one eye closed, Cham touched my hand with the tip of his gray pointer finger. When it didn't hurt, he opened both eyes, delighted. He patted my forearm, and inspected my freckles. To my surprise, Dorl and Surm reached down to pat me too. I laughed, and so did they.

"Now," interrupted the king. "It's time for you to see what I ride."

He led me toward the keep and we peered through the silver bars. The dirt floor of the structure glistened with discarded strings of besmonn thread. Trees grew inside, mostly stripped of their blossoms.

"Look up," the king whispered.

I did. High above, in the dome of the cage, swirled birds the size of horses. Bigger than horses. Besmonns. Huge besmonns. Some flew, their powerful wings swishing through the air. Others perched on branches and metal rods.

"What do you think?" the king asked.

"They . . . they're huge. I saw a small one in the village." How could both birds share the same name? The differences were enormous.

"You've only seen a field besmonn. They're useful to the Croppers for fertilizing the ground. But, to Regents, these are the true besmonns. I'll go first so you can see how to ride."

"Wait." I measured the distance from the ground to the top of the dome with my eyes. A wave of nausea and panic washed over me. "You expect me to ride one of those? I can't go up there."

"You need to," the king said. "If you want the ceremony to take place."

I looked at Von. "You never mentioned this." Of all the things she had tried to prepare me for, she should have covered this most of all.

"She likely didn't think of it," the king said. "Most Croppers aren't part of the queen's wedding traditions. It's something kept among Regents."

"You don't understand. I'm scared of heights." I knew I sounded pathetic. My knees were already shaking at the thought of flight.

"It's necessary." The king tightened his jaw.

"Why?" I would do anything to get my miracle. But only if I had to. Why did it have to involve heights?

"It's tradition. A king and a queen face challenges during their reign together. Some things can't be fixed with a gift. The besmonn ride allows a bride to prove herself to the king, and to the people. It shows courage, and patience. It has to be done, and the Regents have to hear about it. That's why the Watchers came. They'll take a report to the city."

I tried to slow my breaths. The hooded figures stood on the edge of the grove, attentive and silent.

"And what if they bring a bad report?"

The king looked straight at me and lowered his voice. "It is easier for a king not to be at odds with his people."

Dorl knelt beside me. "Riding is not dangerous like it used to be.

Our last queen had to ride a wild besmonn. But now, the king has tamed a whole keep of them for himself. With Cropper help. These animals are gentle. Messengers ride them between the cities."

Their last queen died, and I didn't want to walk in her shoes. I wasn't here for a crown. I was here for healing. If only the two weren't connected.

Proce leaned against the keep. "Croppers could have tamed them long ago, but there was no reason. The smaller besmonns are better for our fields. We are too large to ride these creatures. But we are still the best at keeping them." Proce patted Surm on the shoulder.

"I did catch my share," Surm said.

Once again, the Croppers were happy to work for the Regents. They took pride in doing what they were good at.

I held onto the bars of the keep, eyeing the besmonns. They were beautiful, their graceful wings rich with shining feathers. And they terrified me.

For Andrew, I would have to fly. It wasn't the worst thing that had been asked of me.

I turned to the king. "Okay. I'm ready."

I didn't feel ready at all.

15

"Watch me first," the king said. "Then we'll put you on an old bird. One that won't fly too high."

Cham climbed several feet up the silver bars, tilting his head back to look at us. "That's no fun. I'm still small enough to ride, like you. And I like to go high."

"Today is not about you," said Dorl.

"Cham might as well ride too," the king said. "He's learned well this year. Let him show Alora."

Clever. If a child could do it, then I had no excuse.

Cham followed the king to a wood barrel at the edge of the keep. They each took a glass tumbler and dipped a cup of glossy liquid out of the barrel.

"What is that?" I asked Dorl.

"Nectar. To reward the besmonns. They do not like to be caught without an incentive."

Cham and the king entered the keep through a hinged gate, made of the same silver bars as the whole keep. The king held his tumbler high, his stance wide. Cham did the same.

"Aviore!" the king shouted.

A bird with spotted wings and a high crest descended. It hovered above the king, dipping its slender mouth into the nectar. It was larger than the king, a beautiful monster with sharp talons.

The king caught the bird at the base of its wing. In one swift

motion, he pulled the creature down and swung his legs across
its back.

The besmonn floated into the air, as if carrying a rider required
no extra effort. It was gifted flight, beyond what should have been
possible.

Next, Cham called his bird, a gray creature with clear wings like
glass. Its talons shone jewel-black.

As Cham mounted, he faltered and lost his balance, then
corrected himself by clutching a fist full of feathers. His besmonn
let out a sharp whistle and darted into the air. Cham fought his way
onto the bird's back. Together, they flew to meet the king.

The riders circled within the keep, wind blowing through
Cham's wild hair. They flew higher, into the tip of the dome.
Too high.

"Proce?" I asked. "Their wings look too delicate. How do they
hold a rider?"

Proce was delighted to answer me. "Besmonns are gifted." He
confirmed my theory. "In flight, and in other ways also. Regents
and Croppers will always obey the King's Gift. We must. Besmonns
are different, and not easily tamed." He looked down at me. "I
wonder if humans might be different too."

Even if the besmonns were different, the king had still tamed
them. He had found a way. My sickness gave him power over me.
How many days could I live without his healing?

After a few more turns around the keep, Cham and the king flew
near the gate. Dorl swung it open, and their besmonns scrambled
through the opening, as if this might be their last chance. They
soared into the open sky, along the ground at first, then higher.

The king gripped his halter with only one hand, letting the other
wave free, balancing on his seat. He laughed.

Cham swooped and dipped, flying faster than the king.

Surm watched with a proud smile.

"How did you become a besmonn keeper?" I asked, making
small talk.

"My father—" Surm began.

He was interrupted by a scream.

Dorl's scream.

"CHAM!"

I looked up. Cham's besmonn was descending quickly. Too quickly. Cham slipped from his perch and clung to the halter, his legs dangling in the air. He was going to fall. From that height and speed, he would die.

The king pulled at his bird's halter and flew toward Cham. He reached for the child, but the besmonn wings were between them, blocking his angle. They continued their frantic descent.

"Hold on!" Dorl cried, helpless to save her son.

But Cham couldn't hold on. He fell through the air, separated from his besmonn.

The king pulled his halter down hard, forcing his besmonn into a dive. He reached forward, gripping the bird with only his legs, and wrapped his arms around Cham's body.

At the last moment, the king's besmonn spread its wings, slowing their fall. The three of them skidded into a pile in the grass. Regent, Cropper, and besmonn, limbs tangled.

Cham's riderless bird didn't stop. It careened toward me at full speed. I held up my arms, ready for impact.

But the impact never came.

The creature stopped and hovered beside me.

I stood still, my heart pounding. What did it want? Was it going to attack me?

The besmonn rubbed its smooth cheek against my arm and closed its eyes lazily.

"Cham's not moving!" Dorl said.

Cham lay where he fell. We ran as fast as we could. The Croppers outpaced me, reaching the crash site first. Dorl and Surm fell to Cham's side. Proce raced to the king, faster than Von.

"Does he live?" Von cried.

By the time I reached the others, the king stood up, cradling his arm. He was hurt. The king's besmonn floated above, unharmed.

"I am well," the king said to the giants. "But Cham . . ."

At a stiff run, he rushed to Cham.

"He's not breathing," Dorl sobbed.

The king laid his hands against Cham's cheeks. A bright noise crackled through the air. He was using his gift.

Cham gasped, and then his body went still.

Dorl let out another sob, and Cham sat up.

"We flew so fast!" he said.

"You will never fly so fast again," Dorl laughed, tears in her thick white lashes.

"He wasn't badly injured," the king told her. "He just lost his breath for a moment."

"I do not understand," said Surm. "Why did the besmonns dive? I have never seen them behave like that. Cham has flown a hundred times."

"I think I know," said the king. "They're as drawn to color as we are. Maybe more so." He eyed me.

Cham's besmonn had followed behind us. The other bird descended to join him. They landed on either side of me, their wings folded neatly.

"See how they stay near Alora?" the king asked. "They must have spotted her once they reached the air. I should have guessed."

"I . . . I'm sorry," I stammered. Cham was almost hurt, because of me.

Nobody said anything for a moment. I glanced at the king's arm. Something dark and gray oozed from a narrow gash where his shirt was torn. Blood. Regent blood. My stomach churned.

"You're cut," I said. "Can you heal yourself?"

"Normally, yes. But it was the besmonn's beak that pierced my skin. They're full of their own gift. It's how they fly. A gifted wound can't be healed with a gift. Or, more exactly, it would take too much of my gift. I'll be fine. It's a shallow cut."

He removed a silken scarf from his pocket and dabbed at the blood. I wished he would cover it up.

"Let me." I took the fabric and tied it around his arm. "Aren't your Watchers supposed to guard you? Why didn't they run over here?"

"Because I didn't need them. What kind of a report would they bring to the city, about our flight, if I needed help with a cut? Now, they'll talk about how you ran to me. They'll say you're a compassionate wife."

Dorl held Cham close to her, smothering his face into her ribcage. "Thank you," she said to the king. "You saved our son."

"From the looks of it, I won't have to do any more saving today. Those besmonns would do anything for Alora. She'll ride easily."

The besmonn to my right nestled its beak against my shins.

"It's your turn." The king pointed to the bird with the spotted wing, the one he had ridden. "You should ride Aviore."

"What about an old one? A slow one."

"Now that I've seen you with Aviore, I don't think you'll have any problems with him. It's time. No more delays."

Not long ago, I had climbed the waterfall cliff, running from the giants' cottage. My fear of Proce and Von had been greater than my fear of heights. Now, I hoped my love for Andrew would be greater than my fear of flying.

"Do you need me to lift you?" Proce asked.

"No," the king answered for me. "She'll do it herself." He turned to me. "If you lean forward, Aviore will come closer to the ground. When you lean back, he'll fly higher. Nudge him with your legs to turn. But really, he can pick his own path. Just hold onto the harness."

I ran my hand along Aviore's feathers. The bird let out a deep whistle, soft and hollow.

Cham detangled himself from his mother's arms. "That noise is a good sign. Aviore likes you."

In a strange way, I liked Aviore too. Up close, I couldn't help but admire his round, innocent eyes. That didn't mean I wanted to ride him.

I placed my hand at the base of Aviore's wings. He unfurled, ready for flight. I hummed a calming lullaby, to myself and to the bird. The others didn't exist anymore. They weren't coming with me, off the ground. It was just the two of us.

I climbed onto Aviore's back and found a seat in front of his wings. I'm sure I didn't look graceful. Not even a little bit. But I was riding a besmonn.

As soon as Aviore flew into the air, I gripped his halter and leaned forward, my nails digging into my palms. Forward was toward the ground. Toward safety. We stayed low, skimming along the grass. Not high, but fast. Why hadn't I asked how to slow down? Aviore navigated through the trees and left the grove behind. Cham's besmonn came with us. I leaned to the left, and Aviore turned left. I leaned to the right, and he turned right.

We circled back to where the others stood. Aviore didn't stop, but he slowed as we passed. I rolled off his back and landed on the ground with a painful thud.

I wasn't a skilled rider. I didn't need to be. As long as it was enough for the Watchers to accept.

The king helped me to my feet.

"Is that all I needed to do?" I asked.

"You flew well."

"You're lying. I couldn't have done much worse."

He laughed. "All right. You didn't do well, but at least you did it. That's what counts."

Surm took hold of the besmonns' halters and led them toward their keep. The birds flapped their wings and tugged away from him. They wanted to stay near me.

"I'll walk them back," I offered.

"It seems you will have to." Surm handed me the straps of the halters.

As the besmonns followed me to the keep, the king stayed at my side. "My Alora, the besmonn tamer. I wonder how a wild besmonn would respond to you? I hope we can ride together again."

I wasn't his. And I didn't ever want to fly again. But I wouldn't mind seeing the besmonns in the future. They were the only creatures in the gray earth without a plan for my life.

"Maybe I can visit Aviore sometime?"

"All the time," the king said. "When we're married, we can ride as often as you want."

I coaxed Aviore and the other besmonn into their keep. Surm gave them a sip of nectar before they flew away and perched in the dome.

Before we left, I clasped hands with each member of the Cropper family, fingers laced. "Thank you. Your keep is wonderful."

"Someday, I hope you bring your children to meet me," Cham said.

It was the same request Aggi had made. A playmate. They would both be disappointed.

We followed the river back to the city. At first, I walked with Proce and Von.

"Surm should be careful," Proce said. "Meg might replace him as the best besmonn keeper in our fields."

"I'd rather not," I laughed.

"Alora's color is a gift." The king corrected my name.

Proce and Von exchanged a look. Had they heard of my name change? Or did most of the Polaris residents still refer to me as *the human*?

"Human color is remarkable," Proce said. "There is more to it than we know."

The king nodded. "It took me twenty-six years to fully tame my first riding besmonn." He looked down at me. "You might have done it in one day."

"Aviore was already tame," I pointed out.

"Still. You're different, and the besmonns sense it."

After a while, Proce and Von outpaced us, leaving me alone with the king. I suspected he had given them some kind of signal, but I didn't protest. I took it as an opportunity.

"I want to ask you about the Croppers," I said.

"I'm sure your friend Proce is more of an expert. What do you want to know?"

I walked fast, trying not to slow the king. "Maybe it's more about the Regents . . . Proce told that story earlier, about how the Croppers made a Regent their king, to create some kind of power balance."

"Regents tell the same story," the king confirmed. "It's our shared history."

"Then . . . why does it seem like the Regents don't like the Croppers very much?"

He glanced at me. "Proce and Von have probably told you things about the Regents. What did they say? We're proud, or delicate, or narrow-minded? That would explain it."

"They never said anything quite that bad. I think Von called you particular. But I want to hear it from you. What do Regents have against the Croppers?"

The king was silent for so long, I thought he might not answer. Then, he spoke.

"We are proud. I won't deny it. The Croppers appear simple. They don't build cities or write books, but they're powerful, deeply traditional. Croppers are woven into this earth, soul and body. They're bigger than us, and they have giftings we can't begin to understand. We needed them, long before they needed us. Regents don't like to be reminded of that. We don't see ourselves as weak. Regents view Croppers with feelings that range anywhere from mild affection to full hatred."

"And what about you?" I asked. "You seem to be friends with Cham's family."

"I see the Croppers as another gift, given to Regents. A gift to be used wisely. I've known Dorl and Surm since before I was king. Besmonns can't be coerced with my gift, but Dorl is big enough to harness a wild besmonn. To catch it and control it. It's wise to keep his friendship." The king smiled. "And I can't help but like him."

It seemed I was a gift to be used wisely too, like he used the Croppers.

"Then it sounds like the Cropper elders were smart to make a power balance."

"They were," he agreed. "There were Regents who would have

made the Croppers slaves. Or, at least tried to do so. There could have been terrible wars. But our King's and Queen's Gifts are half-Cropper. We're united. Without Croppers, there would be no healing, no music, no plants. I can't grow things with my King's Gift, but the power of it helps me to move the earth, the stones. It's how the cities are made now."

But it wasn't a true power balance. Not since the queen died, and the Croppers lost their sleep. Why was this happening now, after thousands of years? I tried to imagine the gray earth without trees and fields, without the scent of flowers. If the Croppers died, everything good would be gone from this place. The king knew that too.

The Polaris stood tall in the distance, its black walls reflecting the sun.

"Why build walls around your city if you're not at war?" I asked.

"Why do you build walls around your mind?"

My stomach tightened at his question. I looked around at the empty valley and the far mountains. "You want your privacy?"

The king gave a knowing smile. "Long ago, the walls kept the mountain beasts away. Now, they block the wind. I'm sorry I don't have a more interesting answer for you. But I'm glad you're curious about your new home."

Home. The word triggered half memories of human voices and yellow sunshine. I tried to hold on to the images, but they flowed like water through fingers.

When we reached the city, Proce and Von waited at the gate.

"Our time has come to an end," the king said.

"I see . . ." Proce said.

"Thank you for letting us join." Von's eyes lingered on me, as if she were saying a silent goodbye. Heavier than her words expressed. She bowed. "It was a gift."

"Wait." My hand flew up. "I'd like a minute alone, before you go."

"Why?" The king stood beside me. His mind searched mine, without success.

"I want to thank them," I told him, "for everything they've done."

"You need to be alone to do that?" the king asked.

"Yes." I looked him square in the eye, daring him to say no. If he outright withheld Proce and Von from me, he would have to give up his pretense that I was free in his house. It was time to take advantage of the ruse.

"A Watcher will stay outside the wall with you." The king hesitated, then walked away.

I stood in the shadows of the Croppers, cast by the afternoon sun. All was silent outside the city wall, except the sound of the river.

As soon as I sensed the king's presence recede into the Polaris, I turned to Proce and Von. We were far enough away from the remaining Watcher to have privacy.

"I'm thankful," I said quickly. "I really am. But that's not all I need to say. Has the king been keeping you away from me?"

Neither giant would look at me directly.

"Proce?" He would be the most likely to spill a secret.

Von answered for him. "The king thinks it is best for you to focus on the marriage ceremony right now."

"Is that what you think is best? I'm all alone in the King's House, and the Regents aren't kind to me." I knew Von wouldn't like to hear that.

"We must honor the king."

"What about earlier today?" I asked. "You didn't tell the king when I stole Proce's gift. Proce lied to him about his hand. Couldn't you come visit me at night, when no one's looking? You can honor the king, but he doesn't have to know everything."

"I did not lie," said Proce. "The king can see our thoughts. We simply have become good at not thinking about certain things at certain times."

"We should go," Von said. "The king will be waiting for you."

"No." I held on to the hem of her tunic. "Not until you promise to come visit me tomorrow."

Von looked around to see who could hear. No one was nearby,

except the Watcher, who was still out of earshot. "I cannot promise. But we will try."

"I must warn you," Proce said. "Do not tell the king that you stole my gift away from me. It is a strange skill, one that he may fear. He is not easy by nature. Not even for a Regent."

The Watcher approached us. "Lady Alora, I will escort you through the city."

I gave a last look to Proce and Von. "I am thankful."

The Watcher led me through a gate of shining black glass.

16

Regents offered smiles and bows as we marched through the city. None spoke to me.

"Where are we going?" I asked my escort.

"The King's House."

The Watcher's hood did little to hide his features in full daylight. He was younger than the others I had seen. Where a human's eyes would have been white, his were gray. He wore his cloak well, fabric layered over a strong frame.

"Yes, but it's a big house," I said. "Which part?"

"The king's auditorium. You'll share a meal."

"I know the way. I can go by myself." I could see the king's towers above the city.

The Watcher stayed with me. "I'll honor the king's request to guide you."

"I'm not going to run away or anything. Where would I go?"

A Regent passed us in the street, pulling a wide cart, loaded with bags of grain. We moved to the side to let the cart pass.

When the Regent laid eyes on me, he bowed low and snatched his hat from his head. "Didn't mean to inconvenience your path, Lady."

"It's okay." I gave a little bow back.

The Regent took hold of his cart again and scurried by.

One of the bags brushed against the Watcher's cloak, causing his hood to fall.

I stole a glance. His head was shaved, and a ridged scar marked the side of his neck. He snatched his hood and laid it back into place. His eyes darted to me, as if gauging my reaction. Was he embarrassed?

"It's like the Regents are avoiding me today," I said, trying to make conversation. "Without the king here."

The Watcher said nothing.

"Do you know why?" I prodded.

"You belong to the king. Not to them."

My jaw tightened at his answer. Once again, I was a possession.

"You're talking to me," I pointed out.

That observation led to a long silence between us.

I didn't know much about Watchers. They reported to the people, and spread news. But it seemed like they answered to the king. Were they soldiers? They were all big enough to be intimidating. Except this one didn't scare me. Not after I saw his embarrassment.

After a while, I tried a question again. "Are all Watchers men?"

"Now they are. A long time ago, the females also Watched over the King's House. Now they have their own order, in the mountains."

I had never thought of having a conversation with a Watcher. It wasn't exactly like talking to a normal person. He was still guarded. But at least he answered my questions. For a Regent, he was decent.

"What's your name?" I asked.

"It's not for you to know." The Watcher stiffened. "It will be better if we don't speak anymore." He pulled his hood forward, burying himself deeper in shadow.

"Oh . . ."

So much for a conversation.

I wouldn't have minded saying the young Watcher's name, even if it gave him power. He didn't want me to say it. That made him safe.

I was silent for the rest of the journey through the city. When we reached the auditorium, the king was waiting, leaning against the archway glass.

The Watcher turned to leave.

"Goodbye," I called to his cloaked back.

He paused for the slightest moment, so brief I might have imagined it. Then he disappeared into the hall.

"You must be hungry?" the king asked.

I hadn't eaten all day.

"I'm fine." I already needed too much from him.

The king ushered me into the auditorium, toward a table set with trays of bread, soup, and white fruit. We sat.

"Eat. It's hard enough keeping you well. I don't want you starving yourself."

I took slower bites than I wanted to, breaking off polite corners of the bread crust. I wouldn't show my dependency on the king's kindness. Not outright.

"Tell me," he said. "Why aren't you sleeping?"

His mind was there, an eavesdropping thread. Had he seen into my thoughts? No. I would have felt it. I tightened my guard and felt a rush of satisfaction at its fortitude.

"I've been sleeping fine, thank you."

"I heal you, remember? I know you were exhausted this morning, before we went to the keep. Anyone would have known by looking at you. I can offer you a drink to make you sleep tonight. It can be difficult to rest in a new place."

"No . . . it's not that." I didn't want any strong drinks. "My door was locked. I felt trapped. That kept me up a bit, I guess. You said I could explore the house." I kept my tone pleasant.

"We could explore together. Where would you like to go?"

"Anywhere. But alone. I need some time alone."

"Someday, you'll want to go places with me. Not away from me."

Today was not that day.

"It's just a walk through the halls. Walking helps me to think. All of this . . . it's a lot to process."

The king nodded, considering. "I can understand that, but you need to rest when you're done."

"No Watchers?" I asked.

"Just you," he promised. "After you've looked around the house, I'll come to your rooms for dinner."

I drank my soup as fast as I could, ready to leave.

"Slow down." The king put a plate of fruit in front of me. "You should eat more than broth. And I want to talk with you."

I took a bite of the fruit. It was shaped like an apple, but it tasted like a berry, filled with juice. Thoughts of red berries gave me a nostalgic feeling. And when had I last eaten an apple? The question made my head hurt. I'd had this white fruit before, at the Regent banquet. It was delicious.

The king ate nothing. "If we're going to be married, I'd like us to know each other. It's going to be more than walks through the city and smiles for the people."

I set down the fruit. "What else should I know about you?"

"Maybe I want to know things about you."

"What kinds of things?" I wasn't sure how much I should share. Or how much I would remember.

"Tell me about your mother." It was a request, not a command. He didn't press my mind for an answer.

My mom. I sifted through the shadows of memory, until I could picture her face. Freckled, like mine, framed with smooth curls.

"She died. A while ago." This truth was something I hadn't told the giants. Something I hadn't said out loud in a long time. Sharing this with the king didn't mean anything. It was a fact about me that would placate his curiosity. Still, I swallowed back a surprise rush of feelings.

"And you still remember her, even after crossing into our earth. You were too young to lose a mother."

"I was." My voice sounded heavier than I wanted. Even with my mind guarded, there were some things that were hard to hide.

"It was the same for me. With my father too. I still miss them, though I'm grown. More than the person, I miss the feeling of family. Belonging."

He knew what it was like, shared my grief without reading my thoughts.

"What else do you want to know?" I asked.

"Let me tell you what I do know. Your name is Meg, you have the most beautiful hair I've ever seen, and your favorite food in my earth is berkels. You're loyal to your human, even though he's in a different earth now. You're scared of heights, and a little bit scared of me, but you'll face either if you have to. You're alone among my people, against your will, but you still treated Cham with kindness. I also know that you can't go home. Ever. And I know your future."

I listened to his list, but he didn't know anything about me. He didn't know how I missed yellow sunrises, and the smell of the dirt from my earth, and he didn't know I was more than a little scared to face him. I was terrified. Or maybe he did know. Most of all, I hoped he didn't know my future.

"What's a berkel?" I asked.

"It's the fruit on your plate. And if you're not going to eat the rest of it, you might as well go for your walk."

Before he could change his mind, I hopped out of my chair and raced toward the exit.

"Don't return to my auditorium," the king called after me. "I'll come to your rooms."

I waved goodbye on my way out. Regents didn't wave as a custom, but I didn't care. He could figure it out, since he knew so much about me.

I was finally alone and unguarded. No Watchers in sight. I ran my hands along the glass walls in the hallway and examined the coned sconces. Their glowing light burned cold. Was it gift-powered light? I would ask Proce later.

Now it was time to explore and I knew exactly where I wanted to go. I had seen the King's House from the outside. They called it a house, but it was really an endless collection of domes and walls and bridges.

With only three towers.

On one side of the house stood two spired towers. On the far side, a domed tower overlooked the city. The singer had been in the domed tower. To reach it, I would need to go deeper into the halls than I had ever been, far beyond my human rooms.

The passage I was following should have led to my chamber. It didn't. It curved to the right, then stopped in a dead end.

There had to be another way.

I backtracked and chose a different corridor, opening doors along the way. Some of the doors led into empty rooms with high ceilings and glass floors. Other doors led to new hallways. Some were locked.

When the hall took me to another dead end, I picked a different door at random. If I covered enough ground, I was bound to find the tower.

The whole house was perfect, as if untouched. Surfaces gleamed dust-free. The air in the halls smelled of nothing. Not food or perfume or people. I saw no one. Cut-crystal windows let in sunshine, beaming onto walls and floors. Still, cones glowed in expectation of my approach, adding extra light. There were paintings and murals, images of Regents and blossoms. None of the artwork was evocative. The faces of the Regents were serene. No joy. No anguish. In my memory, I could picture flashes of colored artwork from my own earth. Paintings of battles and lovers.

I climbed a spiral staircase, wandering the upper halls. All the passages looked the same, colorless and lavish. After a while, I came to an identical staircase, spiraled and glass. Or could it have been the same one as before? Was I going in circles?

I flung open a door beneath the stairs, one I hadn't tried yet.

White daylight poured into the hall. An exit.

The doorway led into a courtyard garden, larger than the garden in my rooms. Leafy vines grew up the sides of surrounding walls. A narrow stream wound through trees and silver grass, edged with bell-shaped flowers. I smelled fruit and something spicy I couldn't name.

The most interesting thing in the garden was not actually in the garden. It was above it. The domed tower looked down on the courtyard from the other side of a wall. I had to tilt my head all the way back to see the upper window, where the singer had been.

There were no other doors in the courtyard walls. No visible way to get to the tower. I ran across the grass and inspected the wall. Climbing it couldn't be worse than climbing a waterfall cliff, or worse than riding a besmonn. Those challenges had been faced for good cause. What would I do to hear that song again?

The leaves on the vines were succulent and soft, but they grew on thick branches, covered in spiny thorns. Could they support my weight? I dug my hands into the silvery plants, feeling the stone beneath.

Instead of a wall, I touched something cold and round. Something metal. I pulled the plants aside, scratching my arms in the process. Little beads of blood welled up. I ignored the blood and kept digging into the vine.

The round thing was a handle. A door handle. A small wooden door was set in the garden wall, hidden behind shrubbery. The metal was rusted, neglected by time. It didn't belong in the king's perfect house.

I turned the handle.

It made a grinding sound as it turned. When I pulled, the door didn't budge.

Nothing could ever be easy.

I leaned back, putting my whole weight into the second pull. A branch cracked off the wall and the door swung toward me. I fell onto the grass, landing hard on my tailbone. Dust motes swirled from the wall.

I stood, feeling the bruise already forming on my backside. Sunlight peeped through the crack of the door. The branches wouldn't let it open all the way. But it was enough for me to squirm through. As I pressed against the vines, a thorn scratched my pinky finger. I put it in my mouth and tasted dirt. Not the rich, dusty taste of dirt from my earth. It was bright, and almost sweet. The smell of the land. The smell of Croppers.

You couldn't call the other side a garden. Not like the others. It was an unkempt patch of grassy weeds. Bits of stone crumbled from the wall and the vines were bare of leaves.

But I didn't care about the garden. I cared about the singer's tower. It was there, right in front of me. My heart beat faster. Stone steps sank into a tunnel at the base of the tower. There was no other entrance. To go in, I would have to go down.

I crossed the grass and stopped at the edge of the tunnel. Damp cold drifted up from the shadows, void of any gifted cones of light. I wrapped my arms around myself, prepared to explore the dark.

"Lady Alora." A voice came from within the tunnel. I jumped. A Watcher stepped out of the shadows, squinting in the sunlight. I knew his face. This was my nameless Watcher. The one with the scar on his neck.

"Are you looking for the king's gardens?" he asked. "I can take you there."

"Thanks. I'm actually just heading into the tunnel."

I stepped to the side, to pass where he stood.

He moved to block my path. "Let me take you to the garden."

"The king said I could go anywhere. You'll have to fight him on this one." I kept my tone light, teasing.

"I would never go against the king." He looked worried. "It's against my oath."

So the Watchers did answer to him. It was hardly a balanced form of government.

"Do all Watchers take that oath?" I asked.

"I don't know. But I did. I'm part of Kalmus's personal guard."

It wasn't lost on me that he used the king's name. This young Regent had given away his power. Had he been taught to say it, like the king wanted me to?

"Then you should let me through," I said.

The Watcher raised his hand above my head. I flinched. A tone-deaf hum filled the air, the sound of a Regent's gift.

As he lowered his hand, a stone gate closed over the entrance to the tunnel, locking us both out.

"You need to leave this place," he said. "We both do. The king has called for me, and I can't delay."

I heard a scuffle from within the tunnel. The Watcher turned around.

A croaky voice spoke from the dark. "It's bad enough having to come here. Now you Watchers are locking me in? Open this gate!"

The Watcher raised his hand. The gate rose with it.

Out from the tunnel ambled a rotund Regent woman. The blind seamstress, Garlian.

She carried a tray of empty dishes. Her expression was sour.

The gate closed again with a rumble.

"I apologize," the Watcher said. "Lady Alora is looking for the king's garden. I didn't want her to end up in the cave. I need to go now. Lady Alora, the king will meet you later."

Garlian finished climbing the steps. "Yes, I'm not stupid. I sense her color. Come with me, human. I'll take you to the garden. I know my way around this house as well as anyone. At least I did, until that fool of a Watcher closed the gate on me." She stomped toward an arch in the garden wall on the other side of the courtyard. "Come on!"

I eyed the Watcher. He wasn't going to move until I left. The door I had come through was overgrown with vines, barely visible from this side. I was thankful to know of the open archway in the wall. I would pay attention so that I could find my way back later. I followed after Garlian, running to keep up.

"Why did you bring that food tray to the tower?" I asked.

"I'm happy to work for the king. I am. But why are there always so many stairs involved?"

She hadn't answered my question. Could Garlian be the singer in the tower? I doubted it. Not with that Regent voice.

We turned a corner and then another. Were we going in circles? After a while, we entered the hallway next to the spiral staircase.

Right where I had started. Directions didn't make sense in the King's House. Would I be able to find the tower again?

"The king's garden is through that door." Garlian gave a half bow. "Now I've got other things to do." She started down the hall.

I hadn't asked as many questions as I wanted, and now she was leaving.

"Wait." I ran alongside Garlian's fast steps. "Who lives in the tower?"

Garlian stopped, her eyes squinted and unfocused. "You shouldn't be asking such questions. I've never seen anyone in that tower."

She never saw anyone anywhere.

"Have you heard someone? Maybe at night? A woman—"

Her hand shot out and grabbed my wrist, so tight it hurt. "Don't ask me about this again." She let go and hurried down the hall.

I didn't follow.

17

Alone in the hall, my heart pounded. Hot anger flooded my cheeks. The anger I hadn't allowed myself to feel, held back while I bargained and schemed and kept my mind guarded. The king had trapped me again. Despite his promise that I could explore, a Watcher had stopped me from going the one place I wanted to be.

I didn't think the king had sent the Watcher after me. Otherwise, why would he call him away? But it was clear I wasn't allowed in the tower. I was locked out. Just like I had been locked in my rooms. Just like the king had kept Proce and Von away from me. And we were all supposed to pretend none of that was happening.

If the king was so deceitful, how could I trust him to keep his other promise, the one that really mattered?

My temper carried me through the halls, toward the king's auditorium. I knew I was supposed to go to my rooms instead. I didn't care. Dirt smudged my skirt and shoes. My braid hung limp, wild hairs loose in my face. My arms were lined with scratches. Larlia would have been ashamed.

The auditorium entrance was unguarded by Watchers. Good. I hoped the king would be alone. I put up my mental walls and prepared a speech, ready to confront him as tactfully as possible. It was time to remind him of his promises. I wouldn't be so easily confined.

I rounded the corner, through the archway. The room was

empty. No king. No Regents. No one to direct my frustration toward.

I paced back and forth in front of the king's desk. My stomach growled, ready for a second meal. My feet ached. How many miles had I walked that day? To the keep, through the endless halls of the house. But the sun was still up and it would be a while before dinner, when the king was supposed to come to me. The auditorium was the best place to catch him before then.

At the back of the room, the king's sofa was pushed against a wall, beside a miniature tree in a stone pot. If I had to wait, I might as well sit.

As I headed to the sofa, something caught my notice. Light flickered from a vertical crack in the wall panel behind the tree, as if a fire burned on the other side. Was there another room?

I crept toward the crack, curious. The air hummed, charged with a gift. I edged around the tree and peeked through the wall panel. My eyes watered against the bright light of the other room. This was a door, disguised as part of the wall. I could see the hinges now that I was close enough.

My eyes adjusted. In the other room, the king and the nameless Watcher stood facing one another. Instinctively, I pulled back. The wall around my mind grew miles thick. Had they seen me spying? Neither of them had looked at the crack. Slowly, I peeked through again. What could have been so urgent for the Watcher to rush back here?

The Regents stared at two crystal bowls of liquid, sitting on a wide table, one in front of each of them. White flames flickered beneath the bowls, boiling their contents. Something blood-red shone in a third dish at the center of the table. It was submerged in water. Was it a gem? It was the right size.

Any color should have been a comfort. Instead, my stomach tightened. This didn't feel right. I didn't like looking at the red object. But I couldn't look away. What were they doing?

Thin tubes of glass curled between all three bowls, connecting them. The king closed his eyes and placed his fingertips into the bowl closest to him. The gifted hum grew to a crescendo. My ears itched, and an acidic smell burned my nostrils. The red object melted and trickled through a glass tube, toward the king.

The Watcher placed his hand into his own bowl. His off-pitch hum joined the king's, and the two acrid tones clashed. My hands flew to my ears.

Glass tubes exploded, blasting shards across the room. A tiny piece lodged into my cheek, through the crack in the door. I picked it out.

The red substance from the tubes hung in the air after. It didn't act like a liquid should. The color burned bright and collected into a blinding mass. It was red lightning, expanding and contracting at erratic intervals. With a deafening crack, it also exploded. Electricity struck the floor tiles and the glass wall. It burned the table.

And it pierced the Watcher's chest.

He screamed and shook, then crumpled onto the floor.

The king kneeled beside the Watcher and peered at his wound. A thick pool of gray drained from his chest, wrapping around the king's black shoes.

Regent blood.

Nausea washed over me. I backed away from the crack in the door. What had I just seen? My breath came in ragged heaves. The Watcher. He needed help.

Without thinking, I pushed the door open and rushed to the Watcher's side. He was still, eyes rolled back in his head. I gathered the hem of my skirt and pressed it against the wound. It wasn't enough. His blood poured from his body.

For the first time since entering the room, I looked at the king. "Why aren't you healing him?" My voice caught.

He stared for a moment, face calm. Then, he stood. "What are you doing here?"

A second door flew open at the back of the room. Two Watchers marched to their bleeding comrade. They pulled my hands away from the wound, replacing my skirts with white linen.

"He's bleeding. He—"

"We know." One of the Watchers poured a thick black liquid onto the linen.

Without a word, the king took me by the elbow and ushered me back into his auditorium. He slammed the door behind us and forced me onto the sofa.

I sat on the edge, my insides quaking, my eyes on the shut door. What could they do for him? I wrapped my arms around myself, suddenly cold.

"Why did you come here?" the king asked.

His face was smooth. Gray blood still clung to his shoes.

I stared at the blood, silent. It matched the gray that coated my own fingers.

He pressed against my mind until I thought I might break.

I gasped and he relented.

"I should have posted Watchers at the door," the king said. "The others know not to come unannounced. Apparently, you do not."

I found my voice. "Can you heal him?"

"No."

I had already guessed this answer. "Because it's a gifted wound?"

"You're learning." The king sat beside me on the sofa.

"You didn't even try." My breath was uneven.

"It would be pointless." The king sounded like he was explaining an interesting fact, not like someone was dying. "I can't spare that much of the King's Gift. Gift-made wounds aren't supposed to happen. They're rare. His body might heal on its own, if he's strong enough."

Another lie. The Watcher had lost too much blood. His chest was burned through on both sides. How was he supposed to heal from that? My throat ached with a sob, and my hand covered my mouth.

I barely knew the nameless Watcher. He had served the king and kept me imprisoned. He was ugly and inhuman. But I didn't want him to die. I had watched his life spill out onto the stone floor, hot, and gray, and final.

"I'm sorry you had to see that." The king reached for my hand.

As if he hadn't been the one to cause the explosion. As if he hadn't stared, unfeeling, while his Watcher bled. He didn't even try to help. This was the man I had to trust with my life. With Andrew's life, and Proce's and Von's.

If I could see his thoughts, as he saw mine, what would I find? If I pressed into his mind, would I see any remorse? Sadness? Empathy? If it was there, it didn't show. The king could charm his people, even without his gift. But all I had heard from him was calculation and duty and strategy. Not love for the people he protected. He had called the gems for them, to increase their birth rate. But had I ever heard him express remorse over the Croppers' lost sleep? Or their lost people?

As the king held my hand, I could feel the gift beneath his skin. Power hummed in his veins. It coursed beneath the surface, near my color.

I wasn't trying to steal the King's Gift. But I was thinking about it. I imagined what it would be like to see inside the king. To read his thoughts.

And the gift heard me. It answered me, leaping to my will.

The hum grew at the connection between our hands. Gray on color. My vision went dark. I held the king's hand tight and something pulled inside of me. My vision cleared. I was seeing through the king's eyes again.

It wasn't the mindreading I had thought of. But it was something. I knew I should look away. It was wrong to steal. Instead, I turned the king's eye inward. I couldn't hear his thoughts, but I could see inside him, where his power lived.

Something wasn't right.

Last time, the gift had been an electric blaze. Now, it barely flickered. His gift was wounded. Drained. What had he been doing with the Watcher? What had taken so much of the King's Gift?

I opened my eyes and broke the connection. Had he noticed that I stole his power? I had only taken a little bit of his light, to look into him. Had he felt pain, as Proce had when I stole from him?

The king studied my expression. He showed no sign of alarm. Proce's gift had felt thin and reluctant when I stole it. The King's

Gift, though wounded, came willingly, ready to move. Even flickering, even drained, it was a deeper hum of power than Proce's could ever be. Apparently, the king hadn't noticed my trespass. What I stole was a drop in an ocean.

"Your gift," I said. "You drained it. When you made that red stuff explode."

He eyed me. "You're partially correct."

I pulled my hand away and stood. "You hurt him. And you hurt yourself. You could spare the King's Gift for that?"

Was he still strong enough to keep his promises? Something was wrong. Seriously wrong. The way his light had fizzled made me feel sick.

The king's expression grew cold, harboring danger under the surface.

That was when I realized my guard was down. For a moment, the king had heard everything I thought. I put up my walls, but it was too late. Now he knew what I had done.

"You always see more than you're supposed to, don't you?" he said. "But you have no idea what you're looking at. Even drained, I have more power than anyone else in this earth."

He closed his long fingers over my forearm. His gift hummed, and my scratches disappeared. The sting on my face faded, where the glass shard had cut me. He even healed the bruise from Garlian's harsh grasp.

"Then you can still heal Andrew?" The question was bold, but I was afraid of the answer.

The king's fingers dug into my skin. "With my mind, I'm holding up the walls of this city. Yes, there was an accident today. It took more of my gift than I anticipated. But once I have the Queen's Gift, I'll be more than restored. Don't ever doubt me."

He pulled me back onto the sofa, beside him. "How did you cut yourself?"

"I'm fine." I thought of the Watcher's wound. "There are other things for you to worry about."

"I'm a king. There's always a crisis at my door. That doesn't mean I don't care about you. Even the small things."

I looked into his icy eyes. "Then care about the big things. Healings. The Croppers' sleep. One of your Watchers had a broken finger. Your gift sensed it, but you never healed it. Von heals your Regents. What was so important that you had to use up your gift? What were you doing with all that glass?"

The king considered me for a moment. "I'm about to tell you things no one else knows. If you're going to trust me, I have to trust you first. Can I do that?"

"You can trust me to keep my promise. I'll go to the ceremony. Will you keep yours?"

"Yes. And I'll tell you the truth about what you saw. If you want it."

"I do."

"Good."

I saw through him. He trusted me because he had all the power over me. My future, my health. I wasn't sure how much sway he had over his people, but apparently his grip was loose enough to keep secrets from them. But not from me. I was an outsider, unproven and untrusted by almost everyone. Who would believe me, even if I spilled his secrets?

"We've been experimenting with color," he said. "You walked in on the end of the experiment. Halor wanted to participate. He knew the risk, and he believed it was worth it."

Halor. Now that he was gone, the nameless Watcher had a name. I would never be able to call him by it.

"Did he believe it was worth it?" I asked. "Or did he swear an oath to you? Everyone obeys you. They have to."

The king looked me up and down, as if deciding how much to reveal. "They don't. I can see in their minds. I can direct their dreams. There's reverence for my gift. But my people have a free will. Even the Croppers. Especially the Croppers."

"Even the Watchers?" I asked.

"The experiment was important." He ignored my question.

"The color in our stones enhances our gifts. But I believe it could be so much more than we currently know. We wanted to make it stronger, to combine the color into my gift. I separated the color from a red stone and called it to me. Halor was supposed to destroy the stone. The color would have stayed with me, unable to return to its home. But he faltered. It was too much for him."

Tears stung my eyes. "It was for more power."

That's what Halor died for? That's what the king spent his gift on?

"Power to save lives. It's what you want too. If the experiment had succeeded, I might have been able to heal your human right away. The King's Gift, amplified. It almost worked. I could feel it."

"Almost." I weighed the emptiness of the word.

"It was a risk." He moved closer to me. "But the Queen's Gift is my fail-safe. After the ceremony, I'll be stronger than I was before the experiment. Stronger than any king has been."

"And then you won't need me anymore." Would he still spend his gift on healing me? "Except for my color."

"That's not true," he said. "Not even close to being true. You're worried that I'll try an experiment on you, to take your color?" He laughed, as if the idea were funny, not horrifying. "You're different than a gem. You're alive, so your color constantly renews. I wouldn't waste that. I won't waste you."

Until the day I died, I would be a commodity to him. A source of power. He wouldn't waste me, but he didn't seem to mind wasting his King's Gift. "Why didn't you bless the Croppers' sleep? You had so much gifting before today. It seemed endless."

The king's mouth went tight. "You're right. You've seen inside me, more than anyone." He paused for a long time, then let out a breath. "I could have blessed them. But you don't know the kinds of choices I've had to make."

"Then tell me." What could he possibly say to make it right? My face grew hot again. I tried to bury my anger where he couldn't see it, but I was sure my cheeks were pink.

"The sun is setting on the Croppers and the Regents. Each

generation is smaller than the last. Gems have helped our birth rate, but it takes a toll on my gift to call them. During the last cold, I had to choose. I could either use my gift for gems, or to bless the sleep. I knew only a few Croppers would die. The old and the weak. The ones we lost were too old to have more children. Do you think I would risk the Croppers? We need them. I'm preserving their population. It was the right choice. Even still, with gems, it's not enough. No one likes to think about it, but in time, our numbers will dwindle."

What about the Croppers who were alive now? Proce was likely too old to have a child. The king would consider him expendable. It was monstrous. Inhuman. But the king had never claimed to be human.

"Most couples have two children," I said. "They replace themselves. It would take generations for you to die out. Hundreds of thousands of years."

"It's too little, too late. At our current rate, in twenty thousand years, our cities will be half their size. We're a dying people. Just dying slowly. A king reigns for a thousand years. Long life was a curse, given so long ago we've forgotten what actually happened. All we have is fable. But, once, we covered the earth. And I'll be the king who restores that. I'll be remembered through all time." His eyes grew bright. "After the ceremony, when the cold comes again, I'll be ready for the Croppers' sleep. I'll be able to do anything, like no king before me."

He was taking lives to solve a problem twenty generations from now. This wasn't about birth rates. It was about power. Proce and Von were deceived. The king never needed me. They wouldn't have needed me, if not for him. But here I was. And I needed the king.

"No more experiments after that?" I asked. "The ceremony will be enough?"

The king hesitated before answering. "I don't want to hide anything from you. Even with the Queen's Gift, I'll still need more color to make my own thin place. I'll keep trying my gem experiment. It's nothing compared to your color. You're living.

Powerful. But if I can possess the gem color also, it might be enough. I want to call more things from your earth. Larger things. Living things. Humans can have Regent children. Lots of them. More of my people should have human wives."

I stared at him in horror. He wanted to call humans from my earth.

Human girls.

Like me. Torn away against their will, into a place of poisons and forgetting. They would never see another blue sky. They would be married off to monsters. Most of them probably wouldn't even survive the crossing if they fought against it.

"They'll be prisoners," I whispered.

"No. They'll be adored. Their children will live for a thousand years."

"Whether they choose it or not. Like Halor chose death. Like the Croppers chose to stay awake. They didn't choose. You chose for them. They deserve to know the truth." My anger was too much now, too hot to hide.

"I've told them everything they need to know." The angles of the king's face sharpened. "And that's all they will know, if you want to save your human."

I wanted it more than anything, and the king knew it.

This had been his plan all along. The king had once said that he trusted his people's faith in the Writings. He wanted a human wife. He knew the Croppers would find a way to get a human, if their sleep was in danger. Had it all been to bring me here? To trigger the Writings and send the Croppers on a mission? And now I was his, to use and to keep. He would call on my color. He would make me participate in capturing more humans.

I imagined the king, free to access my earth. In his kingdom, I had no rights. No citizenship. Would it be any different for the other humans? I could pretend it was my choice to walk into the ceremony, because I had bargained for it. But I was fooling myself. The king would have had his way, eventually.

I had never allowed myself to consider my life after the ceremony.

Those thoughts were locked away in a secret part of my mind that even I couldn't see. As I sat with the king's gray hand in mine, I admitted the truth to myself. After the ceremony, I didn't want to have a life. Not as the king's wife, in a poisonous world, as a weapon against my own kind. Once Andrew was healed, what choices would I have left?

18

I refused dinner. I couldn't eat after what I had seen. The king escorted me to my rooms and followed me through the door. My eyes glossed over the wall of mosaics, the plush floors, the crystal curtain. My gilded cage.

"I'm going to make sure you sleep tonight," the king said. "You won't take care of yourself, so someone has to." He sat on the ottoman. "I'll wait here while you prepare for bed."

During my time in the Polaris, I had never prepared for bed. I had fallen asleep in my day clothes, unwashed and unsettled. Somehow, Larlia managed to hide that each morning, removing the dark circles under my eyes, bringing fresh life to my hair.

I started by washing Halor's blood off my hands. When I returned from the bathroom, I avoided the king's gaze and ducked into the enormous closet, closing the door behind me. What if I crawled under the Cropper bench and spent my evening in the library, or the garden? The stars would be out soon.

But the king was waiting. He would come looking for me.

I dug through rows of lacy dresses, searching for suitable pajamas. The king couldn't see me behind a closed door, but he could press my mind. I pushed him away, and my breath caught from the effort. An ashamed part of me craved the battle. It was the only time I felt my own power. My color was a force I could only access when faced with a gift.

In the back of the closet hung a modest night dress. Perfect. I slipped it on as fast as I could. Woolly cloth draped from my throat to the tips of my toes, adorned with thick frills. I wrapped my hair in a black scarf, another layer between me and the king. All my color would be hidden.

Beneath my dress, I tied a second scarf around my thigh, fastening my tiny sword in place, within reach. I unfolded my paper note. Creases cut through the penned words, but I could still read them. There was something about the letters. They were from my old language. English. I could hardly register the difference, but it was there. Beneath the gift of language that scrambled words in my brain. I ran my fingers over the writing, then put the note under the bench. It felt better to leave it here, away from the king. A part of myself, kept safe.

When I emerged from the closet, the king stood, taking in my frumpy dress and scarf. He smirked.

"I'll fall asleep right away. I don't need your help." I opened my mind a crack and poured out my fatigue. It was real.

"I'm not taking any chances." The king took my hand and led me toward the bedroom. "My gift will put you to rest."

I would be alone with him. In my bedroom.

I planted my feet and freed my hand. "We're not married."

"Do we need to be married before you'll sleep?"

"Unmarried people don't sleep in the same room," I said.

"I won't be sleeping."

That's what I was worried about. I didn't move.

The king smirked again. "You're a cautious soul. Always worried. Making bargains. Planning ahead. Believe me, you have nothing to worry about tonight. I'm patient. Your sleep is my only agenda. If it makes you feel better, go ahead of me and get settled." He stepped aside.

I marched past him, through the curtain, into the bedroom. I hid my body in the bed, piling blankets around myself. More layers between us.

After a time, the king followed and stood beside the bed.

"I'm going to use my gift now. Don't worry." He brushed his fingertips against my cheek. His gift hummed.

The king was always finding reasons to touch me. I was growing used to his hand in mine. Almost. But this was different. I was so vulnerable. A chill ran through me and I clamped down my mind.

The bed was soft, the room dim. Exhaustion weighed on me, enhanced by the hum of the gift. But I wouldn't surrender. Not alone, beside the king.

Von had made me sleep once, but that was before I had learned to resist the king's mind. Was it my color that allowed me to guard myself? I could steal power. Use it as my own. The Regents said their gifts were drawn to my color. Made stronger in my presence. Maybe it was more than that. Maybe I could repel a gift too. Would the King's Gift listen to me now, if I resisted it?

I closed my eyes and imagined my color as a thick blanket, keeping the King's Gift at bay. It worked. I stayed awake. Sleep was a deep water, and I was treading the surface, sipping air.

The hum grew and then stopped.

"You're fighting me." The king's voice held an edge. "You're not gifted, but you're stubborn."

I was more than stubborn. I was alone. Desperate. Every scrap of freedom meant something to me. Right now, freedom was choosing when to sleep.

"You're right," I said. "I need to rest. But no more locks on my door. No guards. It makes me feel trapped. I promised you the ceremony, and it's not like I'm going anywhere." I opened my eyes. "If I'm going to trust you, you need to trust me. You said that."

The king thought about it for a moment. "If you sleep, then no more locks."

"Good." I closed my eyes and made my face look peaceful, sinking deeper into the pillow.

He pressed his palm onto my forehead and the hum began again. In the hidden parts of my mind, I stayed alert. Outwardly, I took deep breaths and relaxed my body.

It was time for an experiment of my own. Could I lie to him with my thoughts? I conjured the feeling of slumber, black and dreamy, then poured it outward, toward the king's mind. Instead of a wall, intended to keep the king away, I wrapped myself in imagined sleep and invited him to see it.

His mind encountered mine and I almost faltered. But his gift saw the lie and pressed no further.

He believed me.

I fought to keep my breath steady.

The king lifted his hand from my skin. He was silent for a while. My breath was the only sound in the room.

"You're going to change everything," he whispered, closer to my ear than I had anticipated.

Then the king left. The crystal curtain tinkled and the outer door latched.

I waited, tense beneath my façade of sleep. The thread of his mind stayed with me. The king was in the hall. After a while, it receded. I was alone, the thrill of the lie gone.

I flung my blankets off and tiptoed to the door.

It wasn't locked.

Finally, one promise kept. I relished the twist of the handle as I left the human rooms.

I barely knew myself anymore, the ungifted girl who could fool the King's Gift. It was my secret, another piece of protection, like the knife tied to my leg.

No Watchers waited outside my room. On bare feet, I wandered the halls of the King's House, searching for the tower courtyard. Which way had Garlian taken me? I strained my ears for the sound of Watchers, hoping to hear the voice from the tower again. Maybe she only sang at night.

I explored countless rooms, but found no sign of the courtyard archway. It should have been right around the corner. I began to suspect that the King's House was gifted, full of illusions and changing passages. The halls were too perfect. Artificial. Like the Regents, they never showed their age.

After a while, I came to the spiral staircase, beside the entrance to the King's Garden. Since I couldn't find Garlian's passage to the tower, I would have to try the tiny door in the garden wall again. It would mean squeezing through thorns and branches.

Outside, the stars shone bright, and the garden stream rippled beneath the moon. White blossoms shimmered, releasing their perfume into a soft breeze.

I marched straight to the back wall, searching for the place where the tarnished door had been.

Nothing. I found nothing.

The vines were undisturbed where they should have been torn from the wall. I dug my hands into the branches. No knob. No door. The foliage was even thicker than before, full of thorns. Blood welled up from the tip of my thumb, another wound for the king to worry about.

This had been done with a gift. I remembered what the king said—with his mind, he held up the walls of the city. With his mind, had he sealed this wall?

I searched up and down, left and right. The door was gone, as if it had never existed.

What time was it? My teeth ached from grinding them and my eyes were dry, ready to close for sleep. I sat in the grass, admitting defeat. Or, at least, admitting exhaustion.

If I slept, that meant I was one day closer to the ceremony. I wanted it to happen. I'd pushed for it. But after that, I would be bound to the king. Better to remain in this moment, unmarried. Right now, I knew Andrew would be healed. It was something to look forward to. After that, what would I have?

For a while, I was safe beneath the moon, nestled in the garden grass. I kept my eyes open, determined to cherish the rest of the night.

I could still remember the moon from my own earth. I could remember who I was with when I looked at it on a summer night. Only one night. One memory. But that was enough. Maybe it would be easier to forget what I could never have. After the ceremony—

The music came, low and sweet, interrupting my thoughts.

I sat up, and a light flickered on in the tower window.

"Hello?" I whispered, afraid to raise my voice. What if the Watchers heard?

No reply came, except for the rise and fall of the music. I lay back and hummed along, finally content to sleep.

In my dream, I sat in the secret library of the human rooms, at the table with the large book. My hand held a brush, wet with black ink. On a page, I painted orbs in the sky.

Balloons.

They were from my earth.

Familiar words lined the page, from the Writings. It was the passage about me. Eyes of hue. Golden skin.

A line stood out to me. The letters glowed with a light of their own, and I leaned closer to read.

Oh gift, thou art wielded as a sword

Proce had explained that line to me once, during one of his long speeches. He thought it alluded to the gift of sleep. How it had turned against them. Once a blessing. Now a curse. But in order for a sword to be wielded, it needs someone to hold it. The king.

I turned the page of the book. The next was an image of the king's garden. A stream flowed through the middle of silver grass, surrounded by black walls and white blossoms.

On one side of the stream, a Cropper lay lifeless, eyes cold and staring. On the other side, the king's limp body leaned against a wall of vines. The drawing was his perfect likeness. Sharp blazer. Soft hair, tied back from his face. Silver blood flowed from a wound in his chest.

My hand picked up an ink pen. I didn't tell it to. It scrawled an ugly word between the two bodies.

Choose.

I didn't understand. Without the king, the Croppers would die. There was no choice between them.

My hand wrote again.

Choose.

19

When I woke, there was no music. I pulled myself from damp grass and wrapped the top layer of the nightgown skirt around my shoulders. It was a wobbly trek, through the king's garden, back into the King's House. After a few doors and halls, I crawled into bed, waiting for Larlia to arrive.

Time passed. No one came. I slept through the morning, into the afternoon. It was a dreamless, void sleep.

Larlia clattered her tools onto my bed stand. "Wake up. It's your marriage dance tonight and you're going to have puffy eyes."

I expected Garlian to appear, ready with something for me to wear. Instead, a young Regent lady brought my gown. Not Kahlea, the one who had made lace.

The new girl gave a shy smile and a quick bow before leaving. I wished she would stay. There were plenty of Regents who didn't hate me, but I was stuck with Larlia. Because of her family's status. I still had so much to learn about the Regents. Every society has a hierarchy. Here, there were Watchers and councils and exclusive dinners and I didn't know any of the rules.

Larlia took the gown and held it out for me to see. "The King ordered this to be sewn before you even arrived. Garlian made sure it would fit, once you got here."

It was the most elaborate dress yet. And the most revealing. My back was completely bare and the skirt had been sheared away in the front, exposing my thighs. Costly red streaks swirled through the ~~shimmering bodice. I knew, even without my memories, that I had~~ never worn anything like it.

The king was showing me off, revealing as much color as possible.

"We need more hair pins!" Larlia shouted, raking my hair into a braid.

The other Regent moved to answer the demand.

I leapt out of Larlia's reach. "I know where they are. I'll get them."

The other Regent sat down and I scurried through the curtain of crystal beads.

Inside the closet room, I retrieved my note and hid it in the front of my dress along with the little sword-knife. They were my empty securities, one for protection and one for remembering. I scooped up a handful of silver pins from a crystal jar and returned to the Regents.

Larlia curled and pinned my hair into a work of art, painting my face with mechanical precision.

Today, the Watchers didn't wait outside. Seven of them entered my rooms, their black robes decorated with silver streamers.

"Is she ready? The music has already started."

"Almost." Larlia took a bright green gem from a velveteen box and pinned it into the crown of my braids. "Now she's stunning."

The compliment wasn't for me. Larlia was admiring her own work. I was the canvas.

As I followed the Watchers through the halls, tiny white flames drifted above us in midair. Gifted light, conjured to celebrate my marriage. Like fireflies. I didn't fully remember what fireflies were, but it sounded right. Night sky peeked through the windows. This was my last night before the ceremony.

As we approached the king's auditorium, I could hear Regent laughter. And music. It wasn't the voice from the tower. It wasn't even Cropper singing. This was something deep and rhythmic. Someone was playing instruments.

The entrance archway, now painted with silver swirls, had been enlarged to twice its usual size. More of the King's Gift, wasted.

White, smokeless fires burned on either side of the arch, casting light onto hundreds of crystals hung on besmonn thread.

A line of Regents waited for entry, dressed in more finery than usual. Heavy white gems hung from the ladies' ears. Gossamer dust powdered their sculpted curls. The men wore polished shoes and tight pants with gleaming buttons.

One by one, they noticed our approach. Conversations hushed to whispers and the line parted to let us through.

I wanted to shrink away, to cover the bare parts of my legs and chest. Instead, I forced a smile and walked tall.

In the auditorium, a thousand pale fires hung above crowds of gray people. White petals coated the floor and heaping dishes of food sat on long tables. On a high dais, Croppers tapped complex rhythms onto wooden drums. They wore their usual tunics, though the fabric looked more tightly woven. None of them wore shoes. The female Croppers had braided rows of silver beads into their hair.

Regents danced on one half of the room, Croppers on the other.

The movements of the two peoples were different from each other. The Croppers linked arms in concentric circles, jumping and stomping their feet in measured patterns. The Regents paired into couples. They spun and twirled, trading partners without any semblance of order or timing.

The Watchers faded into the crowd and the king appeared beside me. We bowed to each other, then turned to watch the dancers.

"Humans could find their place in this dance too," the king said. "Among Regents and Croppers. We'd all be better for it."

Which side of the room would humans choose? There was no room in between. I was too small to dance with the Croppers. I couldn't make sense of the Regents' dance. Humans wouldn't be worried about dancing. They would be struggling to breathe poisoned air.

The king glanced at the dress he had chosen for me.

I refused to show my discomfort. My mind was the only defense I needed. "Humans don't even get along with other humans. There have been a lot of wars in my earth."

"That's because you're all the same. When you have different gifts, you need each other. Maybe you need us."

The song ended and the Regents cheered encouragement, shouting short phrases, one by one.

"Well done!"

"Good song!"

Soon, the Croppers drowned the Regents out with a flurry of whistles and stomped feet.

The king slid his hand into mine. "It's time. They expect us to dance."

Everyone crowded to the edge of the auditorium, jostling one another. From silver pitchers, Regents poured streams of dark liquid into clear goblets. The Croppers ate large spoonfuls of grain.

When the music began again, they all turned to face the dance floor as the king led me into the middle of the room.

The crowd quieted.

The king stood in front of me, resting a hand on my waist. I looked up into his pallid features. It had never been his appearance that unsettled me. It was something else.

"I don't think I know how to dance," I whispered.

"Follow me."

We moved. The king was right. All I had to do was follow. With firm pressure on my hand or my back, he could guide me through the steps. It was a simple dance, without rhythm, more focused on spinning than on music.

The Croppers whistled their approval and the Regents shouted unintelligible encouragement.

Soon, other Regent couples joined us on the floor. The Croppers circled around, singing along in a booming chorus. I wished I knew the lyrics. I might have sung. The music sped up, faster and faster, as the king spun me in wild circles. Giddy sounds rose up from the Regents. Nonsense words.

"Aha!"

"Heroo!"

We spun so fast I could hardly keep up. All I could see was

the king. All I could feel was him, moving me through the steps. Then, the music ended. The room filled with peals of laughter. The Croppers applauded, a chaos of drums and stomping feet.

All the spinning made me dizzy and I stumbled to one side. The king caught me and held me up, my cheek pressed to his shoulder. I looked up and he smiled at me, as if we were sharing a joke.

I stepped away from him, my face warm from the dance. "I need to get some water."

"I have something better." He pulled me to a table and poured a goblet of the black drink.

I eyed it, unsure.

"Try it." The king handed me the goblet.

It burned my throat, bitter and strong. "I don't think this stuff is for humans."

"It'll make you enjoy yourself more. You'll be carefree."

Carefree was the last thing I wanted to be. I needed to care. I needed to be careful. After a closed-mouth sip, I pretended to swallow. "Thanks."

I scanned the room for a jug of something more refreshing. Instead of water, I spotted Proce and Von. They wore finely spun trousers, fringed with tassels of besmonn thread.

Four Regent men clustered around Proce. He was speaking to them, or maybe even singing. They leaned in, riveted by whatever he was saying. Was he talking about me? Proce and Von knew me better than any of the Regents in the city. Aside from Larlia's disdain, most Regents were curious about the human, though they were too polite to ask questions.

The king followed my line of sight. "I hope your friends will still visit the Polaris after we're married."

"Visit?" I asked. "Won't they stay?"

"Croppers can't be happy in the city for long. They have their lands."

"And you think a human can be happy here?"

"I know a human could be happy here. I'll do whatever it takes to make her happy."

He was right, in a way. Healing Andrew would make me happy. Or maybe happy wasn't the right word. Relieved?

Love was different than I had thought. When Andrew was injured, I wanted him to wake up so I could be with him. I couldn't stand the thought of being alone. Now, even though I would never see him again, I needed Andrew to live for his own sake. My life was over, and that was okay. It was going to have to be okay.

I turned to the king. "If the Croppers are going to leave the Polaris, I shouldn't waste time. Can I go talk with them?"

"So eager to get away from me?" the king asked. "Or maybe to see your human. I know Proce helps you monitor Andrew's illness."

He knew what Proce could do. What we could do together. Had he seen it in Proce's thoughts? I did want to check on Andrew. That was true. But I also wanted to see my giants.

"Is it impossible that I might care about a Cropper?" I opened my mind to the king and pictured my hands clasped with Von's. In my thought-image, she showed all of her teeth and congratulated me on my marriage.

I hid any thoughts of Proce, or Andrew, and projected the image as fiercely as I could toward the king. My temples throbbed with the strain and I felt a familiar surge of pride as my mind met the king's.

"I know what you're doing." He looked at me closely. "You'll wear yourself out. There's no need for trickery between us."

I clamped my thoughts shut. Had he known I was lying about my sleep last night? Had he known I would wander the halls? His house was gifted. I hadn't found the tower and I hadn't found the Croppers. Maybe that was on purpose.

Freedom was an illusion.

I shoved his mind away from mine. For just one moment, I thought I saw him flinch. Then his face smoothed.

"If you want to talk to the Croppers, you can do it in my presence," he said.

I set my goblet on the table, still full. "I don't want to anymore."

The king laughed. "Another lie. At least this one was with your voice, not your mind. It's easier to detect."

I took a breath to respond, but it caught in my chest and turned into a cough. The king hadn't healed me in more than a day. The earth's poison was beginning to take effect. I wheezed and recovered my composure.

He brushed his hand against my shoulder. I expected the familiar hum of his gift, healing me. It never came.

I looked up into the king's eyes. Would he make me ask for my healing? He usually jumped at the chance to fix every scratch and cough.

He knew what I was thinking without seeing my thoughts.

"I'm saving my gift for the ceremony," he said. "I'll need every bit of it."

"You're not going to heal me?" By the time the ceremony arrived, I would be fevered, maybe worse. Did he really need to save his gift? Or did he want me to be weak? Fear pinched my stomach. I suddenly felt sick.

An excited buzz of conversation filled the room and the music died down again.

The king spun me to face away from Proce and Von, as if we were dancing again. "Come with me. It's time for our blessing."

In an orderly bustle, every creature lined up in two rows, facing each other. They formed a winding aisle of glittering people, snaking throughout the auditorium. Three Croppers traveled up and down the walkway, scattering the floor with more petals. The coned lights dimmed and the Regents lit miniature flames in the palms of their hands. Fire danced against their skin without burning. They became an avenue of stars, twinkling in the dim room.

The king directed me to an opening in the aisle and leaned low to whisper in my ear.

"You greet to the right. I'm to the left. Don't bow. You represent the king now." He stood straight again and faced the rows of people, his shoulders back.

The Regents' cheeks glowed hollow, flickering in their gifted flames. There were more Regents than Croppers, but the Croppers stood out among them, their size making up for their numbers.

I studied the people on the right side of the walkway. They looked back at me with keen eyes. What emotions lay behind those expressions? Joy? Maybe from the Croppers. Jealousy? How many of the ladies in my line had hoped to be queen? They might still be, when I died. Unless the king found another human by then. I caught eyes with a familiar face. Von was on my side of the aisle. Proce stood beside her.

The king nudged me forward and turned his back to me, greeting the first Regent to the left. As told, I faced the right.

An elder Regent man was first in line. He bowed low, his curly hair oiled against his scalp. "Blessings to you. And may your marriage yield many children."

"Thank you." I felt sick to my stomach, but I managed a smile before I moved to the next Regent.

The aisle of creatures stayed still while the king and I moved along, making our way to each individual. I greeted a girl next, her bow even deeper than the man's. She looked about my age, but I knew she wasn't. She was probably decades older. Maybe a century. A white gem sparkled against her forehead and a pink ribbon wound through her hair. Decadent color.

"May I?" she asked.

"Umm . . . yes?" I had no idea what I was agreeing to. Regents didn't usually ask for permission. Larlia liked to pull my hair without so much as a warning. How would this girl have responded if I had said no to her question?

She spread her sharp white fingers and hovered them an inch away from my abdomen. "May you be blessed as a patient mother." She spoke with feeling. Tears shone against her pale cheeks.

She moved her hand closer, to press against my stomach.

I recoiled. "Are you using your gift?"

"No. I'm wishing you my same joy." She smiled and spread her hand over her own rounded stomach. She was pregnant.

I gave an awkward nod and moved along.

With each encounter, I received a new blessing. Some wished me a long life. Others wished me a happy marriage. They were ungifted blessings, hopes for my future, and the future of their king. Every Regent and every Cropper mentioned children. After a while, I stopped looking into their eyes. I couldn't accept their blessings, or their wishes for a life I didn't want.

Out of the corner of my eye, I noticed the king. He smiled up at an especially wiry Cropper. I tuned out the blessing of the Regent in front of me and listened to the king's voice instead.

"It's a good thing all my subjects can't sing as well as you," he said.

"Why is that?" the Cropper asked.

"We wouldn't get anything else done. We'd just sit around and listen."

The Cropper chuckled, delighted by the compliment.

Next, the king moved to a young Regent man. "Your mother is dearly missed," the king said. "I love to walk over the bridges she designed, in the north of the city. Seeing them must make you proud."

The king knew exactly what to say to everyone. It was more than his gift that made the people loyal. It was him. He saw their thoughts and spun his words. How had Proce and Von ever seen this king as a broken man, mourning the loss of his wife? A king who needed saving, so he could save them from the cold. To the Croppers, he had played victim and hero all at once.

Had he loved Queen Elia? Her death hadn't weakened his gift like Proce thought. But maybe it made him hungry for power. Grief is a strange thing.

"Lady Alora?" The Cropper in front of me could tell I wasn't listening to her.

I stepped back and arched my neck to see her face. "I'm sorry. I was listening to the king."

"It is good that you are getting to know him. We can see how he loves you. You are new in years to carry this burden, but do not be afraid." She clasped my hands and hummed a tune, her long fingers laced between mine.

Her gift flooded me with an artificial sense of calm, a calm I didn't want to feel. When she let go, the comfort faded. Had she sensed my fear of the future, or only guessed it?

After five more Regents in the line, I would reach Proce and Von. I didn't want the king within earshot, so I took as long as possible with each blessing. The king kept moving. I asked pointless questions and let awkward silences linger, until the king outpaced me. I was left behind. He was three Regents ahead in the aisle. That would have to be enough.

Proce and Von didn't bow. They lowered all the way to their knees so that I could look into their eyes. It was an undignified move compared with the other Croppers.

Von held out her hands to me, but I didn't take them. Instead, I leaned in and wrapped my arms around her long neck. After a pause, she hugged me back. My throat tightened. How long since I had been hugged?

I turned to Proce, wary of touching him. What if I accidentally stole his gift again? I didn't want that, though I wanted to see Andrew.

"I need to ask you something." I lowered my voice and hoped the Regents on either side couldn't hear. "About Regent history. Can it stay between us?"

Proce's eyes darted to the king, then back to me. He nodded, just once.

"Thank you." I clouded my thoughts as thickly as I could. "Has anyone ever lost their gift? Has it ever been taken away?"

Proce thought for a pause. "The gift of sleep was taken away last season. We would have never believed it to be possible."

"I'm not talking about the gifts of the land, or the sleep, or children, or grain. I'm talking about the gift inside you. Your power. The light."

"The queen died," Proce said. "We lost her gift, and more."

"What if the king lost his gift? Would it go to a new king? Maybe a better one?"

Proce spoke so quietly I could barely hear him. "Such a thing has never happened. The King's Gift is always transferred when the king is dying, in a ceremony. It is one torch that lights another. If the fire went out, I do not know what would happen. There is no other way. Why are you asking this? The king has done well for the Croppers. He has given us gems to increase our birth rate. He has—"

"He hasn't blessed the sleep," I hissed. "The more Croppers are born, the less value each life has . . . What if he uses up his gift? Wastes it?"

I was risking everything, hinting like that. The king had threatened to break our bargain if I revealed his choice. But I needed to talk to someone. I had questions, and Proce always had answers.

"Enough." Proce's whisper was sharp. "He would never go against his purpose."

Von rested her hand on my shoulder. "Do not worry about these things. After the ceremony tomorrow, all will be well." She sounded like she was trying to convince herself too.

I looked back to Proce. "We both need the King's Gift to live. But I can tell you don't trust him. Not fully. You've kept your secrets. How much power will be enough for him? How much power should he have?"

Proce set his jaw. "What are you saying? The king needs this ceremony. We all do. Even you. At first, we thought we had done wrong in calling you to cross over. You were so scared of us in the meadow. But then we learned of Andrew. He is the reason the Writings brought us to you, of all humans. So that Andrew could be healed. If you do not give the king what he asks, he will not be able to help the boy."

"You think I don't know that?" I guarded my mind, in case the king was listening. "But I'm scared of the consequences. It's not a normal ceremony. The king wants the Queen's Gift. I can't carry it. I'm a human. So it will go to him." How much of this did Proce understand?

Proce eyed me. "I am going to show you your human, so that you can remember what is at risk." He clasped my hands and closed his eyes.

I held myself back from stealing his power. It only took a split second for his gift to flow, but in that instant, I had to fight for self-control.

Proce's voice hummed, and I saw Andrew, shaggy hair against white sheets. His eyes were sunken. Plastic tubes protruded from his nose, and his lips were almost as pale as a Regent.

I felt his injury, black and spreading. It left blank spaces in his mind. Although his body breathed, his spirit was fading. How much of Andrew would be left, once the king finally got around to healing him?

Meg? Andrew's thoughts were more distant than before. He was weak. But I could hear him.

I'm here, I said. *Andrew, keep holding on. Just a little bit longer.*

It's so dark here. It keeps getting darker. Meg . . . I don't know where I am.

Tears fell down my cheeks. What could I say to him? How much would he understand?

Do you remember looking at the stars in your yard? When you showed me your song for the entrance exam? The dark was never so bad when we were together. I'm here with you now. Soon, it won't be dark anymore.

There was a smile in Andrew's next thought. *I wanted to kiss you that night. I should have done it.*

Warmth filled me.

I would have liked that. Andrew—

Proce pulled his hands away and the vision disappeared. I fought back tears. He had shown me Andrew to remind me of my purpose. It had worked. I remembered what I had to do. At any cost.

"Wait." I reached for Proce's hand again. "I need to—"

He spoke in an artificially loud voice. "We bless your marriage, Lady Alora. We hope to visit you, and the king, soon."

I looked down the aisle. The king was watching us, his eyes narrow. I had spent too long with the Croppers. Proce was covering for me.

"Thank you for your blessing." I bowed to Von, despite what the king had ordered. I would give honor where it was due.

The giants were my only friends, and at the same time, I wished I had never met them. I would never have done what they did, stealing my life to save their own. Not even if it meant saving Andrew. Nothing could justify the choice they had made for me, what they took from me without permission. And yet, now that I was here, now that it was done, I couldn't watch them die in the cold. Yes, they were wrong. But they were good. They were gentle creatures. Patient. Ancient.

There was still the problem of the humans. After the ceremony, if the king was powerful enough to use his gift for the Croppers, he might be powerful enough to steal more human brides. And so, after all, I would be doing what Proce and Von had done to me. Was I trading Cropper lives, Andrew's life, for the lives of unnamed girls?

I didn't remember much from my earth, but I knew things about myself. I was a quiet soul, content to stay on the ground. I wasn't the type to go fast or far or high. And now I was being asked to do just that. To career toward impossible choices. How high would I go for Andrew? For Proce and Von? Would I let the king use me to hurt others in order to save people I loved?

Reluctantly, I moved on from my Croppers, leaving them behind in a crowd of Regents.

The line of blessings lasted for at least another hour. More than one lady touched my stomach, blessing my future children.

I wanted to yell, to tell them to stop. Instead, I moved along to the next Regent, and the next.

When the blessings ended, the cones glowed bright and the Regents' flames disappeared. Everyone drank more goblets of black and played a skipping game on the dance floor. From what I could tell, the rules involved jumping on one leg, having better balance than your opponent.

I watched, as if through glass, the merriment a thousand miles away. How had Queen Elia felt when she married the king? It had probably been easy for her to smile at each blessing. She would have known exactly what to say to the Regents. To the king. Had he been her version of Andrew?

The king stayed at my side. We sat at the edge of the room on hard chairs. With one hand, he held mine. With the other, he sipped from his goblet. Thankfully, we didn't dance again, though the other Regents spun in the middle of the room.

"How long will they dance?" I shivered in my scant dress. Days were hot in the gray earth, but the air cooled at night, enough to need more clothes than I was wearing.

"Until morning," he said. "You're worth celebrating."

I crossed my legs, one over the other.

The king set down his goblet. "You're tired. I know the blessing wasn't easy. They watch your every move and evaluate every word. I'm still not used to it."

"I doubt that."

"I would like nothing more than to leave this room and to be alone with you."

I looked away, unsettled by what I saw in the king's eyes. "I should get some sleep before the ceremony tomorrow."

"One more song. Then I think we can get away with an exit."

A Cropper woman stepped up on the dais and belted a raspy tune. It was a silly song, about a besmonn who fell in love with a flower and wanted to marry it. When she finished, the Regents cheered and hooted.

The king stood and raised a hand. Everyone silenced.

A single voice yelled from the crowd. "Tomorrow, you marry the human!"

The Regents cheered again. In their drunken state, I wasn't Lady Alora. I was simply the human, caught and kept.

The king lowered his hand and they quieted.

"Tomorrow, the Watchers will report on the ceremony. There will be a feast prepared for the whole city. Before then, Alora and I need to rest. You have celebrated well, and I am thankful. Just because I have to sleep, doesn't mean you have to. Enjoy my house!"

With chalky laughter, Regents downed their goblets. Croppers hit their drums. Everyone shouted, their words lost in a deafening noise.

The king grabbed my hand and the unruly crowd parted, shoving one another aside. I trailed behind the king as we ran through the auditorium, out the archway. A moment later, we were alone in the hall, hurrying away from the fading whistles and shouts.

When I couldn't hear the party anymore, I stopped and leaned against a wall. The king watched me. At least there was only one of him. The pressure of all those inhuman eyes lifted from me.

For a moment, I was relieved. Then, it struck me as absurd that I was relieved to be alone with a creature like the king. Not long ago, he would have terrified me. All the shock and fear and pain of the past several days welled up and brought tears. I didn't cry. I laughed. Maybe I did both.

"What's funny?" The king looked concerned.

"Regents." I wiped tears from my cheeks. "You look funny and you talk funny, but you think you're so fancy."

One corner of his mouth turned up. "You might have a point."

"I definitely have a point." I regained control of myself, suppressing the giggles and sobs. We were almost to the human rooms.

The king bowed to me at my door. "I enjoyed dancing with you tonight. I think you enjoyed it for a moment too, though I doubt you'd ever admit it."

Maybe, in another life, if I knew less, I might have enjoyed dancing in a glittering dress beneath gifted lights. If things had been different, I might have been impressed by this king, with his assured manner. But I had seen too much. Lost too much.

"Rest your gift," I said. "Tomorrow, we have a promise to keep."

20

As soon as I woke up, I tested my lungs. They burned, and I couldn't breathe at full capacity. This wasn't a good start. How long until my lungs bled, or closed, locked shut by the gray earth's poison? By the end of the day, the king would have his ceremony. I had to last that long, and then long enough to ensure Andrew was healed. And then, how soon after that would the king try to open a thin place, to call another human here?

The bedroom was quiet in a way that only mornings can be. Fresh sunshine illuminated the finery around me: tapestries, luxurious carpet, shimmery stone walls. All of it paled next to the blue curtain, hung beside the bed. Now that I knew more about the Regents, I wondered at the luxury of so much color in my room. It was a gift from the king, for me. A costly thing, meant to please. It would never replace a blue sky.

I sat up and slid off the silk bed sheets. Would I really be married by the end of the day, to the king who owned this house? I felt numb at the thought. A girl should be happy on her wedding day. At the very least, she should be marrying a human.

Would Andrew have asked me to marry him someday, when we were older? I imagined him on one knee, in a field of yellow flowers. I would have said yes. I no longer remembered Andrew's favorite color, or all the songs he had written, or even exactly how long I had known him. But I remembered how I felt.

I would have said yes.

Larlia brought a tray of sweet rolls and tea. The moment she set it down, I snatched a roll and took an enormous bite, my stomach growling.

Food in the King's House had been offered sparsely, aside from wedding feasts. Even then, it was difficult to eat with so many eyes on me. Maybe the king wanted me to eat only with him. Or maybe Larlia had been starving me, against his orders. A couple of times, a Regent lady had brought a morning drink, spicy and sweet and thick, but it had always been taken away as quickly as it was given.

I was beginning to feel weak, and I hoped the roll would help. Was the food here poisonous to me too, like the air? Nothing felt right without the king's healing. Better to be sick, than to be hungry and sick.

I washed down the roll with a sip from a steaming chalice, then coughed as Larlia tore at my tangles with a silver-pronged comb.

I clinked the chalice onto the tray. "Can I eat before you pull my hair out?"

In truth, Larlia never damaged my hair with her rough treatment. If anything, it always looked somehow thicker and shinier when she finished.

"The king will be here soon to take you," Larlia said.

I froze at her words. The ceremony wasn't supposed to happen until night. "Take me where?"

"Can't say." Larlia shoved a pin through one of my braids, into my scalp.

I bit my lip. Why would the king come for me early? What if he had some kind of experiment planned for me? My stomach knotted at the memory of crackling red light and gray blood.

I hated his gift. I hated it, and I needed it. When I had looked within him, to see his power, I'd seen a pool of something unrelenting and ancient. It was separate from the king, but it pulsed with his breath and heartbeat. Maybe it wasn't the King's Gift I hated.

Larlia dressed me in a silk robe, tied down the back with ribbons. To my delight, the robe had pockets. Pockets that buttoned closed, perfect to stow note and knife. I buried the treasures there when no one was looking. My slippers were sturdy today and my hair well secured. I was dressed for walking. Was the king taking me outside the city again?

"Sit down." Larlia reached for her jars of cosmetics. She hadn't applied dust to my face yet.

"He's almost at the door." I felt his presence before he arrived.

I shoved the rest of my roll into my mouth.

Larlia straightened her tool kit and smoothed the front of her dress. She was breathless, jitters hidden beneath her usual calculated movements. Was she scared of him? No. I realized it was something else.

The door handle turned and the king entered the room, his black jacket crisp and straight.

Larlia went still, a mask of decorum in place. She kept her gaze on the king, expectant. He looked past her, to me.

"I have something for you." The king handed me a silver flower with a long stem.

"Thank you." I slipped the flower into my waistband, ignoring Larlia's watchful eye. "I didn't expect to see you until tonight. In my earth, I think it's bad luck to see your . . ." I didn't know what to call him. Fiancé? Groom? Those words felt beyond wrong for this situation. "To see each other before the ceremony."

"I'm taking you for a surprise," the king said. "And I don't believe in luck."

"I think I've had enough surprises for a lifetime."

He smiled, flashing white teeth. "I suppose you have. But you'll like this one. I promise."

He ushered me into the hall, a hand on my back. The door swung shut behind us, leaving Larlia in the human rooms. It took barely a minute for us to walk through the King's House, out into the morning sun of the Polaris. My guess had been right about the gifted halls. They were a maze for me. For the king, they led directly where he wanted to go.

He didn't speak as we walked, but there was no such thing as an uncomfortable silence between us anymore. Our minds were matched, searching out the edges of the other. We walked through the city, beneath the eyes of curious Regents, though they kept their distance today.

An elderly couple called out to us from their balcony. "Blessed wedding day!"

The king acknowledged them with a gracious nod. He took my hand and the couple whistled.

A Regent man and his young wife carried baskets of rolls down the street. The husband laughed and shook his head at the elders. "Let the king enjoy his bride without a crowd!"

"Fair enough!" The elderly lady linked arms with her husband and they retreated into their home.

The little street led to an arched bridge over a trickling stream. Silver trees cast rustling shadows on the water. There were fewer houses here than in other parts of the city. We were relatively alone. No need for a charade. I let go of the king's hand, but he didn't let go of mine.

"Everywhere I look here, I see couples," I said. "Do all your people get married?"

He pressed my hand and let go. "If they can, they should, for the hope of a new generation. It takes a lifetime for us to have children. Committed relationships are most successful. But marriage isn't always an easy thing for Regents. A long life with the wrong partner can be difficult."

"Don't couples ever split up, if it's not working?"

"That would be . . . a failure."

"Marriage isn't easy for a human either," I said. "If life's short, you don't want to waste it on the wrong person."

"And I'm the wrong person?" He didn't sound offended, just curious to hear my answer.

I decided to tell the truth. He already knew. "Yes."

The king was powerful and fascinating. And he wanted me. Some part of me wanted to be wanted. But he wasn't kind. Not underneath it all.

"Believe me," the king said, "your idea of what is right and what is wrong can change with time."

"I don't think I'll ever have that much time."

The King's mouth curved, as if he were holding back a contrary remark.

"Anyway," I said. "you'll outlive me and find another Regent wife."

"Not likely. I'll be older then. And if I have children, it would be frowned upon for me to remarry. It's not our custom."

"To leave an opportunity for other couples?" I guessed.

"Exactly. There aren't many of us. It's greedy for one man to have children with two women."

"But you could marry an older woman," I said. "For companionship. That way, your people will still have someone to carry the Queen's Gift."

"If I carry the Queen's Gift for you, I hope to keep it past your death. Until the day I die. Two gifts in one. Another ceremony might jeopardize that."

"Do your people know about this part of the plan?" I asked.

"Some do. On the high councils."

"So that's why . . ." I didn't finish my thought.

"So that's why some of the Regents haven't welcomed you?" he finished for me.

"Yes." Their chances were over if all went according to plan.

"You're under my protection," the king said. "No one will harm you. But I can't stop some of them from being jealous of the queenship." He stopped and looked at me, that secret smile back. "Most are jealous of me, that I will have you. A human wife is the secret fantasy of many Regents."

I held his gaze, refusing to be embarrassed anymore.

"Come on." The king grasped my hand and sped his pace. "I want to show you the heart of my city. We're almost there." He pulled me around the corner at a trot.

It took me much longer than it should have to catch my breath after the short run. My sickness was growing, my lungs burning. After a moment, I took in the view.

Dozens of low bridges crisscrossed over a smooth lake, creating an intricate pattern of pathways. Water lapped against the sides. Their foundations must have been built deep beneath the surface. Silver leaves grew on the water, dotted with crisp white blossoms.

Huge boulders jutted from the lake. Some had staircases carved into the sides, so that swimmers could climb up onto them. A Cropper lay on a distant boulder, eyes closed against the warm sun. He was probably tired after the long night of celebration. I was tired.

Across the lake, silver lawns sprawled beneath giant trees. Their branches were pruned into geometric shapes. Tiny besmonns, like the one I had first seen with Urma, peeped among the leaves.

Behind the trees, on grassy hills, were rows of arbors, each with its own set of beautiful chairs and tables. Three Regents reclined in the arbor shade, sipping from tall mugs.

The whole scene was beauty and nature, stretched out over acres.

The king turned to me. "This is the Polaris Conservatory. What do you think?"

The place was breathtaking. "What's it for?"

"It's for you and me. And for anybody who wants to enjoy it. Croppers help the plants grow, but my mother designed it." He strolled onto a stone bridge.

I followed, careful to stay away from the watery edges.

"Is this my surprise?" I hoped that was all he had in store for the morning. A walk in a park. No flying. No experiments.

"Not quite."

"I think I should rest before tonight." My breath was shallow, strained.

Our path led to the grassy shore, ending in a set of descending steps. The king didn't respond to my comment, but helped me to the ground with a steady hand. He walked to the grass and sat, legs crossed. I followed suit, glad for the rest.

"Let's wait here. Our surprise will come to us." A silver leaf floated into the king's black hair, landing just above his ear. For a moment, he looked young, with his perfect skin. Almost boyish.

"What's it like to live forever?" How would he describe it? He hadn't known anything different.

"I won't live forever." The king brushed the leaf from his hair. "I'm as mortal as you."

"You know what I mean." I could breathe a little easier, now that I wasn't walking. "It might as well be forever."

The king plucked at the grass near his legs. "When I was new, the years seemed long. Now, each day passes faster than the last. There's so much I want to do."

"Maybe you've done enough already." I tried to keep my voice light, but I knew what he wanted to do. He wanted to steal more humans.

"Well, I haven't given you your surprise yet." He rose to his feet and pointed up the hill, into the trees. "There it is."

From behind the manicured grove, a Cropper emerged. Surm. His long fingers were wrapped around a tether, leading a glistening besmonn. A riding besmonn. The massive bird hovered over Surm's head, darting back and forth, investigating tree blossoms.

"HOOO!" Surm yelled at Cropper volume and quickened his step, a smile widening across his gray face.

"Surm!" I stood and called back with my small voice.

The besmonn caught sight of me. And my color. It abandoned the flowers and flew in a straight line toward me, tugging Surm at a jog. Surm's smile disappeared as he dodged a tree branch.

Once the bird neared me, it hovered at eye level and preened my hair with its slender beak. I laughed and caressed the soft feathers on its cheek. Its crest glinted bright silver and its eyes held a ring of icy white. It looked like the king and it belonged to the king. But I couldn't stop myself from loving it.

Surm gave a little bow. "I apologize for the chaos, Kalmus. You know she is usually better behaved."

The besmonn was female.

"It's not your fault," the king said. "Nothing is usual about a human."

Surm offered the tether to me. I took it.

"It's good to see you," I said. "How's Cham?"

"Flying every day, despite his mother's grumblings. Blessings on your marriage." Surm gave the king a knowing smile. "It will be best if I leave you two alone now." He bowed, then turned and loped away.

I yelled after him. "Thank you for bringing her!"

He shot one arm into the air, acknowledging my thanks. Then, he disappeared over the hill at full Cropper speed.

The king ran a finger along the besmonn's wing feathers. "Her name is Sky. Do you like her?"

"Yes," I breathed.

She was beautiful.

"Good. She's yours now."

Mine.

Nothing in the gray earth belonged to me. Even my old clothes were long gone, dissected to add a flare of color to various garments. My gowns, my rooms, they belonged to the king. But Sky was a creature, with her own will and thoughts. You could never truly own a creature like that. For the short time I had left, this sweet animal wouldn't belong to me, but she would belong with me.

"Thank you." An idea came to me. "Can Sky stand with me tonight, in the ceremony? I'm sure she won't fly away or cause any trouble." She would be my witness.

"Of course," the king said. "Have you learned anything more about the ceremony?"

"No." I knew I wouldn't have to promise my love to the king, and I knew it would make a miracle possible. That was all that mattered.

"Don't worry, it doesn't hurt," he assured.

Then why would he say that? I led Sky closer to the giant tree blossoms, so she could search for nectar. My lungs ached. "How does the ceremony work?"

The king leaned against the tree trunk and watched us. "Tonight, I'll give you a portion of my gift. If you were a Regent, it would call the Queen's Gift to you. Since you're a human, I hope the Queen's Gift will come to me instead."

"You hope." My spine went rigid. "It's another experiment, isn't it? Like the color."

He didn't acknowledge my question. "The gifts will be whole, unsplit between king and queen. It's how it always should have been."

How it always should have been. According to who? He didn't want a wife as an equal partner. He wanted to hold all the power. Unease spread through me, deeper than sickness. Did the king have any idea what he was doing? I should have argued. I should have run away. But I needed it to work for Andrew's sake, so I said nothing. I was ready to get married.

21

We returned to the King's House with Sky. She had to waddle through the halls. More than once, she spread her wings to their full span, stretching from wall to wall. I thought she might damage the lights, but the cones were solid against her feathers. Sooner than should have been possible, we reached the king's garden.

"The ceremony is always held under moonlight." The king took Sky's tether and tied it to a tree. "My parents were married in this garden."

Had he also married Queen Elia here, where we were standing?

Sky wasn't happy when I turned for the door. She flapped her wings and pulled at her tether.

I turned to her and tried to make my voice soothing. "I'm coming back tonight."

It seemed to work. Sky folded her wings and watched through slitted eyes as I left the garden with the king.

In the hall, beneath the staircase, the king bowed low to me. "Ceremony aside, I'm glad you'll be my wife. You. Meg. Not just any human."

He had only known one other human. And she had been an old woman. I half bowed, palms forward, lips tight. I couldn't picture that kind of a future between us.

We parted ways. Three Watchers escorted me to my rooms.

Larlia directed me to the mosaic bathroom, where she filled

a crystal basin with hot water. I thought of the simple days in the waterfall ravine, when I had bathed in the streams with sticky Cropper soap.

My memories of my own earth were more than patchy now, but I knew I had been ordinary. A normal, human girl. I could never have imagined anything more strange than the Croppers. But here I was, bathing in a palace, promised to marry the king of the giants.

When Larlia left the bathroom, I slipped out of my robe and sank into the basin, hiding my body beneath a layer of soapy bubbles. The hot water eased my sore muscles. When would I be alone again? After the ceremony, would the king and I be expected to sleep in the same room, as husbands and wives did?

The king wanted children. I knew that. But I hadn't promised anything beyond the ceremony. Not to him, and not to myself.

"At this rate, you'll never be ready." Larlia stormed into the bathroom and poured a decanter of fragrant shampoo over my head. "Wash your hair, or I'll do it for you."

She'd done it once before, on my second day in the Polaris, and she hadn't been gentle. I made an overeager show of lathering the suds on my head. Larlia left. Somehow, Regent soap never burned your eyes. When I finished washing, I wrapped myself in a feather-soft towel and returned to the bedroom.

Larlia, assisted by two other Regents, laid my wedding gown across the bed.

"We started making it years ago."

The coal-black gown absorbed light, like a deep shadow against the white sheets of the bed. It was an odd fabric. Matte, and fluid. Wedding dresses weren't supposed to be black, not in my earth. But this wasn't a wedding. It was a negotiation, my life traded for Andrew's. Black was fitting.

I pulled the dress behind the curtain and forced my body into it. It fit well, sturdy against my damp skin. The neck was low, but secure, my shoulders bare, as always.

Larlia swept my hair into a cascade of artificially perfect curls, then lined my eyes with glittering black ink. On my head, she fastened a silver crown, inlaid with frosted stones.

She brought her face close to my ear. "Just because you're dressed like a queen, doesn't mean you are one."

I looked into her eyes without defense. She was right. It wasn't a real Queen's Ceremony.

Larlia slid my feet into silver shoes. Traditional wedding shoes. I doubted they let Von weave them, as she had once promised me.

She will walk upon silver.

The words from the Writings played in my mind. The Croppers had placed all their hope on this ceremony. I hoped they were right.

"That's as good as she gets." Larlia clapped her hands twice in the air. "Everyone out."

The other ladies scurried from the room.

Larlia turned to follow them.

Words tumbled from my mouth before I could think. "You're in love with the king."

She spun to face me, her cheeks aglow with an odd shade of ash, her voice a husky whisper. "It should have been me in that dress."

"I wish it were you."

Her nostrils flared. "They didn't tell you about me?"

"No." I wished I could give her a better answer.

"Even the gossip is over, then." Larlia's eyes hardened. "I didn't marry when I was young. It's rare, but it happens when a match falls through. Then no one wanted me. By that time, my chances of having a child were low. But there was still a chance. After we lost the queen, the king gave me that chance with him. It never happened. We weren't married. Then you came."

He wouldn't have married her. He was holding out for a human, so he could keep the Queen's Gift for himself. Even if he married a Regent, it would have been a young one. He had used Larlia.

Despite all her stabbing combs and unkind words, I felt pity for her. "I'm sorry he made you dress me." I really was. "I know about your grandfather and the council and everything. But there had to be someone else."

She sniffed and turned her face away. "Regents like beautiful things. Hair and clothes. They matter in the King's House. I dressed Queen Elia before . . . my time with the king."

"I'm sorry." I repeated my apology. An apology for the king's actions, as if my words could make it better.

Larlia gave me a dry look, then spun on her heels and marched out the door.

The king kept her on the end of a string, still in his house, still in his presence. The hope of being reeled back in made her want him more than ever. Why was she so blind? I shook my head. They all were.

My lungs continued to burn. I hid my cut-glass sword in the wrist of my sleeve. My useless weapon. If I began to lose myself, under the pressure of the king's mind, what would I be willing to do with it?

My paper note fit tight between my skin and the silk lining of the wedding gown. I would carry it with me no matter what came, evidence of the true words in my heart.

Only one Watcher came for me that night, a Regent I had never seen before. He led me down an unfamiliar hall that somehow took us to the garden door beneath the staircase. I no longer questioned the irrational pathways through the King's House.

I had expected the courtyard to be full of guests and lights and decoration. But no one greeted me as I entered the garden. No fires burned. No music played. There was nothing but moonlight on silver grass. I looked up at the tower window, visible over the garden wall. The light was off. Would the singer witness my ceremony? Beside the stream stood the king, alone except for Sky, who hovered at the end of her tether.

I crossed the grass to face him. "Where's everyone else?"

"The ceremony is always private. The Watchers will report on the gift born between us."

The Queen's Gift. It would try to come to me. What if it overwhelmed me? I looked up at the moon, identical to the one from my earth.

"We should begin," the king declared.

Red silk peeked from the edges of his jacket. The collar was higher than usual, embroidered with midnight thread. From his pocket, he removed a tiny black book.

"We'll read from this. We both have a part to say for the ceremony."

"Is it an incantation? To make the gift come?"

The king smiled. "No. The words are traditional, to remind a king and a queen of their bond. But these words don't make the actual ceremony happen. It's the intention of the heart, the will. And the way I direct my gift."

"Do I need to . . ." I hesitated. "Make an intention?"

"Your will won't make a difference. Normally, a queen should intend to receive the gift. But, you're a human, so I'll receive it. You're here to incite the Queen's Gift, then reflect it to me. It will be as if I were giving a gift to a mirror. There will still be a bond between us, but it's different from what I would share with a Regent wife."

I took a breath. My lungs ached as I nodded my head. "Then I intend to get you what you need."

The king looked at me. "Ready?"

"Ready."

The king opened the book and read in a solemn cadence.

> "I pour out my gift to you,
> my queen, my wife.
> I need no gift from you.
> You are my gift,
> and a gift to our people."

The king handed me the book and pointed to a line of squiggles. "You read this part."

I held it, and squinted at the page in the moonlight. For a moment, my mind struggled to make sense of the language.

"Can you not read?

"Wait," I said. "It takes me a moment."

I had never acknowledged it before, but on some level, I had always resisted the gray language, the same way I resisted the king's mind. I looked at the words, and stopped fighting them. Quicker than before, the letters came into focus.

> "I receive your gift,
> my king and my husband.
> Between us, it becomes more than it was alone.
> The Queen's Gift will seal our bond
> and serve our people well."

I stumbled over the word *husband*, but I managed to continue on. Reading those words didn't make me a wife, just like handing my possessions over to a thief wouldn't make me generous. Love can't be demanded, or bargained for.

The king placed the book back into his pocket, then took both of my hands and held them in front of me. He looked at me, long enough to unsettle me.

"What now?" I tried to keep my voice calm.

"Just like we read. I'm going to pour my gift into you and it will grow into something more. The Queen's Gift will come to us."

I thought of Andrew. "What are you waiting for?"

"We're about to step over a ledge together. We'll cross a line and we can't come back. I wanted to remember this . . . to remember what you look like."

I met his gaze, though I couldn't match his emotion. He held me there until he was ready.

After a moment, he closed his eyes and the familiar hum of his gift resonated in my mind. The gift didn't heal my aching lungs or ease my burning throat. Instead, it pooled inside of my arms like liquid light.

I closed my eyes and focused on the light gathering inside my bones. I felt like someone else, something else, a million miles away from human experience.

As the light grew, I sensed its voice. It had a will of its own. It called out, reaching toward something beyond sight.

The Queen's Gift.

The light called and pleaded, but no answer came from the unseen place. The voice in the light grew shrill and stretched, frantic for reply.

The king gripped my hands tighter, his fingers sharp. The full force of his gift rushed into my arms, wild and unchecked.

Too much light.

It filled me up, screaming with electricity. First, my bones itched. Then they were on fire. The light burned. It reached the limit of what I could hold and kept pushing against me. My skin felt like it would tear from my body. The light's voice was deafening now.

"Stop!" My eyes flew open. "It's hurting me!"

This wasn't how it was supposed to go.

The king's fingers only dug deeper into my wrists and his gift rushed faster, forcing a fresh wave of pain. My heart beat dangerously fast and I couldn't get enough air into my lungs. The light wasn't just hurting me. It was killing me.

I was going to die.

I hadn't wanted to live. Not trapped. But I couldn't die. Not now.

It didn't matter how desperately the king called to it. The Queen's Gift wasn't coming. I could guess why. Maybe this was never going to work. Maybe the gift wasn't meant for a human, or it wasn't meant for him. Whatever the reason, the king wouldn't give up.

If this continued, he would completely drain his gift. The Croppers would be left to die when the sleep came. Whether he chose to bless them or not, he wouldn't have enough gift to do it.

I writhed against the pain, pulling my hands away from the king. He clamped down on my wrists, holding the connection. Through tears, I tried to focus on his face. His cold eyes stared into mine. He was calm. He saw my pain and terror and he felt no pity. Not even a hint of discomfort.

Moments earlier, he had looked at me with affection. He

had said he wanted to remember what I looked like before the ceremony. This wasn't romance. It was twisted science, and I would be sacrificed.

But not willingly.

With barely enough breath to scream, I threw myself to the ground and kicked my legs into the air, aiming at the king. One foot met with his thigh and I jerked a hand free.

It didn't matter. He grabbed my wrist with both hands, pouring his scorching gift into my body.

"Stop fighting me, Meg."

I barely heard the king's words beneath the scorching light, but I felt him say my name. As he said it, the pain eased by a fraction. For one second, I was able to resist the flow of his gift.

There was power in a name.

I took in a deep breath. As I struggled against the king's grip, a thin piece of glass slid into my free hand. My sword. It dislodged from its hiding place in my sleeve.

My dream from the garden loomed vivid in my mind. The king had laid on one side of the stream, the Cropper on the other.

Choose.

But choosing to hurt the king would hurt the Croppers. And letting him waste his gift would hurt them too.

I gripped my little sword in a tight fist. Would I be strong enough to plunge it into the king's body? If he died, Andrew would die too. Proce said the King's Gift had to be passed on before the king died. I couldn't leave the Croppers without a king.

And then I remembered, he would heal. A knife couldn't kill him, only stop him. Maybe long enough for me to get away. And after he healed, maybe he would see reason. It might even save the King's Gift, the little that was left. Whatever ended up happening, I wouldn't last much longer unless I did something.

My vision clouded and I tightened every muscle in my body, stifling a convulsion of agony. With all my remaining strength, and a sound that tore my throat, I thrust the bookmark upward. It met

with resistance. My hand pressed against the king. Warm liquid
trickled onto my skin.

Blood.

The king released my wrist. Instantly, the pain stopped. Light
drained out of me, lifeless, crackling against the grass. Where it
landed, the plants turned black, burned away and smoking. The
power was gone, used up for nothing.

My vision cleared and the king stood over me, panting. He
clutched the handle of the glass bookmark that protruded from his
chest. Gray blood soaked his hand. Surprise had played across his
features. Now there was anger.

He grabbed my arm and jerked me to my feet at an odd angle.
My shoulder made a loud pop, searing at the joint. It hurt, but not
as much as the ceremony had. I held back a cry.

He was strong. Stronger than I had imagined. The king marched
across the grass, dragging me along. I tripped as I tried to keep up.
He pulled harder. My shoulder flared.

Now I heard Sky, trilling and fighting her tether. How long had
she been making that noise? She knew something was wrong. I
wanted to go to her, to comfort her, but I had no comfort to give.

The dangerous look in the king's eye warned me not to speak.
I had only been able to stab him because he didn't know I would.
Now that I had lost the advantage of surprise, I was helpless.
He was stronger than me. Every creature in his whole earth was
stronger than me.

We left the garden, my legs shaking. He pulled me down the
hall to my rooms and pushed me through the human-sized door. I
fell onto the carpet, gasping for air. Pain stabbed my shoulder. How
badly was I hurt? All of me felt torn.

The king entered and slammed the door shut. He paced back
and forth for a moment before speaking.

"Do you know what you've done?" His voice was steadier than
I expected.

"I stopped you from ruining your gift."

"You stopped nothing. You only delayed the ceremony. It takes more of my gift to heal myself than to heal another. It will take time to replenish after this wound. Maybe weeks." Something unreadable flashed across his expression. "I hope, for your sake, that your human will last until then. If not, you've killed him."

He wanted to try again. He still wanted the Queen's Gift.

I had to say something. "You . . . I would have died."

The king knelt down and brought his face close to mine. "Do you think I would let you die?"

Yes. I did. I knew he would, despite what he believed.

But that wasn't the answer he wanted, so I remained silent, my mind guarded. I knew the truth. He hadn't been in control. He was so focused on his goal, he would do anything.

We had both made a false promise to the other. I was never going to be his wife. Not in my heart. He was never going to be able to heal Andrew.

The king stood, his hand over the bloody part of his chest. "No one else in my city would try to stab me. It would be entertaining under different circumstances. I'll come back to heal you when I can, tomorrow. You should last that long. By then, I may have forgiven you."

He turned to leave and I rose to my feet. "How long until you attempt the ceremony again?"

How long until I died?

"As long as I want." His face was controlled now, a cool smile on his lips. But when he left, he slammed the door shut.

22

I sank to the floor, my cheek laid against the carpet. There was no need to check the door. I already knew it was locked.

I was so stupid.

In my own way, I had started to believe Proce's prophecy. I had thought that something good, somehow, might come from walking into that ceremony with the king. Hearing some nameless voice, singing from a tower, convinced me that there was more to all of this.

I was an idiot.

Those writings weren't about me. They weren't about anything, and no amount of magical gifting would ever be enough to change the fact that people died. Andrew would die. I would die. My mother was already dead, buried somewhere in my own earth.

Even the Croppers would disappear with time. No long life. No new life.

Would I ever see Proce or Von again?

Andrew would die. A cough shook my body. I had only been able to do this because I knew he would live. Without that . . . I couldn't let my thoughts go there. My mind felt numb.

My little sword was gone. What had I intended it for all along? A fantasy of escape, perhaps. But that's all it had been. A fantasy. This was reality.

I coughed again and tasted blood in my mouth. Despite what

the king had said, I doubted I would last through the night. I had been through this before. The coughing, then the choking. When the time came, I hoped I would accept it. Let it take me easy. At least I was away from the king, my thoughts and my body my own. I would rather gasp for air than be burned alive in his ceremony.

Maybe this was how it was always supposed to be. Afterward, would the king give up on his experiments? He would see his own madness, after killing me. Maybe he would bless the Croppers, when his gift replenished. If it replenished. Could this be what the prophecy meant? That I was destined to die.

What a waste of life.

At least he would never have his thin place. He couldn't use my color to steal more human brides. And that was something. But I had wanted more than that. For me and for Andrew. Home and healing and a future. But now, after seeing the evil the king could do, I would have to settle for stopping him.

Andrew . . . I pictured his messy curls. I thought of his fingers on his guitar. My throat tightened. That was more a memory of a memory now, but I had no tears. I couldn't let myself cry. It was hard enough to breathe already.

Then, an almost hopeful thought came to mind. If I went to my courtyard, the little garden in the human rooms, I would be able to look up at the moon again. It was the closest I could get to Andrew. Sky was still outside, in the king's garden. Maybe I would be able to hear her trill.

Arms and legs weak with fever, I made my way into the closet. Slowly, I crawled through the passage under the bench, wincing as I moved. I half considered searching the library for another bookmark, but my body kept going, carrying me onto the soft grass in the courtyard. I sat on the silver lawn and held my torn shoulder.

No lights appeared in the tower above. No music drifted from the window. It didn't matter who the singer was anymore. She couldn't help me now. I leaned against the courtyard wall and focused on breathing, my eyes closed.

That was where the Watchers found me.

"Lady Alora, you need to come with us." Two of them stood in the courtyard.

I tried to stand, but faltered. "How did you get in here?"

"The king can open doors, even where they don't exist."

He was right. There was now a door in the courtyard wall, where one had never been. Apparently, the king still had enough gift to do this. I remembered what the king had said, that his gift held up the walls of the Polaris. Maybe this was easier for him than healing.

One of the Watchers appraised me with his eyes, then looked to the other. "Send for the Croppers named Von and Proce. Lady Alora needs healing, and the king needs to rest his gift."

"Only the king can heal my sickness," I told him.

"Von's healing will fill the temporary need."

The second Watcher bowed. "I'll bring the Croppers and meet you where you're going." He ran around the corner of the courtyard walls, out of sight.

"Where are we going?" I asked.

"I'm not supposed to tell you."

He must have known that the ceremony was unsuccessful. We weren't going to a wedding celebration in the auditorium, full of lights and Regents. That's what might have waited for me, if everything had gone right. Or maybe, I would be dead, and the king would have celebrated without me. As long as he had the Queen's Gift.

What would happen if I tried to resist leaving? Would the Watcher take me away by force? It wouldn't be hard. Wherever we were going, at least I would see Von. I stood on shaky legs, strengthened by that thought.

He led me through the crude arch the king had apparently made in the courtyard wall. It was an ugly thing, a sign of the king's failing gift.

I counted the doors we passed, trying to keep track of my location. Nothing was familiar, until we came to a door beneath a spiral staircase, the door to the King's Garden. My heart lifted a beat.

I would see Sky.

Maybe the king was sending me to collect her, to bring her to the besmonn keep? No. Not in the middle of the night. Not in my current state.

I pushed through the door and scanned the garden. Sky was asleep, curled up and nestled beneath her tree. Two large figures rushed to greet me.

Proce and Von.

They kneeled beside me and I could tell Von had been crying. At the sight of them, I wanted to cry too. I wanted to let all the fear and pain wash away, to be back in the meadow, where Von would gently pat my back and comb my hair. But the giants couldn't help me now.

"You're here." I reached out to clasp Von's hands.

She didn't let me. Instead, she laid her hand against my arm and hummed. The sharp pain in my shoulder disappeared and the general ache in my body calmed. Her gift did nothing to ease my lungs.

"Thank you," I whispered.

Von didn't reply and she wouldn't meet my eyes.

I thought of what all this would mean for them. How could I even begin to explain myself?

Proce broke the silence. "Is it true that you injured the king before the ceremony was complete?"

I bit my lip. Everything they believed was a lie. A lie so big, they couldn't see through it. But what did I have to lose now? The king had no more threats. Proce and Von deserved the full truth, nothing spared.

"Yes," I began. "But it's not what you think—"

Von cut me off. "It is not too late to fix this. You must do exactly as the king says."

The king.

I should have sensed him, but my focus was fading. His mind

was present in mine, a dark shadow. He sat on the other side of the garden, beneath a tree. The scene looked exactly like the illustration from my dream, a wounded Regent beside the crystal stream. Except now, in real life, a thick bandage ran across the king's chest.

He rose to his feet and approached us. "I've forgiven you sooner than I thought I would." A gray stain marked his bandage.

"You're still bleeding." The bandage was all I could look at.

Did he have enough gift to heal himself? Or maybe he was saving the gift for something else. Von could heal him. Yet why would she offer? In her mind, the king could do anything. She didn't know about what he had wasted.

"That's not important right now." The king faced me. "We need to restore the Queen's Gift. I understand the process may be uncomfortable, but I need you to cooperate. It will be over soon."

"Uncomfortable?" I backed away from him.

He was insane. Or he enjoyed hurting me. Maybe both. I looked to Proce, my eyes pleading for help.

Von clasped my hands in her Cropper way. "It is important. Meg, please. I know you understand. We have told you what this means . . ." Her voice broke off.

Minutes earlier, alone in my rooms, I had thought of death with numbness, almost acceptance. Now, reality brought a flood of grief. My hands shook in Von's.

Tears finally came.

I shed tears for the fear I saw in Von's face. I shed tears for all the Croppers. For Cham and Urma and Aggi, who would face death when the king wasted his gift. I cried for Andrew. Especially for Andrew. And I cried for myself. For everything I had lost, and everything I was about to lose.

And I cried because I was afraid of the pain.

Von hummed, trying to comfort me with her gift, but it was no use. My grief was a river, and her gift was a teacup, trying to stop the flow.

The king took my hands from Von. I went stiff.

It was happening again. It was happening, and nothing could stop it.

In an instant, his gift flowed. The same as before, it collected inside my body and called out to the Queen's Gift. No answer came and the king pressed on, surging light through my arms.

The pain took away what little breath I had left. I gasped and tried to pull away. The light burned me and stretched me. I clenched my teeth and my body quaked.

"You are hurting her!" Proce's voice was distant in my ears.

The king didn't listen. The pain worsened.

Proce barreled toward the king, as if to knock him down. A wall of gift stopped the attack. Proce pushed against it, unable to come close. Von stood back, unmoving, her hands over her face.

No one could help me.

As I felt my life slipping, stolen, I found something inside myself that I had not encountered before. A wild defiance. This wasn't right. I wanted to live.

Even if I had to face the king every day. Even if I never escaped the gray earth.

I had tried everything to save Andrew. It hadn't been enough. Dying would prove nothing. Andrew deserved for me to say goodbye, at least. Proce and Von deserved the truth about the King's Gift. Without me, who would tell them?

Most of all, the king didn't deserve to have my life. With nothing left to lose, I wasn't afraid to fight him anymore.

I gathered all the power of my human color and pushed the light away. I imagined a cascade of water, washing out all the pain. I built walls around my arms and I fortified them with my will to live.

The pain decreased and I fought harder.

It was working.

As I pushed the light out of me, it had to go somewhere. It wanted to go into the living things around me. The plants. A thought crossed my mind. What if the light burned Proce or Von? But in that moment, all that mattered was getting the gift out of me, stopping the pain. I had already gone too far.

White light blazed in front of my eyes, pouring out of my body. It hung in the air, expanding and sparking with deafening cracks.

The mass grew until it burned my eyes to look at it. The king let go of my hands and backed away. I couldn't see his face through the light.

I took a step back and covered my ears as another spark exploded. It shot in every direction, burning trees and disintegrating blossoms. With a final spark, the courtyard shone brighter than daylight, then night returned. A disturbing smell hung in the air.

For a while, the king and I faced each other in the moonlight, eyes wide. Then, the sound of labored breath drew my attention away.

It was Proce.

He lay on the ground at an odd angle, his face contorted. Von crouched next to him, both hands pressed against his hip.

My stomach lurched, cold ice running through my veins.

Where Proce's leg should have connected to his body, there was nothing. Only a pool of ashen blood. Von's shoulders heaved as she hummed. Proce trembled violently.

His leg had been torn from his body.

I raced to Proce's side. The king knelt beside me, his face tight.

"Heal him!" I grabbed the king's hand and forced it against Proce's bloody skin.

The king pulled his hand away. "I can't. It's a gift-made wound. It would take more than I can afford to give."

Life was full of wounds and diseases and minds that couldn't be healed. But not this time.

Not Proce.

Bumbling, long-winded Proce. Proce who hid his thoughts from the king for me, who tried to stop the ceremony for me, who carried me when I was sick. I wouldn't accept it.

Proce wasn't innocent. He had stolen me from my earth, but he didn't deserve this. He had trusted me to save him and his people through my marriage. Instead, I had hurt him.

I might have killed him.

I took the king's hand again, my grip tight with anger, despite my sickness. If the king wouldn't use his gift, I would steal it.

I called the light to me. The King's Gift hummed and came, drawn by my color. The light didn't pool into me, like it had in the ceremony. Instead, it flowed through my will. I called it for a purpose, a purpose it wanted to fulfill.

It happened fast, but the king realized what I was doing this time. He didn't have much gift left, so he could feel the drain.

He tried to free his hand, but I held tight. I called the gift and wrapped light around our hands, lashing our fingers together. He couldn't get away.

The king gave a short laugh, though his eyes flared. "My Meg, always with a new trick."

At that, more of his gift poured into me, this time at his will. The light he sent burned. It felt as if I would lose my hand where we were lashed together.

I tried to ignore the pain. The ceremony had been worse. Did the king think this would stop me? I focused on the healing.

New skin crept over the edges of Proce's wound, fresh and pale in the moonlight. I urged more of the gift toward Proce, but its flow slowed to a trickle. Even the pain the king sent grew thin. All that remained was the light that bound our hands.

"What did you do?" The king's voice was full of fury.

I ignored him. There had to be more light, more power.

I left my own vision behind and looked deep within the king. His gift sparked and fizzled, barely alight within his body. It wouldn't be enough. I pressed further, through the cage around the king's heart. There, a remnant of his gift blazed. A wealth of life and healing and goodness. It was the last core of the King's Gift, the part even he wasn't willing to spend.

Strong fingers closed over my throat. I couldn't breathe. With my free hand, I tried to push the king away. He was choking me.

I wouldn't be able to stop him with my hands. I turned to my only resource. His gift. The well of light in his chest fought to escape the cage. It wanted to help, to heal, to be free and good. And I would be the one to let it go.

I called to the light. It came.

Proce's bleeding stopped. His skin grew. I urged the light forward, willing life and wholeness into Proce's body. It took the very last drop of the King's Gift before the wound healed over completely.

As the gift drained from the king, his grip on my throat loosened. I gasped, breathing in precious air. When all the light in the king was gone, our hands fell away from each other. The king's eyes rolled back and he fell into the grass.

I collapsed beside him and took shuddering breaths.

If the Croppers couldn't have their sleep, at least Proce could have this. He had lost his leg forever, but he was alive. That was the only miracle any of us would get today.

My lungs burned, and tears streamed down my cheeks.

Proce was alive.

He would live.

And I would die without the King's Gift to heal me. It was gone. I had taken all of it. At least it had been spent on healing, rather than more experiments. I had laid it to rest well, honoring its final wishes.

Then, a deep roar echoed through the courtyard and the ground rumbled beneath me. I sat up, scanning the garden for the source of the noise. A crack ran up one of the stone walls, and the high towers swayed.

My tears dried and we all froze for a moment. Von spoke first.

"What did you do?" She stood over me, raw fear on her face.

I crawled to my feet, fighting for breath. "I stopped it. I stopped him."

The ground stilled and the roar quieted.

Proce moaned and reached a shaking hand to feel the place where his leg should have been. Not long ago, he had carried me to the Polaris when I was dying, his legs strong and his arms careful. Now, he would never walk again. I had destroyed something beautiful, to save my own life. And even that hadn't been enough to save me.

Or to save Andrew.

Proce removed his hand from the scarred wound. Carefully, he lifted his head and met my gaze. "The King's Gift is gone from him. We cannot sense it, and we are afraid. The city will fall. The roads. The towers."

The king lay on the ground. Von stared at his unmoving body, her hands limp at her sides.

"Meg," Proce said. "Explain what you did. What has happened?"

I tried not to look at his severed leg, lying in the grass, but I couldn't keep my eyes away. The bare foot was already turning a lighter shade of gray. I swallowed the acid that filled my throat.

"Please explain," Proce repeated.

I swallowed again. "The king wouldn't stop. The ceremony wasn't working . . . He was killing me. I ended it, but . . . your leg." My throat burned again. "He wouldn't heal you. I knew he was saving his gift, holding it back. So I stole it. It wasn't enough to . . . it only closed your wound. I tried to do more . . . but I couldn't."

Proce sat up. "Do you know what happens if a gift is used beyond its ability?"

"It's going to replenish," I said. "It will—"

"No." Proce's voice shook. "It is like a fire that has been extinguished. His gift is gone, and he has no ember to light the next king. In all our histories, this has never happened." The ground rumbled again. "Even now, the Seven Cities may fall. Sickness will come, long held at bay by the king. I can only guess what else may come."

Von wrapped her arms across her body, her expression far away.

I searched for words, unable to think. I hadn't wanted Proce to die. I had done what I could to keep myself alive. Then to keep him alive. That was all I had.

The garden door flew open. Three Watchers rushed to the king. They felt his throat for a pulse.

"I can't sense his gift," a Watcher said.

Another turned on me, throwing back his hood. "What have you done, human?"

"The gift . . . it wanted to heal Proce," I said. "I helped it."

The Watcher's face twisted into a dangerous expression. He turned to the others and they began to whisper. What would they do with me?

I stood there in the dark, surrounded by Watchers, cut off from Proce and Von.

Then, a familiar light flickered on in the tower window. Haunting music filled the garden. It shouldn't have mattered to me then. I knew I should ignore it and listen to the Watchers. There were more important things than the voice.

But the song called to me, stronger than before. It was enough to drown out my fear and my guilt. I wanted to hide in the melody, to lose myself in it. It carried me away and buried the ugly memories of the ceremony.

A different Watcher stepped toward me with the same question. "What happened?" His words were muffled beneath the song.

The melody soared to a high note, lifting my attention to it. Couldn't the Watcher hear it? As if in a dream, all I could see was the bright spot of the tower window, high above the garden. If only there were some way to climb to that window, to float away. Or to fly.

Sky.

I had hardly noticed her trills in the chaos of the ceremony, but she was awake now, flitting at the end of her tether. And she was my chance to scale the tower.

I didn't want to face the Watcher's questions or look at Proce's bloody leg again. I didn't have answers for the Watchers, or for Proce and Von, though I owed it to them. There had to be an explanation, a way forward, but I couldn't think with everyone staring at me. I would die in the morning, when my lungs closed. Right now, all I wanted to do was slip away into the dark, to clear my mind for a moment, and Sky was my escape.

The Watcher stood between me and the bird.

"Answer me." There was a dangerous edge in the Watcher's voice. "Give the king his gift back."

I rested my eyes on the king and walked toward him.

The Watcher let me pass. To the Regents, I wasn't just a young girl. I was a human, a creature from another earth. I'd broken their king, and they hoped I could set him right. I wished I could do what the Watcher asked, but I didn't know how. It wouldn't help to spend the rest of my short life, maybe only hours, as a prisoner.

Once I reached the king, nothing stood between me and Sky. Beneath my skirt, I slipped my feet out of my silver shoes, digging my toes into the grass for traction.

All eyes were on me. I drew a deep breath into my tight lungs and bolted through the garden. Every movement hurt, but I fought through. I pulled up my skirt and forced my legs to move as fast as they could.

It wasn't very fast.

Sky greeted me with a triumphant shake of her beak. I didn't have time for her to nuzzle my hand with her cheek feathers. I pulled her toward me by the base of her wing and unbuckled her tether.

An urgent whisper rose to my lips. "Good girl. Sweet girl."

The Watcher sprinted toward us, a dark shadow in his black cloak. He had figured out what I was doing. I swung my legs onto Sky's back and urged her upward with my knees. She spread her powerful wings, drawing us into the air. Barely. It was more of a hover than flight.

I leaned back, pulling on the tether. Sky listened, beating her wings into flight.

Just as we took off, my dress caught me at the waist, threatening to pull me away from Sky. The heavy skirt was caught on something.

The Watcher.

In an outstretched fist, he clutched the edge of my trailing hem. I leaned forward and hugged Sky, pulling at my dress with my body. The Watcher pulled back. I slid downward.

"No!" I choked.

Sky chirped in protest as I hooked my foot around the base of her wing, anchoring myself to her body.

Fabric ripped away from me, torn at the seam. The outer layer of my dress floated through the air like a burnt rose petal. I was free. We soared, leaving the Watcher behind.

I scrambled to find a sturdy perch and leaned my head against Sky's neck. "Thank you."

Flight wasn't so bad in the dark, when I couldn't see the ground. I was more scared of the Watchers now than I was of falling. A cough burned my throat and a cool breeze ran over my back as the besmonn circled the tower. I could have lain like that for a long time, fighting for each breath.

Then, I heard the song again. The voice in the tower.

I nudged Sky upward, toward the window with the light. She moved at my slightest touch, as if she knew I was too sick to properly guide her.

A ledge jutted out from the open window, just large enough for Sky to land on. She touched down, and I slid off of her back. I didn't look down as I clung to a metal rod on the outside of the window frame, my legs shaking.

The voice stopped singing.

Now that the gifted music was gone, my fear of heights reared up with full force. The open window was just wide enough to fit my whole body through.

I lunged forward and tumbled into the tower, landing on a knitted rug. My night-adjusted eyes watered against white light. The tower room was round, furnished with rich wooden desks and a canopied bed. A Regent-sized bed.

Now that the call of the voice was gone, I felt awkward about climbing into someone's bedroom window. Was this where I would be when my lungs stopped working? I could already feel my airways tightening.

"Gifted evening," said a woman's smooth voice.

It was a Cropper greeting, but the speaker was a Regent. She stepped from behind the bed curtains and placed an orb of light onto a desk. I backed against the window and doubled over, coughing, my eyes still on the Regent.

I had never seen her before. Pale hair fell loose in ringlets over her long, delicate neck. She had pure white skin, without a hint of gray, and her eyes were black to the rims.

I knew this voice. She was the singer.

And it was more than the voice. It was her presence, her mind in the room. In the same way I could sense the king, I sensed this Regent. She didn't search my thoughts, but she was there, at the edge of my awareness. Her mind carried the same allure as her melody.

What if she could see my thoughts? She would know about the King's Gift, about how I had stolen it. Worst of all, she would know about Proce's leg. Shame rose to my cheeks and I inched closer to the window.

What if I flew away now, on Sky's back, before the Regent started asking questions? I didn't want to face this elegant lady, not in my broken state. Not with my blood-stained conscience.

She spoke again, her voice like bells. "You fought hard to be here. I hope you're not leaving so soon?"

I tucked a loose curl behind my ear and forced air into my lungs. "I'm sorry to intrude. I heard you singing."

"It's not an intrusion when you're invited." The Regent sat on the edge of the bed and smoothed her silken dress over her knees. "I'm glad you heard my call. Please, come sit. I can see you're unwell." She patted the blanket next to her.

I reached for the window frame to steady myself and glanced out at Sky. She was curled up on the ledge, her feathers ruffled in the breeze. Would I have the strength for another flight? The Regent was right. I had come this far. Why would I leave now?

I crossed the room and collapsed on the end of the bed, trying to look stronger than I felt.

"Why did you call to me?" I asked in a hoarse voice.

"You're the first one to hear me sing in a long time." The Regent smiled. Her angular features suited her face better than the other Regents. She was almost beautiful, in a clipped, peculiar way.

"Your song was nice," I said. "It . . . it made me feel less alone."

"Me too." The Regent leaned toward me. "Will you allow me to heal you? It'll be easier to talk when you feel better."

"Only Croppers can heal," I said.

"Well, I'm a Regent, and I can heal."

It didn't matter what kind of gift she had, she wouldn't be able to heal me. Not completely. Now that the King's Gift was gone, nothing could. How much longer until I would cough blood?

At least if she tried to heal me, I would hear the hum of her gift. Would it be beautiful, like her voice? She was different from the other Regents, warm and musical. I held out my hand to her.

She took it in her milky fingers and the music began. As her gift flowed, she sang. Her voice followed a different melody than I had heard before. It didn't call to me. It blew over me, cooling my lungs from the inside out.

She let go. I took a deep breath, expecting my sickness to stop me.

But it didn't. It was gone.

My eyes went wide and my heart pounded. To make sure I wasn't imagining things, I took another breath. And another, each one a victory. I felt better than I had in days. What was happening? A moment ago, I had been dying. Now, I wasn't sure. And that was impossible. Her gift was impossible.

The sickness was gone. My mind cleared. Had the king lied to me about his gift, creating a false scenario so I would have to rely on him? Maybe anyone could have healed me all along.

No. That couldn't be true.

Von was the strongest healer in her village, and even she couldn't save me from being poisoned. On the night Proce had carried me to the Polaris, she would have healed me if she could have, even if the king told her not to.

I stood from the bed and faced the lady. "How did you do that?"

She folded her hands in her lap. "You're asking the wrong question."

"Then tell me what I'm supposed to ask." I was tired of games. Bowing and obeying and trying to be polite.

"What's your name?" she asked.

"Lady Alora." I hated the name the king chose for me, but it was a Regent name, and I was speaking to a Regent.

She shook her head. "Neither of us like Alora. Let's stick with Meg. Now, ask me what my name is and you'll know how I healed you."

"What's your name?" Would the answer mean anything to me?

The Regent stood and gave a deep bow. "I'm Elia. Queen Elia. It's an honor to meet you face-to-face."

23

The queen flashed a brilliant smile. Perfect teeth, full lips.

The queen.

As soon as she said the words, I knew they were true. She had a Regent voice that could sing like a Cropper. She carried the gifts of both peoples. No one else could have healed me and no one else had a mind like hers, except for the king. She was the only match for him.

But if she was alive, nothing I had learned made sense.

"You're the first human I've ever met," she added. "I felt your color as soon as you arrived in my earth."

I stared at the queen, the wife of Kalmus. Why would she stay hidden in a tower while her husband took a human bride? She would have known about the ceremony. Everyone knew.

And how was the king supposed to call the Queen's Gift to him when it already belonged to Elia? She had watched the whole thing happen from her high window. What had they hoped to gain? I didn't understand.

She had stood by while I was tortured.

With any other Regent, I would have expected that. But I felt like I knew the lady. I knew her voice. She had comforted me in the dark.

"You knew," I said, hurt. "And you let him burn me." And she let me burn Proce. I had been a cog in some machine I didn't understand.

She gave a nod. "I did know."

I shook my head and my crown fell to one side, snagged on a

curl. I ripped it loose, pulling my own hair, and looked down at the frosted jewels. It was a beautiful thing, made for royalty. On my head, it was a joke. My mind whirled, trying to make sense of everything, until my thoughts landed on one thing: something clear and easy and simple.

Anger.

I was angry.

Andrew was never going to be healed. All of my time in the King's House had been for nothing. It was a waste. And she knew.

Suddenly, I couldn't stand to look at the crown.

"I never wanted this. It belongs to you." I tossed it her direction.

The crown sailed toward her, then stopped, abrupt. It hovered in the air for a second and then fell onto the carpet as the queen hummed her gifted song.

She stood at her full Regent height and her eyes glinted an alien black. "There are things you don't understand."

She was right about that. "Then tell me. No more songs and poems and lies. Why did you call me up here?" Fresh tears escaped my eyes.

The queen softened. "I wish you could have come sooner. I tried to reach you, but I've been imprisoned. You of all people know what that's like."

I searched her face, looking for honesty. If what she said was true, Proce and Von needed to know. I had to tell them that their queen was alive. They were down there, terrified. A moment earlier, before I was healed, I had felt the same.

"Imprisoned?" I asked. "They say you're dead."

"I think Kalmus would have killed me, if he could. I undertook the Queen's Ceremony a long time ago. Under the stars, the same as you. I was barely old enough to marry and I loved the king. Looking back, I don't know if he ever felt the same. But Kalmus gave me a portion of his gift that night. It grew into something more, the Queen's Gift. It linked us together. Later, I think he feared that harming me would harm his own gift."

"If he was afraid of harming his own gift, he shouldn't have tried his experiments." A hopeful thought occurred to me. "Do you still have the Queen's Gift? The Croppers . . . they need their sleep."

"I do have the Queen's Gift," she said. "Kalmus almost stole it from me tonight. But I wouldn't let go so easily. However, it's the King's Gift that blesses the sleep."

Shame pierced at me again. What had I done to Proce? What had I done to all the Croppers? I would never be able to face them.

"I'm sure you have a lot of questions." Elia lowered back onto the bed. "Let's sit and talk."

I stayed put. How could she be so calm?

"Don't you understand what happened to the king tonight?" I braced for her answer.

"Yes." She tucked her hands into the draping sleeves of her dress. "I know more than you think."

"Are you listening to my thoughts?"

"You know I'm not."

It was true. I felt her at the edge of my mind, keeping a graceful distance.

"Then you saw?" I asked.

"Yes. What you did was more than many could have managed. You saved a life. You healed your friend."

I saw Proce's leg again in my mind. My stomach burned. She might as well know the truth.

"It was my fault Proce needed saving," I told her. "I fought the ceremony to save myself. That's why the King's Gift exploded like that. Stopping him wasn't brave, it was self-preservation. It accomplished nothing," My voice shook. "And now, the Croppers . . ." And Andrew.

Elia patted the spot beside her, inviting me to sit again. "You can't change the past, Meg, but you can see it more clearly."

Proce and Von were probably still in the garden. Still scared and confused.

"My friends," I blurted. "They should know you're alive. It will be their first good news in a while."

"They're fine for now, I promise," Elia assured. "I can sense them with my gift. This conversation between us is important. I'll help you see what has happened."

"Do I want to see?" I swallowed the lump in my throat. I didn't want to think about what I had done. But it was all I *could* think about.

"Yes." Elia's smile was so warm, so gentle, she could have almost been a Cropper in that moment.

If I wasn't going to die, I needed to make sense of what had happened in the garden. Shouldn't the city have fallen already, without the King's Gift to hold it in place? I needed answers.

I sat on the bed beside Elia. "I stole the King's Gift." I needed to say the words out loud. "All of it. I put everyone in danger."

"I wouldn't call it stealing," Elia said slowly. "More like using. Maybe even freeing. I'm not sure exactly how it works. I haven't known any humans. But I do know one thing: none of us can receive a gift unless it chooses to come to us. It goes where it wants, and it chose you. Of course, it couldn't rest in a human. But it went to your task. It went gladly. You fought hard tonight, and you can't blame yourself for what Kalmus lost."

I wanted to believe her, but the consequences of what I had done were too much to forgive. Unless the consequences weren't what I thought.

"How are the city walls still standing?" I asked. "Isn't the King's Gift gone?"

"That's the right question." Elia took a breath. "I'm going to start at the beginning. You know that I married the king, and I was gifted as queen. You also heard of my death. Every Cropper and Regent heard the news. They didn't know it was a lie."

"Garlian knew something," I said.

"She can't see, and Kalmus blocked me from speaking to her. After years of bringing my food, she may have guessed. But to go against the king . . . that would be more than I could expect her to bear."

"But what does this have to do with the King's Gift?"

"Kalmus was the one who spread the rumor of my death. I should have known what he intended. He had gone astray. That's why he wanted to get rid of me. He hoarded his gift, withholding it from our people. I argued with him. He said it was progress, saving his gift for a new purpose. I said it was greed. He convinced himself that I was an enemy, but truthfully, I believe he began to see his own shame when he looked at me.

"He caught me by surprise one day, and my gift couldn't match his. He snared me in this tower and restricted my voice." Her face tightened and she continued. "I couldn't sing my gift out loud. The Queen's Gift is similar to a Cropper gift, and I needed my voice. He hid the minds of our people away from me. I had no way to communicate, even in thought."

"But you sang to me."

"Only in your mind. He couldn't hide your thoughts from me. You're not our kind, and your mind is free. I couldn't call to you in words and Kalmus knew that. But he never understood music. He never considered that a melody might speak to you."

"What about the secret door I found in the garden?" I asked. "Did you create it?"

"The cities are held together by the King's Gift. And this house is at the center of the cities. In some ways, the King's House is part of the king's mind, bending and shifting with his thoughts. There are sometimes corners of our own minds that we forget about. You found one of those corners for Kalmus: a door, too small for him to remember. He always underestimated small things. Of course, after you found the door, he got rid of it."

"So you're free?" I asked. "Now that Kalmus lost his gift?"

"I am." Elia gave a broad smile. "Because of what you did."

How could she smile? What about the Croppers? "I'm sorry about what the king did to you." I was now at the edge of the bed. "But don't you understand? There's no gift left for the Croppers since there's no king to bless their sleep." And it was my fault.

A part of me wanted her to be angry at me. I deserved it. I wanted her to tell me that what I had done was wrong. Awful.

She didn't.

Instead, she kept her smile and spoke with weighted words. "What if the King's Gift isn't gone? What if it has gone to another Regent?"

"But I used it all."

"Yes. What was given has been taken away."

"You're talking about the Writings?" She sounded like Proce.

The queen sat straight. "Every time Kalmus twisted the purpose of his gift, it broke away from him a little bit more. I sensed it through our bond. By the time you met him, he was a half king, diminished and diluted by his own choices. He would never have recovered from his attempt at the Queen's Ceremony tonight. You called the last of his gift away. It was happy to leave him. This has never happened before, but it was foretold."

Elia sang the Writings to a Cropper melody, her voice rich and smooth.

> What was given is taken away
> Oh peace, return through the new one small
> She will walk upon silver
> Oh sleep, return upon her call.

The memory of pain and gifted light crackled in my mind. "But I took it all. How could it go to someone else when it's all used up?"

"If I burn through my gift, it's lost to me. But it's not lost to the giver of gifts. The King's Gift was not taken away from our people. It was only taken from Kalmus."

I looked at her. "How do you know?" Then, "Who's the next king?"

"We don't have another king. We won't have one for a long time."

I ran a hand through my tangled curls, frustrated. "I don't understand. Can you please just tell me what you're trying to say?"

One corner of Elia's beautiful mouth turned upward. "We don't have a king, because the King's Gift was given to the queen."

24

My hand fell to my lap, exasperated. "But you said you couldn't bless the Croppers' sleep."

The queen's head tilted slightly. "No. I never said that. I told you that only the King's Gift can do it. Not the Queen's Gift. I have both now. How do you think this tower is standing? I'm holding it. I'm holding it all."

My eyes widened. "Both gifts in one," I breathed. "That's what he wanted."

"Yes," Elia said thoughtfully. "He did want it. And I received it. To be honest, I'm not sure why. Maybe so that the next king doesn't get stuck with me as his queen? He should have the right to choose his own wife, and that can't happen until I die. Or maybe the King's Gift is meant for a child, one who isn't ready yet. Or even born yet. I don't know how long I will have the King's Gift, but I intend to use it well. I can feel its purpose. It pulls at me."

"You'll bless the sleep?" I asked, very hopeful now.

"I will. When the time is right. We feel the cold. It's coming soon."

A burden lifted from me, heavier than I knew. I thought of Urma. She would live.

"It doesn't seem cold at all here," I said.

"We feel it on the inside first. Then, one day, it's winter."

"I think it's different in my earth . . . the weather."

"A lot of things will probably be different here than in your earth." Elia's black eyes rested on me. "I hope you can learn to accept them."

Her tone made me uneasy.

"Like what? Everything has been so different already."

"We'll talk about that later."

Later. The future. Something I had let go of. I thought of Andrew. How the injury was making his mind dark. Could I ask the queen for more, when she had already healed me? I had no bargain with her. I had nothing to bargain with. But after everything, I wouldn't give up.

"I have something else to ask you," I said.

"I know. I promise I haven't trespassed into your mind. But, with two gifts, it's hard not to overhear some things. You think loudly. Who is Andrew?"

I put up a half-hearted wall around my mind and swallowed back emotion. "He's what brought me here. He's why I did everything. Except, in the end, I failed him."

"How?" Elia asked.

"The king was supposed to heal him, in exchange for my cooperation with the ceremony. Andrew is dying." My voice faded to a whisper. "He could . . . I don't know how long he has."

"I see. And what would you give me, if I tried to heal him?"

My eyes snapped to hers. It didn't matter what she asked. Anything. I would give anything, if I thought she could do it.

"What would you want?"

"What if . . . you faced Kalmus for me. What if you stole his gift, and set me free, and fought for the Croppers, and healed Proce's leg?" She smiled. It was what I had already done.

"That's it? Nothing else?" There had to be a catch. I knew that kind of healing would take a lot of her gift. Probably more than she would want to give. I stared at her. "Why would you help me?"

"Facing Kalmus was more than I would ask of any of my own people. And you're not one of my people yet, are you? You're human, and you don't feel you belong here. But I want you to belong. I want it very much. How can you settle in, when you can't forget your past? It will eat at you, every day. You'll hate me, eventually, if I have the power, and I don't at least try to heal him."

She wasn't wrong. How did she know me better than I knew myself?

"You'll really do it?" I was afraid to believe her. I wanted it too much.

"I'll try. That's all. I won't give more of my gift than I should."

There was the catch. How would I know how hard she tried? How much gift she would use? But it was all I had.

"Will it take a lot of the gift?" I asked her. "I was never sure if the king was telling the truth, or if he was saving the healing as a bargaining chip."

"Every gift comes with a purpose. The King's Gift, and the Queen's, are meant to help the people, here, now, as needed. Anything outside our earth won't be as easy. The gift doesn't go as far for things like that. As Kalmus discovered when he called gems and started his experiments."

"I don't think he really believed he would lose his gift." I remembered his intensity. "Even at the end."

"I won't hear excuses for him." Elia's eyes darkened. "He knew the consequences."

"He seemed to think it was for the best."

"Maybe he told himself that. But his gift knew it wasn't true. I knew. So did you. After he lost his parents, Kalmus started to believe he was owed something, to make up for the loss. Greatness. But a king's purpose isn't to be great. It's to serve the people."

"But I'm not your people. Andrew isn't your people. You'll use your gift for us?" I didn't want to make her think twice, but I was beginning to wonder if she would really try.

"Are you so sure you're not one of my people?"

I didn't answer.

"You're here," Elia said. "That makes you mine. The boy is different. But I'm so full of light right now"—her eyes glazed for a moment, as if looking inward—"I can spare some gift without disregarding my purpose. And, who knows? Maybe the gift will find purpose in this too. Perhaps. And it will need to be soon, while my power is fresh."

"Now would be good," I pressed. "He doesn't have much time."

"First, answer something. You could have waited years before marrying Kalmus. Engagements are usually long. But you pushed forward, didn't you? To heal a boy you're going to forget. Why?"

"I need him to be okay," I whispered.

"No. You didn't do it for yourself. You're never going to see him again, whether he's healed or not. And your memories will fade even more."

I thought for a moment, then made my move. "I might not remember him, but I would remember the choices I made. I wanted to be someone who does the right thing, even when there's no reward. Even if I never see him." I met her gaze, as if to ask what kind of person she would be. Maybe that would encourage her to try harder, use more of her gift. "It has to be soon."

She smiled. "Are all humans so determined?"

"Probably." I didn't remember most humans.

"For the sake of what you've done for my people, I'll try."

My heart refused to believe it until it was done.

"First we need to locate him," Elia said. "I've never done this across another earth."

"I have."

She held out her hand to me and I took it.

Before picturing Andrew, I decided to look inward, at Elia's gift. Was it really enough? When my mind's eye focused, the light within her blazed white hot, a thousand times brighter than the king's. If he had been a fire, she was the sun. I only looked, I didn't call her gift to me, but something went wrong. It burned my hand. I tried to hold on, but she pushed me away. Elia rose to her feet, breaking the connection.

"What happened?" I cradled my burnt hand, the skin covered in red blisters.

The queen stood over me, her eyes a deeper black. "My gift wasn't yours to look at." She took me by the wrist, her grip hard.

What was she doing?

Her gift hummed, along with her voice, but I felt nothing. She was trying to heal my burn, and it didn't work.

She let go and sank back into her chair. "I can't heal your hand. It's gift-made." She swallowed hard and looked away. "I was angry when you looked inside me. I've spent years in this room, imagining what I would do if I were free to be queen, to help others." Her voice grew faint. "But my first act was to hurt someone."

She was crying. Her face lost its ancient power. She was still young, for a Regent.

I spoke gently. "I shouldn't have done that."

"You shouldn't have."

"I don't think it's going to be easy, carrying two gifts," I said. "But it came to you for a reason."

We sat in silence for a while. Then, Elia straightened, her mask of royalty back in place. "I'll be a good queen." She was promising herself. "There's nothing I won't do for my people, if it's right. And that starts with you. Are you ready to try Andrew's healing?"

"I'm ready." I dug my free hand into my torn dress and removed the note. I unfolded it carefully, unsticking the sweat-dampened edges.

"What is that?"

"Something to help me remember."

I took Elia's hand and closed my eyes, searching for Andrew in my memory. Brown eyes. He had brown eyes.

Elia's gift flowed, and I saw Andrew. The image of his dusky face flickered in rhythm, along with a soft sound.

Thud. Thud. Thud.

It was his heartbeat, weak and distant. But he was alive.

Andrew! I called out to him with my mind.

"He's too far gone." Elia's voice broke through the vision. "There's darkness in his mind. I won't give that much of my gift."

No. I had come too close for this.

I wanted to steal the Queen's Gift, to force it toward Andrew. But I couldn't. I wouldn't. Never again.

A thought hit me. What about my color? I wouldn't call the Queen's Gift to me, but what if I could give a part of myself to her? I remembered seeing my own blazing color through Kalmus's eyes, the way he coveted it. Could it fortify the Queen's Gift now? Could I make her stronger, help her, the way I helped the Regent to make lace, the king to call a stone?

I allowed myself to be drawn to the queen. This was different than anything I had experienced with my color so far. I was offering myself up, giving myself away. It felt wrong, like loss. I didn't care.

Something warm and painful trickled from me. I sent it to Andrew. I poured myself out, becoming hollow. I thought I had sacrificed everything when I left my earth, when I lost my memories. Now, I found there was more to give, part of myself that I couldn't name.

Sweat ran into the creases of my closed eyes.

Thud. Thud. Thud.

Was it my heartbeat, or Andrew's? The vision flickered and I fell forward. Something hit my chin. My ears rang and I saw black.

When I opened my eyes again, Elia knelt beside me and healed my headache with a touch.

"I passed out," I mumbled.

"Only for a moment."

I sat up. "Your gift . . . did I . . . ?"

"No. You didn't take anything. You gave something. Probably too much."

"It didn't work?" My voice shook. I stared at the stone floor and took in a breath. Of course it hadn't worked. And now I had nothing left to try. The Croppers would sleep. I would live. But Andrew . . .

"Do you think so little of yourself?" the queen asked. "The human is healed."

It took a moment for her words to pierce through my defeat. Andrew. Healed.

Andrew.

Healed.

I stopped the emotion that wanted to erupt, a torrent I wasn't prepared to handle. I needed to see him first, for myself.

"Show me." I held out my hand. "Please."

Elia smiled, and once she took my hand, the vision came immediately, bright and clear. I saw amber eyes. Andrew's eyes, open and blinking.

The black spots in his mind were gone and he was awake.

He was healed.

Andrew. Healed.

I gripped the queen's hand, my tether to Andrew. I could have stared at him forever.

Tears slid from my eyes as I thought of everything that had led to this miracle: my terror at the sight of the giants, my own blood coughed onto my dress, the king's cold hand in mine.

Andrew! I called to him.

He focused his eyes beyond me and moved his lips. No sound came out.

I can't hear you like that, I said. *Use your thoughts.*

He stretched his arms into the air, flexing his shoulders. It looked like he had just woken up from a nap, not from a deadly coma. I took in the color in his cheeks and laughed from sheer joy.

He spoke again, his mouth forming the shapes of foreign words. I couldn't hear him. He was speaking to someone else. Someone who was there with him, beyond my vision. He smiled.

Andrew? Andrew.

He didn't respond.

I spoke aloud. "Why can't he hear me? I need to talk to him."

Elia released my hand and I opened my eyes. "Were you able to speak with him before?"

I wiped tears away. "Only with my thoughts, not words. Toward the end, it got easier."

"I think I see." Elia nodded. "You may have been able to speak into his mind when he was dreaming. This has never been done across another earth, but dreams have a way of telling us what we can't accept while we're awake. Your connection is strong. It's how you healed him."

"I didn't heal him. You did."

"The strength didn't come from me." She looked me up and down. "There's something I think you need to see."

Elia stood and beckoned me across the room. I followed in a daze. Andrew was healed, and my goal was accomplished. It had kept me going. Beyond that, there had been nothing for me.

I knew I wanted to live now. Especially since I didn't have to marry the king. But what did life hold for me in the gray earth? What was beyond the healing?

Andrew. Healed.

I felt myself smile as fresh tears clouded my vision. My lips trembled. My face was probably pink.

The queen stopped beside a richly embroidered curtain. She took me by the shoulders and guided me to stand square in front of it.

"Look." She pulled back the curtain to reveal a floor-length mirror.

A foreign reflection stared back at me. My brown eyes and my golden freckles were the same as always, a shock of color in the gray earth. My cheeks were indeed pink from crying, though not patchy as they had been before Urma changed me.

It was my hair that made my breath catch in my chest. My hair was not my own. Instead of brunette tangles, I now possessed a mane of white. It had lost its color.

I had given it away.

I ran my fingertips through the pale strands. They felt the same as always, fine and limp.

"How?"

"There's so much about humans we don't understand," the queen said. "But I think you sacrificed your color. Without it, I doubt the boy would have lived. I wouldn't have spared that much gift for him."

I pulled my eyes from the mirror. "The king tried to do something like this. He took the color from a crystal . . ." I tried not to picture the pool of Halor's blood, spilled onto the auditorium floor.

Elia's mouth tightened. "Some things can't be taken. They have to be given."

I turned back to the mirror. Would my hair always be white? For now, it was a sign that Andrew was awake, and so I decided to love the way it looked. Beneath the appearance, though, it was more than color. A piece of me was gone. I had a feeling I would never get it back. My brunette was traded, displaced by the gray earth.

"Meg." The queen said my name gently. "We have to leave this tower now. I've been with you too long already. My people need me."

I looked at her, curious. "Why didn't you just come to the garden when the king lost his gift? Why did you call me up here? You were free."

"I thought we needed a moment alone together. You deserved that. I didn't expect you to make so much demand on my gift." Her smile returned. "I should've known you'd still have some fight left in you."

Elia waved for me to come with her to the window. "Hopefully you didn't use up all your courage. We're going to see Kalmus."

25

Outside the window, Sky sat on the tower ledge, wings folded, eyes closed.

I had another question. "Why didn't the Watchers follow me up here? They could have gone for a besmonn."

Elia laughed. "They tried. But the King's House can be surprisingly difficult to navigate."

I had been lost in the halls myself. The Watchers had no hope of finding their way up here if the queen didn't want them to.

When Elia stepped through the window, Sky stretched and let out a chirp.

"There are stairs," the queen said. "But this will be faster for us to get down. And more fun."

"There's no way we can both ride her at the same time." I clutched the window frame and eyed Elia's height, sizing her next to Sky.

"She won't be able to carry us for long, but we'll make it onto the ground safely. Your besmonn is a true beauty, and strong too."

Before I could protest any further, the queen swung her legs onto Sky's back. The movement was practiced, as if she had ridden a thousand times before. Elia held out a hand to me, an invitation to climb out the window.

An invitation to the garden below.

Not long ago, I had wanted nothing but an escape from the

garden. But that had been when I was dying. Now, I couldn't hide in the tower forever. There were things I needed to face.

Elia regarded me. "What are you waiting for?"

"I don't know how it will be down there . . . now that everything's changed."

"It's changed for the better," Elia pointed out.

"In some ways," I agreed and took a breath. "And now I have to change with it."

I took Elia's hand and let her pull me onto Sky. The queen whistled and kicked her heels, then we tumbled into the air.

Sky beat her wings as we descended. The ground rose to meet us, faster than it should have. Sky spread her wings, slowing the fall, but it wasn't enough.

"We're going to crash!" I yelled.

The queen laughed. "That's the fun part."

What if Sky's beak and talons cut into me, uncontrolled in the tumble? It would be better to hit the ground alone, in my own broken pile, than to take my chances on Sky's back. When the silver sheen of the garden lawn grew close, I jumped, pushing away from the besmonn with all my strength.

My knees buckled when I hit the ground and I rolled over prickly bushes. A few yards away, Sky landed next to the stream, her wings flailing. After she caught her balance, she regained her composure and ruffled her feathers, as if the landing had been routine. The queen dismounted, the hem of her robes flowing behind her.

"See?" she asked. "Fun."

I stood, brushing dirt and grass from my blistered palm. "I lightened the load for you. You're welcome."

She only laughed again. "The landing would have been safe for both of us. I'm glad you didn't hurt yourself by jumping. When things are settled, you need to practice flying. You're the perfect size for it."

I never wanted to fly again, but I didn't tell Elia that. My attention was drawn elsewhere.

In the moonlight, on the other side of the stream, sat Proce, his back against the courtyard wall, his one remaining leg stretched out in front of him. He watched us, his shoulders straight, I couldn't make out his expression from this distance.

My stomach knotted. I wanted to run to him, and at the same time, I wanted to run from him and never see him again.

Elia led the way. We crossed the footbridge over the stream until we stood in front of Proce. I lingered behind, unable to look directly at him. A black cloak lay on the grass, covering a shape that had once been his leg.

I finally dared a glance at Proce. He watched Elia, a question in his eyes.

Elia stepped forward and clasped his hands in the Cropper way. "You're Proce? Son of Urma?"

"I am." Proce bowed his head, lower than ever. Then, he looked up to search her face.

"I remember you." The queen smiled. "We met in the Polaris library, during the celebration for my marriage. You're the most word-gifted Cropper I've ever known."

Recognition lit his expression. "You recited the Twelfth Act of the Seven Cities that day."

Elia nodded, then began to sing.

"Gifted stones too high to stand—"

Proce joined the song, his voice steady.

"Cities held by a king's hand.
Roads follow where rivers wind.
Gates open to every kind."

Their voices blended into a harmony, then faded to silence.

"You must have questions," the queen said. "And I owe you answers. I owe you more than that."

Proce furrowed his brow. "I . . . I should ask how you are still alive . . . but I am afraid I will not like your answer. Our king was not who we thought he was. When the gift left Kalmus, I was afraid. But, I sense its protection now. How?"

"I carry it."

"What was given was taken away . . ." Proce clenched his jaw. "Even when Meg hinted at the king's folly, I doubted her. I have been a coward."

"No." Elia laid a hand on Proce's shoulder. With Proce sitting, they were almost the same height. "I know what you've done. You entered a thin place, unsure if you'd be able to return. You challenged the ceremony to protect Meg. It's more than most would be capable of."

Proce lowered his head. "I was only able to challenge the king because his gift had weakened. Still, I failed. But you are the king now, and the queen. I feel it. Is this possible?"

"I can bless the sleep. I know that's what you're thinking of. But I can't restore your leg. It was taken by a poisoned gift." Her hands tensed and flexed as she spoke, as if remembering what it felt like to harm someone with her own gift.

"Yes," said Proce. "I suspected."

"I'll give you anything else you ask for." Elia's voice grew round and full. "You'll be honored among Croppers and Regents for generations. My word is a binding agreement." Her voice softened. "But for now, there are other things to consider. You need to rest, and I need to see Kalmus."

"The Watchers took the kin—I mean, Kalmus—to his auditorium. They are not sure what to do with him."

"Are other Croppers coming to help you?"

"Yes," Proce said. "Von went to get Erno. He is in the city for the celebration. He can be an obstinate Cropper, but he is from our home village, and he is very gifted. They will be here soon."

Elia turned around and rested her eyes on me. I twisted my fingers together, wishing to stay invisible.

"Meg, I've decided it's best if I see Kalmus alone, for now. I need the Watchers to witness my gifting, and to hear the truth of the Queen's Ceremony tonight. Besmonn riders will take the news to the other cities. I fear what kinds of stories may have already spread through the Polaris. In my absence, don't trust anyone, except for Proce and Von." Elia turned to Proce. "Can your family see to Meg's needs tonight?"

"We would be honored to do so."

The queen bowed her head to him. "Thank you. It is a gifted night."

"It is a gifted night."

Elia spun toward the door and marched away, the train of her dress billowing behind her.

"Wait!" I stopped her. "Will I see you again?"

She looked at me over her shoulder, a twinkle in her eye. "You won't be able to get out of it." Then she left through the courtyard door.

Sky was on the other side of the garden, sipping nectar from blossoms. Except for the besmonn, Proce and I were alone. I stood across from him, my eyes on the grass, my hands hidden in the folds of my skirt. A heavy weight sat in my stomach. What could I say to him? Maybe it would be better if I left.

"Proce . . ." His name felt wrong in my mouth. "I know the queen asked you to watch me, but you don't have to. I'll go—"

"You will not go. I gave my word."

I glanced at him out of the corner of my eye. He sat at his full height, still two heads taller than me.

"I would never break my word," he said. "Not intentionally."

His words stoked my guilt. He was talking about me.

"You're right." My voice was hoarse with emotion, my throat tight. "I broke my word. I promised to help you . . . instead . . . Proce, I'm so sorry."

He cocked his head to one side. "For my injury? Yes, I am grieving. But, you did help. Because of tonight, the Croppers will have our sleep. It was I who broke my word to you. Andrew was not healed." There was regret in his voice. "I trusted the king. And now, I fear Andrew does not have enough time."

"You still care about that? After everything?" I was louder

than I meant to be. His worry for Andrew made it worse. Made my shame burn. He deserved the brutal truth. Tears rolled from my eyes as I spoke. "Proce . . . your leg. I knew the King's Gift might burn you or Von, but I did it anyway. I was the one who pushed the light away from me, during the ceremony. I saved myself."

We were both silent for a while, reading each other's faces, mine wet with misery, his unnaturally still, guarded.

Proce spoke first. "We have both stolen something from the other. Something we would give back, if we could. How can we face each other, then?"

He had stolen my earth from me. But while I was alive, there was still a chance to go home. He would never have his leg. He was a Cropper, a farmer, meant to lope across fields. That was gone.

"You're right," I said. Fresh tears spilled. "I would give it back." I had already tried. Already failed.

"Give me something else, then. Something in your power." I paused. I had nothing for him. "What would that be?"

"Give me your forgiveness." Proce reached up with his long fingers and tilted my face to look at him. "I offer you mine."

I swallowed. "How can you?"

Proce let his hand fall away. "Because I have done wrong in my days too. And because I need to believe that broken things can be turned into something new. Broken friendships, and broken bodies. Never the same, but mended. And because I think I would have given my leg to keep you alive, if I had been given the choice."

This was too much from Proce, too good, and it made me cry harder.

Would I have willingly left my earth in order to save the Croppers? Not back then. Now, if the Croppers ended, a part of me would end too. Their husky songs, their fields, their healing gifts. They needed to go on.

My tears had to slow before I could speak. "The queen healed Andrew. Without you and Von, he would have died. You were right to bring me here. There's nothing to forgive. And there's nothing I can do to repay you."

Proce closed his eyes and took a long breath. The lines in his face smoothed. "Thank you." He opened his eyes. "The boy is awake?"

I ran my hand over my white hair. "He is. I was able to help Elia with his healing by giving up some of my color."

Proce nodded. "I noticed the change in your hair, but I thought it was a delayed effect from the ceremony, so I did not mention it. Von would be proud of my politeness. We must write these happenings down in the King's Library. Humans are still a mystery. I would like to learn more about you."

I laughed and wiped my running nose. "I'd teach you, but I don't understand it either."

"Then we will learn together."

When Von and Erno arrived, Proce took charge of filling them in about the queen. He didn't leave out a single detail.

At the end of his story, Von burst into tears and clasped my hand, too tightly. She tried to say something, but I couldn't understand through her sniffles. But she was smiling. They were happy tears.

Erno listened with a solemn expression, then spoke. "Many will need to see the king and queen for themselves."

"Kalmus is no longer the king," Proce reminded him.

"We will speak of this later," Erno said. "Tonight, we must attend to your leg."

Von and I stayed with Proce while Erno went to a tree across the stream. He placed his hands on the trunk and sang a baritone hum.

"Erno is exceedingly gifted with plants and water," Von reminded me.

As we watched, a new tree branch formed, growing from beneath Erno's hands. It grew long and straight, with a flat stub at

its end. After it had reached a certain length, the branch fell from
the tree and landed in the grass. When Erno picked the branch up,
I recognized what it was.

The smooth wood had grown in the perfect form of a Cropper
leg, with a cup at the top to fit over Proce's healed wound. Erno
carried the gift to Proce.

"Does your injury still hurt?" Erno asked.

Proce dared a glance at his hip joint, then looked away quickly.
"It does. But not in the place where it was burned. My missing leg
pains me. I know it is only in my mind."

Von laid a hand on him. "My gift may be able to ease the pain."

Proce shook his head. "I think only time will help."

Erno knelt and placed the wooden leg at Proce's hip, padding
the connection with a piece of cloth. He hummed a gifted song, and
the cup shrank over the joint. The leg extended from Proce's body
as if it belonged to him.

"It will be enough for tonight," Erno said. "Later, the Regents
will build a better one that moves as it should."

The giants helped Proce to stand. He shifted his weight, testing
his balance. He took a clumsy step forward and then another, and
another.

"This will do."

As we left the garden, Proce's empty bag fell from his shoulders.
I picked it up and slung it over my back. It hung all the way to my
feet, and I struggled to carry it. Von moved to take the oversized
load from me, but I stopped her.

"No. I need to do this." I would have carried Proce himself, if
possible.

We walked through halls I had never seen, toward the Cropper
rooms. Here, the ceilings vaulted higher and the doors were taller.
The usual glass walls of the King's House grew rough, like the
Croppers' stone. Von led us to a wooden door and turned a key in
its knob.

Beyond the door, a fireplace sat in the corner of a large room.

Windows peeped out onto a moonlit river and white orbs of light glowed among thatched rafters.

"It looks just like a Cropper's cottage in here," I said.

Proce eased into a chair. "They got some things right. But there are never enough cushions, and it always smells like Regents."

"I don't smell anything."

"That is because you are a human," Proce said. "It is the only thing about you that is not impressive. Well, also you are slow."

I sat on a silken cushion. "I'm pretty sure the Watchers aren't impressed with me, after the ceremony."

Von joined me on the floor. "Soon, everyone will know that what you did tonight was right."

Erno snorted from his corner of the room. "We will see . . ."

"Do you doubt our word?" Proce asked.

Erno leaned against a wall. "I doubt what I do not see with my own eyes."

"Then there is much to doubt."

Erno tensed and took a step toward Proce.

"We need to sleep." Von stood. "All of us. It is nearly morning now. Meg has been through an ordeal, and she is young."

"The human is not a child," Erno said. "No matter how much you wish for one."

Von took a deep breath, then turned her back on him. "Come, Meg. We will sleep in here."

I followed her into an unlit room and stretched out on the nearest pillow.

Von placed a blanket over me and lay down nearby. "The night is a gift, Meg."

I smiled in the dark. "Goodnight, Von."

For the first time in a long time, I wasn't tired, I wasn't sick, and I wasn't scared. I lay beside my giant, happy to be her prisoner.

26

While Von slept, I let my mind go over everything that had happened. Andrew was healed. I closed my eyes and relished that truth. He was healed, I was alive. But what kind of a life would it be in the gray earth? What kind of a life would Andrew have, knowing I had disappeared into the forest? He would eventually think I was dead, if I never returned. When I never returned.

But I couldn't think like that. I had seen more miracles than I deserved. I had made my bargain.

Early morning arrived and I finally slept, but not for long. Something wasn't right. When I opened my eyes, Von was gone, her cushions left untidy. The door to the outer room was cracked open.

A noise had disturbed my sleep. Erno stood outside the open bedroom door, whispering to a Cropper I had never seen before. Their voices were tense.

I threw off my blankets and stood. "Where's Von? And Proce?"

Both giants turned their heads to me. The look on their faces made me back away. They stepped inside of the bedroom and closed the door behind them.

Erno's companion was a weathered Cropper with an uneven jawline and heavy brows. He spoke first, in a grinding voice.

"We will ask the questions. You will answer them."

I held my ground, though I was tempted to run to the window.

When I had first met Proce and Von, they were terrifying to me. But they had never been threatening. These giants were different.

"You are awake." Erno looked down his nose at me. "Good. I must tell you, we are not fooled by your false claims about the queen. You may have charmed Proce, but I will not be taken so easily."

The hostility in Erno's voice shook me. "I . . . Proce saw the queen last night. He doesn't lie."

The weathered Cropper spoke. "If the girl will not tell the truth on her own, we might shake it out of her."

He lunged forward and tried to take hold of my arm.

Before he could tighten his grip, I darted under the Cropper's legs and scrambled toward the door, but Erno was there to block my way. I kicked him in the shin as hard as I could. He barely seemed to notice. Then, there was a roar from outside the door.

"Enough!"

It was a voice I knew well.

The Croppers turned and Erno pressed his hand against the door, blocking it from opening.

After a moment of stillness, the door flew wide open, pushing Erno aside.

The queen entered, clothed in black silk and bright green ribbons, her dark eyes narrowed, her mouth stern.

The Croppers stared, then shot glances at each other.

"Are you well, Meg?" she asked.

I nodded.

Elia faced the Croppers. She was half their size, but her presence filled the whole room.

"Erno, son of Saun, is this what you needed to see?" She threw out her arms and spun once, putting herself on display.

Erno bowed his head low, saying nothing.

"You can sense that I carry the King's Gift," Elia said. "Do you wish to interrogate this child further?"

"We did not know," Erno began. "We thought—"

"You're right," Elia interrupted. "You didn't know. But now

you do, beyond all doubt. Return to your village and tell the other Croppers what you've seen. Hopefully they'll listen better to you than you did to Proce."

The queen looked at the other Cropper. "Deg, son of Usa. Leave my city. If I see you again before I come to bless the sleep, you'll regret it."

The giants bowed again and left without another word. Elia kept her eyes on them as they lumbered away from the Cropper rooms.

When the outer door closed, we were alone.

"Thank you." I inclined my head and brought it back up. "Where are Proce and Von?"

"I looked into Erno's mind," Elia said. "He woke them early and told them they were summoned to the garden by the king's Watchers. He lied."

"How did you know to come help me?"

"I didn't," the queen admitted. "I was already coming to you. When I arrived, I sensed Erno's darkness. I waited to see what they would do. When Deg touched you, I knew their character. Proce and Von were too trusting. I must speak to them about that."

"We should go get them." I reached for the door handle.

"They can wait in the garden while we continue to talk for a moment," Elia said. "You should know, most of the danger has passed for you now. I've met with all the Watchers and I guaranteed their loyalty, but there's still confusion outside the Polaris. Erno isn't alone in his doubt. I've sent letters, gifted by my own hand. I'll eventually go on a tour to see the Croppers in person. Some of them don't accept change easily."

"What about the king?" I asked. "I mean, Kalmus? I guess there's not a king." I wasn't afraid to say his name anymore.

The queen sat on a cushion. "You're right. We have no king. I hope that will change in the coming years. I can carry both gifts, but this isn't how things were originally meant to be."

"Is Kalmus . . . is he still alive? They said he was taken to the Auditorium, but I wasn't sure what that meant." A part of me hedged at knowing the answer.

"Yes. Though he is wounded. And he's drained of all power. To him, that was his life, and now it's gone."

I didn't know how to feel. I was relieved that I wasn't a killer, but still the queen was right. In a way, I had stolen Kalmus's life.

"There's something else." Elia eyed me curiously. "His wound, where you stabbed him. Did you use a glass knife?"

"Yes." I tried not to remember the king's sticky blood trickling onto my hand as I punctured his flesh.

"If you had used anything else, he would be healed now," Elia said. "But that knife is an unusual object. We found it in the garden. It's old. Older than we can remember. And someone poured their gift into it, a long time ago. The wound is gift-made. I can't heal it."

"Is he going to be okay?" My stomach still felt queasy that I had stabbed someone.

"His body will probably heal on its own, and I can keep the infection away. My Watchers will get rid of the knife. Weapons aren't allowed in my cities. Especially gifted weapons."

"But it's not a weapon," I told her. "Or, it wasn't meant to be. I found it in my library. I think it's a bookmark."

Elia's eyebrows rose. "I'll look into it further, then. There may be another purpose for your weapon."

I hoped Kalmus would heal soon. He didn't need any more lingering reminders of what I had done to him.

"What did he say to you?" I asked. "When you saw him?"

"He conceded my queenship. Then he tried to convince me that you would still want to marry him." Elia's face was expressionless. "I think he was hoping to steal your marriage gift. At least that would be something for him."

My stomach knotted. "He's crazy."

"So you don't want to marry him?" Elia's eyes were shadowed.

"You know I don't."

"I wouldn't have allowed it," she confessed. "Either way. But I'll give you the chance to see him again, if you choose. There's a fine line between love and hate. Both are powerful emotions that might require closure."

"No."

"He can't hurt you now." Elia's voice was gentle.

"It's not that I'm scared," I said. "Well . . . maybe I am. But it's more than that. I don't want him to matter to me. Not in any way, good or bad. Right now . . . he left an impression in my mind. If I never see him again, if I don't need closure, that's a first step."

"It may not be as easy as you hope, to forget some things."

"I know you loved him once. I'm sorry."

"I did love him," Elia said. "And I hoped he would love me. But now I see that he isn't able to love. He can only want."

"So what's going to happen to him?" I had never heard of a Regent prison, but I assumed one existed.

"I don't know for sure," she said. "I imagine his pride will keep him away from the people. He might go to the desert, or seek the spirits in the mountains. It's up to him."

"What?" My heart beat faster. "You're letting him go? He killed Halor. He tried to kill me. He's a criminal!"

"He is." Elia agreed with a slow nod. "Things are different for us than they are for humans. You have unimaginable numbers of people. There are so few Regents, we need each one. Someday, Kalmus's mind could be mended. I'll never speak to him again, but he could start over in another city."

"It's not safe," I insisted. "He's not safe."

"You don't have to worry," the queen said. "I'll watch over him. And you. You're part of my house now."

It was the same thing Kalmus had promised. Safety. Belonging. Would Elia, despite her kindness, also want something in return? She was still a Regent, despite her Cropper gifts.

"What next?" I asked and immediately began to prepare for her answer. "With two gifts, maybe you could open a thin place—"

"No," Elia said, an edge in her voice. "I won't risk that kind of an experiment. You know why. You've seen the consequences. A burnt, dying gift. And we are not likely to find another natural thin place in your lifetime."

"But if we did find one," I persisted. "You would try to send me back?"

The queen avoided my question. "Do you realize you're one of the most valuable things in my kingdom right now? Kalmus was wrong to try the ceremony. The Queen's Gift was meant for a Regent. But your other potential still remains."

"What potential?" I didn't like the direction this was going.

"Only eleven human women have ever entered our earth," she said. "They wandered into thin places, too deep to return to their home. We rescued them."

"But you never send anything to my earth?"

"Never. Proce and Von came the closest. When we find a thin place, we want to extract color. Why would we want to send something through? A human is precious. A treasure. Each has blessed the Regents for generations after. If you marry a Regent, you could have children. A lot of children. Every new life protects our future, and every drop of color in our bloodline strengthens us. As queen, I can't ignore that. I will do what is right for my people."

Heat flooded my cheeks. The queen was talking about me as if I were an animal, meant for breeding. She was serious. She didn't want me for herself, but she wanted my future. Sweat formed on my face and I fought the urge to storm out of the room. Where would I go?

It was the same as before with Kalmus. The game hadn't changed.

Except I was different. No longer desperate, but still a bargainer.

My nails dug into my blistered palms. "You can't make me get married."

The queen narrowed her eyes. "There are good Regents in my cities. Kind Regents. You'll grow to love one of them."

I wouldn't. I knew I wouldn't. But what if the queen thought I might? I made myself relax my shaking hands, trying to look calm.

"Maybe I could get married . . . someday," I said. "But only if you'll make a promise to me now."

Elia's mind scratched toward mine, as if she were tempted to read my thoughts. I put up my guard for the second time with her.

"What do you want me to promise?"

"It could be a long time before I get married. If we find a thin place before then, would you help me to go home?"

"You don't know what you're asking us to give up," Elia said. "Your children would replace the lives of those who were lost to the experiments."

There had been more than just Halor?

"You said the chance of finding a thin place is slim. So it's a pretty low-risk promise for you. If you agree to it, I could be open to marriage. If you don't promise . . . how far are you willing to go to force me?"

The queen's lips went tight. "Your life is short. You'll need to marry within five years, if you're going to have children. Your body will age."

"In ten years, I'll still be young."

"Five." The queen's eyes hardened.

In five years, I would be twenty-two. I couldn't wrap my mind around what the queen was asking of me. Did I want to be a wife and a mother? Let alone the wife and the mother of people who weren't humans?

But five years was more time than I'd had before, when I was promised to Kalmus. A lot could happen in that time.

"In five years," I said. "I'll consider marrying a Regent. Only if I'm in love." I could barely say the word love. "And only if you promise to send me home, if it becomes possible," I amended.

"I want you to be happy here," Elia said. "So I'll agree to your terms. I promise." The queen bowed her head to me. "My word is a binding agreement."

Over the next weeks and months, life in the Queen's House settled into routine. I moved back into the human rooms, though I still spent every mealtime and evening with Proce and Von in the Cropper suites. My door stayed unlocked at all times, and I wandered the streets of Polaris almost every night, just because I could. Elia insisted that I stay inside the city walls, unless accompanied by my giants or a guard of Watchers. Doubts of the queen's gifting still lingered in distant cities, and some creatures feared the human who had wounded their king.

"Fear causes us to do things we normally wouldn't do," Elia told me.

Sometimes, I saw Larlia in the halls. We never spoke again. It was different with Garlian.

She came to Elia's rooms one day when I was there for my healing.

"Forgive me." Tears streamed from Garlian's pale eyes as she addressed the queen. "I didn't know. I didn't know." She bowed low enough to bend in half.

Elia rose from her plush chair and stood over Garlian. "You didn't want to know."

Garlian sobbed harder.

"But I will do more than forgive you." Elia placed a hand on Garlian's back. A lovely hum filled the room.

The elderly Regent made a garbled noise and straightened. Her eyes were wide, roving. She blinked, then stared, then blinked again. "But the king said . . . he always said . . ."

"Kalmus told many lies," Elia said. "The truth is, he could have healed your sight at any time. We were both trapped by him."

That was the last time I saw Garlian before she returned to her city to be with her children.

Often, I joined Von on visits to her village. She was their most gifted healer, and they invited her home frequently to fix sore throats and jammed thumbs. Sometimes they sent messages with the besmonn riders, who flew in and out of the Polaris keep every day.

The first time I went with her, Von received word of a crushed arm. A stone had fallen on a Cropper named Gad. She packed to leave the Polaris.

"Will you come?" Von asked.

"I'll slow you down."

"It is not that urgent, and your color extends my ability. I might be able to do more with you there."

"What about Erno?" I asked. "What if the others—"

"My people are not stupid. For the most part, at least. They listen more to Urma than to Erno. Trust me, you will be welcomed as before."

Von was right.

The healing trips became our tradition. My color was a good excuse, but I would have gone with Von anyway, just to be with her. She never apologized for stealing me, or for pushing me toward marriage, but I forgave her anyway. Von had been afraid, and that was something I could understand.

I loved the comfortable silence between us as we traveled the gifted road to the Croppers, surrounded by silver fields and groves of fruit trees. Once the healing was done, we would stay up late into the night, gathered around white fire with the other Croppers. Urma and Aggi were always there, though Erno stayed away.

The Croppers insisted that I sing with them. After my first few trips, I lost my shyness, joining in with high harmonies that only a human could sing. The music was rich, all voices blended into one sound, more whole than the queen's song.

With all that beauty, I should have known Von would want to leave the Polaris.

On the night she told me, I cried.

We were in the Cropper rooms at the Queen's House. Proce hadn't joined us for dinner.

"He is too busy with his duties as a library keeper to eat with us." Von laid bowls of grain and fresh herbs on the table.

"Well, you know, he is the very first Cropper to ever hold the position." I did my best to imitate Proce's voice, saying it in the same way he would have.

Von laughed. "Yes, he keeps reminding me. I am still surprised the queen allowed it. He is gifted enough, but it is not natural to have a Cropper live in the King's House."

"The other keepers don't seem to mind." I poured an oversized bowl of tea for Von and a small one for myself. "He's memorized all the books they wrote, word for word. I think they're flattered. Besides, there are other Croppers in the King's House. You live here."

Von's expression grew serious. "Do you remember Gad?"

"Of course. He was our first healing trip together."

Von sat in her chair, her slim ankles tucked neatly to one side. "His brother owns the fields near the city of Perennial." She paused. "And soon, I will be his wife."

There was an immediate lump in my throat. What was she saying? Von, a wife? It was the last thing I wanted to be right now. But for her . . . I thought of the cradle in her cottage, empty for too many years. I had so many questions, but I asked the one that weighed heaviest.

"When?"

"It has been intended since I was young. I feared he had changed his mind when I left my earth for all those years." A funny smile curved her lips. "But he waited for me. I will need to make preparations in his village before the marriage. I am leaving soon."

Von had received plenty of letters during our time at the King's House, but I had assumed they were from relatives or friends— thank-you notes for healings, not love letters.

I forced a smile and blinked away the tears that were welling. "What will Proce do without you?"

What would I do? I couldn't imagine the Polaris without Von.

"He will stay here with you. Meg, do not cry. Be happy for me. I have waited a long time. Longer than I should have. The cold will be here soon. We trust the queen . . . but after the last time, when Croppers were lost, we will always fear the cold. I want to marry before then. We will go into the cold together."

I thought of everything Von had faced: the crossing, the years in the meadow, the King's Garden, where Von had watched her brother lose his leg. It was too much for someone as gentle as Von, someone built for singing and mending and caring. And now this was her chance for all she had dreamed of. She was leaving me. But wouldn't I have done the same thing, to be with Andrew?

I laughed through my tears. "I am happy for you. More than you can know." My voice trailed to a whisper and my smile faded. "Von . . . can't I go with you?"

"You know you cannot." Von's eyes were gentle. "Though I would take you if I could."

She was right. I needed the queen to heal me almost every day. Even two nights away from Elia in the village left me breathless.

"I will come to visit as often as I can," Von said. "But I cannot stay in the Polaris forever. I need to be with my own kind."

I would never be with my own kind again. But Von deserved to be. It's why I had fought against Kalmus. Not only for my life, but for the Croppers. To be together, and love each other, and sing, and marry, and sleep, and live.

"It's so soon . . ." I already knew what I was about to say was wrong, but I couldn't stop myself. "You'll live so much longer than me. Would another year make a difference?"

Von's face fell. I was hurting her. It wasn't just another year. It would be a long sleep, more separation from someone she loved.

I shook my head. "I'm sorry, I didn't mean that. You shouldn't have to wait until after the cold." I tried to cheer my tone. "And, who knows? You might already have a baby in a year."

Von smiled. "It does not happen that fast for us."

"You'd better get started then." I winked, a very un-Cropper gesture.

"The queen also thinks that now is the best time. I am going at her request, and with her blessing."

My stomach sank. Of all Cropper affairs, why would Elia comment on this? Elia and Von weren't close. Did she want the Cropper away from the Polaris? Maybe the queen and I needed to have a conversation.

The next day, I walked with Von all the way to her village, accompanied by Watchers to escort me back to the Polaris. Von would have to walk another four days before she reached Gad. It would be even longer for my human-sized legs. How fast would Sky be able to fly to the city of Perennial? Probably not fast enough for me to go there without the queen.

Von bent down and clasped my hands in farewell.

I reached up and wrapped my arms around her neck. "This is how humans say goodbye."

When the hug ended, I saw tears in her eyes. They mirrored my own.

"Bring Gad to meet me," I said.

"If all goes well, we will bear a child within your lifetime. Because of you. Meg, thank you . . . for everything."

I wanted to say nothing. To believe that Von knew my heart and that tears between us were enough. But during my time in the gray earth, I had found my voice. This was my chance to use it, even when it was hard. Especially when it was hard.

"I love you." I squeezed Von's hand as tight as I could. "I didn't at first, even when you loved me. But now . . . there are places in my heart I never knew existed. You're there. And Proce. And you always will be."

Von gave a deep nod, almost a bow, and her cheeks turned a deep gray. A Cropper blush. "If I have a daughter, I will name her Meg."

I laughed. "Kalmus said Meg sounds like a Cropper name. I took that as a compliment."

"It is a compliment." She hesitated. "Meg, the life I imagined for you here . . . I thought you would be happy, but now I am not so sure. You are not at ease among the Regents. I am grateful you crossed earths, even if you are not. But I wish . . . I wish I could put you back."

"I don't regret crossing. I don't regret meeting you. Healing is more than your gift. It's who you are. You deserve to go home."

"So do you." Von gave a sad smile.

With a last hug, we parted ways.

I walked back to the Polaris in silence, the Watchers trailing behind. What would the gray earth be like without Von? Even Proce would be gone soon. The Croppers would sleep for years. They never knew how long the cold would stay. It could be a decade. Maybe many decades.

Some Regents wondered if the cold made the Croppers sleep, or if their sleep helped to make the earth cold. I suspected the second theory. Croppers were warmth. They said it was a mild winter, when they stayed awake and suffered. After this sleep, when Von finally awoke, I might be old. Even dead. She would still be young enough to have a child. Time was nothing to them.

I could live among the Regents. I wasn't afraid. The gray earth's poison hadn't beat me yet. But it was still a struggle. I could feel the air, battling to take my breath, always reminding me I didn't belong. Von had a journey ahead of her. Did I?

I had found a new home among the Croppers, but my old home still loomed in my memory. It was the place my mother was buried, the place where Andrew still lived. I hadn't forgotten that I was human. I had a people and a past of my own. Would there ever be a way back?

After the Watchers escorted me to my rooms, I went straight to the library to see Proce.

The Queen's Library was a thousand times larger than the one in my rooms. It had domed ceilings, high windows, and bookshelves too tall for even a Cropper. At the center of the library stood a massive tabletop, carved with a topographic map of the Seven Cities.

There were more books than any human could read in a lifetime. Maybe more than a Regent or a Cropper could even read. Proce took that as a personal challenge. He was determined to memorize the full catalogue.

Afternoon sunshine filtered through the windows onto the table where Proce sat examining a stack of papers.

"You didn't come to say goodbye to Von," I accused.

Proce didn't look up from his work. "It is not goodbye. I will see her soon, at her wedding."

The queen had already made it clear that I wouldn't be attending. She was too busy to go with me, and I couldn't go without her healing.

"Now that Von is away, I'll be in the library more." I climbed onto a Regent chair.

I could read the Regent script well now, though it still took concentration, and it hurt my eyes. I read every day. The illustrations in the books were incredible, made with metallic inks and precise brush strokes. Regents liked to paint their cities—the buildings, the streets, the people. One book had a map of all the cities. Perennial, the city near Von's new village, was built on a foundation shaped like a sunflower. I could lose myself in those illustrations. But that wasn't the only reason I read.

I was searching for something. A way home.

"Have you found anything new for me to look at?" I asked.

Proce knew what I meant. "I have already shown you the full history of thin places," he said. "Do you want to read the biographies of the human mothers again? If I find anything else on the subject of your earth, you will be the first to know."

"I know. Thank you."

Proce didn't believe I would ever be able to go home. He didn't agree with my search, but he couldn't say no to my thirst for knowledge. It was a drive he understood.

"For now, you can help me with my composition," Proce said.

"Go ahead."

The queen had agreed to let Proce add a book of his own to the library. He was writing an in-depth study of his experience crossing between earths. Proce always said he wanted my help with the composition, but that wasn't true. The thing he really wanted was an audience, someone to listen to him.

I made myself comfortable in the oversized chair while Proce read his descriptions of human soil. He kept calling it red, or yellow, which were apparently his words for brown. Color language was not as precise in the gray earth. They only knew the basics.

After an hour, I needed a break.

Proce took a breath in the middle of a sentence. I took the opportunity to change the subject. Something had been weighing on my mind, and Proce was the person to ask.

I cleared my throat, obviously trying to interrupt.

Proce looked up. "Yes?"

"The gifts are supposed to be good, right? Always given for a good purpose?"

"Yes." Proce's eyes drifted back to the page, ready to keep reading.

I kept talking, before he could speak. "And you said the gifts and the Writings come from an unseen giver? An unnamed power?"

"Right."

"So if the giver of the Writings knows the future, enough to give a prophecy, why would it still give Kalmus the King's Gift? He didn't use it for good. The giver would have known Kalmus was a bad king."

Proce set down his pen and leaned back in his seat, resigned to conversation. "Who said Kalmus did not do good things with the King's Gift, along with the bad things? He was given a choice for both. In the end, he chose more wrong than right, and he lost the gift."

"But people died. Others suffered. If the giver already knew . . ."

My eyes darted to Proce's leg. The Regents had made him a new prosthetic with hinges and straps.

"Was your human not healed?" Proce asked. "Andrew may have died if you had not faced the king. The giver of gifts was alive long before we were born, and he will remain when we are gone. He does not owe us anything. But still, good came from the wrong choices Kalmus made. Who knows what good may come from our other losses?"

Proce laid his palm against his thigh where he had been burned.

I gave him a soft smile. "Can we check on Andrew before bedtime?"

"Of course."

"I'll bring you dinner," I said. "I assume you want to eat in the library."

Proce had helped me to look in on Andrew every night. I suspected he enjoyed the ritual almost as much as I did. It was Proce's chance to see into the human earth. When awake, Andrew was unaware of my presence. He went about his day. Brushing his teeth. Reading a book. In my visions, I could never see anyone but Andrew. Even his immediate surroundings were hazy. But I was pretty sure I had seen him in class once. He was in school. Where he belonged.

I loved to catch him while he was sleeping. Sometimes, in his sleep, Andrew would smile at the sound of my thoughts, or even murmur my name. But he never again heard me as clearly as he had during his coma. We couldn't talk to each other.

When I returned to the library that night with a tray of food,

Proce was acting strange. Usually, he read until the last possible second before dinner, his eyes glued to the pages. Tonight, he met me at the library entrance.

"You took so long," he said.

"I guess you're hungrier than usual." I set the tray on a table.

"Never mind food. I have something to show you."

"What's more important than food?" Now I was worried.

Proce limped to his usual work seat and picked up a tiny object. When he offered it to me, I didn't take it.

27

I took a sharp breath. "My sword."

In Proce's large hand, the tiny bookmark looked like a sliver of glass. The last time I had seen it, it was lodged into Kalmus's chest. It had once made me feel safe. Now, I didn't want to touch it.

"It is not a sword. The queen's Watchers just brought it. They had no idea what it was. Really, they should have come to me sooner. I did not see it before, when you . . . used it . . . in the garden. I would have recognized it right away."

I barely heard Proce. My eyes were stuck on the bookmark. Had its wound left a scar on the king's chest? A permanent reminder of the human who attacked him.

"Well," Proce said. "Are you going to ask me what it is?"

"Oh." I blinked. "What is it?"

"It is the study key." Proce flashed a rare smile, revealing teeth that looked like Von's.

"And that's a good thing?"

"Before today, I had only read about the study key." Proce laid the sword flat on his palm. "It belonged to the library keepers, long ago, and it has been lost for many years. No one knows how it was made, but we do know what it does. It still works."

"Works how?" I asked. Why was Proce so excited to show me?

"Let me demonstrate." Proce closed his hand over the sword and shut his eyes.

A tiny hum, like the sound of a flying bug, came from his hand. Light glowed from between his fingers, then dimmed.

Movement caught my eye behind Proce. A book was moving on its own, floating through the air toward us.

Proce snatched the book from the air and the hum faded. "See? You hold the study key in your hand and think of any topic. It will call a book to you with the most relevant information. The glass is gifted. It has knowledge."

"What topic did you think of?" My mind whirled with possibilities.

Proce flipped open the book to a page with an illustration of a tiny sword. "This is the story of how the key was lost, years ago."

My heart beat faster. There was only one topic I wanted to know about, and this bookmark was my chance. It had been there all along, tucked into my dress, hidden under my pillow, plunged into the king's chest. Had I sensed its gift? Is that why I kept it close during those dark days?

"Can I use the key?" I held out my hand. Out of the millions of books in the library, there had to be one with an answer. A way home.

But he closed his huge hand around the sliver of glass. "What if you find nothing? I am concerned. Will you be able to bear it?"

"I won't be able to bear it if you don't let me try." I raised my hand higher. "I have to."

"I know. But do not rest your future on something that may never happen."

I was getting impatient. "Don't pretend to know the future."

Proce's mouth tightened, but he dropped the sword into my open hand. The cool glass was familiar against my skin.

"Do I need your gift to make it work?" I asked.

"It is already gifted. Meg . . . before you use it, I am curious. They said you were the one who found the lost key. Where?"

"In the human rooms. There's a library hidden there, through a small tunnel. I think it belonged to Analese, the last human."

"And you sensed the gift in the glass, so you took it?"

"Maybe." I hesitated. "No. I took it because . . . it was sharp."
People in this earth didn't have weapons. I felt like I was sharing a
dirty secret. But Proce deserved the truth.

"I understand." He lowered his eyes. "When Analese died, her
husband could not bear it. He left the city without warning. Some
say he lived out his years in isolation, in the wilds. Some say he took
his own life. He was Baltus, the head library keeper. When he left,
no one could find the key. It has been lost since then. At first, the
scholars searched. They even searched Analese's things. I have not
heard of such a tunnel, or a library in the human rooms. I would
like to see it. Perhaps only the King's Gift knew of that place during
the search. But those were the days when the previous king began
to die. The end of his time. I doubt he had strength to help look for
the key. Then, Kalmus did not value such things. He probably never
looked. It took a human to find it."

We sat in silence for a moment and I pondered Proce's story.
Had Analese's husband really loved her so much that he didn't want
to live without her? Kalmus had seen me as something to possess.
He cherished my power. Was it the same for Baltus? And why had
Analese needed a secret room? I had looked for clues about her life
in her library. But all the books were full of poetry and drawings.
If she had left a journal behind, I couldn't find it.

Proce interrupted my thoughts. "Are you ready to use the key?"

I was more than ready. "I just think of what I want?"

"Yes. Hold the key tight and think. It will hear you."

I closed my fingers and spoke to the knife with my thoughts.
*Can you find a book that shows how to cross back into my human
earth? Please . . . and thank you. Thank you more than you know.*

For one awful second, nothing moved. Then, a book from a
nearby table rose into the air and floated to me.

I had expected some dusty book to travel from the furthest
corner of the library. Instead, the book that came to me was
familiar. I read the title, printed across the front in gilded letters.

THE ANTICIPATORY WRITINGS

It was Proce's copy. The same Writings I had first heard about in the meadow. The same Writings I had read in Analese's library. Proce knew the full text word for word. I had skimmed over most of it by now, though I didn't understand a lot of what I read.

"I am sorry," Proce said. "It seems there is nothing new for you to learn about thin places."

I ignored him.

The book hovered in front of me. I wrapped my hand tighter around the sword.

Isn't there anything else? I asked with my thoughts. *Or . . . at least, could you tell me which page to look at?*

On its own, the book opened and lay flat, as if it rested on an invisible table. The page it opened to was familiar. It was the passage I knew best, the verses that had inspired Proce and Von to call me to their earth.

My heart fell. *Are you serious?* I thought. *This is useless.*

With a flurry of dust, the book snapped shut and edged away from me.

Wait, I'm sorry . . .

Slowly, the pages opened again.

I need help. Exactly which part tells me how to go home?

Next to the last verse, at the end of the poem, a little ink dot appeared on the page. It hadn't been there before. I knew it hadn't. I read the verse aloud.

> "Where the sky of seven colors
> Meets the waters of our lands
> When the new one has walked on silver
> Eyes of hue and golden hands."

Proce shook his head. "The foretold thin place has already

closed. The key has nothing more to show you. Let us put it away and eat our food."

"I asked for a way to go home," I said. "It showed me verse 1127. It's saying that's how I go home."

He eyed the page. "The study key only shows books, not verses."

"Maybe you never asked it politely." I pointed at the ink dot. "This spot appeared on the page when I asked. It was an answer."

"Hmmm." Proce didn't sound convinced.

For the first time, something about the verse struck me as odd.

"Past tense," I said.

"What?"

"Past tense!" I grabbed the book out of the air and held it closer to me. "When the new one has walked on silver. Has. At the beginning of the poem, it says she will walk on silver. Will. At the end, it says has."

"Yes. I have seen this discrepancy. It may have happened during the translation from the old languages, before we all were gifted with one tongue."

"What if . . ." I took a breath. "I mean, I've already walked on silver . . . and the verse is describing the thin place after that, using past tense. Sky and water and land and everything. What if the thin place is going to open again? At the waterfall?"

"A thin place has never opened twice." Proce reached for a bowl of soup. "The tense of one word can't change that fact. Sit and eat. It will calm you."

"I don't want to be calm. I want to talk to the queen."

"Meg . . ." Proce met my gaze, concern in his eyes. "If there was any way . . . I would send you back. Even if I had to go in between earths for another hundred years. But I fear you are hoping for too much. In the morning, talk to the queen. She may let you journey to the falls. I will speak to her for you, if you need me. I cannot deny my doubt. But I have doubted you before, and I was wrong."

"Thank you. But I can't wait until morning." A wave of nervous energy turned my stomach. "I'm going now."

Proce gave a solemn nod.

I clasped his hand, fingers locked. A brief goodbye.

"And yes, you can eat my dinner."

As I ran from the library, Proce reached for my bowl of soup.

Elia's favorite Watcher, Calen, met me at the gem-studded door to the queen's rooms. The queen never used the auditorium for her gatherings. Instead, she conducted business in the garden, or the study adjacent to her lavish chambers.

"The queen isn't here," said Calen. "But you could join her at the besmonn keep. I'll escort you. She wouldn't mind."

"I'm sure she wouldn't." I didn't try to hide my annoyance.

Elia was convinced that I would be the best besmonn rider in the Seven Cities because of my size. She didn't take into account my personality. At first, I had visited the keep with her often, to see Sky. But Elia always insisted that I fly higher than I wanted to. Higher than the besmonns liked to go. Naturally, they preferred to stay close to the ground, where blossoms grew on trees. Unless they were trapped in a keep, taller than it is wide. Unless they were urged upward by their rider.

It was another thing to love about the besmonns.

Once, the queen had refused to heal me all day until I forced Sky to a ridiculous height. Since then, I had visited Sky on my own time, avoiding the queen's trips outside the city walls. In fact, as much as possible, I avoided Elia.

Calen accompanied me through the Polaris gate, all the way to the keep. As we approached, Elia circled down to greet us, mounted on the back of Claws. The besmonn's name suited him. His glossy talons curled into sharp points, longer than most, and his eyes glinted full black, like the queen's.

Elia jumped to the ground, Claws's tether in her grip. Her hair was smooth, her white skin blushed with gray from the evening warmth.

"So you've decided not to hide anymore?" she asked as a greeting. "You're not due for a healing until tomorrow."

"I need to talk with you about something."

With Elia, it was always best to be straightforward.

"I'd be happy to talk with you." She gave me one of her crooked smiles. "As soon as your feet leave the ground."

We'd been through this before, and I knew she wouldn't relent. "I'll get Sky."

The trick wasn't getting Sky to come to me—it was getting *only* Sky to come to me. Every time I entered the keep, a swarm of besmonns descended.

I squeezed Sky out of the gate, managing to keep the others corralled.

She whistled, pleased by my color.

Elia soared above us. "We'll fly to the clearing in the grove."

I climbed onto Sky's back. We followed the queen, skimming just above the grass, the way Sky and I both liked it. Air whooshed past my ears. Sky wove a zig-zag flight pattern, playful, enjoying her freedom.

The queen would have corrected our height, but we outdistanced her, zooming ahead to the clearing. I leaned back, slowing Sky so that Claws could catch up. As we hovered beside a tree, I plucked a silver leaf and tucked it behind my ear.

When the queen reached the clearing, she swooped to our level. "Sky is a strong bird, but she's lazy. She could do so much more."

It was our usual argument.

"You call it lazy, I call it smart." I stroked Sky's feathers and slid off her back, landing on my hands and feet.

The queen dismounted from Claws more gracefully and released his tether. Both besmonns flitted to nearby trees, grazing for nectar. They wouldn't stray far from my color.

"Let's walk." Elia led the way through the clearing.

I doubled my steps to keep at her side.

"How far do you think Sky could fly in one day?" I asked.

"Is this about Von's wedding again?" Elia stopped walking. "I've already told you, it's unwise for me to leave the Polaris right now for that long. Von will come visit you. And we both know it's better for you that she's gone."

I had meant to get straight to the point, but I couldn't ignore Elia's last statement.

"It's not better," I confessed. "What are you talking about?"

"You've been in the Polaris for almost a year now." She resumed her pace.

"A year? It's been less than six months. You're rounding up."

"Regents don't measure time in months," she said. "That's a human invention."

"Half a year, then," I said.

"I think it's time you start taking an interest in Regent things. Look at you." Elia raised her brows, gesturing to my heathered pants and long tunic. "You're not a Cropper, even if you dress like one."

"I'm not a Regent, either."

"Exactly," the queen said. "And that's what makes you special. You have no idea how many Regents are interested in meeting you."

"Oh, I'm aware."

She was talking about Regent men. They didn't want to just meet me. Some of them wanted to marry me.

After Kalmus lost his gift, I had spent little time with the members of the King's House. There were no more dances and parades to attend. Larlia no longer came to dress me in the mornings. And I only explored the city at night, when most Regents were in their homes.

Once, Elia had invited me to a Regent dinner. My entire table was seated with unmarried men, eager to make small talk with me. Mostly, they boasted about the houses they owned. After that, I had declined Elia's invitations.

"You only have four more years until your marriage." Elia kept walking. "You can't keep hiding from your future."

"Four and a half years." I darted forward and stopped in front of the queen, halting her progress. "Listen, this isn't what I wanted to talk about. I need your help."

"I've done nothing but help you," Elia said. "Do you want to be healed more often?" Her mind teetered on the boundaries of mine, threatening to cross.

The mental skirmishes were another reason I liked to avoid the queen these days. I could sense her elevated gift, drawn to my color in a way that connected us. I hated the rush of my own power as I guarded my mind. Though the queen didn't pry like Kalmus had, her presence still made me feel unnatural, as if there were a part of myself that wasn't me. The power of my color only lit up in her presence. Did she feel something similar?

"I want to return to the thin place," I said. "Where I crossed into your earth. It's a day's walk past Von's village, if you're a Cropper. Human legs are slower."

"Why do you want to go?" Elia's mind collided into mine.

I put up my barrier. "I need to see for myself that the thin place is gone."

"Of course it is."

"I could go fast enough on a besmonn to be back before my next healing. In theory. But I need you with me . . . in case I find what I'm looking for. You promised to help. To send me through if it was there."

"You're referring to our bargain?" Elia asked. "I said I would use my gift to send you home, if it were possible. I see no evidence of possibility. Only a foolish errand. And we can't take the besmonns. There are no nectar trees beyond the Regent cities."

"I've seen besmonns in the Cropper village."

"Those are field besmonns," Elia said. "There are certain types of trees that riding besmonns need to survive. Kalmus destroyed all the trees outside our city regions. That's how he grew his flock. Flying besmonns used to be rarely sighted, spread at great distances over all the valleys."

I imagined a company of Watchers, armed with axes. Or maybe

they used their gifts to cut down the trees. Had the Watchers fallen that far under Kalmus, to use their gifts to destroy?

Elia continued, "We can fly between the cities, where there's plenty of nectar. But we can't journey into the wilds. The besmonns can't carry enough food. They drink too much."

I blinked away tears for the besmonns. Would their habitat ever recover? I mentally shook myself. I couldn't think about that now. I had other things to worry about.

"So we'll walk there." I wouldn't give up.

"I can't be gone for that long." Elia walked past me and continued along the edge of the clearing.

"You promised." I stayed put, my eyes on Elia's back.

She ignored me.

Past tense. I was basing all of this on past tense. But I knew what I had seen—an ink dot made by the library key, an ancient source of knowledge. Proce believed in stranger things than that. And maybe I did too now. He had risked his life on an ancient poem to save his people. What would I risk to save my future?

I imagined the gray earth during the cold. No Proce. No Von. No songs or summer. It might last the rest of my life. From what Proce said, the winters were harsh. I would be trapped inside the King's House for years.

What would I gain if I was right? Humanity. Color. Health. Even with the Queen's healings, I still felt the poison. It was always there, sinking into me. I had proved that I could survive here. But if there was a chance to go home, how could I live with myself if I didn't take it?

And then there was Andrew . . .

That would be too good. Too much to hope for. Right now, I would just think about going to the waterfall.

"One year." I opened up my mind and let the queen see my intent. "If you go with me, in one year, I'll marry a Regent."

Regents counted years by the stars, which were the same on both earths, despite the queen's exaggeration.

She halted, but didn't turn around. "If nothing is found, you'll give up?"

"Yes . . ."

The queen turned and smiled. "We'll find a good husband for you."

I fought back revulsion. It was so easy for her to plan my life for me, like I belonged to her.

"And you know about good husbands?" I immediately regretted my retort.

The queen's face stilled. She didn't say anything. I didn't need to see her thoughts to know I had wounded her.

"I'm sorry . . ."

Elia's expression softened. "I know this isn't easy for you."

"There used to be someone else. It's hard to forget."

"You should have forgotten your entire earth by now." Elia said. "What still remains?"

I took my note from the front pocket of my tunic and handed it to Elia. It was a battered and stained scrap, the ink barely legible.

"I wrote this when I first arrived in your earth to help me remember my life. So I could remember I'm someone who loved someone."

Elia glanced at the words on the note, then handed it back to me. Had she been able to read my human writing? Would the gift of language translate? Either way, it didn't matter.

I tore the paper and let the shreds fall into the grass.

"I don't need it anymore," I said. "I won't forget. Not ever."

Elia and I traveled back to the Polaris before sunset, a wedge of silence between us.

28

Three days later, before the queen and I left for our journey, I went to the library.

"This is for Von." I pulled a thick envelope from my travel satchel and handed it to Proce.

Proce stowed the envelope in his shirt sleeve. "I will ensure she receives your letter." He adjusted his artificial leg. "I am sorry I cannot travel with you today."

He would slow us down and we both knew it. A familiar well of grief opened at the sight of his missing limb.

"It wouldn't be fair if you found a thin place twice." I forced a smile. "Do you know how many songs the Croppers have written about you already? Save some glory for everyone else."

Proce frowned. "Do not be disappointed if you find nothing. A thin place has never opened twice, despite what you may hope. Prepare your mind now."

This was Proce's way of caring, but I still bristled at his words. "How is it that I have more faith in the Writings right now than you do?"

"You must remember that we have never sent anything to your earth," he said. "We have only gone in between. It is dangerous."

"But I'll have the Queen's Gift. And the King's. Impossible things have happened before. You know they have. I'll make it through."

"Or you might get stuck."

He wasn't saying anything I hadn't considered already.

"According to you, the thin place is gone," I pointed out. "So there's nothing to worry about. But, just in case, I wrote a letter for you too."

As I handed the second envelope to him, everything became real. I was leaving. This might be my last conversation with Proce. Our last argument. His last chance to teach me something.

My eyes filled with tears. "I wanted you to know . . ." My voice cracked. "You have no idea—"

"I do have an idea," Proce gave a watery smile. "You are my second sister."

I held myself back from hugging him because I knew it wouldn't mean as much as words. Words were his way.

"I'll never stop missing you and Von," I said.

"You were never ours to keep. We should have known that."

In a way, I wished they *could* keep me. We were family now, split between earths.

"You know," I said. "You're a lot wiser than Von gives you credit for."

"I hope you wrote that in her letter."

We clasped hands, my small human fingers folded in his large Cropper ones, maybe for the last time. I held on longer than normal. Then I left.

From the road, I looked back at the Polaris, bidding a last farewell to its glossy towers and walls. Walls that had once been my prison and my home. Seven Watchers accompanied us on the road, the full number of the queen's guard. They walked in a line, our trailing shadow.

Elia strolled beside me, slow for a Regent, fast for a human. "When we return, we should have a dance. It's been too long since I've danced."

"You should do that."

The queen was silent for a while. When she spoke, her tone was artificially light.

"What would you do, if you returned to your earth? Besides looking for your boy?"

I decided to give her the truth. "I would visit my mother's grave. I want to remember my past."

We bypassed the villages. It was faster that way. At night, we slept on thick blankets, laid out by the Watchers. Calen was never far from us.

On our second day, as my feet grew sore and the sun began to dip, I spotted someone ahead of us on the horizon. We were in the thick of the trees now and the only open space was the Queen's Road. The figure ahead stood square in the middle, facing us. He was too small to be a Cropper, but tall for a Regent. I couldn't see a face at our distance.

"Why would a Regent come this far outside of the city?" I asked Elia.

"They wouldn't. Unless they wanted to be away from other Regents. Unless they wanted to see a human. You've finally noticed him? It's about time."

"Who is he?" But I didn't really need to ask.

"He's here to talk to you," Elia said. "I've seen that much in his mind. Should I tell him to leave?"

We slowed and I thought for a long moment. "I'm not going to run from him. Will you watch us and keep me safe?"

"I can keep your body safe. I can't promise anything for your heart."

I looked away. "You don't have to worry about that."

"Let's make him come to you." Elia led her Watchers forward while I stayed behind.

As if released, the figure moved toward us.

Kalmus.

They passed him on the road like he didn't exist. Then Elia turned and watched him approach me.

I had said my heart would be fine, but now I wasn't so sure. It beat in my chest so hard I was sure Kalmus would be able to see. He had hurt me once. My body still remembered what that felt like.

What would he say to me? Was this his chance for retribution? If he tried to attack, Elia's gift would stop him. I hoped.

I braced myself, feet firm, and met his pale gaze.

He stopped in front of me and smiled. As if nothing had changed. As if I had never buried a knife in his chest. Was his wound fully healed? The scar would be hidden beneath his slim blazer, black as always, with a hint of red silk at the collar. The wrinkles in the silk and the dust on his shoes were the only signs of his exile. Smooth skin, high cheekbones. He was the same. And yet, something was missing.

His mind.

It didn't press into mine. Its weight was gone. Cautious, I let down my guard.

"Meg," he said. "That was the first word you ever spoke to me. Your name."

"Kalmus." I tried his name as an experiment. Nothing happened. My thoughts were my own.

His smile turned up at one corner, teasing. "You're still testing my power. Even when the battle's over."

"Is it?" I asked. "Why are you here?"

"Do you wish I had been punished?" He kept his smile. "I won't fault you. You're not the only one."

"I'm glad that's not my decision." It was the truth. "I don't know what I wish Elia had done."

His tone grew serious. "I wish it had been different."

I didn't know what to say to him. Did I wish it were different? If I had never come here, Andrew wouldn't be alive. But I owed that to Elia. Not to Kalmus.

"It could have been different," I said.

"Some things, yes. But I'm not sorry I got to know a human. And I'm not sorry for my experiment. It worked."

I shook my head. "What are you talking about? Nothing worked."

"Two gifts in one. It happened." He looked back at Elia. "It should have been me, not her. But she's carrying it well."

"She shouldn't have to."

"She's stronger than you think," he said. "I'd be more worried about what she can do with all that power than what it might do to her."

"What do you mean?"

Kalmus would have done evil things with two gifts. Was he projecting that onto Elia?

He gave me that smile, then changed the direction of the conversation. "When I proposed marriage, it wasn't just for the ceremony. I hope you know that. I never lied to you about our future."

I laughed, an unhappy sound. "We both lied. Neither of us were going to keep our promise. You were never going to heal Andrew. I was never going to be yours. I'm sorry I played along." He had no power now. I was done pretending.

"Don't say you regret everything about our time together." He stepped closer.

I held my ground. "I don't."

"Tell me." He was close now.

It wouldn't be what he hoped to hear. "Before I came here, I was scared a lot of the time. There were things I couldn't say." I thought of Andrew. Would I ever be able to tell him that I love him? "But now . . . I'm not scared anymore. In the end, I faced the worst and kept breathing. I didn't know I could do that."

He laughed. "Humans are smaller than I thought. And also bigger."

I looked up into his eyes. There was an odd sensation, as if I were seeing Kalmus for the first time. Past the gift. Past the kingship. He was just a Regent.

"Is this why you came here?" I asked. "You just wanted to talk?"

"Think of it as a first step. Maybe, with lots of time, you'll want to talk to me too."

I wouldn't. He was still overconfident. Was it an act?

He raised his hand with a flick. At his movement, a blossom floated from the trees to hover in front of me.

My heart raced. I snapped the guard into place around my mind. How was he doing that without the King's Gift? Outwardly, I tried to look calm.

"Your gift . . ." I didn't know what else to say.

I glanced at Elia, standing guard at a distance. She didn't move. Was this a surprise to her?

"I'm not a king anymore," Kalmus said. "But I still have my first gifts from when I was new. Nothing like my power as king, but it's something."

My heart slowed and I let down my guard. I was surprised to find myself almost happy for him. I hadn't taken all of Kalmus, when I took the King's Gift.

"I thought only Croppers could use their gifts for plants and earth?" I plucked the flower from the air.

Kalmus looked away, uncomfortable for the first time. "I'm not growing anything. I'm not changing the shape and nature of stones. I can move things with my gift. Small things. That's all."

"It's something," I said.

"It might be more. In time."

Was he planning more experiments? I didn't want to be around to find out.

He snapped his pale fingers and the flower wrapped its stem around my wrist, like a bracelet. It was a pantomime of the jewelry we had received on our parade through the city.

"Do you know where I'm going?" I asked.

"I have a good guess. But you'll be back."

"I won't." I slipped the flower off my wrist and held it out to him. He didn't take it. "We'll see."

I looked up at Elia, fifty paces away. She took my cue and stepped forward.

Kalmus stiffened. "Goodbye, Meg."

I bowed to him, low, like Von had taught me. "Goodbye, Kalmus."

He waved. A human gesture learned from me.

Then we parted, walking in opposite directions on the road.

On our third day of travel, my surroundings grew familiar. I heard the waterfall before I saw it. We emerged from a grove of trees and looked out over the ravine.

White rapids crashed. Grass glinted silver beneath a colorless sunset. Not a scrap of blue sky shone above us, or green forest below.

I ran ahead and stopped, one step from the edge, searching the cliffs for any spot of color.

The landscape was unavoidably gray.

The queen caught up with me. "Don't stand so close." She took my arm and guided me away from the edge.

We stood side by side. I had placed everything on one word in the Writings. Past tense. But how was I supposed to know when the thin place would open?

"How long can we stay?"

"We'll wait until morning, then turn back," Elia said. "There's nothing here. I'm sorry."

But I knew she wasn't sorry.

For hours, I stayed at the edge of the ravine. My eyes traced the forest below, searching for color. I found nothing.

One year.

The thought kept coming into my mind. With it, I pictured the faces of Regent men I had met. Which one would I have to marry?

The one with the greasy curls? The one whose eyes were flat gray, without pupils?

I clenched my fists and searched the ravine again.

The sun set and the Watchers gifted a fire to heat water for tea. I stayed at the cliff edge. Elia brought me a blanket, then went to sleep beside the fire. The moon arched across the sky, a dupe for my own earth.

Would I even recognize the human earth? Would I be able to speak my own language? I wanted the chance to find out. The Polaris would never be home. Not with the cold. Not with Kalmus free.

And I could never be free. Not as long as Elia had to heal me every day.

She had the weight of a kingdom on her. She was supposed to take care of a dying people, and I was a tool in her belt. My fertility was part of her plan.

I wanted to be a mother someday. But I wanted it to be in my own timing, in my own way. I had met one of Analese's children in the Polaris. A woman who had outlived her mother. I couldn't see any human in her.

When morning arrived, the sun didn't bring its usual heat. I sat up from my blanket and my breath formed a fog in the chilled air.

Cold. This earth was never cold. At least, not yet.

Everyone was still asleep.

I wrapped my blanket around my shoulders. The icy breeze was familiar, though I had no memory of the last time I had felt anything like it. I searched the ravine. Still no color. So why was hope fluttering in my chest?

A bird called in the distance. Not the peep of a besmonn, but the caw of something nostalgic. The sunrise shifted, brightening.

That was when I saw it and everything changed.

Color.

On the horizon shone a barely pink swatch of almost-color. Then, the sky flamed into blistering red and sunshine yellow. The river in the gully below flowed blue, a bright thread sewn into deep evergreen. Ice hung heavy on the branches of spindly pines.

This was my earth.

I didn't know where the thin place ended or where it began. But it was open, and the Writings were true.

At first, I didn't move. All I could do was drink in color, reunited with something I barely remembered. The giver of the Writings had seen the future. Could he see me now?

"Thank you," I whispered.

My throat was tight with emotion, but my eyes remained dry. There was too much to see. Too much to think.

Footsteps crunched in gravel.

The queen came to stand beside me. I pulled my eyes from the color to look at her.

She stared at the horizon. Tears glistened on her cheeks. "You never said it was so beautiful."

"You never asked."

"You've gotten everything you wanted." It sounded like an accusation.

"And I'm scared."

"As you should be." Elia wrapped a blanket around herself.

I turned to face her. "Will you keep your promise?"

Her warm breath made a flurry of mist in the cold air. "You know I will. But are you sure you want me to try? The boy we healed may have moved on from you by now. Who do you have in your earth? Here, you're wanted. You could belong in the Polaris."

"Kalmus wanted me. That didn't make me belong."

"A part of you will always belong in my earth." Elia smoothed a strand of hair behind her ear, reminding me of my own white tangles.

"You're right," I agreed. "There are people here I love. But if there's a place for me in such a strange earth, I can find a way to belong in my own. I don't know how Andrew feels, but I know how I felt when he was almost gone. Now I'm the one who's lost. How can I not go back? Even if I end up alone. Look at this." I pointed at the color. "All of this opened for me. Just like before."

The queen shook her head. "How did you know the thin place would open?"

"I didn't know. I hoped."

"Hope." Elia smiled. "It's what kept me alive in the tower for years."

"It's how I'm getting home."

"You'll need more than that. I'll lend you my gift, but it might not be enough for you to cross over," she warned. "You could die. This has never been done before."

I smiled, trying to look braver than I felt. "That's how it always seems to work for me."

"Do you remember where to go once you arrive?" she asked. "It's cold there. You'll need shelter."

I searched my mind for a memory of what lay beyond the gully and I came up empty. Most of my memories were of the gray earth. I knew the way to Von's village by heart and the name of every single Cropper who lived there. I had finally made sense of the halls in the King's House. But none of that would help me now. It was useless information.

"I know the risk I'm taking."

The queen returned her gaze to the landscape. "Either way, whatever happens, I'm losing you."

"Thank you for keeping your word."

Elia wrapped her blanket tighter around her shoulders. "I doubt it's what's best for my people."

"You're a queen who keeps her promises," I told her. "That's what's best for your people. They're lucky to have you." I looked up at her. "I've been lucky to have you."

Despite her schemes, the queen had given me everything. Andrew's life. My healings. Now, a way home. I didn't want to give her my future, but I owed her my thanks.

We stood for a long moment on the edge of the cliff, our bodies made small by the expanse of two earths.

"It's time," I urged. "Before it closes again."

"You would have been a gift to us, Meg." The queen reached a hand toward me.

Familiar pain erupted along my spine, burning like cold iron. It was the pain of crossing earths. I fell to my knees and committed myself to it. Any resistance would make it worse.

This time, instead of fading into black, the pain increased. It was like being pushed upstream, against a swift river.

This wasn't right. I wasn't moving fast enough toward my earth. I was willing, but only my mind was racing forward, not my body. I felt it when I hit the barrier, the place where Proce and Von had stopped. In between.

But this wasn't far enough for me. There would be no way back, no way forward. I had to go all the way to my earth. If my body caught up to this in-between place, I would be torn apart without a gift to hold it open.

Desperate, I opened my mind to the Queen's Gift, offering any part of myself to it. The brown from my eyes separated from me, joining in the effort to send me home. It hurt to lose more color. But I let it go, a sacrifice. Not for Andrew this time.

For myself.

For my way forward. This was the future I chose.

The pain intensified and I screamed. Cold poured into me and I tumbled into a bank of snow.

Before I opened my eyes, I smelled the pine trees. My cheek was numb against the frozen ground. I clutched my blanket and climbed to my feet, my head pounding.

The meadow looked different than it had when I was between earths. Now, snow carpeted the once green grass and pillars of ice stood where the waterfall used to flow. The winter sun shone at its full height. It shone in a blue sky.

Blue.

Gone was the eternal twilight of in between. Gone was the gray of the other place. I had made it all the way through, without stopping. A smile spread across my face and I let out a short laugh.

The sickness didn't linger from this crossing, as if my body knew it had gone the right direction this time. And yet, I was like this meadow. Once vibrant, now covered over in white. I felt it. My lack of color. Like I was bringing part of the gray earth with me.

I spun in a slow circle, ice melting into my summer shoes. Which way had I entered the gully on the day I met Proce and Von? My eyes trailed along the forest, landing on a split in the tree line.

A path.

That's what I had been searching for when I first ran away from my giants.

As I entered the forest, my lungs felt more free than I could ever remember. The air wasn't poison. It was meant for human life. For me.

Red berries gleamed on a bush. I stopped for a moment to look at the color, despite my bone-chilled limbs. I ran my fingers over the red, then kept going.

The patchy trail was clear of trees, though slick with white. As I climbed, the height made me queasy, but I trudged on. My legs were strong from days of walking between the Croppers' village and the Polaris.

I began to hurry along the path. I had no idea where I was going, but I wanted to get there. Several times I nearly slipped. By the time I reached the top of the ravine, I couldn't feel my toes.

The first sign of humans was a house. Its gabled roof and high windows peeked through the trees. Red lights were strung along the gutters and a garland of greenery adorned the porch rails.

I stopped.

Something about this place felt familiar. At least, I thought I did. Maybe it was just hope. My memories were still out of reach. What if they never returned? What if I was changed forever, an outsider to my earth?

It was too late for doubt. I had come this far, and this house would be a shelter from the cold. I walked to the front door and tapped my frozen knuckles against the wood beneath a wreath of red berries.

The door swung open. A human stood on the other side of the threshold. My first human in full memory. She had rosy cheeks. Delicate features. I could have stared for a long time, silent, just looking.

An animal sat near her ankles, whining and shaking its tale.

A beagle.

I knew what it was called.

The woman was small, even compared to me. Amber eyes peered out from her aged face. I didn't know who she was, but there was something about those eyes. They were the same as Andrew's. Did all humans look like that?

She stared back at me. What was I supposed to say?

"Hello. My name is Meg . . . I'm lost."

When I spoke, she blinked, confused.

"Meg . . ." She said my name, followed by an unintelligible string of words.

I didn't understand her. She didn't understand me.

I had lost my own language. The gray earth was gone, but it had left its speech in my mind.

The woman's words sounded like a jumble of soft vowels. From the tone of her voice, I knew she had asked a question. How was I supposed to answer her?

More questions spilled from her lips, in rapid sequence. When she was done talking, she waited, expectant.

"I'm looking for someone named Andrew." She wouldn't understand me, but maybe she would recognize the name. It was the only name I knew.

Her eyes widened. A flurry of words followed. She stepped outside and closed the door behind her, looking over her shoulder.

But almost as soon as it closed, the door flew open again. On the other side stood someone I recognized.

The only person I would have recognized.

Andrew.

His eyes darted from me, to the woman, then back to me, where they stayed fixed. He stepped onto the icy porch. His mouth opened and color drained from his face, leaving him pale for a human. He didn't look into my eyes at first. He looked at my clothes, my hair, my shoes.

My breath stopped. I couldn't move.

Would he recognize me, the girl who had disappeared, now returned with white hair and gray eyes? Would he hate me for leaving? I never had a choice, but he didn't know that.

"Meg." He said my name, the only word I would have understood.

It sounded wonderful, when he said it.

I expected questions from him, but he didn't speak. He just moved. Before I could respond, I was wrapped in his arms, his cheek against my white hair. I hugged him back, as hard as I could. I had worried he might seem like a stranger to me, after so much had happened, but his hug felt more like home than anything ever had.

He held me tight, then let go to look at my face. His eyes shone through tears and he wiped his nose on the sleeve of his green sweater.

That's when the questions came, tangled and urgent. It was a garble of sounds to me, but I watched him speak. Every expression on his face was perfect, beautifully human. Andrew, as I remembered him. As I had seen him in Proce's visions over the past months.

But now it was in person.

I took his hand and held it tight. "You won't know what I'm saying." My voice was thick with emotion.

Confusion shadowed his expression as he heard me speak gibberish. Would he think I was crazy? Or worse? I tried not to panic. What word might he know? Any word. My mind scrambled.

"Andrew," I said.

At his name, a hint of recognition played over his face.

Then, another word came to me. "Christmas . . ."

Andrew nodded, slow.

The red berries, the snow. That was why Andrew was in the forest now, with his family. It was their winter cabin, where they spent the holiday. If a memory had returned to my mind, and a human word along with it, then there was hope. There was room in my head for two earths.

And then, I realized that I did know more human words. How could I not? I had traced over the shapes of the letters too many times to count: the words written on my crumpled little note, the one I tore to pieces. I wasn't sure I could say the words, but I remembered what they looked like. The writing was human, rounder and shorter than the letters in Proce's books.

I took a step back, off the porch. Kneeling, I wrote my truth in the snow with one steady finger.

I love you Andrew.

He looked at the writing, then me. He was smiling, all his color sparkling.

The moment was a gift.

I stood and laughed, a short burst of pure happiness. We both breathed for a moment, taking in the other.

I had so much to say and not enough language to say it, so I spoke in my colorless tongue as I looked into his amber eyes. "Someday, I'll be able to explain. I'll tell you everything, if you want to hear it."

Whatever it took, however long it took. I was home now. No matter what that held for me, I wasn't afraid.

29

Five years later, on my real wedding day, I refused to wear a tiara or a veil. I let my hair fall loose and unkempt, decorated with flowers.

"I like it this way," Andrew told me that night, curling a white strand around the tip of his finger, tilting my chin back for a gentle kiss.

My hair has never returned to brown. A part of me still thinks of it as a loss, but I'm glad for it too. It reminds me of my time with the Croppers and the Regents. How can I forget them when I see them in the mirror?

Every once in a while, on warm evenings, I go outside to sing. There's a stone bench in our yard I like to sit on. I look at the moon and I sing songs that only I could know. Sometimes, Andrew joins me, though he can't pronounce the lyrics. I try to teach him. He plays along on his guitar.

I don't mind being outside in the temporary gray of night. It holds no power. A yellow sun will rise again in a sky of seven colors.

THE END

ACKNOWLEDGEMENTS

To my husband, Jared Nelson, for your patience and love. You were right.

To my mother, Dian Roberson, who introduced me to our earth and many others. Thank you for reading to me.

Special thanks to the amazing Makenna Albert for believing in my story down to the last annoying detail.

ABOUT THE AUTHOR

Rachelle grew up reading fantasy novels and getting her clothes muddy in the pine forests of Idaho. These days, she still loves hiking through mountains and libraries, though she is a bit less fond of mud. She doesn't write true stories, but she writes about truth. When Rachelle is not reading and writing, she sings in a band with her talented husband, who makes her happier than should be legal. If you like adventures, good food, and honest conversations, you are her favorite kind of person.

To receive a short story by Rachelle, you can sign up for her newsletter at rachellenelsonauthor.com.